10⁰⁰

3/22

D0862563

The Dilligaf Heiress

by

Sebastian Graham

Wordclay
1663 Liberty Drive, Suite 200
Bloomington, IN 47403
www.wordclay.com

© Copyright 2010 Sebastian Graham. All rights reserved.

No part of this book may be reproduced, stored in a retrieval system, or transmitted by any means without the written permission of the author.

First published by Wordclay on 9/8/2010.
ISBN: 978-1-6048-1786-7 (sc)

Printed in the United States of America.

This book is printed on acid-free paper.

For

JC

("if you want to win at doubles, choose your partner wisely")

Outline

She's frequently kind and she's suddenly cruel
She can do as she pleases, she's nobody's fool
And she can't be convicted, she's earned her degree
And the most she will do is throw shadows at you
But she's always a woman to me

(v. Billy Joel)

Prologue

*And now these three remain: faith, hope and love. But
the greatest of these is love.*
-- 1 Corinthians 13:13

You lose, she wins… Life's a zero sum game to The Dilligaf
Heiress, my fatwa imama of Locust Valley.

No one ever said marriage would be easy…then again, no one ever
said it would be this hard. I'm a big believer in the wisdom of Erma
Bombeck, 'Marriage has no guarantees…If that's what you're
looking for, go live with a car battery.' My ex was society's Lucy
('Lucifer') Van Pelt, pulling the ball away every time I was about to
kick.

I'd have swum across an ocean for that woman…and she'd drown
me when I was furthest from land. When I asked for rope…she
handed me a noose. I'd have gone through hell for her…and that's
exactly where she wanted me. In the end, hers was simply anger as
pleasure. Well…, nobody's perfect. This is a Balzac talking head
tale of consumerism, social disconnection, political stagnation, and
modern malaise. And that's just my marriage. Please call me Seb.

I'm studying the evil ex syndrome in detail these days. My tentative
conclusion: my ex has 'em all beat. Her victory and reach were
made all the more possible by the nature of her smoldering
beauty…simply and declaratively stunning. The trust fund merely
underwrote her mayhem. There was never a day of rest for her
wickedness and her dystopia view of humanity was shuddering.

She plumbed pathological depths scientists and psychologists hadn't considered reachable, a cosmos of malice that only theory had been attached to prior to her arrival, and I've asked the pro's… Ultimately the only act she didn't commit was first-degree murder, not that she didn't give it the old college try. A thousand years will pass before another human gets close to just ten percent of her depraved accomplishments. I can now appreciate the extent of her diabolical bent though: it must say something about me, that I could have married such an overachiever.

She was a biblical assault in Oscar de la Renta. She has a Futurist psychology where she examines certain events not yet come to pass but which she simply appropriates as having already happened. She has a Preterist psychology, a casual dismissal of historical events when it suits her fantasies. She has a Historicist psychology where she identifies with certain historical people and events, but only when it flatters her self-love (and only at very large parties). And finally she has an Idealist psychology, not in the sense that you and I might think, but rather where she trumpets events that support the triumph of evil over good. In other words, she's the Book of Revelations but ass-backwards.

My wife infected me like the simmering Thais to Alexander the Great, taunting him to needlessly burn down the glorious city of Persepolis, Thais' sexual attraction mocking Alexander's strength. When he agreed to burn the city, that one useless act forever ruined East-West relations (and when an act committed in 330 BC still has legs 2,000+ years later, it's epic…my wife will affect similar glory).

Before we start, I should tell you a little bit about me. I think (and even she'd concur) I'm stranded in the wrong time, as if someone teleported me to a future I never belonged to. I shave acoustic and grow holiday beards, I'm hypnotized by hotness but respect all, and about the very worst you could say about me before her was I had cobra yawn.

I came from a one-horse town in North Carolina…we weren't where it's at, we're more where it wasn't. Bronski Beat 'Smalltown Boy' was my soul anthem. I've always lived life in tune, a dreamer on vinyl wax…my concert resume was strong. Never jealous and never can be, I don't have the bone. Maybe a sin I now have is Playlistism, an elitist sense of musical taste.

I'm above average height and I should admit, reluctantly but tellingly, Episcopalian. It used to be helpful saying you were Episcopalian…I just don't know anymore. We can be wild-eyed socialist homosexuals or arch-conservative straight ticket Republicans. It's all good. I'm a southern wasp, not a Brahmin wasp, so I didn't really concern myself with society optics.

I've never been hyper social but I wasn't exactly a recluse either…okay, maybe a semi-recluse who much preferred playing ping-pong. She'll tell you I was anti-social, almost urban Amish, but if you knew the town where she and I eventually lived, anti-social means you only go out four nights a week….we lived in the shoulder surfing capital of the world. Spending valuable time on parties for profit never seemed very fun to me.

I hate but two things in life: large parties and 70's light rock… Manhattan high society axis parties are basically social dog parks, where the navy blazer army manically sniffs each other to make sure no one's a threat. She loves large parties (which actually means she hates them…this will take some explaining, but for now, assume that what she loves she hates and what she hates she loves…the world was always upside down for her, an eternal inversion of truth, a truly dizzying way to live). Those parties box-locked me and drained my accounts for good measure. My ex loves Steely Dan (which come to think of it, I should have paid more attention to…Steely Dan is named after a vibrator).

I think I'm the kind of guy you'd want to make the dreaded middle-of-the-night emergency phone call to, half because I'd be there for you no matter what and half because I'm an insomniac anyway. Reliable, loyal, and never a complaint. I never complain, I don't gossip, and I don't go to doctors. I happily shovel snow at 3 AM, my driveway and yours.

When I met my ex, I was a wannabe rock musician with too many useless poems and not enough paying fans, a dreamer with no solid ground. My clark-kent job was a trading position at Shearson American Express (which then became Shearson Lehman Hutton which begat Lehman Brothers…I'm not sure staying there wouldn't have worked out better for me in the end!). Financial services was a clip-on wasteland for me. My superman job was as yet unidentified, but I always knew it was out there.

Eventually I got fired or quit (depends on whom you ask) and went to work in Russia starting my consulting company. I probably should have gotten away from financial services then, but I was trapped in a marriage whose foundations (I believed) rested solely on my checkbook.

I made money mostly by not being an ass unlike the competition. I listened to clients and was honest about whether we could deliver. I never referred to employees as my people…every banker in Manhattan loves to say that, almost as if they need to convince themselves they're first class even when they're on the Titanic, neglecting the outcome so long as the image soothes. When I hear someone refer to employees as my people, I walk away. Stockbrokers now are financiers…yuck. There's no letup in the Manhattan marketing game.

As a dad, I loved my kids almost too much and still it grows every day. They're my most trusted eternal friends because they know me and she can't figure out how to sell her fantasies to them. I had my children, dog, garden, music, and sports to keep me sane. Even loved that wife of mine back then, only sort of still do now (I more or less laugh anymore in appreciative, lustful delusion that all will work out in the end…not). I'm forever resigned to the twin afflictions of optimism and hope.

The only thing I can point back to and see was a continuous chink in my armor was her, a veritable eye-watering feast of smoldering beauty and defying chartless lunacy, my Yahtzee to Nazi in a minute debutante. I wanted to get with her the second I met her…she wanted to kill me about the same instant. We were MFEO…made for each other, me for love and she to kill. That girl was big pimpin' in the Mortimer's-Swifty's-Doubles milieu.

I've run out of words to describe her. Chérie, tu es ravissante ce soir. She's so damn gorgeous but narcissistic to the point of being utterly, unhumanly recognizable. She's the fifty-fifty wonder, hurting you, nursing you enough, then hurting you all over again except worse each successive time. Eventually you just die from the pain.

If you paid the right price she was yours…death became you. Her narcissism eats you alive…she couldn't slow down if she wanted, and she didn't…she keeps artificially busy.

The core manifestation of all that narcissism was her private and public opinion on marriage: charitably you could term hers an eternal struggle, a hand to hand combat to death, a daily test where even if you won the battle du jour, there'd be too much hell to pay later…so you could never really win. She definitely doesn't believe in unconditional love! She also doesn't believe in small matters like church oaths…nothing is sacred to the devil when she's in her little black dress.

And yet, I adored her, all through the madness and hellish flames to the bitter end. She's the Woman of Halves. When she was on, my world stopped…it felt like love. But when she was off, whew, man…heartless of a nature not yet seen, her bat shit signal was deafening. It wasn't so much that no girl could be that mean, it was that no human could be that mean. My blood wasn't only on her hands, it was on her lips, the party dress, the invitations, the shoes, and in her stomach. She was my peroxide blonde Jennifer Barrett, 'love means never having to say you're sorry'. My ex had life figured out alright.

It wasn't the way it should be for any normal relationship but the fact is I never wanted to leave. She had, still has I guess, an ass that's remarkably unassailable. I'm pathetically weak about that…it's always been my first and most obvious failure. It keeps me awake at night and in trouble during the day. It enfeebles me like a child with a shiny new red toy. I should by all rights hate her by now, but I just can't bring myself to do it. Anglicanism is so beat…we need more anger. I look at the stars and still think they shine for her, if not perhaps slightly dimmer (that should shock you by the end of this book).

I'd been stupid because I forgot to heed the old yarn about foreseeing who your wife will become simply by knowing her mother today. And I'd been insane because I kept trying the same thing for fifteen excruciating years hoping for a different outcome…the thing is, Albert Einstein never met my ex or he'd have asterisked his theory on insanity. You know what Einstein's theory on marriage was? 'Women marry men hoping they will change, Men marry women hoping they will not. So each is inevitably disappointed.'

My ex is neither stupid nor insane…she just likes her men that way. She's high society's answer to the Deep Sea Anglerfish, otherwise known as the common black devil…she baits prey with her beauty. And she always has a plan…she has contingencies for contingencies and never a sign of guilt. She doesn't mess around because she's only here once. Eve herself is the only comparable mess she made of her man Adam and that only because of the epochal eternal fuckup. They had the Garden of Eden…and we had Westbury Gardens.

So what is she in the end? A tough-as-nails, steely, ice-cold, unsurpassably vengeful, evil, feminine, sexy-as-shit, narcissistic, split-personality, schizophrenic vortex of a society thug. She's a Gwathmy house, trust fund, insecure, berating, over-controlling, vulgar queen who occasionally has great sex when absolutely necessary. Does that sound confusing? That's what she is, or was to me anyway. I could never express myself perfectly and probably never will. She crippled what was left of my mental acuity, I'm toast.

So when did the little girl in pink Lilly turn into a heartless, adulterous, quasi-murderous, thong-wearing assassin of one? What triggered that metamorphosis? Was it me? Was I so powerful as to create this modern-day Goebbels clone? Or was she simply following in her mother's footsteps? Had her mother's never coming clean about her heritage and being humiliated by Locust Valley in the process, helped convince the daughter that ex-husbands are not to be heard or seen?

You won't believe the story; you'll likely chalk it up to being bitter and vengeful…I'm neither, I swear. I'm miraculously appreciative of my wife still in the demented ways of an excessive Anglican forgiver. And that's saying something…my forgiveness should be canonized.

She even had the shovel in her hand at the end, digging furiously, guilty as charged but definitely not shamed…more re-energized, a bloodlust energy boost, the Stranger in her macabre glory. She had social engagements to attend so the work needed to be expedited.

And if ever charged with a crime, she'd simply tell a judge to go fuck himself. She's mastered the art of vulgarity and self-righteousness. She has what they call Bad Boundaries...other people are simply extensions, so she controls all.

Here's the essential key to my wife's soul... She doesn't care one whit if you or I think she's the devil...actually, she'd prefer it for no other reason than she has a pathological obsession with universal intimidation.

The pavement she walks upon burns and I have the scars to prove it, they're my marital souvenirs. Sadly she left me no screwvenirs. And for my part, I no longer think she's the daughter of Azazel, King of the Devils...even he couldn't control this force of life. So here I am, not feeling too great thank you very much, in a place as far removed from my dream locale and as far away from my dream girl as can be imagined.

I was married to Somers Gillette of Locust Valley, New York, from 1992 to 2009. Fifteen years of the most mismatched twosome in the history of heterosexual relations (fifteen years of marriage, and two additional years of useless divorce proceedings for me, two very useful years for her). How to get from there to here...? A long, sad story...

Oh yeah...I forgot. I'm in the Bing now, on the loose in my dreams but locked up in reality. She got freedom and I got time and it's the greatest travesty in the history of the world. Because she's the one still hustling life's weaknesses, steamrolling artificial enemies, creating orgiastic fantasies, and selling pernicious lies.

I never did understand why me, a nobody of the lowest order, how did I get trapped in her Megiddo world... Luckily, before the Bing, I had a chance meeting with a lady I knew many lifetimes ago, at the corner of 78th and 2nd. She knew I was looking for answers so she showed me the reason, the purpose, the Rapture, and the End. I'll let you know at the end of this novel what she had to say.

This story is one for the books. The lesson learned: be careful of a fake plastic girl playing three-card Monte with your soul, because when you lose…she definitely wins.

there's a heartbreak beat playing all night long
down on my street and it feels like love
got the radio on and it's all that we need

(v. Psychedelic Furs)

A Phallic Narcissist

"This is no time to make new enemies." The last words of the philosopher Voltaire uttered when a priest asked him to renounce Satan.

She was the bar star at a cacophonous Upper East Side restaurant at 78th and 3rd. I'd gone there simply to watch a basketball game and left with my life in tatters. When we met, I'd been closed up to love, but after that night I wasn't sure I could get through another day without her.

The musical pulse was British-accent canyon echo rings (Smiths, Pet Shop Boys, Bronski Beat), upbeat tempos, percussive drum pops, synth chords and string section fill, a lyrical runway of angst and sorrow. Your marital omens start the second you meet and music has always been my channel marker.

The bar was called Hunter's and casino air was pumped in to keep the people frenzied. Everyone knew the place…the jackpine savages simply followed the money trail scent, charging the booze and memories to their latchkey parents. Manhattan bars are dream oases, sprouting up in the concrete every night to fool the patrons…even boarding school kids have dreams. The partiers' mouths were perma-open like a million starving emperor penguins, living it up on a Monday night. The bar manager had the music cranked high, the noise descending on the birds. High society was not yet decamped to the Hamptons, Millbrook, or Fisher's for the summer.

Amstel Light was it. No cell phones, Poland Spring, internet, Wi-Fi, and barely any cable. Yoga was practiced in India only. Lawyers knew judges and judges knew lawyers. A man could be anonymous, innocent, and tap water was fine.

I'd ventured out that night with a friend, Paul Auerbach, but I was really more or less on my own in that city, notwithstanding Paul. We'd gone there to watch the 1992 NCAA basketball Championship: Duke-Michigan, no Cinderella's that year. Duke had Bobby Hurley, Grant Hill, and Christian Laettner. Duke's my alma mater, UPenn his. I'd have gone to a real sports bar instead, but Manhattan didn't have them back then...you just went to whatever was closest to where you lived, and I lived at 75th and 3rd.

Paul was a secular Jew from Scarsdale New York but every Jew from Scarsdale is secular. He happened to have a much better-paying job than me at Shearson, but I've never been jealous of anyone's success, especially good guys like Paul, so that was fine. I didn't even read the Wall Street Journal. And let's be real, all I could really do was dream in tune. The lights of Manhattan didn't inspire me as much as overwhelm. Cody Jarrett and I had nothing in common...I'd never yell 'look at me Ma, I'm on top of the world'. It was more, how do I get out of here, Ma.

The bar was wall to wall snob, 50/50 girls-guys I'd say. Snobs despise everyone below but idolize everyone above (until they get above...then they hate again...). Mostly these were the Hermes-tie, tassel-loafered, manicured, boarding school, komsomol types. They didn't look like athletes, that's for sure. The LLBean cretins were swarming.

Like every other dolt without a sister to provide moral compass, when Paul went to take a leak I looked around the bar to see if there was a girl I might be attracted to (as if that was the real purpose to going out, which I suppose it half-was...). Paul and I were the only ones who weren't wearing ties and I think we were the only ones watching the game... I half-thought the bar wouldn't even let us in the door. I was drinking Bud so the waitress thought I had scurvy. When I enthusiastically informed her Coach K was a god, she reached for the phone to call the narco-police…she thought Coach K was a cocaine derivative I was looking to sell.

A silver-spoon crowd of twenty scuds came through the front door…scuds look good from afar, up close they can be kind of rough. I'm not sure how the manager made room for them at the bar but he did…must be VIP trusties I thought. I'd never go to a bar with twenty people, it seemed so desperate, a shout out for self-love. These were Phallic Narcissists: sounds horny, it's anything but. A phallic narcissist is an elitist, a "social climber", superior, admiration seeking, self-promoting, and empowered by social success. As you know, omens begin the second our life changes.

Wait a sec…Whoah…Stop the presses…Holy shite…Who's that?!…

A table queen came into view among the two-hundred preppy doppelgangers, as intoxicating a face as I'd ever seen, front, mid-center, ground zero of the bar's layout. She had a Grace Kelly look, neon-blue eyes set off against a gentle, sun-kissed skin, a full exterior package that discreetly, quietly, and confidently whispered wasp. I mean, she sure as hell looked wasp: detergent clean, sporty lean. Potentially a 420 stoner, but not over the top. Her camisole wrap was the softest cashmere, a hued periwinkle blue.

I stared from fifteen yards, me up on the raised level of the exterior tables, she down below…I was mesmerized by her glowing radiance. She stood out like color in a sea of black and white. Her aura was enchanting, magical, and practically hypnotic.

That was my kind of woman, as if Southern California had accidentally dropped one of its natural-blonde surfer chicks in Manhattan and the Quest crowd outfitted her. Ethereal, wonderfully pedigreed, a button nose, thin country-club ankles, shoulder length golden blond-streaked hair, drops of summer, muted vacation-rest makeup, a toothpaste atmosphere smile, and wind-swept-off-your-feet visual attention.

I wanted to play tennis on Har-Tru and make love to her at the same time. She'd probably wear one of those cute little white tennis skirts and her legs would go to the sky. We'd be floating on the Milky Way within seconds. My heart skipped....shooting stars were arcing across the firmament like so many fireflies. This was the closest to heaven I'd ever feel, mostly because it was the one and only time she hadn't messed my head up yet...I had no more than fifteen minutes of freedom left. My sentence was determined before the crime even committed.

A soft overhead light had settled on her flawless face, showcasing skin that had never seen a single blemish, further setting her apart from the besotted revelers lost in the dark scrum of the bar. Okay, the face had hardness to it, but not so much that it overly concerned me, and I was easily waylaid by the songs anyway. The scene just buzzed. Seeing your girl in a pulsating environment is intoxicating enough, it's also why you never want to meet her there. Everything's easily manipulated in a bar. In hindsight, I wonder if she paid the owners to throw the one directional light her way. You just can't trust her...

Her girl friends looked one hundred percent protestant, not as clean and lean as she, but clean enough anyway. They went by names like Bunny, Muffie, Flotsie, and Polly...sea horses with blocky, birth control glasses, saying 'ewww' every couple minutes. These future suburban mavens were afflicted by The Talbot's. They were trying to copy her swagger, hitching onto her social ride because they could never get there on their own. Eventually they fall prey to Darien, a Volvo, clubs, school functions, the cocktail circuit, no-foreplay no-movement no-screaming no-kissing, get-up-throw-the-condom-away, turn-the-tv-back-on sex, and then hear about a

neighbors' in-shape husband making a killing with his hedge fund…
Je dois aller à la maison retrouver ma petite femme…pas!

The game came back on…Paul was tugging my shirt. I bet when that girl shoots, she scores…all net no doubt.   She sets trends, doesn't follow them.   Duke looked good.

The young men were polished, hair above the ears perfectly parted, starched French cuff shirts, remarkably similar, dark-grey, Brooks Brother suits, ridiculously expensive Hermes ties with kitschy animal drawings (giraffes, elephants, lizards, cocksuckers…okay, not the last one but you get the point, nearly Brokeback boys). Their shirts were tightly fastened all the way to the neck, not an ounce of relaxation among them. They were in frantic competition to see who would be oldest first…cookie-cutter Rockefeller Republicans, moral equivocators. The young men of Choate, Deerfield, and Hotchkiss, Lake Forest, Main Line, and Greenwich, Hobe Sound, Nantucket, and Northeast Harbor: nothing to look forward to except a lonely Metro-North future and an oddly impressive GHIN score given their otherwise unathletic bent.

Note to crowd: move to the East Village not Darien.

This girl, my future ex-wife, looked enchanting in a way you didn't see back then…she'd keep her man fit, he'd need to be fit to handle that. She definitely knew how to do the wild thing (so far as I could imagine anyway by staring at her from 15 yards and never having met…but then again, nothing held my imagination back in my 20's). She wasn't preppy by definition but she was clean like a preppy.

Laettner was unstoppable…nice dunk.

She had the smallest hint of the devil-may-care. The perfect amount, enough to intrigue a man. The way she carried herself, you knew she wanted the spotlight. A narcissist's Travis Bickle stare, a 'you talkin' to me' dare to anyone who crossed paths with her. *'You talkin' to me? I said, you talkin' to me?!'* Wow….She seemed at odds with her own self. Perhaps she was a born-on-third and thought she hit a triple, but what did I care…it wasn't as if she was my wife…haha.

I'd gladly trade an aneurism for making love to this bar star…if I'm going to go out Lord, please let me go out making love to a woman of unparalleled beauty, otherwise known as the Nelson Rockefeller syndrome, though I'd prefer it to be known forevermore as the Sebastian Graham Syndrome, with my own variation. The weird thing was, she looked like she wouldn't mind if you died making love to her, or at least had a brain-stopping aneurysm trying. I'd have been first in line….of course.

Her only freak flag was that distant smirk and hardness…I should have paid closer attention. She had the feminine thing down and was American to boot. She wasn't a crazy I complete-you woman, but she was the best you'd find in Manhattan. She'd tell you a thousand times don't forget this is my life….and you wouldn't.

Paul was steamed I wasn't more into the game…he didn't even graduate from Duke. Hill was draining corners.

Those dark suited banker types were all over her. I'd never been so physiologically struck by a woman, dumbed down again to 2nd Grade when I dropped pencils on floor to stare up into Mrs. Davidson's skirts (the payoff being her granny panties). Most men have the testosterone level of adolescent apes at an adult-ape cabaret. *"Get your stinking paws off me, you damned dirty ape!"* I understood Charlton, Jesus, God, and Bogart. The odds were daunting for the five of us against her.

I was hooked on an invisible two-hundred pound test line. She turned my way, looked up and smiled at me, like a seasoned, confident stage director enjoying the performance of her cast. She sensed my sexual crudity. You could tell she smelled great, and who doesn't love that? She laughed because I wasn't watching the game… We weren't two lost souls swimming in any fish bowl… one of us was lost and he was being reeled in fast.

Her High Bidder

"Of all the gin joints in all the towns in all the world, she walks into mine"... Bogart had my future violent destruction down cold.

Was she a bad girl? Did she have Pine Manor morals and USC cheerleader looks? I had no idea she was the original heiress Black Widow, willing to kill without remorse, able to underwrite murders. Some talk, others walk...she walked and you knew. If someone had told me the whole pestiferous deal right then, I'd probably have gone for it anyway...she was a dare you couldn't walk away from. That's why the Black Widow never runs out of willing mates, men are supremely predictive, aren't we? I was an easy pickoff at first for this girl.

Duke was playing not to lose...first halves make me puke.

She wasn't a woman that slept around indiscriminately. I could envision three guys, if that. I was watching her every motion. Her face suggested few meaningless one-night stands, that would be for the lesser lights.

Like any hopeless romantic, my fantasy of her was now eternally seared into my empty brain, even when the evidence suggested a cold shower and wholesale lobotomy. Later, I'd learn that she could toss memories aside like yesterday's refuse...I hold them to my grave, even the afterlife.

The more I stared, the more she took my breath away. Most men at 29 can crash through cinder block walls to get to a woman they desire, so even when expectations are low, the risk of failure never seems too daunting…especially to idiots like me. Frankly, I never considered the consequences.

Duke was up but not by much.

Like a demented Moses to the burning bush, my wild light in need of company, I began the walk across the cloister of yuppie hedonists. Paul couldn't believe it. I'd given in to temptation…to the Fallen Angel. Sin was born that very moment. She'd never be consumed by her own fire, the devil's outstretched hands patiently waiting.

I muscled my way through and around the impenetrable wall of bodies, drunken Andover dark-suited I-banker types, some of whom looked vaguely familiar, and Madeira trusties who'd spent one too many hours around horses. I edged ever so closely to the girl…she kept turning her eyes to me. Her friends mouthed empty words as I elbowed around them and pried apart their disturbingly vacuous high street souls. Even their eyes were on their celubutante friend.

I mumbled back, staring at the floor, prying four penguins apart just to make one step. No way those girls owned thongs yet and they could have used them…a thong would tip their guy friends over. Finally a song I knew…The Smith's "There is a Light That Never Goes Out"*… I hummed it to myself.

'…Take me home tonight…In the darkened underpass, I thought O God my chance has come at last, but then a strange fear gripped me and I just couldn't ask…'

These people were drinking liquor like a bacchanalian orgy of money excess…and this was just a Monday night and it wasn't even a sports bar. The markets must have been raging (not that I would have known, even though I was supposed to…). For my job, I was simply a ticket taker selling popcorn, not caring if the movie was good or bad. That's what investment banking ultimately comes down to, don't let i-bankers fool you.

I could see Hurley dribbling the ball up the court practically through the legs of the UM defenders.

I had nothing prepared to say to her once I got there of course. What do you say to someone you don't know but already love…. can I kiss you for a few minutes? I needed a wow line, something Oscar Wilde and Shakespeare couldn't dream up if they had weeks to prepare, not may I kiss you etc... I needed her name. With a name, a man can go places but without a name, the man can go to hell. Or in my case, I'd get her name and go to hell…(this would never be a match made in heaven…spoiler alert).

I could only think one thing…don't screw up buddy.

'…where there's music and there's people, driving in your car, I never ever want to go home.'… *

Every man ends up in this spot eventually, where your instinct is to be beyond-witty and stand out from the others who'd fallen before you. You put too much pressure on yourself this way; it's a girl, why so ridiculously strategic? Why such pressure? I mean after all, it's not as if she's going to kill you, right? Ha…

She was everything good in my life, and if Duke won, an historical evening.

I was flying naked. Ten feet from the bar star now. The noise was deafening up there, the music, the penguins, the horses, and even the tiny voices inside my pathetic head.

She was in pristine shape....Tall, maybe 5'9" with battleship grey eyes...from across the room I thought they were neon-blue, up close they defied description. I'd never seen eyes like that. They were North Atlantic seawater in a cold dark storm... haunting, hurt, wary, foreboding, but also tough, determined, purposeful, strong, an evolutionary testament to survival and reproduction. Everything in one eye was at odds with the other, like half of her was good and the other half evil. I should learn more about omens. Mistake #2.

I stared at her for the final thirty seconds it took to navigate the last of the penguins and horses, and she back at me. Some Hotchkiss boy was talking to her but she'd stopped paying attention to him. She was pre-occupied with me, a mortally-wounded gazelle appearing on her horizon, one who had come inside her feasting boundaries, and she was measuring its weaknesses. Her irises lasered in on my presence like a puma cat before pouncing.

I inched closer. You should have seen her... I was flabbergasted, dumbfounded, reduced to a teenager again...my mind spun like a drunken top, its stunted sexual development laid bare for the world to see.

She was wearing faded blue jeans, but not normal jeans...they were super skinny, not a popular trend back then...in fact, not even in stores. These are the skinny jeans girls wear today, with tight ankle grips and low waist lines. Sexy and revolutionary then. I assumed she didn't have cactus legs or a tramp stamp...if she had a backdoor stamp, I'd simply, regrettably, inescapably, prematurely, and mortifyingly ejaculate at the mere sight right there at the bar (or I'd Nelson Rockefeller myself)...just get the mop mate. No girl had tramp stamps back then. You put a tramp stamp on a woman as fine as this, you're talking wasp freak and Protestant boys implode (her tattoo stamp now would be the devil with horns is my guess…).

'…if a double decker bus crashes into us, to die by your side, is such a heavenly way to die,'… *

Her ass was flawless, undefiled, without error. She thrusted backwards ever so slightly showcasing its near perfect half moon form, and yet she simultaneously grinded forward, her front pelvis straining against the steel zipper, the final gate to this wasp boy's Promised Land. She was squirming, all fire, youth, and hunger. I was enfeebled intentionally, like the heretic Venus flytrap to the unsuspecting naïf. There was no escape from the curves, symmetry, femininity, and wonder…those jeans allowed for few doubts. I needed Lamaze before I knew what Lamaze was…breathe in, breathe out…

Her ass was ridiculously clean…it must have been. Is that a weird thought…? Maybe my previous girlfriends had issues or maybe I was deranged to some extent. I'm just being honest. You could eat a five-course meal off that ass and be confident. I wanted to frame it like Monet, an artist sketching a masterpiece for the world's enjoyment.

In other words, I was…sold: her highest bidder. I couldn't survive without her.

Her shoulders were insane, delicate and precise. I wanted to embrace them for all eternity. She didn't have big breasts from what I could tell, but then again no one had big breasts back then…every girl was flattish. No tucks or silicone, so I thought… She was an angel as well as diabolical fiend…heaven help me but this wasn't going to be easy. I needed to talk God, maybe at this bar, and beer was proof that God loves us anyway: La bière est la preuve que Dieu nous aime et qu'il veut que nous soyons heureux.

'...Take me home tonight, take me anywhere, I don't care,'... *

I suppose it couldn't have been windy inside there, but I swear I saw perfect periodic wind gusts. They would sweep her golden blond-streaked hair over her winsome shoulders every few minutes. Everything moved delightfully with each toss of her head and twist of her body, in slow repeat form. The game would have to wait. She was female perfection and I was male imperfection, the story of all civilization.

I was five feet away now.

Our staring had become total, desirous of each other for very different reasons. We wanted to devour, animatedly/sexually for me, mentally/emotionally for her. That's an easy trade for a young woman but a horrible one for a young man. I wanted to be with her...she and I could last forever and it was making me shake already. I began to wonder why I even came.

With five more bodies elbowed, I made it, she still half-sitting, half-thrusting on the stool, me brain-exhausted from the thousand-step path I had taken. Since I don't have much mental bandwidth to start, I was in retard territory by then, the gazelle completely defenseless, the puma licking her chops, or was that the vampire licking her fangs... I could feel her heat, like being too close to a bonfire.

She looked down at my Budweiser. Fuck.

Sometimes a moment can last a lifetime when you meet someone. I wonder what she thought…likely she didn't think much, probably just here comes my next victim, but this time he's got a Bud and not even an Amstel. After this book, her memory is bound to get pretty caustic, so don't believe her if you ask….she was probably fairly agnostic at the time.

That other guy was still yapping at her, not shamed by the girl's complete disinterest in what he was saying…I'd keep talking too if Darien was my future. The guy stopped and stared at me. He saw the Bud and sneered. I saw his fingers and thought what I always think of guys in Manhattan: this guy gets manicures...a Facebook pussy fifteen years ahead of Facebook time.

She and he simply waited for me to trip over my tongue, which was as good a bet as any that night. I stood there Quasimodo-like, dumbed down mostly, but it must have looked to him as if I was daring him to go first. The band was hitting a crescendo and the players were leaving the court. He lamely slunk away, a Volvo surely in his future.

'…there is a light that never goes out,'… *

For me, I could write a thesis on the moment when my eyes held this girl's…civilizations have been built on lesser meaning. I felt like a hibernating bear that'd emerged from a cave in need of potassium, if not a tranquilizer dart to my scrotum. I wanted to get with her. She smiled her broken smile, and she had a gap tooth. She was here to lure me away from goodness. I loved it. I was game for her evil, and I had approval from corporate.

She went first, in a Fanny Brice imitation, "Hello Gorgeous."

Then her tone immediately shape shifted into something more ominous and epochal, but enough of a boyfriend voice to melt me at the same time, "I've been waiting for you."

The Public Flogging

Crickets chirped. Clock hands ticked. I could hear a single clap in the back from a Duke fan. A metronomic bass beat pounded out of my chest, or was that my heart? Before I could say a word, a future Facebragger penguin waddled up to her, remarkably oblivious to me, and said,

"The plan is the Surf Club in an hour, cool?"

"Ned, sit and spin, and then can you fuck off. I'm talking to someone? Jesus fucking Christ."

"Ewww.... Hey, no probs. Period much...? God."

That guy must have gone to Trinity-Pawling. This boarding school robot of neckwear strangulation spun away as fast as he came. She intimidated me already with her cursing. It was my turn at bat,

"Were you playing tennis in Central Park this weekend?"

Imbecile! So flipping stupid! Could I be any more transparent? It was a total fart of a follow-up to hello gorgeous. How about saying hi, or mentioning the basketball game at least? Something safe, topical, the weather perhaps? I'd stay up all night with her if she was game…I bet she hated Bronski Beat.

I didn't belong to any clubs in New York, not yet anyway, so I wasn't schooled in the local country club nomenclature, where guys let girls know they're members of the society crowd. I knew the Central Park tennis courts were Har-Tru, Har Tru is waspy, waspy was good, and she looked waspy. A dishonest start to a bad relationship only makes it tragic in the end. Mistake # 3. But she bit…a sleeper cell in her womb was hungry…

"Huh? What did you just say (the way she said this was less like she was confused, and more like she was accusing me of asking her to show me her breasts…)? Do we know each other? You look kinda familiar. Talk."

Done…I was hung up on her with three lines. You know the great Brendan Francis quote: "A man is already halfway in love with any woman who listens to him,"…that was me there.

She had a naughty voice, not Lauren Bacall husky but definitely not sweet or innocent, sparkly, challenging, worldly, and invitingly tipsy. Maybe she did sleep around, maybe my across-room assessment had been wrong. She was intoxicating….seas would rise at her word. This one had to worry Daddy, if she was human that is and I wasn't sold on that part yet.

The music amped. The second half of the game started. I could barely hear myself while I took her in and tried to find solid ground. It must have looked like New Year's Eve from the outside, with the beat, booze, and crowd…Everyone was pulling on her, like peasants asking the Queen for dispensation, and the Queen lapping it up, reveling in the adulation and carnival atmosphere. The Phallic Narcissists were cheering, waiting for my head to get chopped off.

Big Audio Dynamite was at full throttle… '…*All the chances that I've blown, All the times that I've been down, Situation no win, Rush for the change of atmosphere…'* The crowd was bouncing in tune, like a concert of mating flamingoes stuck in a cage.

"No. Don't think we know each other. But, uhhh, okay, who do you want me to be, to make you sleep with me?"

"Are you always full of crappy 80's music responses, or do you have a wittier answer to who you really are? By the way, I fucking hate Animotion!"

She talked tough, like a longshoreman at happy hour. You've never seen a finer looking woman with a more gutter vocabulary.

"Argh...I hate them too. Impressed you know the song though, with just one line! You should be on one of those music trivia shows."

"I'd win…I always win. At everything. Join us. You sure we haven't met? I know everyone. What's your name, and don't lie this time for fuck's sake?"

She was teasing me before we even knew each other, laying me out like a seasoned pro. No wedding band thank god, she struck me as a girl who might be the one to slip off a wedding band…normally that's a bad guy's role. She could feel fear in her enemy's eyes…or the wounded gazelle's anyway.

"They call me 'Jesus of Nazareth'… But some people just call me Sebastian, still more call me Seb. Only a few call me Jesus…actually, now that I think of it, no one does. But my mom's name is Mary if that helps. Can I buy you a drink, uhhhh, ummmmm, or just give you money?"

She laughed…good sign. She was babysitting her drink which looked suspiciously like vodka and tonic. This was her stage. The world's a stage for the front burners.

But behind the bravado, she was skin and bones scared about something in there, but for the life of me I couldn't figure it out. In my head I was drawing masterpieces, writing Joycian odes, blasting perfect clay sculptures, silently bleeding with the passion of a rectitudinal Protestant. Any more of this and I guess I'd die an early death…not on the cross so much, but rather at a hospital for the lovelorn insane. I was in the presence of something holy, like holy hell.

'…I wouldn't change a single thing even when I was to blame'… *

She would definitely not sleep with a nobody from North Carolina. I knew that without being told. Like most losers, I had a deeply ingrained sense of self-loathing, all musicians do. And most musicians have a Jesus complex as well. I wouldn't sleep with me, why would she (then again, I wouldn't sleep with any guy…how women do it is beyond me…). I subscribed to the Oscar Wilde maxim that the man who says his wife cant' take a joke, forgets that she took him. I knew exactly where I stood.

"Well Jesus, I mean Seb, I always take the cash, so no to the drink. How come we've never met, or have we in some other life? That's always possible, you may not know it yet…I'm going to call you the full 'Sebastian' by the way…I like that name much better, it suits you."

She now owned my name and she was answering my questions with questions. At least I could hear her. My senses were getting sharper, if still one-dimensional. She seemed somewhat interested in me but time was going to go by quickly, you just knew. She was sniffing, baiting, reeling, but I wouldn't have all night to take the test. I was on her bar star clock.

I was hypnotized, she had the juice. I should have met her when I was five, fallen eternally in love by seven, stopped looking up Mrs. Davidson's skirts by eight, and created the world's first super-family by twenty-four. I could avenge her honor like the great gladiators of yesterday.

Duke was pulling away.

The devil feasts on weakness. Look how the crowd cried for her. Look how the crowd hates Duke.

"I don't know. I just moved to the Upper East Side actually. Crowded bar….Do you hang out here a lot?"

I was trying to do anything to move her eyes away from the Exeter crowd pantomiming gay Oscar Wilde last century, to separate her from her never-orgasmic Frick Young Collector girlfriends, hinting to her in painfully obvious ways that I could not believe someone that radiant was hanging out with hangers-on and dozens of them at that. Why wasn't this girl in Monaco sipping champagne on a mega-yacht with the Prince of Monaco, debating UN resolutions while making starry-eyed love? She was in a crap bar with crap friends meeting a crap guy like me…and I wasn't even the 'Prince of Fuckup' yet.

"I know the owners; do you? What do you do by the way Sebastian?"

I'd been to Hunter's once in my life…tonight. How would I know the owners? Of course though, why wouldn't she. Like a banker handing out umbrellas only when it's sunny, she didn't even pay for her drinks. And I hate discussing careers…argh… Boring and mine-fieldish, the last reliable refuge of the Manhattan cocktail circuit…the rest of the country talks weather, we talk career.

"No, I don't know them. Looks like they're doing well though. Umm, well, I work at Shearson, but truthfully I want to be a full-time musician."

"What instrument do you play (kinda cool she didn't ask more about Shearson…)?"

"Uhh, rhythm guitar. Mostly rock, you know Pink Floyd, Queen, Bowie. That kind of thing. Tough to get enough volunteer musicians together in this town to play those bands' tunes, so I do acoustic stuff, my own, theirs. I also write."

"Would you write a song for me? Can you write one now?"

"Here with these people?…nah. Not a good idea. It'll end up being an ode to suicide. Later tonight, I could write you a poem that could become a song…I'm still learning instruments so I'm really just a role player on stage, and a total spaz on overall song production. But sure, why not. Hey, want to sit down in the back with my buddy and me? I need the company…he's a good guy and all, but boring as shite. It's fairly loud up here. C'mon on."

We were already at a crossroads, I'd shot my load with the musical interest comment, and no one liked the music I liked anyway. The penguins loved Air Supply and Toto…argh, all tune wedgies in my head. And Diablo loves Foreigner! This was my full court press moment.

"I'd really love to, but my friends are all here at the bar. Come on back after you and your friend are done. Promise?"

Had she just said 'Why don't you come up sometime and see me?' Was she the Lady Lou of the Upper East Side, or was I Hollywood delusional?   She had the juice…

"OK. Sounds good. We'll stop back when this thins out. See you then."

Semi-humiliated but not yet completely dead, barely alive but still breathing, I began my walk away, unsteadily like a wounded boxer being sent by the ref to his corner. I wanted to see this through…nothing could ever make me love her less.

'…how I'd love to be your man through the laughter and the tears, situation no win,'…*

That's it…I turned from ten steps away. She was still staring…friends of hers were as well. I think everyone was aghast at my ignorance as to who she was, my head still intact on its shoulder…they knew the slaying was soon. I shouted over the din,

"Hey, what did you say your name was again?"

"I didn't say my name Jesus… Just call me Hell, since that's what I'll be to you…You have to work a lot harder for my real name. It's worth the effort though. (Whisper) Trust me."

She mouthed the words 'trust me', she didn't actually speak them, the implication being that just between two of us if we have crazy sex, you'll die a very happy man indeed (that's what went through my head anyway…). She had balls of steel. They called her Hell. I loved it. Weird.

"Huh?" I was stuck in stupid gear. She got down from her stool, the seas parted, and she floated over to me. That was easy. She put her hands on my shoulder, leaned in, and whispered,

"There's a side of me you may never want to know. We'll go out soon…just get my name and find a way to reach me. And…you will give me a poem and it better be fucking good. I've been expecting you for a while Sebastian, I had almost given up."

God she smelled great but she was a tough crowd.

Lost in love's crazy embrace for a nanosecond, she then laughed…at me, not hysterically, but conspiratorially. I'd been set up by the Angra Mainyu, the unholy destructive spirit of Miss Porter's and trust funds. Who says what she said and laughs, as if she knew this was a challenge of hopeless and ultimately self-defeating ends? What kind of woman was this?

I was in love, lost and confused. A trifecta strike of modern male enfeeblement.   Maybe I could love her less. She was a smoldering piece of ass called Hell.

*'…If I had my time again, I would do it all the same, situation no win, rush for the change of atmosphere.'… **

Did she call me Sebastian? I said call me Seb, not Sebastian…only mother Mary calls me Sebastian. I don't have mommy issues by the way, but she needed to know… A young man goes from feeling like he will never desert his woman to agony in the blink of an eye. Stars dim quickly when the sun rises…

I stared at her and at nothing, physically incapable of moving or thought. All I could do was twitch my eyes and fingers like some kid with erratic epilepsy, listening to the pulsating toms beat away at my hopes. She was a full-blown drama riot. It was SRO at the bar of humiliation. I was too ashamed to cry.

Some of her friends saw her laugh so they laughed too, like a school of nervous fish, buzzkill shoulder surfers. I was in the town square being mocked and ridiculed while the Queen held court…I would have preferred the guillotine. A thousand vuvuzela's were blaring in my general direction and I was without thought lost in the cacophony. Quasimodo's bells had never been more deafening. My forehead was on fire. Even Michigan scored…

It sure helps to be witty or more instinctively intelligent. I could have replied, Hey you know what, you work for it, sister, a Jimmy Cagney sneer, yeah that's the ticket, See, See! I didn't say that of course, since I had already offered up my own name within a nanosecond of meeting her…smooth move. Mistake # 4.

I turned to go, my urban Amish tail tucked snugly between his legs, no longer chasing hopeless dreams. Duke was up safely.

A curiously less raucous choice from the house DJ, The Kink's Celluloid Heroes, "…you can see all the stars as you walk down Hollywood Boulevard, some who succeeded and some who suffered in vain, success walks hand in hand with failure…" Music was all the art form I ever needed to paint my life stories.

It was a lonely path to Paul in the cloister. Note to self: it's easier walking away from a fire than toward one. I turned to look when I sat and she was still eyeing me, self-pleasantly smiling. She had orgasmed from the beatdown, squirming on her stool. Baphomet had a gap tooth.

God, I loved her…

Somers Gillette

I knew I would always meet a girl like her…her good half that is. When a guy like me meets a girl who has already taken Manhattan but he's unaware of it, ironically the odds are in your favor.

In the back of the restaurant, I could hear myself. Paul was holding up a score card with the number ZERO on it. Just another wretched four-letter word that seemed to capture my spirit all too well. He had the grin of a man who feasted on his buddy's failures. He knew I'd never see her again. That was correct so far as my head told me, but my libido was saying otherwise. Geez, I wonder who will win that debate…

Paul spoke,

"Here comes Loser #1! She's good looking dude. You should stay after her if you can take rejection. Way to cheer your team on by the way. You're up 10."

"She's unreal. I can't explain it…I don't think she likes me at all, but she wants me to try anyway. What's that all about?"

"Move along… Let her chase you or else it'll be doomed before its starts."

He was so much smarter than me. I was stuck in the English countryside of the 1400's, forever resigned to the bludgeon tools of the times, whereas Paul was winging it in the 23rd Century, Bluetooling before Bluetooth was a word. The Jews were pulling ahead of the Protestants, Duke was pulling away from Michigan, and the Frick would be the Schwartzman soon. I wanted Paul to be my mentor, and yet we were the same age.

From where we sat, I could barely make out the bar scene anymore, which seemed to grow in size each second, sucking that beautiful girl deeper into the massive void of arrogance pretending to watch hoops. Every so often I'd momentarily catch her flawless visage, when she would toss her head. I think she'd steal a fleeting glance my way. I wondered if I was caught in her trap. I already felt like I was in a trap of my own making.

"Hey Paul, what's going on?"

Two girls approached our table. They looked to be about mid-twenties, dark hair, dark eyes, dark makeup, awful outfits, nasally accents, New Jersey for sure (or so I thought)…The exact opposite of the girl at the bar. The game was now into garbage time.

Paul knew one of the girls from Shearson, a secretary. Paul was an I-banker. We worked on different floors and got paid wildly different salaries. Paul was integral to the firm and I was useless, not that these two girls knew any different (like a lot of people on the outside of an investment bank, they assumed if you worked at one, that everyone makes the same amount as the CEO…why ruin the fantasy).

The girls had decent bodies from what I could tell, but my heart wasn't in it. They'd been drinking hard, as only (what I thought) Jersey girls can. You could tell in the first minute they were game-on…for anything, because they laughed at everything we said. When girls laugh at what you say and you're not a comedian…the laughter is a full plumage mating call. The liquor…that's just an excuse for Daddy.

I wish I'd had a sister growing up…

We paired off conversationally, Paul talking to Cindy and me with Jessica. Jessica was actually not from Jersey…she was from a town called Framingham in Massachusetts. She was Jewish, which I only knew because she said so within the first minute of talking. And I didn't follow up with the classic, that's funny, you don't look Jewish! But, the thing was, she didn't…

Jessica didn't make me work for her name or for much else for that matter. I could no longer see any sign of the white blouse girl at the bar…I was hoping she was still inside somewhere, wailing at her loss of me to Jessica. She would never leave without saying good-bye…would she?

The final buzzer mercifully ended for Michigan…we won by 20. Anti-climactic really, even a tinge of March sadness though my team won. I felt like my soul had been zapped by a new bracketology. The night wasn't looking historical.

I should have been honest with Jessica and simply said that I had zero interest in her, no matter what went down.   Mistake #5.

The DJ cued up James' Laid, all military drum procession and acoustic six string sweeps, *'…she only comes when she's on top…you're like a disease without any cure…you're so obsessed you're becoming a bore…I locked you out you cut a hole in the door…'*

I didn't know where Jessica was taking me…I just knew it would be too far. Coach K was on his way to the Hall of Fame and not the cocaine trade. I had an awful feeling that I let slip the one human in my life that I'd ever truly wanted. It was an emotional death shot. The rabbit died. The casino air just blew out the exhaust vent.

We got up to go. When we reached the front door, I told Jessica I left something back at the table. What I'd left, I had no idea, not that she needed to know. I just needed an excuse to go back and trace the other girl. Where it began, it would not end, not tonight anyway. I wanted to pull the rabbit out of the hat.

"Let me just run and get it…it will take me a second, so stay right here".

I walked over to the serving station and asked the waitress if she knew the group that had been there earlier. She didn't, but she said I could check with the manager in the music room, just off to the side of the serving station. She pointed the room out to me, I thanked her and walked over. I poked my head in and it was loud there as well.

I wanted to march in with Gats in hand, have the guy hit the floor, and say to him, "OK, give me the girl's name and no one gets hurt…"

Instead…Episcopalianism raised its clean head,

"Hey, sorry to bother you, heard you might be the manager here. Great restaurant by the way. Was wondering if you knew who was here earlier tonight, a big group at the bar, maybe thirty or so people? There was a girl in a white top with blond hair...gorgeous. They call her 'Hell'?"

A young man, with eyes of the purest blue I had ever seen, was hunched over a stereo system…I could see he was holding David Bowie's Heroes CD single, ready to insert,

"Yeah mate (an Aussie), that's Somers and her gang…they come here every few weeks when the owners want 'em around…hang out for a few hours, then split. Her friends are a little obnoxious, but she's okay. Nice Sheila, eh?"

"Somers, huh? Not Hell?…What's her last name, do you know?"

"Surname's Gillette. Works for a magazine. Uhhhhhhh, Fortune (what was Fortune? I didn't read business magazines…). Yeah, that's it. Doesn't write for them though mate. She manages events, like the Fortune Sponsored Dinners (hmmm, party for profit planner…sounds fun if a little below her…)."

"Thanks man. Somers Gillette. Somers Gillette. Thanks."

"Hey mate just a warning: everyone wants Somers, but no one gets her. She doesn't give in to just any bloke (I wish everyone would stop assuming I'm just 'some' bloke…isn't doing anything for my confidence btw…). Her ex-boyfriend messed her up in the head real good a few years back, or she him, so she's on the Revenge Tour 1992! That's why she calls herself Hell. She'll eat you the wrong way, if you know what I mean…she has what we call 'bad boundaries'…a bird without a soul."

He laughed hard, but in the most magically decent way I had ever heard another man laugh. My laugh. My kind of guy.

"Yeah…Thanks. See you around."

I had a name. That would be all I'd need. To heck with Aussie advice for the moment, they ruined Bon Scott.

Jewish Oral

Somers Gillette was racing through my stone-crazy brain. Tomorrow, I could triangulate Somers' address from the White Pages based on the streets where residents lived in Manhattan. You had to figure that this Somers Gillette would live on the UES, probably the 80's or 70's, east of Park. And who had a name like Gillette…what a strange last name.

Just not tonight…Back to my jumper, Jessica, who was holding onto the red door for support, slightly wobbly from the booze.

"Hey sorry Jessica. I thought I brought my briefcase, but must have left it at my apartment. You want to get another drink somewhere?"

"No not really, just take me back to my friend's place. I don't live in Manhattan, I live in Norwalk CT. I'm staying at my girlfriend's apartment here in the city (hmmm…)…you met her, she went home with Paul. I work for Honda, did I tell you that (no, but interesting….kind of…)."

I am using my girlfriend's apartment and she's gone for the night: code words for let's go back and do things to each other that are still illegal in Alabama. My Boston-born, Jewish, regional New England Honda-auto parts sales manager and me. Take me home tonight, Sebastian.

We walked outside and I nearly tripped over a bum lying on the street. I stooped down to give him a dollar. He looked vaguely like the stereo guy inside Hunter's, except this guy's hair was down to his waist and his clothes were ratty. The same blue mesmerizing eyes though, the same face even. He was decency, dignity, and grace, even in this state. I gave him a dollar, and this is what he said to me,

"The Rapture is coming Sebastian. The Lamb is in you."

Protestants don't have superb guilt consciences but I do for some unexplained reason. I was so bummed this guy knew my name...I could see my soul in his eyes, I could see my sins in his grace. He was dying for me and I didn't deserve to be standing above him...you just knew.

Jessica grabbed my arm and ripped me into a dingy yellow cab with no legroom. I stared at the bum as we pulled away, but Jessica had already begun to massage my groin. I couldn't put a name to the face of that guy, but we'd met before a long time ago. He looked like me if I hadn't shaved for sixty months.

Jessica was tonguing my mouth so deep I thought she wanted my dinner. Her hands were all over me...the Indian cabdriver was having trouble keeping his eyes on traffic. In the foggy haze of the 90's, little things like your girlfriend massaging a screaming boner were of little or no concern to cab drivers, Muslim, Hindi, or Jewish...everyone loved it. Farting hadn't been criminalized yet, but guys like Giuliani were warming up to write a law against it. My mind was back at Hunter's...that bum's presence was powerful and consuming, it even knocked Somers Gillette off a pedestal and that would piss her off.

When we got to Cindy's apartment on East 50th, we barely made it inside the front door, all quiet no noise except for two amoral humans wrestling. I fumbled for a light switch, but Jessica wanted nothing to do with that...

"Kill the lights Seb for God's sake!"

Jessica, my Jewish Jessica, proceeded to perform the single greatest, twenty-minute blow job in the history of global blow jobs, a standing in the hallway, grand symphonic, double rainbow, back to the wall, arms behind head, trousers crumpled on ground shoes still on, she on knees, hands mouth and head manically engaged like the UN General Assembly, culminating in the heretofore relatively-rare…swallow. The aria lived. White doves were released. This was L'extase des sens.

Jewish girls must love this I thought (ahem…). Slim Browning had never been more prescient, "You know how to whistle, don't you, Steve? You just put your lips together and blow."

All my life I had been trying to wrap my arms around the world…it finally gave back, perhaps in a less moral way than I had anticipated, still…. So this is what it feels like to be Mick Jagger… I could never do what she just did…must be a nurturing thing. We collapsed onto a couch.

Miraculously, I woke up in the morning at 6 AM. The apartment had a woman's light air touch and good smells. The early morning traffic smoothed down the avenues…you could hear the sanitation trucks on the side streets.

I was sure this blowjob would lead the evening news that day. Peter Jennings would have an ABC field reporter standing outside the apartment building and the guy would intone in a very earnest bass-baritone, Last night Peter, the greatest blowjob ever given, in this instance by a young Jewish woman from Framingham Massachusetts… I left the apartment slightly hungover, very tired, tripping, and completely spent, but no reporters were standing outside waiting for my quotes.

I called Paul from a payphone and demanded that he meet me at a diner back in our UES 'hood so we could swap stories (or more accurately, I could tell him mine…). He needed to tell Cindy to leave and go back to Jessica. He would have needed a threesome to compete with my story, and since we didn't live in LA, that wasn't happening.

We held our summit at a 24-hour diner at 75th and 3rd, right across from Mortimer's which was the physical and spiritual epicenter of Manhattan wasp high-society in the 80's and 90's. When we sat down, he was already in hysterics. Cindy had told him that Jessica was a sexual deviant and had been on the prowl that night…she chose me simply because Paul knew me. She was getting out of her system what she needed to get out because she was to be married in six months, and would never give her husband head. That was funny…Jessica never mentioned anything to me about being engaged. OK, maybe Paul wasn't the worst wingman…

We ordered scrambled eggs, bacon, and fries. My brain and body needed sustenance. Frankly, the story alternately inflated and depressed me. I was exhausted. No pursuit is ever worth the reward when there's no meaning behind it. Dreamers like me get old quick, you'll find us working as ski instructors in Taos or gigging for house bands in Jackson Hole.

Paul – "You ever find out that other girl's name, the one you acted like a school-kid with?"

Yes. I'd been thinking about her ever since I woke up.

"Yeah, actually I did get it. And I ain't giving it to you, you bastard!"

"Dude, I could really give a shit."

"Alright…You can't call her though. OK? Somers Gillette. Somers Gillette is her name. Works at Fortune."

Paul stared at me as if I had just given him the missing piece to some long-lost treasure map holding the directions to Atlantis.

"Don't you know who that is, man?! That chick is New York Society! She rules the old-money crowd. On the cover of Quest every month (what the hell is Quest?…). Wow, never knew what she looked like in person. Taller than I thought; much prettier too. Interesting… Anyway, I heard she's a bit of a fruitloop. And out of reach for you I would say."

I didn't know what he was talking about, or what New York Society meant. I'd never heard of Quest Magazine…I barely knew what Fortune was. I didn't care though. I just thought Somers was ravishing, and those shoulders... She was the perfect young American.

I'd gotten an epic blowjob the previous night, regaled the story to my pal, and all I could think was the one that got away. I'd never seen shoulders like Somers'. That's mostly what I remembered, those shoulders, more so than her face. But those shoulders….wars would be started over those shoulders. So soft, pure, feminine, sleek. All I had to offer in return was something called love.

And so far as New York Society goes, the wasp girls had started to intermarry. Guys like Paul were making more money than their boarding school cousin reruns. Still, the sons and daughters of Round Hill, The Racquet, Links, Brook, National, Stoney, Southampton Bathing, Maidstone, Bailey's, Lyford….they knew each other and respected the patrimony. Reruns are for sure their history and become comforting in a stale way.

Someone else was getting her best last night, so I needed to act fast.

We finished eating and walked out the diner to a still sleepy city. Loud street sweepers were blowing dirt from the one empty alternate side parking side to the other…so useless. And yet there was orchestral symphony to their massive brooms grazing the concrete.

"Whatever. I am going to somehow find her. Call you later."

My life had changed that night, and I didn't even know it. I met the girl of my dreams…she owned me and my name. I felt like a newborn. I had a life obsession now, to die by her side. Her name was Somers Gillette. To die by her side…

Pink Peonies and the 7th Mistake

I left for work that morning with my Walkman headphones on, better to avoid conversation.

'I still don't know what I was waiting for'…(v. David Bowie*)

I hoped I wasn't playing where I shouldn't be playing. I had massive amounts of ambition, lust, and sex envy. Enough to get me in all sorts of trouble with a girl used to wealth and grandeur. What I was feeling inside, I couldn't explain, but it was as if I was possessed, bitten by le Diable.

I made it to my Orwellian trading desk that day at 7:30 AM, me very alive in the land of stock and bond zombies and credit whores. The floor had begun its daily machinations, about a quarter full, the hive responding to a new day's sunlight, the night traders goofing off as their work day ended. Each voice in the canyon was disconnected, as if I was in a huge echo chamber but far from anyone. I was lost in music anyway, unable to disconnect the melodies and lyrics from my life.

I grabbed the White Pages from a colleague's desk and began my spade work…I didn't know what I was doing really, but it felt good. The mental tune was nothing if not rebellious for a young guy like me.

'…A million dead end streets'… *

There were two Somers Gillette's in Manhattan, one on East 79th and the other East 1st. She couldn't live on East 1st, that would have been about seventy blocks south of the Social Register DMZ. I found it strange that there were two Somers Gillette's…that wasn't exactly a common name. I mean, Stephen Smith, no problem…but Somers Gillette? The only Somers I knew were guys from Bermuda or the UK. I didn't know any Gillette's.

I didn't have the time to get my hands on The Social Register, and I certainly wasn't about to call my Mom. The Register used to be one hundred percent Episcopalian…the members' idea of cultural assimilation was saying hello to a Presbyterian while passing on a street. In order to be listed anymore, you shamelessly lobby the membership committee… like a 7th Avenue schemata for an apparel directory. The Register has as many Catholics as Episcopalians now, not that there's anything wrong with that, except for the fact that the Register Catholics don't want you to know they're Catholic…they're the self-hating kind… Mostly The Register's just friends who never show.

'…But I've never caught a glimpse, Of how the others must see the faker, I'm much too fast to take that test'… *

For some people like my future ex, there's no more important annual body of work. The Register is their standard-bearer, the final determinant in all matters of importance and prestige. They focus on the addresses, schools, emails, cell phones, and club affiliations like a banker reviews a credit applicant.

Back to my dilemma, thinking about all those lonely nights. There was no such thing as Caller ID in 1992 so I could always call and hang up if I heard a voice and chickened out...which was very likely. I swallowed hard and impulsively dialed the East 79th number from my office. After two rings, the answering machine came on…yes!

The voice was a woman's, natch, but it sounded harsh, business-like, and too scary for a home phone. I hung up. Whoa. Plan B.

The other traders at my desk had begun to file in solemnly, determined to make a killing that day, completely immune to small matters like their hearts, buddy pouncers with Kodak courage only. Those were the days for bondsexual traders, thinking of all the great things they could do without the SEC up their butt…Artists without portfolio's, or pas de couillons.

I dialed Fortune Magazine's general information number, to find out if I could get a direct dial number for a Miss Somers Gillette. To my delight, that's indeed where she worked. How far would I go to have her, I wasn't sure…But I was on point.

"Hi, you've reached the office of Somers Gillette. I'm not available to take your call, so leave your number and time of day when you called, and I will get back to you. Thanks a lot…Ta-ta!!"

Her work tone was not nearly the business-like sergeant-at-arms mien as her apartment answering machine. It was as if she had confused her home and business message recordings. She was chirpy at work, yet guarded at home. Odd. I hung up. I'm such a wimp about girls, especially when thirty other traders are staring at you like a fuckwit, seeing through you like the office ghost you are. This girl's spirit was haunting me already….

I collected my thoughts to determine what I should say in my message…if I left one. The problem with voice messages was they left no room for error…what you left, you couldn't take back (errr…once you fuck a horse, you're always a horse-fucker…). I decided to give it a rest for the day and gather my wits. Tonight would not be a good night.

'...I watch the ripples change their size, But never leave the stream,'... *

But before all of my wits were collected, I called a flower shop on Sixth Avenue, still on company time, and ordered a dozen pink peonies to be delivered. I thought I should prepare her for my call, you know, so she remembered who I was. Stalker much…

The girl at the shop wanted to know what I wanted on the card. I sat no more than two feet from a European equities trader on my right and two feet from a LatAm equities trader on my left, and I didn't trust them at all. They were staring at me intensely, amazed that someone had such complete disregard for the job they loved.

"(an exasperated half-smile on my face…) Can you guys go back to work, or am I your entertainment today?"

Me to the flower shop girl – "Uhhh…I don't know, perhaps you can help. I just met this girl last night and she doesn't know me. What would you want to read if you were her?"

"Well, make it a mystery…girls love that. Say something like, 'perhaps we'll meet again?'…Something open-ended."

Yeah, well, this is going to be a mystery for sure…!! I'm not even sure this girl remembers me.

"OK. Hmmmm. Let's see. Uhhhhh. I got it…Why don't we write, 'Seems That Every Time I had It Made, the Taste Was Not So Sweet…I'll Call Soon…Seb'. How's that? OK? (it was derivative, it sucked, but I was from Wrightsville Beach North Carolina, not Greenwich Connecticut…at least it wasn't Journey!)"

"Hmmm. I don't really understand it, but hey, it's sufficiently mysterious, if too obtuse."

She didn't know Bowie obviously. The heart is a total stranger to the brain…one acts and one thinks. My heart had found a warm friend to play with so flowers were on the way, and my brain was looking out for a black widow spinning its web in the bouquet…The flowers were ordered, a semi-broken heart looking for grace. Dreamers get steamrolled eventually.

'…Time may change me, but I can't trace time'…*

I wondered as I looked around the massive football-sized trading floor if anyone else had such wasteful pursuits going on, or were they actually earning money for the firm to pay my salary. Two clients had called me from Fido while I was doing the flower ordering…I simply asked the assistant to give the flow to a colleague rather than take the call. You could sense where my trading career was headed.

For the rest of the day, I couldn't get Somers out of my head. I wondered what she would think when she saw the flowers. I bet Goldman didn't spend their days arranging dates.

Anyway, the brain is not a great multi-tasking agent. I'm a believer in uni-tasking, where I focus on one task and do it well. Once completed, I can move on to the next one. I have made most of my mistakes while trying to do too many things rather than just sticking to one thing.

'...So the days float through my eyes, But still the days seem the same,'... *

I needed her, I missed her, if I could just see her again...Waiting for her call would be a heartbreaker. I hoped she'd never set me free when we met again.

My Polish-born trading boss, Rojek (that was his last, first, and only name: the Madonna of institutional equity trading...) desperately wanted to fire me, his least favorite office ghost among a thousand stock sluts...he clock-blocked me every day with some futile task at 5 PM, making me stay another hour or two while everyone else scattered to their real lives. I hated him in a non-personal kind of way...I just hated what he stood for, the politics and stuff. His ego wall had a billion awards and diploma's...argh.

I also felt sorry for all the young Deerfield Hermes-tie komsomol that bowed to him, my Astroturf boarding school colleagues....no one had a soul. I needed to work for a small company with real products with real people, I was giving too much valuable time to Mr. Shearson.

It was never my intention or plan to only think of her... it just felt better. Mistake #6.

At about 7:30 pm, I finished for the day, the day really being me thinking about Somers' shoulders for twelve hours, tapping my keyboard out of boring purposeful deceit to my employer. My heart was pumping. I decided to walk the thirty blocks to my apartment at 75th and 3rd. Mini-skirts were everywhere. Hope was on the streets and women's thighs.

'...and these children that you spit on, as they try to change their worlds, are immune to your consultations,'... *

Home bound, practically floating on air, passing thousands of empty faces. My mind cleared as I walked past the endless shops, making my way around the suits of misery. I was physically tired but mentally wide awake. Between Jessica's blowjob and thoughts of Somers, I hadn't gotten more than two hours of sleep the previous night.

I grabbed a slice at Ray's and a 24-ounce Foster's oilcan from the Korean grocer…about as healthy a dinner as any 29-year old can hope for in Manhattan. I had a fifth-floor girlfriend-ready studio above Juanita's, the rat-infested screen door Mexican restaurant that had the uncanny talent to make my suits smell like stale ground beef every day…

Were other boys blowing up her phone all night? Should I get in line? Was she out until sunlight? What was I missing?

I flopped onto my new futon, turning on the non-flatscreen television which by any haphazard geometric calculation occupied at least an eighth of the entire apartment…in other words, I paid about $250 of apartment space each month just to have the physical presence of a TV, let alone the cable bill.

I turned on some channel called ESPN. I half watched a game and half stared down 3rd Avenue through my window. I stared at my Jewish Jessica's red Honda logo and wandered if Honda corporate knew they had a sexual deviant on their hands. I bet she was a good sales manager for the parts division…

I could hear the background noises of a baseball game and the city streets filling the cool night air. Bowie was waxing quixotic.

'...Changes are taking the pace I'm going through...look out you rock and rollers'... *

Jack and Annie Come Up with a Name

I woke up the next morning at 6 AM, a new day rising, I was swimming with hope.

Come on Eileen* ushered in the sunrise on my clock radio. The hum of the city's streets at 6 AM was sunbreak smooth…you can hear cab hoods bounce harmlessly against their chassis as they cruise unmolested down the avenues. I couldn't get my mind off of Somers. I couldn't define how I felt, I simply felt light. From a chance meeting only, you had to know she knew I wanted her. Aaah, but it's just a delusion in the end, isn't it?

I went for a run around the Central Park Reservoir which on a typical spring day, you'd likely bump into people you knew and people you wanted to know. There's so much ambition in those runners. Exercise sometimes seems to be the only thing that helps me re-focus. I finished two loops, came home, showered, and dressed for work. My Ibanez six-string lay in the corner lonely, gathering dust.

As soon as I got to work all monkey suited up, I dialed Somers' office. Her voice came on as clear as yesterday, perhaps more so. Pleasant, chirpy still. Truth be told, I knew she wouldn't be at the office by 8 am…no one in publishing gets in before 9 AM. My confidence was misguided even with that.

But, I could feel it more than ever. In my best male baritone, I let it go, throwing caution to the wind,

"Hey Somers, Seb Graham here. We met the other night at Hunter's. Anyway, hope you remember me, because, well, uhh, I remember you. And I sent you something. I worked hard for this number. Impressed? Hope so (because I'm starting to screw this message up…). Anyway, I would love to take you out for dinner sometime (preferably tonight…). Japanese. My number is 212 922 1575. Call me when you have a minute and let's get it on (whoops…nuclear explosion…)."

I hung up fast. Moving forward…not.

Let's get it on?!?! How lame is that? I swear I am the dimmest at dating. All I was trying to do was leave a message with an uplifting tone. She would probably think what I really wanted to do was nail her on the first date…you don't bang your wife on a first date if they look like her. I was trapped in a thick cloud of fear.

My latest faux-pas would ice me for the day at Shearson. I needed a tea. I should have done"plastics", not banking.

I walked over to the trading floor cafeteria, a sterile food oasis situated squarely in the middle of the back wall. The guys at Shearson were from all corners of America, if by all corners you meant New England boarding schools. The Deerfield guys only hung out with each other, the Andover guys with Andover guys, Groton the same, Hotchkiss, on and on and on. It's almost as if when you decide what boarding school to attend, that will define everything about you for the rest of your life. These guys had their own handshakes and code words, they were gutless but connected.

I was a southern boy who had gone to a high school in Lake Tahoe to ski {hopefully} professionally, which apparently did wonders with deadhead stoners in Telluride and Taos, but was about as useful in New York as air conditioning in Iceland. I was a social outcast at Shearson...they drank coffee, I drank tea. I was sure they drank coffee only because everyone else did. These guys were bond and stock lemmings with high social aspirations if that makes any sense. They also loved Bon Jovi, but only because apparently they thought everyone else loved Bon Jovi...Bon Jovi sucks (that song Wanted Dead or Alive is one of those forever awful ear worms).

I never wanted to feel this way. Shearson was making me something I was not, resentful, spiteful, dismissive.

I grabbed a tea and pac-manned my way back to my grey-flecked Formica trading station, ready to plug the headset in so I could stare emptily at a computer screen for the next eight hours....living the dream, not. It was 8:10 am. My voicemail light was already blinking with a message. Naturally, I guessed that I'd missed the only trade that day from Fidelity. Where the heck was Erica our desk assistant? She was supposed to handle all incoming calls for thirty traders starting at 7 am.

I pressed the message button. A woman's voice came on,

"Hello Sebastian. Somers here. Sorry I missed your call; I was on with Europe (what, all of Europe?...why do people say it like that?...). Thanks for the flowers! How the heck did you get my number and work address so fast (libido frankly...). Most guys need a few weeks to scrounge up the courage to find my number, let alone call (well, I'm gonna get fired soon so I figured I'd make the best of my last few days...)! I'm a little busy the next few weeks, so let's try to get something in the books for May. Cinco de Mayo? Call back Handsome!"

Cinco de what-o? I hadn't celebrated that one yet, not many Mexicans hang out on the Eastern Shore of North Carolina. No use letting on what a rube I was. May? Was she kidding? Who the heck did this society puma think she was. The month of May was years from now. She couldn't find one free night to figure out if she and I were ideal matchmates? I wanted her so badly, I could taste her (so to speak…). Still, this was a giant step for mankind…it should have been televised.

I couldn't believe that anyone in publishing got in by 8 am. Strange. I couldn't call her back right away, that would have looked super-desperate…I didn't exactly rule my world yet, though I always had a backbeat perception that I'd lived other lives, much fuller than the one today.

'…at this moment you mean everything, with you in that dress my thoughts I confess verge on dirty,'… *

I froze. The day went by about as slowly as any one person's day can ever go. I stared at the clock four thousand times, so I told Rojek I wasn't feeling well. He couldn't have cared less, about my being sick or my leaving, and he wasn't going to clock-block me today. If he could re-assign my accounts without my running to HR to complain, he'd be a happy man. He was just biding time, waiting til the day I got taken down by the Alphabet Boys selling rock to Goldman's CEO, Rojek's two-for-one personal Rapture.

At 4:30 PM I walked home, aimlessly meandering back and forth across the side streets, taking two hours for what would normally take 30 minutes. The streets of people looked so alive versus the video-game staccato of a trading floor.

'…come on Eileen, I swear, well he means, Ah come on let's take off everything,'… *

My sad apartment phone rang that night at 8 PM. It was my friend and old neighbor, Annie Jackson, who'd gotten married and moved to Philadelphia's Main Line. Annie and her husband Jack were coming to New York the following day for a long weekend and they wanted to get together. Sometimes New York could get kind of empty, so their presence would help.

Annie was my first apartment neighbor in New York. There was no sexual chemistry between us, but I could always see why the other guys liked her. She was the first girl I knew who wore a thong…I saw it on her one morning when I walked into her apartment unannounced and she was passed out on a sofa. When she woke up later that day, I wanted to know all about that thing called thong…it made me mental.

We met later that night at Mortimer's. Mortimer's was gallantry and smoke, a bit Frank Sinatra but more Noel Coward, the city's home-grown paean to the good people. A piano's keys delicately produced some idle music every night and the younger trust fund crowd took up seats at 9 PM. The staff marched with the purposefulness of real careers…these guys made professional money.

Annie and Jack looked great as always, and Annie was already working on baby number one…the goalie was pulled. She'd be a great Mom and an even better wife…Annie's not evil. Married couples like them find a single guy's dating life really funny…it only seems funny from the outside, inside its dark and depressing. It isn't as if you're wishing your days away so much as wishing your days would change.

I mentioned to them that I met a girl I really liked, someone who for the first time in a long time I was actually intrigued by. The girl was in a class by herself for reasons I wasn't exactly sure. I described her without mentioning her name. I also asked them for any referrals themselves, in case this one didn't pan out. Surely they knew one girl they could recommend… The piano player rose to take a break and a sound track came on…Tony Orlando and Dawn, Knock Three Times…

Here was the weirdest collision of parallel thought in my life, not Tony Orlando and Dawn, but my friends and what they were about to say…knock, knock, knock... They both looked at each other silently, their eyes widened in lockstep, and then their mouths opened, and then their eyes widened even more. It was as if they both had simultaneously struck on a new definition of pi. At the same moment, in the same tone of quizzical hope, they both said,

"Somers Gillette?"

And with that simple utterance, my decision was cemented. There would be no turning back. I would have to get with her.

It was as if I had waited my whole life and I was made to go out and get her. I could hear the knocks on the pipes here at Mortimer's, the global epicenter of waspdom…it had to be one of three choices: a secular omen, heavenly trumpets, or Hell's Gates' opening…I can't win at roulette with a .473 probability, but somehow the Fates stick me with this girl and she was carrying a much lower .33 chance of doom?!! So typical.

Annie and Jack laughed at their mental symmetry, more because they were thinking that the two of them were ideally suited for each other, rather than considering the potential evil lurking inside Somers' head and how that might work out for me in the end. All blind dates need to be treated with such care and concern by the ones making the introduction… A failure can be epic, not simply a bad date.

Jack had worked with Somers at Fortune, whereas Annie had been in Somers' stepbrother's wedding. Like others' views on Somers Gillette, they had a loveless fascination toward her.

Annie – "I don't know Seb. She's kind of a bitch. I don't mean that in a bad way. She's just cold to the point of being really standoffish to most people. Underneath it, I think she might have a heart of gold (important to remember this quote much later…), but something's off there. Her last boyfriend really screwed her over, and I hear things about new ones. She's up for a good time no question, but she's not a commitment girl. You're a little too nice for her frankly. But I see you guys having a great time…She's a little bit of this and a little bit of that, as if she's unsure who she is really. I've been with her when she's fine, and I've seen her more vicious than any woman ever."

Jack – "Dude, she's such a bitch, but a sexy bitch; I bet she'd bang you on the first date…not! Nah, maybe five dates you get in. You won't likely stay with her for the long run though. I think she'll marry an older Newporty kinda guy. The last boyfriend and she had some issues. I hear she knifed him and his Mom!"

"Jack, she did not. That was a rumor."

"Well, whatever, I believe it. She's tough. You're gonna think she's a real bitch. Barbara Hutton's daughter comes to life. Everyone thinks she's a bitch. She's high society New York, man. Not likely to want to hang out in the 'burbs with you! I will say this; something isn't quite right with Somers; never been able to put my finger on it. I saw her turn on a colleague once for the stupidest reason…that guy was great; he was fired in less than two days. Everyone said Somers planted a false story about him to senior management. But, she was the sexiest worker at Fortune by a mile. Go for it."

I'd heard all I needed. We paid the bill, parted, and I went home, staying up all night staring at the ceiling. I didn't care what they said, to the exclusion of all the warning signals. *On attaque le compte à rebours.* The countdown had started.

"Sake Makes Me Horny"

People always want to fill you with doubt, but nothing's as strong as love. I ignored Jack and Annie's words of caution and decided to call her the next morning. I walked to work with my Walkman reverbing Echo and the Bunnymen's Lips Like Sugar. The trading floor had the early morning buzz of a beehive, all honeycomb purpose and hopes for the kill. I picked up the phone and dialed,

And she answered...

"Hello? (gulp...)"

Yup, she was in. It was 8 AM and no one in publishing gets in that early, I swear. I was thrown.

"Hi Somers. It's Seb. How you doing?"

"Sebastian." My co-signer for life said my first name in full again, in a tone that was both a question of incredulity, a statement of respect, and a declaration of evil mirth...this girl was not linear. Her voice gave me a smile though... She never answers the question 'how are you doing'...that's a waste of time. So my turn again,

"I got your message. Hey, look, a month is too long. What are you doing this weekend? Tonight or Saturday...your pick. I'd love to take you to East if you'd like to go."

East was a Japanese restaurant in my income range, and girls loved Japanese, or so Annie had said.

"Wow, you don't take no for an answer Handsome. I respect that. Well, let me see. It just so happens that I'm not doing anything tonight (hmmm…sounds like maybe someone got blown off…?). OK Cowboy. You're on. East, 8 pm. Make the reservation, see you there and then."

Click. Pure testosterphone! She never waited for a response, never asked if she could bring a safety date to run interference.

This girl was decisive, impulsive, and already bossing me around. And weird, I liked it. How is that for some sort of Freudian case study? You figure it out. She was all business, encased in the sexiest goddam package I'd ever seen. Did she run Fortune or did she simply have bad boundaries, a trust fund dominatrix?

The day went slowly, again. Mr. Shearson must have begun to lose patience with me. With some basic math, it cost Shearson about $1,000 per day in salary and overhead to keep me around. And I was giving them nothing in return. That wouldn't last.

I showed up at East by 7:45 PM, like I was onstage for the very first time with nothing but a broken six string and a voice in need of auto-tune, super nervous and way too uptight. The place was all shogun and Nipponese. I'd wait until 8:10 PM. The ten minutes between 8 and 8:10, I may as well have read Tora Tora Tora. Those were the longest minutes ever, an excruciating Hirohito cuisine water torture.

And then I saw her… I had convinced my very insecure self she wouldn't show. The crowd stepped aside, the star had arrived. I honestly don't think I had ever felt more honored.

'...she calls for you tonight, to share the moonlight,'... *

When she walked in, she stopped the restaurant. The world fell from her face as if nothing else even existed. Six feet of pure, powerful, stunning radiance. I wished she'd owned daisy-dukes…that would have been unreal-surreal, more than a tramp stamp even, more than Jesus' resurrection, more than…ahh, you get it.

She had a seamless tan, which meant she had been somewhere out of New York for the last month. She was dressed less New Year's Eve like last time, but perfectly put together still. It was hard to imagine any woman ever matching her elegance. She was in tight white jeans, a loose navy floral blouse, and high heels. Her jewelry looked like it was on loan from Aphrodite (which should have been a life spoiler alert for me, since Aphrodite was actually born when Cronus cut off Uranus' testicles and threw them into the sea…). She looked like a model with a trust fund and those simply didn't exist. Don't kid yourself that everyone in the restaurant didn't stare either, and don't kid yourself that she didn't know it. She loves being Queen, and who doesn't want to be Queen? She was escorted to my table by a Japanese hostess. I rose and kissed the side of Somers' face. She smelled like heaven.

Time would fly that night: we laughed, I stared, we talked, I stumbled, we ate, I choked. She drank Sake, a full carafe. Maybe she did drink a lot…maybe I would get lucky. She told me about herself but never really asked me anything. I was really impressed that she was on the board of a boarding school in Newport. At such a young age too. And it wasn't one of those boarding schools of self-love…it was the navy blazer army but the kids at this school were good guys and girls.

I made only one near fatal attempt at inappropriate emotion all night,

"Not to be too romantic too soon, but you know Somers, a lot of us search for light in the darkness, and then here you are. I'm just really happy you showed up."

"You're sweet…ugh, I hate sweet. You don't know me Sebastian, yet, so watch out. That light is a locomotive and you're standing in the fucking tunnel. I may be coming right at you and you won't know it until you're plastered. I may need you more than you will ever need me. Just remember that."

She talked about her Dad and that side of the family but she didn't say too much about her Mom. I gathered she had ours, yours, and theirs step and real families. She really was a Gillette, and every time you shaved, you dropped something into her account. Kind of. I didn't really care about that and don't think she didn't notice that, the 'haute heiress' happy that her new man didn't care about dosh or where it came from. My honesty was dangerous to her, or was it my ignorance. I wasn't a Brahmin wasp, I was a southern wasp, the type that doesn't talk much.

She was witty, light, sexy, determined, educated, sarcastic, self-deprecating, and challenging. She never displayed one ounce of evil that night, just a hint of dangerous fun. It was all mental intercourse.

'…she knows what she knows, I know what she's thinking.'… *

I can't recall more of the specifics of the conversation, which is strange…usually I remember everything that a date says. That night however was just a blur, as if time was simply a parallel continuum to the joy of being in her presence. I think I was eloquent, I hope I was; I think she liked me, I hope she did. She laughed enough, but not too much. Who knows? I was new to town and not well-known. She liked that part a lot. She knew everyone, especially the boarding school clutch, but she hadn't examined the Zephyr Cove ski factory as of yet, so she didn't know me.

I know we never discussed prior dating lives or anything remotely uncomfortable. She lowered her walls just a tiny bit that night so I could peek over. I loved what I saw, but the real problem was, I've always been blind to false fronts.

At 11 PM, she asked that I walk her home…it was a sensible hour and she had her safety buzz on. I was more nervous than loaded.

'…you'll flow down her river, but you'll never give her, lips like sugar,'… *

For any other girl I'd ever dated, you'd assume that if she asked you to take her home and she was buzzed and it was a Friday night, you had grounds for sexpectation. But for Somers, I only wanted to protect her, to get her home safely and away from the marauding hordes of Manhattan boarding school Scratches. If you know Somers, she doesn't want to be protected by any man let alone me, but she has a way with all men, making them convince themselves they know what she wants. The fact is, it's always diametrically opposite to what she's really after.

It only took five minutes to reach her apartment block on East 79th and 2nd. She lived in a pre-war, red-brick co-op, natch. This was our first moment of dating awkwardness, where hard decisions needed to be made and not regretted. Her doorman was ten feet from us and staring and she was thinking that perhaps we might possibly take it upstairs, just maybe not that night. She had another game plan for me. She also didn't want her doorman to see us do anything at all and he looked like a formidable presence with his walrus mustache and security guard-like uniform.

She grabbed my hand and reversed our progress a block, to 78th and 2nd, away from the prying eyes of her doorman. The way I felt when I was in her hands that night is not describable, it was all Oliver Barrett IV and Jennifer Cavelleri, except we had switched genders. She stopped me at the northeast corner under one of the blinking yellow pedestrian Stop/Go signs, but it was broken…the lights on this block were all out for some reason. I saw a tarot card reader shop and a woman in the window staring at us…ladies of the paranormal have always haunted me.

We stood there for a minute in a Mexican standoff, heads bobbing and weaving. Then Somers did it….She inflected me with the poison from which I would never recover. It was the perfect moment, a perfect time to kill, time slipped, and I was fully unaware. Mephistopheles does his best work at night.

Somers leaned in, wrapping her arms around my pounding chest, slithering her cool arms past my neck, gliding her fingers through my hair which was on end, rubbing my scalp with perfectly edged nails…she arched her flawless head up, and our lips met…passionately, slightly drunkenly, but purposefully and effortlessly, no awkwardness, no teeth click. She had more strength than I expected.

Time stood still as New York's endless stream of foot and car traffic sped by. We were oblivious to the world and for all I knew the world was oblivious to us. We held on for a minute or so… The stars and heavens collided and I was in love, smote by what only a woman can offer: a life-altering, super-attenuated holistic embrace, a tender touch, exquisite warmth coursing through lips touching yours, tongues soft as skin, body to body contact where height is a perfect fit, elevated senses so wonderfully new, freezing all thoughts and awareness of motion and presence, causing a man to cave like an imbecile, enfeebled by the power of superior love and care.

She neutralized me like a snake before devouring its victim. She was loosening me up for Homer's even sweeter wrath…

We came up for air, out of breath, with her mouth no more than a centimeter from my left ear. I was wobbly. She leaned in for the final slice, the silver bullet, the cosmic artery cut,

"Sebastian, you're really fun. I like you. And I know you want me. But, I'm warning you now: I don't know if falling for me will be good for you in the end. I have to go, it's late and I have to be up early tomorrow (Saturday?...), but I need to tell you one very important, very private, between-us only thing…Never repeat this to anyone, OK, or I'll kill you. Seriously, I'll kill you, and never fuck around with me when I tell you a secret. OK? Ready? Are you really ready Handsome? Cause I'm only gonna say this once: Sake makes me horny."

*'…just when you think she's yours, she's flown to other shores, to laugh at how you break,'… **

Lump in throat, testicles ball-tilting on axis confusion, hearts melting, my soul being draft-sucked into the night sky…What did she just say?!! Sake makes her horny…?! She had a full carafe of that crap!! This loving made me feel so right. I was Icarus flying straight into the Sun on a contented suicide mission. That kiss would never be enough.

She then walked away, a Humphrey Bogart swagger, a 'here's looking at you kid' kiss-off, from a woman to a man no less, back to her apartment building, the she-Oliver Barrett in control. Time to say good bye…il est l'heure de partir et de vous dire au revoir.

I was stunned, twitching and gasping for balance, frozen, staring at this blond society Aphrodite sashaying down that city block, the eddies and currents were in full force. Her ass was the northern star of perfection, moving back and forth as she strode her city block with her traffic smoothing by. Forever feet off the ground, I was delusional, I'd follow her to the ends of the earth if indeed that's where she lived. I was dizzy.

The trap had been set, I was going multiball.

"These People Like REO Speedwagon for God's Sake!"

Sometimes beginnings aren't so simple. One date and I didn't know if I could live without her….god what a fool.

It would be almost two months before I'd see Somers Gillette again. Two of the slowest months in the history of boy-girl relations…in other words, since Adam and Eve. I thought we were in love standing there at 78th and 2nd, the world stopped and Somers and I would be together every day for the rest of our lives, right? Who turns their back on that, who tells you sake makes them horny, and then leaves you high and dry? I'll tell you who…

She was the fly-fishing expert of attraction with no parallel…she baited, teased, and dared you to strike, and when you struck, she'd pull back hard on the rod, ripping your mouth open, and then throw you back in just to do it again... I was swimming upstream as hard as a man could, rocking and rolling, trying to avoid the grizzlies and bait, stoked to get to the spawning grounds, completely oblivious to my mounting odds. I should have turned around and said good bye. Instead…

"Sebastian, that sounds soooo fun…I wish my sister hadn't organized this stupid party for profit in Katonah this weekend. And I just got back from Nantucket…I really don't like that place anymore. Can we try for something different in maybe two weeks?"

She was snowing me…teasing me, making me uneasy. She'd offer the kind of turndown where you wouldn't necessarily be discouraged from calling again…but unfortunately for me, it wasn't as if I had an immediate follow-up plan.

I was driving myself mad, stumbling in my bid, not boyfriend psycho, but boyfriend malaise. My work suffered tremendously. Not that I was operating at Shearson from any elevated position, or had senior protection. I was an awful big-company employee. Memorial Day weekend was coming up. I'd be doing nothing better than standing on a corner, staring at freaks and ghouls, high as a frigging kite, anything really to stop thinking about her.

She said was that she was going away with girlfriends. Somers doesn't have girlfriends, like in a normal sense. Somers sees all women as competitors so she keeps them closer than real friends. It's a relational trick, snaring you into believing she likes you when in fact she hates you. Not that I knew any of that then…heck, she seemed heroically great on our only date.

On the Wednesday morning before Memorial Day, I was at work. Trading floors of holiday weeks are perceptibly quieter than normal weeks, with most of the office bosses slipping out quietly well ahead of the masses that can't leave for their share house in the Hamptons or New Jersey until the closing bell. I called Somers one last time at her office…8 AM. I wasn't going to call again if she didn't answer. Waiting for her call, I was done with that….I'd be on to new challenges. She picked up, as if she had been expecting me…

"What's up Sebastian?! And, how are you doing today?"

She slowly said the last sentence, since I had teased her the other night that she never asks anyone how they are before launching her battles…

"Uhhh….how did you know it was me?"

Can I charm a woman or what! Perhaps I should have just responded to her question, or maybe asked her how she was…instead, I farted, yet again. She couldn't know my troubles with God…I couldn't speak let alone confess.

"You dummy…you're the only one who calls me at 8 AM at the office. Every other guy waits until the afternoon when supposedly I'm less stressed (what other guys?…)… Of course it's you! By the way, I think you're the only one who knows the real me, because I'm a morning person, happiest at this hour. You knew that, right (no, not really…I'm just desperate to see you naked…)? That's why I like you".

OK, OK. So now you're thinking, sounds like she likes you. Well, that's what I thought too, her words and inflection gave me confidence…I was feeling new again, a man back on a mission. But words are also weapons, potentially even landmines. That every other guy comment made it sound as if there was a conga line of suitors behind, or in front, of me. I had to compete.

"Hmmm. Well, I like you too. What are you doing this weekend?"

I could only stumble over my thoughts and tongue, putting my foot in my mouth with the least impressive lines imaginable. And don't you think she didn't know it. She liked that I was urban Amish, she could mold that kind of ignorance.

"Well, I'm headed with some girlfriends to the Adirondack's. We're hiking for a few days (yeah right…my mild sarcasm…)."

I called bulldust on that, to myself anyway. Only a fool always plays it as cool as me. I should have called her out. This girl would not be going to the Adirondack's over Memorial Day…no one else was up there yet.

"Oh…Sorry about that. I wanted to invite you to Montauk to go paddle-boarding."

Wheee. I'm sure that was less than impressive. Paddle-boarding is fun only if you know how…otherwise, it must sound like work.

"Sebastian, we're going to have to know each other better than that, ya know, before we sleep in the same room Sweetie (I got a slight tingle with that statement of the obvious…sharper than a knife this one…). I'm glad you called though. I have a present for you. I think you'll like it. What's your office address? I'll send it over."

"What's the gift?"

Argh….Again. Stupid! Slow down boy…Let her run with this…

"Don't worry about that…it's a surprise. I think you'll like it. And it will give you something to do this weekend, you know, besides thinking about me handsome (I do a few other things besides think about you, like avoid thinking about you…again, not psycho!...)."

How the hell did she know all I did was think about her? Do all women know that? Or only Somers? I gave her my address and told her I'd call sometime after the weekend.

"Let's get together after Memorial Day, Mr. Handsome Graham…Call me then. Ta-ta!"

I was part elated and part crestfallen, again. I was sure the gift was a joke and she'd forget to send it and that she was going to be having sex with a boyfriend who loved his job. My insecurities were piling up at an enormous clip...and in my convoluted head, she was all to blame. Telling me that sake made her horny, kissing me like that...it just wasn't right, I was mush. I wanted to hang stars in her night sky, be her arm candy somewhere, anywhere.

When the head trader from Fidelity called me at 2 pm to check on an open order to buy 200,000 Grand Casino shares at the market, I quoted him $56/share, when the actual price was $12, only a 500% spread...enough of a spread to cause Bat Shit alarms to peel. Rojek buzzed me on the squawk within ten minutes.

"Graham, get in here."

I walked over to Rojek's window office. Shearson didn't really fire people back then for stupid things like mispricing a quote...what they did was re-assign accounts. That's as good as rolling pennies. If I had to cover Farmer's Insurance in Kansas City, and not Putnam or Fidelity in Boston, I may as well become a landscaper and buy insurance from Farmer's, not sell crap security products to them.

"Graham, I've noticed you fucking around a lot in the last few months. Is everything OK? Do you know what we do here?"

"We rob banks, like Clyde Barrow...?"

"Funny. That joke just cost you Putnam. Look, I really like you, you're about the only guy here who doesn't kiss my ass, and I know you think I want people to kiss my ass, but the truth is (when a banker says "the truth is", that means a lie is about to come out...), I hate it (yeah right...my mild sarcasm...)...Look, I-banks are just a huge game anyway; we're here a few years, we make money, and then we leave (wow…meaningful...I feel so much better about myself now…). You're not making money though, for yourself or the firm. So we need to do something. Kammels from Fido just called me. Told me his head trader thinks you're high on drugs. What's up? Are you?"

"Rojek…I'm ok. Just a little tired these days. Girlfriend troubles."

I'd rather have had drug problems though. Maybe she was a drug and I had a habit already… Like Somers was my girlfriend…right! By the way, all those Lawrenceville young Commie apparatchiks knew her, so I could never speak her name around the trading floor. Anyway, real girlfriends have actual boyfriends and I didn't much feel like a boyfriend…more like a male cross-dresser.

"Oh. I've been there young fella. On my third marriage now (what a shock…not…). Third time's a charm, just wait. First one, you're too young; get it out of your system. Second one, she takes your money; let her take it, it's worth every penny to get rid of her. But the third one, now that one, you know what's doing! That one's for life (this guy had a strange interpretation of marriage…). Look, I'm gonna do you a favor, why don't you take the rest of the week off, it's slowing down for Memorial Day (never trust an investment banker when he's nice…he's selling you…). Get your head on straight and come back Tuesday ready to take over the world (Shearson was channeling Up with People?...)!"

This guy, whose first language wasn't even English, had a perma-grin on his face, even when he was pissed. It was like he was about to screw you, telling you he's about to screw you, and then when he finally does screw you, you have no one to blame but yourself.

If I left for the weekend, if Somers actually sent the gift to the office, I wouldn't get it until the following Tuesday. I was losing my mind and she knew it…shite, I knew it. Somers had messed with my head, even though we had gone out on exactly one date…now that's a specialty. The truth was I couldn't answer the phones at Shearson anymore…I'd probably cause the firm to collapse if I stayed another minute. Four thousand employees would be out of work and I'd be strung off the Brooklyn Bridge.

"Alright Rojek. Look, I really hope you don't re-assign Fido while I'm gone. We've been picking up new business there; we're getting trade votes now. We're on track to double revenue this year. So, please don't' do anything."

"Don't worry about that Seb (I'm grabbing ankles this very second…). Just go get your shit together. See you Tuesday."

When I walked out his office door into the boisterous cavern of the Shearson trading floor, it was plastic thrasher metal music sign language in the encore crescendo, traders whipsawing their heads up and down in infantile pigeon neck motion, rocking out to stealing money and robbing banks, hook 'em horn finger displays cutting the dank air signaling victory. Clyde Barrow had been cloned and his wardrobe updated. I looked back in at Rojek in his office…he was already on the phone re-assigning Fido.

These people listen to Journey and REO Speedwagon for God's sakes! Backstabbing, 70's light-rock music loving corporate thieves everywhere. The Prophets were right...trading careers are destroyed before they take off.

Steinbeck and xx's and oo's

I walked over to Erica, our trusty assistant from Staten Island, who not uninterestingly had made 50% of the thirty person team I worked with wiener cousins, but not me. Her sexual exploits probably accounted for half of all after-work conversations from the guys…they said she was a world-class screamer. She was sweet as pie outwardly…I could never reconcile her outward personality with what I heard from the guys. How can any girl be so sweet and yet so dirty?

"Erica, I'm taking off for the weekend. Larry is to handle any Fido trades for the rest of the week. Also, I'm expecting a package today from a friend at Fortune Magazine. I'll call you later to see if it arrives. If it does, do you think you could meet me somewhere later and drop it off, or I guess I could come back? Actually why don't you call me first and let me know."

"No probs Seb. Hope you have a great weekend!"

Chirpy chick that as well, just not nearly as smart as Somers…about $1/100^{th}$ as smart actually.

"Yeah, you too Erica. Be a good girl and don't go the beach with these animals."

"Ha ha…That's exactly where we're going? Who told you?"

Oh, I don't know, I've only heard every trader on the desk for the last month talk how about how much sex they are going to have with you in their time-share in Quogue …that's how Erica. Stay away from them.

"Uhhh. Just a hunch I suppose. Talk to you later."

I walked off the floor to the elevator, down to Sixth Avenue and into a tight-backseat yellow cab with dirty plastic floor mats. Can we get some London cabs please? I was sure no gift was on the way from Fortune.   I'd be doing one-handed flips in buttocks-exposure hospital gowns at Bellevue if life didn't change soon.

When I got to my woefully small apartment, there were three messages waiting on my home answering machine. I was sure one was from Dr. Guthrie the landlord looking for his rent; what a chiseler, I was a day and a half late. The second message was from my mother who wanted to tell me that her summer house in Wrightsville was ready and I could use it any time I wanted…she was headed down there that weekend so the farm was free to use. The third message was from Erica…a package from Fortune had arrived.

I was here and it was there, of course.

I called Erica and asked her to meet me at Grand Central Station near the center platform clock at whatever time she could make (I just couldn't stomach going back to the office…I was the walking office ghost to every other trader, who would have known by then I had been relieved of Fido). We agreed on 5 PM.

At 5:10, she showed (what's up with girls being ten minutes late…). Erica had a bag from Scribner's on Fifth…a book (erotica I was praying...).   Before she left, I hugged Erica and gave her $100.

I went upstairs, out onto 46th Street and over to Connelly's Saloon, a dark Irish pub where I ordered a pint of Bud and carefully opened the letter so as not to tear the paper. They had some sad Irish music wafting around, about hopelessness, famine, and death...a real pick me up. How did U2 ever come out of that misery? Even Danny Boy is about going off to war.

"Dear Sebastian, You told me the other night that you enjoy books. Well, here is my favorite. Please accept this gift with a note of caution. Although this is my favorite book ever, I'm afraid my favorite character is Cathy (Kate) Trask; I'm just like her. You'll understand after you read the book. Call me Tuesday, or never call me again! If you do call me after Memorial Day, we'll go to my father's farm in Millbrook, where we can start our family...! Just kidding! Jesus...I'm not that easy (but you might get lucky ☺). Don't say I didn't warn you. XO Somers. June 27, 1992."

Inside the bag was a large, 400-page hardcover edition of East of Eden by John Steinbeck, not exactly brain candy. Have you ever been close to an unexplained phenomenon? My college thesis was a comparative study of Albert Camus' La Peste and Steinbeck's East of Eden, portraying among other things Steinbeck's Cathy (Kate) Trask as an illogically formed character. Would a wife really be that devious, that duplicitous, and that genuinely evil...Kate frames two kids for rape, shoots her husband, and abandons her kids. Could I even relate to Somers the fortune-teller? I had never been tested by a woman, but she was testing me...

I opened the cover jacket to the flyleaf. Somers had written one more note inside...

"Sebastian...All my Love...Somers Gillette...5-25-92...xoxoxo"

I was right back at 78th Street and 2nd Avenue, my heart skipping beats. Every little thing she did made me crazy, I had vertiginous disbelief that she had given me East of Eden as a gift. The little things only a woman can do, like place x's and o's at the end of a letter, written in the most magical feminine cursive, for whatever reason can reduce me to my most base element.

I kept staring at the writing inside the book, for an hour almost, because that's what the waitress eventually told me…the waitress looked exactly like that fortune teller at 78th and 2nd. For some reason I remembered that woman's face really well…

Somers' game plan was genius. She was a relationship four-star general, I was a private first class on his first day of duty. There would be no way out of the hole I was falling into, it would either be a Quest death or murder…she must have loved those choices. The battle had begun.

Kate Trask is the most complicated, purely evil character in any contemporary piece of American fiction (before this novel anyway…). There was no act beneath her, no heart worth saving, and no joy worth preserving. She is a sociopath of the most disturbing order. Why anyone like Somers would even consider herself to be similar to Kate was beyond me. There was not a chance that this blond Cleopatra, Somers Gillette, could begin to approach Kate's moral depravity. Somers wasn't a sociopath, right? Our kiss had confirmed that. Hadn't it? Hello?

It was love's happy, hazy lunacy, the delusion of youth and testosterone.

(Oh yeah, I have just one book with me now, trying to see what I missed…)

Millbrook Vasocongestion

This was hopeless. I wanted her, but not as much as I needed her, or was it the other way around? I was dreaming, caught like a fool boy by something called love. I decided I needed one more day of mental rest, so I stayed away from work again that Tuesday.

My apartment walls were bouncing with undulating waves of guitars, percussion, and synthesizers. It was detuned low-frequency synth, sustained guitar tricked out feedback and escalating vocal reverb. It was all grand and heroic, capturing my wannabe life, trader by day, rockstar by night.

I called Somers at her office at 8 AM and she picked up on the first ring, as if she had been expecting my call, no hello, just,

"Well, are you taking me to Millbrook for a weekend stud?"

Was I Jennifer or Oliver?

I arranged to pick her up at her apartment, on Friday June 26m at 4 PM, in my trusty but janky Saab 900S. I plucked a low D and let it howl, pissing off my neighbors. Frets on a guitar are laid out in mathematical ratio spacing of the 12th root of two, so every twelve frets equal one octave. I have 24 frets on my electric guitar and I also have a scalloped fretboard, so when I pick, my chords have a dramatic vibrato effect. It helps me convince myself I'm a better player than I really am. I also like to think I can cover my life in chords, riffs, and tuning. Somers was a low D 0-8-3 vibrato.

No one waits four weeks to go on the actual date after the date has been arranged. But that was Somers and this was her plan, her plot,

Diavolous in drag. Waiting created anticipation and the tension became unbearable.

Needless to say, Rojek re-assigned my Boston accounts to a St. Paul's apparatchik over Memorial Day. The trade to me was Kansas City, St. Louis, and Omaha. I gave up Fidelity, State Street, Putnam, and some new accounts called hedge funds. My projected income fell 50% overnight.

When that Friday mercifully arrived, you could say I was kind of ready… I had all the necessary food groups for the weekend: beer, wine, tequila, and Ho-Ho's. The rest I'd worry about when we got there.

She told me there was a pool at the farm so I needed a bathing suit….check. We were going to play tennis so I needed whites…check. We would help out with her father's cows so I needed Wellie's and jeans…check. The weather forecast was fantastic; mid 70's during the days and mid 50's at night, no humidity at all….check. The traffic broadcast seemed favorable…check. All systems were go…the thousand year Bottomless Pit toss was in her grasp.

What I should have been doing was checking myself into a mental facility.

I drove up to her building at exactly 6 PM, and she was ready, natch. Somers is forever a punctual person, if not wildly self-righteous. She was downstairs talking with the doorman, bags packed. This guy eyed me suspiciously again, just like the date night of two and a half months ago.

Somers was dressed in an Audrey Hepburn outfit, light blue Capri's, white oxford cotton shirt, espadrille shoes, and a tan cashmere sweater. She was so impossibly fragile, yet raw and elusive, I almost felt guilty thinking about sex. She should be in a museum somewhere, not possibly getting sweaty with me. The museum I had in mind at the time was the Met…now, the Menninger Clinic.

Somers pecked me on the cheek…she smelled great. If looks could kill, she was a mass murderer. Stunning, textbook exquisite. She spoke,

"You been gone a bit too long for my taste…!"

I was high on memories of skinny jeans and still couldn't breathe…I smiled.

We got in the car and we were on our way to her father's farm in Millbrook. We drove up 3rd Avenue to the Willis Avenue Bridge, leaving the island of Manhattan in the rear view mirror. When we crossed into the Bronx, Somers perceptibly relaxed, almost a metaphysical exhale. Her smile became real, her shoulders loosened, and her words flowed more easily. You could sense that Manhattan was an anvil of sorts for her.

We drove up I-684, to Rte. 22, through the depressed towns of way upper Westchester and lower Duchess Counties. We drove through a mysteriously abandoned state insane asylum in Pawling. The barbed wire surrounding the facility was shiny, but the place had the look of an old Hollywood movie set for the criminally insane. There were no cars on the weeded property and no sign of life…even the weeds looked dead. The windows of the old brick buildings were caked in decades of grime and mostly cracked. Signs read "New York State Department of Mental Health; Pawling Adolescent Detention Facility".

Mr. Gillette was a gentleman farmer who visited his farm only every couple of months. He owned five residences around the world, and Millbrook was but one. Nick's main home was in Locust Valley, New York, on Long Island. He used his Duchess County farm to entertain guests on fall weekends, and the angus kept his property taxes low.

Somers had been given a cottage on the 500 acres by her father, mostly to help get her mind off the seven-year boyfriend Richard (she never told me his last name), whom I got to hear all about on our drive up. Until then, I had been reluctant to engage Somers in talk about anything concerning old boyfriends, but she wanted to discuss it, so I simply let her go. Richard had been the love of Somers' life. Hearing about another man is so draining, the thoughts of him driving her home at night, taking her dress off, etc…Argh…It kills.

He represented everything that she idealized. He was from Newport, belonged to the right clubs, and wasn't a banker (Somers hated the idea of her man being a banker). She said she liked renaissance men, like Count Dracula… Richard didn't care about society because he was society. He was the real deal, not a social climber like everyone else she knew. With him, she could abandon the maniacal and naked pursuit of society parties for profit and the media maulings of Quest, Avenue, and Town and Country.

After six years of dating, Richard was put off by the twin forces of Somers incessantly demanding a wedding and Somers' mother, Gruella Kincaid. I gather Gruella liked to walk in on Richard when he was taking showers at Gruella's house…she'd use the pretext that he used too much water and she wanted to voice her displeasure directly to him. Every year for six years there was a drought…"Mrs. Kincaid, you're trying to seduce me…aren't you?"

Richard ended the relationship and Somers became the crazy girl…
It took a year to disengage and there apparently was quite a bit of
euphemistic bloodshed, but in the end, at least Richard escaped with
his life…something that could not be said for me later I suppose.
Somers almost committed herself to a mental institution.

Somers' views about Richard weren't so pleasant anymore, as if
seven years of a relationship could be so easily dusted into the fires
of hell, as if she'd never wanted to experience any of it. She
couldn't bring herself to say one decent thing about Richard
anymore actually. Nothing. Her memory was a black hole of fury.
The consequences of that were too ugly to control.

"He's the biggest fucking asshole ever! Do you know what it feels
like to love someone who wants to lose you? I was the last to realize
it. I hope he fucking dies, loser!"

She could curse like no one's business…wow. I actually kind of
like that in a girl…it always seems so incongruous with the package,
deepening the mystery (of course the vulgarity cuteness ends when
the relationship dies…then it becomes frightening, like a horror
movie).

She never asked me one question about myself…mostly because she
already knew everything. I could tell she had a slight issue with ego,
but not enough to scare me before we ever got to second base. The
poison was still in my system. Somers was a bit of a conversation
narcissist. In social situations, conversation narcissists steer the
conversation away from others and toward themselves.
Conversational narcissism is the key manifestation of the dominant
attention-getting psychology in America.

She had high walls built around her. If they ever fully came down, the earth would shake. It sounded like her mom had something to do with Somers' walls.

I didn't have the nuts to ask Somers then if she ended up stabbing Richard and his mother, as Jack had said, but she did admit she almost went into psychiatric care because of the breakup. I could hear in her voice the faint trace of suicidal thoughts. Her anger at Richard was real, the pain incurable. I couldn't imagine that it could have been Somers on the giving end of evil. All my own shite seemed to fade when I was with her, so I trusted her already, even though we really didn't know each other at all.

We finally pulled into the bucolic town of Millbrook at 8 PM and the farm ten minutes later. Not a minute too soon either…my head was spinning from her life story and the seeming 50/50 split personality I was getting to know.

Somers' cottage was a two-story, white clapboard colonial. It had a picture postcard country kitchen and three upstairs bedrooms. She had a small garden in the back and a grey-slate patio that lay under a huge elm tree in the front. The inside looked like a Ralph Lauren catalogue, all cotton white sheets and wicker furniture.

I unloaded the car and the first moment of social awkwardness hit us when the house elf (me) took our bags up the stairs…Somers was waiting at the top in her Hepburn country outfit, arms folded in front like a school marm ready to dole out orders.

"Where do you want me to put the bags Somers?"

"Put your bag in that bedroom, put mine in my bedroom. You can use that bathroom over there (she pointed to a small hallway bathroom on my left). But, you're spending the night in my bed (she pointed to a large bedroom to my right...). I mean, come on, how old are we for god's sake? I don't fucking live with my mother anymore (thank god for that...). But it doesn't mean we're sleeping with each other tonight."

AOL Keyword: *"Tonight"*.

Somers really knew how to take charge. I wasn't used to it...I'd always been the one to control the relationship. It was refreshing to know someone who wanted to run with the ball and I was happy to hand off. Physically, she didn't strike me as the take-charge type...those shoulders were way too winsome, her arms too delicate, her wrists too frail. It's only in those eyes where you see the evil that lurks... It took the edge off though, knowing we wouldn't be doing it. I could relax.

It was daylight outside and we were starving. Somers had brought along some food (the Ho-Ho's weren't enough apparently), and Holly, her father's cook, had stocked the fridge with everything else we could ever want for a month. The most dangerous food a man can eat is wedding cake...and I didn't see any inside the refrigerator.

As for Somers, well, she had already gotten the goods on me and I never have found out how. I still don't trust the East of Eden coincidence. It was probably Annie and Jack unintentionally repeating something to her. She knew where I grew up, where I went to college, how I got my scholarship, who I worked with, my friends, my dogs, my masturbatory habits, etc...Well, maybe not the last one, but when someone tells you something about yourself that you haven't exactly repeated to anyone else, you just assume they know everything else, especially the big things like masturbation and prior weddings...Oh yeah, that....I didn't immediately volunteer that I'd been married several years before, for 36 hours...it embarrassed me more than anything. More on that issue later...

I knew nothing about Somers other than the fact that people called her a bitch. I hadn't asked a soul about her prior to that weekend. People are always talking about other people's reputations and never finding out for themselves...I try to have opinions about people for only what I've done with them. God, why did you make wasps so stupid...? Seriously, it's no wonder we lost this country.

Somers wanted to fire up the grill and cook hamburgers, so she asked me to get it going. The carnivores were about to begin.

"You're in control this weekend Sebastian...just remember that."

I didn't have a clue what she was saying...it was as if she was channeling a centuries old language only remotely close to English that rose up out of the earth's core. In control? Of what?

Somers likes her men to do the grilling...a bit of a test from her to be honest, like that's a hard one, but when you're used to Brokeback City of Museum black tie effetes being the men in your life, guys with Kodak courage only, a grill goes a long way to prove your manhood...

I opened some wonderful (read: expensive) white burgundy, which we drank too quickly. I should have bought sake if I was so in control. Alcohol takes the edge off of any situation, but too much leads to missed opportunities. I didn't want to not be able to perform so I tried to remind myself to slow down.

She didn't have a stereo at the farm and there were no radio stations this far north. Taking music away from me was incapacitating on some level, and again, now I just think she knew. I'd have to barbeque in tune, but that gets very hard when a woman is in the vicinity.

We talked about East of Eden. I told her that Kate Trask did not remind me of her, or her Kate. She told me to just wait, I'd see. She was very confident of that position… When we corked our third bottle (at $40 a bottle, this was now a very expensive evening…) and coming out of our food coma, Somers assumed a more determined, less feminine, more bossy character, practically commanding me to believe her when she said she was Kate. She was an inebriated ferocious hellcat and I didn't want to object anymore to anything she said…maybe she was like Kate Trask. I justified her lunacy as simply a sign of her being incredibly brilliant. I was perversely turned on by the quasi-lunacy and she only got more that way as the night bore on.

Somers had an announcement when her cuckoo clock struck midnight…she was feeling some liquid courage.

"Time to go upstairs handsome. I'm a little drunk for my own good. Take me now or lose me forever."

It sure felt like love, maybe even a little sexpectation. In hindsight, it was a drunken front, but what did I know….all she really wanted was arm candy. I still couldn't believe anything would happen…we were on way different levels.

Still…wouldn't you think we were about to do something? It's time…We're drunk…Handsome. No parent within 300 miles…You'd think we were about to do something, but the way she spoke, nahhh.

We made our way upstairs. Kate, errr Somers, excused herself to her bathroom. She walked straight in without turning around, no Hollywood come-hither moment, no pause for effect. From behind the door she told me to take my clothes off and get in bed. By taking my clothes off, I rightly assumed she meant for me to keep my boxers on, everything else could go. I could hear her getting undressed behind her door.

"Turn the lights off Sebastian…I don't want you to see me when I come out."

Nothing is more uncomfortable than hanging out on a bed by yourself, mostly naked, waiting for your dream girl to join you. A girl can take hours and she can change her mind ten times in a minute. I felt so far from where I'd been, but weirdly, I was supposed to be there with her at that moment too. I felt something so deep inside it made my body shake. One touch from her and I'd incinerate.

Somers opened the bathroom door slowly, a soft light still lit in the background.

All I could say (slowly) was, "Holy Christ". You should have seen that body. "Holy Christ"…that says it all, doesn't it?

If her Dad showed up unexpectedly, we were dead (or I was dead to be exact). Actually maybe he would have been dead, because I had one foot in the sanitarium already and one foot out, staring at his smoldering daughter, not sure if I could let go. She was all fire and smoke…I took the longest drag of any hit ever and the rush made me lightheaded.

I could see the backlight of her white mother-of-pearl nightie. The nightie came up mid thigh. Everything was seen in soft backlight: her legs, thighs, belly, breasts, face, hair. She walked over to me, her female curves swaying like a hissing cobra, and sat down sideways on the spotless white sheets. I nearly fell over from the hypnosis.

She slowly let her hair down, full in its rich golden blond texture. I could make out fresh white cotton panties underneath the nightie. In the pale moonlight of upstate New York, with her ridiculously great figure and translucent skin, in such a feminine outfit, sitting upright, smelling so, breathing so, once again I would have killed and been quite happy to do so. I'd never been so close to heaven as this. Sparkles and pixie sprites were lit up in my tripping eyes.

"Come closer Sebastian."

She wanted me even closer to heaven but the heat made it feel like hell…{oops, spoiler alert}.

I was out of my mind, demented and bazooka loco, full of hormonal combustion, as waylaid idiotic as a man can be. How could I have been so in love? Had I confused lust for love? I couldn't stop whatever was raging inside my head. Sam Spade was whispering in my ear, "The stuff that dreams are made of." I just prayed this wasn't a dream.

Without a word, she lifted her nightie and I incinerated. Well, of course, I didn't technically incinerate…we actually proceeded to grovel, grind, kiss, feel, roll, massage, cuddle…for two hours.

The physical reaction to all this body-to-body action, with little else beside boxers and panties on, is the most uncomfortable of things: a steel bending, horns blaring, earth-moving, bridge-raising, fire-consuming erection, essentially a man's blinking beacon in the raging storm, an act yet to be completed by the actors….and only one of you must pay the price for stage fright. She would make me wait, this play would have many more acts as all tragedies do. I could feel Gog and Magog stirring in the Lake of Gehenna.

"Happy to see me cowboy?"

She had what I needed, but wait we would. She confused me so much…have I mentioned that a sister would have really helped me understand the opposite sex.

I didn't know how to adjust to her commands.

So far as my bursting-at-the-seams, two-hour newsworthy erection, she'd do nothing about it. The result wasn't embarrassment so much, I can handle embarrassment. No, she had caused me an acute case of vasocongestion: aka blue balls. It was basic human biology. It's simply unnatural for any man let alone a Prophet or god forbid a Saint to maintain an erection for longer than fifteen minutes. Two hours is your own little private Armageddon, or at least a hospital emergency. As much as I loved grubbing with Somers, the thing was: I was in real pain, hospital visit pain. I'd rather have given birth to a ten pound bowling ball than go through that. And I can take pain…just perhaps not down there. Torture works best at the midsection.

This was malignant narcissism at its most pronounced. She could derive pleasure from psychological accomplishments played over an extended period of time, with not a thought given to others in the realm of impact. In other words, the worse my blue balls, the more she orgasmed. You lose, she wins. Someone one day needs to give her blue walls.

Somers had obviously noticed the protrusion, since it was practically impaling her. It was simply a loss-leader at the checkout line, she could take it or leave it depending on her whim. She didn't grab it with any real purpose, and yet the penis grab is the ultimate sexual Rubicon for any normal human, it means something to everyone...except her.

And yet, she was meant for me. I would always put this one first...

I felt like one of those hooked tuna's at a Japanese fish auction house, where buyers inspect the fish with gaffing rods, lifting and then dropping it back with a thud. Somers Gillette was cock-teasing in a way the world had not yet contemplated, a two hour test of endurance. It was a lose-lose situation, I was looking for the mini-guillotine

"Sebastian, we can't make love tonight. I hope you understand."

She was breaking my crayons already but what could I really say? This was our second date and for all I knew, she was on her period and that would be that for the weekend. I was head over heels for her. I was happy to be in bed with her, vasocongestion or not.

"It's alright for you to tell me what you think of me, Sebastian."

"Well, I think it's obvious, no?"

"Yeah, well, I'm not gonna be taking care of that tonight cowboy...What do you want me to be?"

"Uhhh, I hadn't ever thought of it like that…A nurse? School teacher? Porn star! Just kidding. I guess I just want you to be you. You're everything I need. More even."

"Funny about the porn star. All of this could be yours (she pointed to her body…). Sleep well Sebastian. We'll see about that, your other issue ahem, tomorrow. Remember, it ain't over 'til it's over."

Somers released me and fell asleep quickly, as if someone turned off her society switch, a sleep slut husbanding more energy for tomorrow. The puma sleeps with the wounded gazelle under her paws, she'll eat him later.

Her white cotton panties had never been whiter, reflected against the moonlight streaming in through the country windows. Her nightie was crumpled on the floor. That figure was crazy-good. Her skin was pure, warm, and soft, and smelled in only the most subtle way of a French perfumery. Her ass, up close, was simply outstanding, Modigliani's last masterpiece. Cleaner than a baby's bottom. A soft country wind blew in through the open windows.

I got the sense that Somers was somewhat devoid of true love. It was in the way she spoke of life, she had some issues for sure. She would only be a carrier, never a receiver. She was Millbrook's Typhoid Mary, the New York City carrier of typhoid fever who could never get sick herself. I got the sense that Somers didn't want love but she could dispense it strategically, ruthlessly, no guilt or signs of remorse, all cold cunning and schemes. She liked her man to kneel but she would never be so weak. Her toughness was not feminine and yet her body was ridiculously delicious. It was the craziest of all sexual conflicts. It was samba, waltz, and metal.

I was as wide awake as at any time in my life while she slept. This girl was either good, really good, or this girl was evil, really evil. I concluded she was both good and evil but the kind of evil I could tolerate. She was pure Jeckyll and Hyde, but unlike Drs. Jeckyll or Hyde, infinitely more stunning. I was hallucinating on some level. Toto, I've a feeling we're not in Kansas anymore.

My testicles really began to ache...a painful, steady arcing pain, causing me to mutter every two minutes, like a Pavlovian dog whose testicles are being electrocuted.

This night would really be unfortunate, and it merely set the stage for later life. I watched the clock flip its number cards for two straight hours. Around 4 AM (I think), I finally, fitfully nodded off. Backed up as no young man had ever been but excited and happy nevertheless. I swore I'd never fall again like this, and yet here I was.

I found the one whom my soul loves.
-- Song of Solomon 3:4

A Day at the Farm

The next morning, Somers shot out of bed at 6:30, wide awake, like Pavlov tasered her feet. The sleep slut was an energy freak, natch. Like a little girl on a summer day, she couldn't wait to go outside. She loudly announced that she was going for a run and would I like to come.

I'd been hoping for morning sex followed by afternoon sex followed by evening sex, and then finally Holly's chocolate wafer cake. What I really needed was a full body, happy ending massage. I rolled over in the sheets, dead to the outside world. The birds were in full whistle throw-down…a comedy of noise that one hears only in the country. I mostly wanted to give Somers Gillette some blue walls of her own.

I couldn't exactly laze it up around her, because she was testing me and I knew it. I slowly got out of that Ralph Lauren bed and told her I'd be ready shortly. I wanted the puma to kill me already, to put me out of misery.

I went to the hallway bathroom (which was noticeably smaller than her own bathroom), leaned over the white sink, propped myself up by my arms, and stared in the mirror. My eyes were bloodshot, like red lightening jags were scratched into my irises. I was hungover but most importantly and even more relevantly, extremely backed up with semen. I felt like total cowshit. My entire groinal area was encased in hard cement. I splashed some cold water on my face hoping that would do the trick. I was not a hurricane, more like the detritus of one.

Somers and I went for a run down a dirt country road adjacent to their farm. I could feel the pain in my groin with every step, slowly chipping away at the mass of hardened clay encasing my waist.

The Millbrook country-side is old-world gorgeous and Mr. Gillette's farm was simply stunning. I guessed he did have some money, like perhaps fuck-you levels of it, gigabucks even. I hadn't thought about that before. The main house of the farm was as fine a country house as you'll ever see, with beautifully appointed interior decorating and lots of old-money family photos. I bet the entire compound could sleep fifty people. There was a tennis court and paddle court (waspy winter game), a rectangular gunite pool (wasps do gunite), three ponds (wasps fish), a complex of barns, and even a grass runway airstrip (wasps fly).

Somers and I did everything that day. We played tennis, we rowed, we fished, we walked, we shot crow, we collected eggs from the chickens. She wanted to see if I could deal, unlike her City of Museum metrosexual crew. So far as the weather, it was picture perfect as promised, not an ounce of humidity, maybe 80 degrees for a high, not a cloud in sight. Good times never seemed so good.

No one had cell phones in the early 1990's, so we were truly on our own, cut off from the outside world. Somers did have a landline in her cottage, but that morning I wasn't certain it even worked. Certainly no one in my family knew where I was, or who Somers Gillette was. And no one called her cottage that Saturday.

I couldn't help wonder what was going to happen that night. I still hurt from the prior night's grinding, nothing made the pain subside. By 7 PM, I was generally OK…not great, just OK. If I ever get testicular cancer, that one night will have been the cause and Somers will own the rights….happily I'm sure.

We took showers at 7 PM, me in my tiny bathroom, she in her palatial one. I made dinner again, a summer meal of corn-on-the-cob, country salad, grilled marinated t-bone steaks, and chilled fresh watermelon. Somers joked that all she could make was roast chicken, and in the end, I found out that was true. She cooks by numbers…bland and blasé about food, not so blasé about liquor. My wine was gone from last night, so we dove into her stash…Chateau Margaux naturally. I'm $40 a bottle, she was $40 a glass...The air had cooled from the daytime and the stars were out in full again.

The way the candles lit her face that night, you'd swear not a better looking woman had ever graced god's green earth… She was definitely the best part of my life, up until that point anyway. She was no user, no way…so I thought.

"Why do you stare at me so intently Sebastian?"

"Seriously, you're so freaking gorgeous…you're like an addiction. I'm sorry. "

"I can make that go away for you…I bite."

I didn't know what would happen. She had taken me the previous night as far we could go without actually doing it, so my confidence wasn't high. I was cautiously optimistic but prepared for the worse. And my nuts hurt so bad, I wasn't sure I could even rally if called to duty.

After dinner, we lay down under the large elm tree, side by side, staring quietly at the night sky, wine glasses in our hands, talking about nothing really, a little about her college, a little about her life plans, and a little about how she despised the crowd she hung out with… I suggested she could hang out with another crowd but she dismissed that with a laugh…as if.

We could hear the crickets, the frogs, the cows…I could even hear the termites chewing on bark. I wanted to lie there all night, forgetting about the world. She had other plans.

There wasn't much to say between Somers and me to be honest…last night had broken me somewhat, like a wild mustang during the roundup, and my break merely served to boost her confidence, as if she had won yet again. Le manque de confiance en soi n'est pas une fatalité. I would need to show better to impress her.

Only because I was so emotionally drained did the night have even a fringe element of relaxation. Otherwise, there was something electric in the air. We were acting married without the real responsibilities. And yet, I still knew nothing about her. She had me where she wanted: unaware, unexpecting, and unprepared.

Margo Channing was screaming in my ear, "Fasten your seatbelts. It's going to be a bumpy night."

A Summer Pool's Priapism

At about 11 PM, Somers decided we should go for a swim. More accurately, she commanded that we go for a swim. She released the locks on my cage…I was coming out, chains undone. I was feeling stripsy.

"Let's take a swim; I'm hot. I know you like me by the way; you don't need to say so."

The thing was, it wasn't really that hot but I did like her. The devil's always hot, I was slightly chilled. But desire is a hunger that doesn't have any natural enemy, except Cravath and mother-in-laws.

The pool was a four-hundred yard walk from the cottage, through a field, around the main house, and down a large lawn. Swimming sounded like a good idea regardless of the temperature because there was no way to avoid body-to-body contact…perhaps she would reconsider last night's diabolic cock-tease. We went inside the cottage, put on swimsuits, and grabbed towels and robes. I couldn't help keep noticing how much larger and nicer her bathroom was than mine...

Something was going to happen, as if she had made an unspoken decision. Somers' mood swung from lazy-carefree married couple to intense-purposeful young animal. It wasn't the Manhattan tense, all stressed out and that, but tense in a determined way. Anything I said was useless to her at this stage. Her conversation lost its sarcasm… She wasn't nervous at all but I was shaking. And she was in a hurry…

The midnight hour had arrived, the witching hour when Black Magic works best.

"Fuck Sebastian, let's get going, are you a woman or what? You take so fucking long to get dressed. Jesus. I know you want it so let's get a move on before we grow old."

It was as if a new human species had emerged in the dark and I was chosen to wrestle it. The Prophets had asked me to wrestle the haute heiress Azazel and somehow occupy her until the Lake of Brimstone was prepared for the next thousand-year spell. Her cute demands became emasculating orders. She was fine-looking though, you had to give her that. We silently walked to the pool, mostly because I couldn't speak…I couldn't even see straight anymore. The New Millennial Battle was about to begin.

The pool sat in the middle of the front lawn of the main house. It was gracefully surrounded by boxwood hedges, not a fence like what was required by law (when you have 500 acres, I think you can get away with that). On the right side of the pool, about two hundred paces away, was a hard-surface tennis court (hmmmm…not har-tru…). There were no lights by the pool, just the full natural moon which bathed the night air in soft aqua. You could hear distant coyote barks and owl screeches.

When we got to the edge of the pool, Somers immediately removed her robe to reveal a light-blue, one-piece bathing suit. She was simply breathtaking, an astonishingly gifted figure the likes of which I'd never laid eyes on (outside of last night of course…it looked even better tonight, as if one day of farm activities had increased her attractiveness another impossible 25%). Only God himself had seen this…no crap, her body was holy. This is what a female Jesus will look like upon her Resurrection. The world could simply feed on her perfection, no loaves or wine needed.

Even with her perfect heiress figure, she was no showoff (at least to me that is…more on that later…). She was unnaturally rigid in any state of undress and yet as sexually charged as Mary Magdalene. She demurely turned to the side so I couldn't laser in on her front. She was unsure if I could restrain myself, like a death row inmate to the guard (she was right to be concerned…). I wondered if she had mace tucked away somewhere. I was gasping for oxygen…she had me on life support…I needed a nurse.

She was also high on something that evening, something that made her feel too feminine for her own comfort, but allowed her to unlock her morals. Her daddy was not going to be happy with what was about to go down… The pool hissed with her heat. The gods were laughing at my impending doom.

I kept staring at her bathing suit through the rippled water….a one-piece was simply incongruous on that exquisite figure. I didn't really care that much, it's just that I would have preferred a bikini. No real hard complaints…I would have been content seeing her in army boots and metal diving helmet. She looked like the real thing and that's about all I cared about.

I could hear the faint bass rolls, double toms, and high hats of Duran Duran playing in the recesses of my head. Come Undone*. I knew that one…I'd played lead a year ago at Trader Vic's, it was all too appropriate.

She was slowly walking around the shallow end of the pool, bobbing her head up and down, subtly suggesting I get the fuck in. Maybe not subtly actually. She wasn't talking, and nor was I…it was like we were two fourth-grade children who really liked each other, and girls are more mature than boys so….

I took my shirt off. I had yellow swimsuit trunks on which reached just above the knees…an acceptably preppy-surfer kind of look. Unlike her, I dipped my toes in the shallow end of the pool, to see what the temperature was. She called me out on that one,

"Grow a pair Sebastian…jesus."

Maybe she was still witty and sharp, even in our heightened moment of sexual tension. Also, she was exasperated that I wasn't being more aggressive, like a man could. I jumped in…I didn't want the emasculation to continue.   She swam toward me and rose up. I was ill, shaking, and out of my element in the lair of Voland.

"Take my hands…"

I can't relay more in the way of conversation, because we didn't say another direct word to each other that night that didn't have an element of sheer terror or pain.

'…mine immaculate dream, made breath and skin, I've been waiting for you'… *

Somers was on a mission. This was a silent, ritualized mating dance, in a pool no less, where two semi-equal aggressors can't figure out how to get to where they need to go. You don't dance on the edge of love. We needed to be careful.

We slowly circled each other, inching closer and closer, arms gliding at the water level, creating arc angel water waves, until finally we were standing so close I could hear her breath.   I could smell her every cell….maybe that was chlorine, or chloroform actually.

She pinned me with everything she had: arms, hands, legs, and torso's, on the pool ledge in the shallow end, grinding, kissing and tasting. Her lips were soft and smooth. Her skin, against the cool air, was hot to the touch. I could feel her cautions willingly evaporating into the night air. She had strength in her arms that you would not expect, given how lithe she was.

'...signed with the home tattoo, happy birthday to you was created for you,'... *

I slid the left top of her bathing suit down, and then the right, down to her belly. Her breasts were wet from the pool water and her nipples were hard from the cool air. I concaved my stomach slightly to allow for my newest embarrassing erection to not poke her belly so much and distract either of us. So embarrassing. We were running out of ways to ignore it.

Somers turned around, her back to my front...there wasn't a paper-sheath of air between our bodies, my chest now leaning into her shoulders, and her arching backward with each thrust. I placed her arms on the top of the pool's edge, supporting the both of us. I maneuvered my erection between her thighs, rubbing it against her...she was on fire, the water itself was ten degrees warmer near her.

The top of her one-piece was down more now. Our hands were all over each other, she bringing hers behind and me reaching around, exploring curves and skin and muscle and other body parts. She would reach down and squeeze my penis extremely hard, almost as if she was working out with one of those wrist muscle gizmos. Honestly, I'd need to see a doctor soon. The thing was bursting to get out and tearing my swimsuit fabric.

If she didn't have sex with me, one of those female cows was starting to look like a fine alternative...a Carolina hag-shag.

She took my hand and pushed it further down onto her clitoris.

She whispered,

"Take me now..."

In hindsight, she must have thought I replied 'ruthlessly crush my innocent heart full of love and goodness'…because that's what she started to do right there and then with my life….

We were now facing each other front to front, in the waist-deep water, the mist now rising off both our bodies. Her lips were so soft…we couldn't stop tasting each other, as if the world was ending and only a minute left. It was all passion and youth.

'…oh, it'll take a little time, might take a little crime, to come undone now.'… *

She gingerly stepped out of each leg suit opening on her tiptoes. I tossed the bathing suit onto the grass. Somers was now completely naked. She didn't have large breasts but her nipples were the perfect shade of pink, even in the dark. Her hips were ideally proportioned to her height.

She was grabbing my penis from outside my trunks. We were both lost in the craziness of sexual exploration. I wanted to last all night but the reality is I thought I might shortly set a new definition for the word premature…if a moth landed on it that very second, I'd probably explode.

Somers reached into my trunks and grabbed the penis with her delicate fingers and massaged it up and down. There was no doubt now we were now left with only two options: we score, or she shoots me in the head with a .357 Magnum… Could have gone either way to be honest.

Somers slid my trunks down and now we were both standing acoustic.

She rubbed my penis some more and I lifted her whole body up with my hands…I could have lifted an elephant I was so worked up. You could have hung dumbbells off my penis. You could have…ahh, you get it.

Score….the cows could come out of hiding, she told the defense to run off the field. My erection felt unusually strong as if it was shaped from steel rebar.

This was as close to a marriage proposal as this woman makes. I said 'yes'…

I carefully and gently lowered her light body down onto hips, swaying to music that didn't exist, and she guided me in, the mothership fully in control of the wayward module. It felt so right, no other way to describe entry. The fit was perfect, a testament to precise evolutionary engineering.

She was on fire inside…I could feel the warmth course through my penis to my hips. The tip felt as if it was melting. The heat was alarming. I could feel her heartbeat pounding my chest. If she was really the Old Hob, then the dark side had a good argument to make to us innocents.

'...we'll try to stay blind, to the hope and fear outside, hey child stay wilder than the wind, and blow me in to cry,'... *

This was the Jonathan Carroll moment when you remind yourself to 'walk carefully in the beginning of love; the running across fields into your lover's arms should come later when you're sure they won't laugh if you trip...'

She wrapped her legs around my hips and squeezed as hard as a human can, cutting off air flow and violently compressing whatever vital organs I had. My ribs cracked. Blood just shot down to my penis, she knew what she was doing: she was squeezing the life out of me, literally. She stared at me silently, no moans or sounds. Jesus, did she hurt...maybe the Old Hob needed to relax a little.

Somers' flawless ass was cupped in my large hands, me now lifting her body to the plane of the water and then back down again, while we thrusted, slowly, and then quicker. The pool water splashed gently, and then madly the more hurried the action got. I was staring at the water's waves and thought to myself: hey, this pool is rocking...must be a party.

Maybe this wouldn't last all night. I don't think I could hold out five minutes, more like five seconds....impressive, not. Note to self: knock one out a day before next time. There was no time to think of consequences.

Somers was grinding down on my hips, reducing my lift ratio with each thrust, as if she had mathematically computed that each thrust required $1/8^{th}$ Inch less lift, so by the 64th thrust, I would produce zero vertical and my penis would be fused inside her. These weren't bodies slapping so much, she had me in a bear hug, an heiress on a mission.

'...words, playing me déjà vu, like a radio tune I swear I've heard before, chill is it something real, or the magic I'm feeding off your fingers.'... *

My penis was harder than it had ever been…it had never absorbed more blood from her crazy-legs python compression. Her legs were choking off all other blood flow, causing whatever protein and blood I had to flow in one direction only, the only escape valve I was born with, and it would explode shortly like a fireworks mishap. She was taking what she needed.

She began to rub her clitoris. Great, now I need help…I can't make you orgasm by myself? Emasculation much…if you'd release that death grip with your legs, I could maybe do my work…

Her eyes began to slowly and methodically close, as if she was entering into a devil's hypnotic trance. When they were fully shut, she buried her face and wet hair into my left neck, biting me viciously on the skin near my aorta, with one arm still wrapped tightly around my chest, the other masturbating her business, and her legs compressing my hips. The black widow was at work…her mate was laughing in lunacy's grip of ejaculation, a Mardi Gras ignorance of the murder but a minute away.

Everything she was doing she was doing hard and rough. I could take what she was dishing, but man, this girl was mildly masochistic. We had the perfect balance of youth, passion, and idiocy…one of us had the idiocy anyway. No one listens to Bernstein making this kind of love.

'...lost in a snow filled sky, we'll make it alright.'... *

That little mustang needed to slow down. I was quickly losing the battle. In a pained whisper...

"Somers, I'm gonna come."

I hate a few words in the English dictionary and come and moist are two and yet there is no better way to warn your partner that you are about to come than simply by saying it. She ground down harder, ignoring my words. She had me in an unbreakable connection.

"Somers, I can't hold it any more. I think I'm gonna come."

Somers was in her own world, eyes closed, biting my neck deeper now, legs, arm, and hips squeezing my body with paranormal strength like a boa, furiously rubbing her business with her free hand like she had the devil in her (ahem...), forcing my erection into her as far as it could possibly go, practically dissolving it with her sexual acids.

I was worried I couldn't get out. Let me rephrase that...I knew I couldn't get out, but I was worried about her reaction to my asking to be let out, like I needed a hall pass from a school teacher and didn't have a solid reason.

"Somers, I'm really gonna come. Seriously, I'm fucking coming."

She was breathing so heavily, there wasn't enough oxygen left to sustain either of us. I needed to wake her up out of whatever sexualized trance she was in, if for no other reason than we needed air. She was rubbing her business so hard I thought an exorcism was going down.

I couldn't slap her…if I did, she'd hit me back so hard she'd knock me out and I'd drown, my twist on the Nelson Rockefeller moment. She yelled,

"Take me now! Don't fucking call me Sweetie...Argggggggghhhhhhhh!"

I didn't say Sweetie….What?

She bit the crap out of me, like Leviathan to a raw steak. She was making primal guttural sounds, not exactly an orgasmic ecstatic moan but more animal self-love. Somers was coming, I was coming, she was cursing. I was having an epileptic seizure practically. She was incoherent and had just said the most non-sequitor non-sequitor in the history of romance.

I was desperately trying to get out of her, but we were locked tight. She wouldn't let go…she had my hips in a practical vise lock. My vital organs began to shut down, I needed EMS.

'...Can't ever keep from falling apart, at the seams, can't I believe you're taking my heart, to pieces,'... *

The water was thrashing, she was screaming into the dark country night, I was gritting my teeth, achily muttering the word motherfucker over and over and over. Things were happening so fast, we both felt dizzy. My penis was in abject pain. Life's a funny thing: I can remember this event perfectly, but I can't remember to get milk at a grocery store...

My body was seizing up and I swear my left frontal lobe was pulsating with everything else. Somers was biting my neck so hard, I had to pry her teeth apart from my skin with the Jaws of Life. When she released my neck, blood spurted like a blown gusher...you could see the red plasma hitting the water like a spasmodic derrick.

Torpedo fusillades were firing every two seconds. The orgasm hurt intensely, I was sucking in gobs of air as my whole body spasmed, my chest concaved. She had blood all over her face, smiling like a psychiatric patient after self mutilation. She was a total freak. I was out of words...The kid is alright.

The 80's IT-girl princess was addictive. I'd need rehab soon, if I lived. The female cows were all mooing: I'll have what she's having.

At the end, I thought I might have gotten out of her perhaps with a second to spare...maybe. I swore then I wouldn't swim in the pool the next day, or the next month, or that year, or until someone sanitized the whole thing....off-limits for a while. My blood gusher was still uncapped. Chlorine alone could not handle the massive environmental damage. The farm animals would have a field day smelling the detritus.

I rolled away from Somers and slowly walked toward the middle of the pool. My penis was throbbing, still spewing every ten seconds, and I was holding it tight with my right hand, squeezing the pain away. My left hand was clamped onto my neck as a compression tool, my hand bloodier than a surgeon's. She'd hit the aortic motherlode…. Was this hen a vampire? It looked as if I had been shot, raped, or both. This was a Kodak moment for the insane asylum.

'…*who do you need, who do you love, when you come undone,* '… *

Ooops…did someone forget to mention birth control?

Somers exhaled. She wasn't panting. She went from crazy to still in less than a second. She stood there naked, with the water level between her belly and pubic region. Except for the blood stains around her lips, nose, and chin, you wouldn't have known what she had just done.

I looked utterly useless, a goat rope and nothing more. I wanted to say, hey what the hell with the neck bite, but with my penis still throbbing and coming (would this never end?) and worrying about the excessive blood loss, it was hard to muster any comment at all. Thousands of fireflies were symphonically dancing in the night air.

Somers calmly walked out of the pool via the steps, wiped her bloody face off, toweled down her freakishly perfect figure, put on a large white bathrobe, and wrapped a large towel around her head. In fifteen years of knowing her, it would be the only time I ever saw Somers Gillette completely naked, and even here, only in the pale blue moonlight.

No post-coital cuddle, I guessed. We'd just had the perfect sex, no doubt, but Somers was finished. This was not a girl who reviewed or graded sex after…some like to do nothing else but talk about and grade the act after…how was I, this is what I liked best, etc…Somers had done her job, the deal had closed, bring in the lawyers…

"C'mon on Sebastian. Let's go."

Baphomet was done.

The problem was I couldn't go. My erection was just not going down…if anything, it was getting harder and larger. I was knocking on death's door with an explosion of the penis. New medical books would be written.

I had a severe and acute case of priapism. I wondered if Somers was the South American Wandering Spider, whose side effect, besides death, is excruciating priapism for the male. Somers was two for two: two nights, vasocongestion and now priapism. She was a masterful debilitator, the exquisite Mastema, a new species not yet detected by the Prophets.

"Uhhh. I think I've got a real problem. Can you just wait a second?"

"What's the matter Sebastian, first time?"

"I don't really know how to say this, but my erection isn't going down. I can't get it down. And yeah, I have gotten laid before, just never vampired. What's up with that?"

Every ten seconds, my penis would throb from somewhere deep in the groin…I was dry-coming.

"I do that to men. Ha. When it goes down, come back to the cottage."

She does that to men? She said it as if she really had done this before, like some professionally-trained KGB sex agent, and talking about dicks was par for the course. She does what she wants…

The song faded. *'Who do you need…who do you need when you fall apart.'**

And then she walked away, clearing out her troubled mind, up the grass hill and out of sight, leaving me, my erection, and my neck wound alone, in the pool, under a moonlit night, in Millbrook New York. Lucifer was howling in the distance.

My heart was singing, my sexual market value skyrocketed.

The Doorman

You know it's love when you want to keep holding hands even after you're sweaty.

This was the game of love, played by professionals only. There was someone else, though only one of us was aware of that. Somers and I never had a day where we laughed til we cried and honest love needs that. A King and Queen should be a Prince and Princess first. If only for one day. Otherwise…she'd never be the friend I'd need, just like her mother would accurately predict later. Never one carefree day. The dreamer would go down swinging, but go down indeed.

Somers was asleep by the time I walked in the cottage door at 1:30 AM, the sleep slut gearing up for reproduction. It was so quiet inside, the bed on fire, air waffles of steam rising off. She looked like a contented Kolski, the Antichrist catching Z's. And like Oliver Twist, I wanted more, "Please, sir, I want some more", but I didn't sense divine benevolence. What do you do after the jump?

My penis was still halfway erect. Only the long walk through the dark fields, with visions of wild coyotes sawing away on it, made it deflate. It still hurt like hell, like last night, but even worse now. If this was how Somers had sex, I wasn't sure I'd ever live to tell my friends about it.

Somers slept in the next day. Until 11 AM. Which was odd. She's a morning person, ready to take charge of the day by 6. At 11 AM, she's conquered worlds and defeated enemies. But true love was her kryptonite and she was zapped. I was awake at 7 AM, not sure what to do. The birds were singing, the bees buzzing, and the cows gossiping. The music however was missing.

My penis was boxer match aqua-blue-red and I swear it would not go down. My neck looked like Count Dracula had been up all night feeding on it...the pillow sheet were toast. Somers was practically comatose, adrift in some hellish comfort of self-design. I grabbed my neck. Vampires don't go back to the same victim once bitten, do they...

I rose from the bed, walked barefoot to my small bathroom, dressed, and went outside. I collected the eggs and talked like a crazy man to the cows (who didn't seem fazed by my words or presence...those bovines are shifty fat fuckers)...I could tell they'd been talking about me behind my back).

When Somers finally got out of bed at 11 AM, my tea had grown cold. She came down the stairs in a soft-blue, matronly-like bathrobe, an outfit and look I hadn't seen before. Steel retainers were clamped to the roof of her mouth (vampires needed roof support after feasting...?). I wasn't sure I liked this look of hers. She was 29 going on 70.

I'd been reading The Times in her very cute living room, just more bad news there, so I stood up and walked over to her. She was leaning against the wall, not entirely steady on her feet. She gave me a peck on the cheek, nothing more. She looked e.x.h.a.u.s.t.e.d. Not radiant anymore. No morning glow, just pale and hollow, like the wan vampire during daylight...with braces. As sexless as a human, or vampire, can be.

She told me she had to call her mother and she asked me to get lost while she did, like they were about to swap insider trading tips. You might find that odd, but I didn't...my body was too bruised for much thought on existential meaning. Their call lasted twenty minutes and I could hear raised voices, like two business titans discussing a bad deal and who would take the hit.

"I don't know Mom. It's fine. Fuck, can you call me later tonight?"

I wasn't hungover, but I wasn't fresh, I had museum feet. Hearing her say fuck to her own mother snapped me out of my loginess.

I felt like I had gotten something last night, something that I wanted, but not something I actually needed. I didn't sense anything would keep us together for long...weird. She'd go on her way and me mine after a few more dates and that would be that. I just didn't think I was going to last…. She was first class and fancy free and I had nothing really to offer in return. She didn't even like the Blue Devils, which stunned me…

For the rest of the day, she and I decompressed, reading the Times twice over, she intently studying the Styles and Obituaries Sections.

For Somers that morning, I sensed that she had gotten something months in planning…for me, well, I'm just a guy, what more can I say? I was sated, although mortally wounded to be sure, a little confused about why she didn't want me to hear anything she said to her Mom, but whatever. I didn't know her Mom and didn't know what schemes she would be up to already. It never occurred to me that a 29-year old woman would discuss sexual exploits with her own mother…

We drove back to the city that day at 5 PM. I top-killed my neck wound with a white gauze bandage. Upon traversing the 2nd Avenue Bridge, I could again feel Somers' body constrict and tense up and the muscles in her jaws protruded again, the Society IT girl back on stage. She was just a different human being in the city for sure. We reached her apartment at 79th and 2nd by 7.

Somers sat in the front seat, not moving for a minute, while she thought what to say, deeply meditative of the next steps.

"Sebastian, I'm capable of anything. I can cut you like no other. You better not betray me. We're going to need to discuss this weekend soon."

I wasn't sure what to say to her exactly. I mean, had we crossed a new divide? Were we boyfriend and girlfriend now? Were we on farting terms? Did sex mean anything impactful for this woman? Had that been the best day of my life, or the worst? I was unsure where I stood, but I sensed that she had definite ideas and not entirely to my liking.

"Somers, uhhh, okay. Why do we need to discuss the weekend though? I was just going to thank you for the weekend, not review it. Did I do something wrong? I'll call you tomorrow. Do you need help with the bags?"

"Look Sebastian, actions have consequences, okay? Don't ask me questions, I'll ask you. Right now, let's just go our separate ways. I need time to think. I'll call you in two weeks."

The doorman was eyeing us, me mostly, and my neck especially. I needed a high collar church vestment to hide the scars. It looked like a deer hunter had accidentally grazed my neck with a .22…the wound had begun to get comically large, as the bluish hue had spread far beyond the borders of my white gauze. I was infected with an evil disease.

She hit the brakes, euphemistically, on our budding romance. We were finished for now. With that, she shut the car door and walked toward the red brick co-op with her doorman. No kiss, no touch, no ready plans, no words of comfort, no nothing, me just looking at that ass s-curve away from me.

Two weeks? Did I hear that right? My heart was still pounding with something like love from last night, a heavy drumbeat of hopeful eternal commitment, knowing the odds were not in my favor. She wanted two more weeks to sort things out in her head? Intense shame should be mutual and not simply one-way. I wanted a fellow idiot in my boat of daisy tripping. She was driving me crazy.

What was she doing in those two weeks that was more important than us anyway?

I slowly drove away, staring at Somers and her doorman in my rear view mirror. They had stopped at the building entrance to talk…he kept shifting his glance to my car every few seconds. Accusatorily. It looked like it was he who wanted to shoot the .22…I almost sideswiped three cars in my paranoia.

Maybe she was right, maybe she was Kate Trask. I don't recall Steinbeck word-painting an ass like Somers', but still…the message was on. She had high walls and only professionals should attempt the climb.

JG Melons and EPT's

Sometimes when the night is upon you, you just can't find a light. So you look to the sky for grace.

Now that she was gone, I only wanted to be with her. I couldn't do much else besides think about her. For the next two weeks, I left her a dozen messages. She'd call back when she knew I wouldn't be around, calling me at the apartment at 11 AM or the office at 8 PM. Hers was a stealth call game, cat and mouse telephoning, slowly sapping me of whatever energy and desire I had left. It was making me more loco by the second, and I'm sure she knew it.

Two weeks after the epically erotic pool session, I was alone in my dark apartment at night, staring out the window, trying to learn a muffled 12-string guitar….I had guitarthritis. Fine Young Cannibals was looping over and over in the CD so I could get a chord scheme down right. I needed two strings for that song, not 12…This was a bass drum, tom, percussive box intro, and a rhythm and lead chord I was wholly unfamiliar with. Classic rock is so much easier to riff than New Age or London synth tempo. She Drives Me Crazy was the tune. I was living life in Drop-D.

It was a Sunday night and the phone rang, loudly (I had it jacked up as high as it could go, just in case…). July 4th had passed…New York was now officially in the summer swing. That can be a lonely time for a young man with nothing better to do than dream. I didn't think I could beat this city. I didn't sense the hero in me at all. I'd dress in women's clothes before winning the battle of Manhattan. I killed the CD.

"Hello?"

"Sebastian, I'm sorry that I haven't been free to speak with you over the last few weeks."

It was Somers, my society sex-freak heiress, she of Locust Valley and Millbrook. She never introduces herself or asks how you've been, she just dives in, her testosterphone on full display. She sounded off that night, business-like but odd, even for her standard ball-busting mien, unsure like a salesperson selling a bad product they didn't believe in.

She was driving me crazy. I wanted to re-orient us toward the standard hello and how are you,

"Hi Somers. How are you?"

"Fine. You?"

No man is truly married until he understands every word his wife is NOT saying. She's like a detective in an interview room…Cut the bullshit and let's get down to brass tacks, do you want to deal you lowlife or not? I wished I'd met her when I was so much younger…what she could have taught me… I let it slide,

"To be honest Somers, somewhat pissed, but I'm sure I can get over it it. You could have called me back, you know."

"I know. It's just that something's happened; we need to talk. Can you meet me in an hour at Melons?"

I hadn't heard Somers sound like this before. She was haunted on the phone, withdrawn. It wasn't stress I guessed. I couldn't pin the emotion down frankly. It was nerves, mirth, and uncertainty, wrapped in a vat of fuck-you you douchebag loser male why did I have sex with you venom...yeah, that's it. Hr voice was a rifle and the scope had me at the end of a barrel. She wanted to beerboard me at a bar and have me confess to something.

'Melons' was JG Melon's, a dark-paneled comfort-food standby at 74th and 3rd. Tons of prepster Buckley/Spence types hang out there on weeknights eating burgers and fries…it's basically an expensive hamburger joint. On Sunday night the place is abandoned, a good time to go if you're breaking up with your boyfriend, or if you feel down.

"Yeah sure. You OK? You sound stressed."

"Yeah, I'm OK. Something's happened though. We need to talk. Just meet me there for god's sakes and stop asking questions."

This was no cuddle call.

"Uhhh, alright, OK. See you in an hour."

Click, she never says good bye…

I felt left out of what I was supposed to be involved with. What the hell had I done?! Guilty as charged on the count of wild sex and no birth control, though she told me she was on birth control (I didn't demand to see the evidence…). Maybe the farmer's wife had seen me walking across the fields with my steel erection baying at the moon (Goodnight Moon would have a new ending), and she called the ASPCA to file a bestiality complaint. That would really help my career at Shearson…Rojek would pay a hefty bounty.

An hour? It was always like Somers to provide a socially acceptable period of time to get yourself together, but I would have happily left my apartment then and there and met her in a minute. I never needed an hour for anything, let alone a girlfriend in need, if she was my girlfriend… Somers was, if nothing else, consistently organized, as if The Book of Manners and In Search of Excellence were her bedside bibles.   Good manners and training ultimately allowed Somers to snow me and everyone else.

When I arrived at the restaurant at 8, Somers was already seated in a dark corner table for two. Which of course was strange since she'd normally be the one socially late. The restaurant was sadly quiet, a stark reminder that Manhattan was away during the summer, especially from the Upper East Side. The bartender looked bored as did the waitstaff.   They had no music of course… a bohemian wasteland.

Somers smiled wearily and rose from her seat to kiss me on the cheek. She looked scared, another look I hadn't seen before. She was dressed in her usual, effortlessly-perfect chic way, faded blue jeans, white oxford polo, and grey cashmere wrap, but her empty smile belied something else going on inside her heart. Her elegance was a Rapture of the material kind. She smelled great, always did, always will. That gap in her tooth drove me wild.

"Thanks for coming Seb (first time she ever called me Seb…). You're going to need a drink, this could take all night. What do you want?"

Without even trying, she crippled me immediately. I was guilty and the charges hadn't even been brought up. I practically held my hands out in front of me for the cuff slap, this marital judge of Shaitan.

"Here, I'll get it Somers (eyeing her nervously). (To the waitress) Beer please. (To Somers) What are you having?"

"Water."

"What's wrong? You seem pre-occupied. Hit me with it…I don't like surprises, and if anything's wrong, I will help you no matter what. Or if you're going to break up with me, I'm not sure we were dating in the first place, so you can save that speech for later, when you really hate me."

"I took an EPT. Twice. I'm pregnant. We're having a baby."

Somers dropped the sentence cold as stone, no lead in. She said nothing else. I stared at her gap tooth and then at my beer. She's a hot looking lunatic that's for sure. What did she just say…? I looked to the ceiling to save me, my vacant-eye bus look...no angels floating there at JG Melon's.

I felt like a heavyweight boxing champ cold-cocked me in the jaw, I couldn't move my mouth. What's an EPT? Did she say she was having a baby…? Wonder who the dad was…? That stinks, because I really liked her, and now she was going to marry that Tennessee dude whom I hadn't even met yet. Couldn't be me, we'd only had sex once. I was 29 years old, had been in love three times (all in vain…), but had never gotten anyone pregnant, ever. I was convinced by then I shot nothing but blanks and I'd be the best childless uncle ever.

"You're the father."

My mind, like any guy who isn't married and has gotten a girl pregnant, simply went blank. A canvas of nothingness. On top of my normal nothingness, this was epic stupidity. I guess one thought was I hoped her Dad wasn't in the mafia….a daughter's unexpected pregnancy can't go over well with a made boss (hey Sal can I call you Dad, because your daughter's knocked up! Bang…dead). Thankfully this family was A-List Protestant…

I had no repartee, no jokes, no words of encouragement, no song, and no books like What to Expect When You Are Expecting. My brothers had no children. I had no cousins. I'd never changed a diaper in my life…I don't think I'd ever seen one. I'd never seen a womb scan. I'd never heard of Lamaze. I'd only started filing tax returns five years prior. I didn't have a sister. I didn't know anything about periods, ovulation, birth control, or really, basic responsibility. And according to Somers, I didn't know 'shit about sex' either…that hurt the most. I had to learn to fly without instructions…we were on the runway and the wheels were already moving, my logbook would have 'crash and burn' as my only journal entry.

How does someone know they're pregnant within two weeks of having sex?! Does it really work that way? Had she set me up? Was she doing in-vitro without my knowledge? What was in-vitro?

I was trying to remember the event of two weeks ago, her grinding my hips, practically ring-suctioning my magnesium penis inside her as deep as she could make it. I wondered if this pelvic exaggeration wasn't some sort of pregnancy advice tip read in a doctor's manual, a Highlights Magazine for the almost 30 year old woman whose younger sister already had her own children…

We stared at each other for two minutes, or two decades the way it felt, not a word spoken. I rested my chin on my hands. I wasn't so much lost in thought as in idiocy. I'd been considering blowing out of Shearson and starting a band again, but living off of ramen noodles wasn't a great way for a new family to begin life. She finally spoke again,

"I understand if this is a bit of shock Sebastian (yea-uhhh, you could say that…). I'm going through with it though. I don't need money, I have money (whenever someone tells me they don't 'need' money, that's when they 'want' money…), and I won't force you to be a full-time father. This pregnancy means more to me than anything ("pregnancy", not child…hmmm...). I have an appointment tomorrow at my ObGyn at 10 AM (again, what's an ObGyn?…). I think maybe just this once you should attend, because you're the sperm father (argh…I hate that word 'sperm'…). And, we'll have to be married at least at the birth date…that's only right. Make it legitimate ("it"?…). You can divorce me the day after (divorce, marriage, 220, 221…). Just don't let me down."

She said the last sentence like a judge on sentencing day, as if I had no say in the matter other than a word of contrition to the aggrieved. On one hand she half-said it was up to me but on the other hand she said it was one-hundred percent you're doing what I tell you. That's an interesting debating style, good for dictatorships and monarchies, deadly for American marriage. All girls intimidated me to some extent, Somers just more than the rest. I'm actually less intimidated by gang members flashing throat-slicing signs than by a woman who tells me she's pregnant.

And that word sperm…add that word to the list of ones I hate. Moist, sperm, and come.

There was no doubt in her head I was the dad. When she's definite sounding about something, you tend to believe her. I've learned since that it's all for show, but back then, I believed her completely.

I had no reason to doubt her. She hadn't shape-shifted yet into the Serpent.

This was all Entitlement Narcissism. Somers had unreasonable expectations of others to accord her particularly favorable treatment and automatic compliance with whatever her wishes were. The reason for this expectation was she considered herself very special, as in the world revolved around her. And god forbid there was any failure to comply…that would be considered a full out assault on her superiority. Defiance of her will triggers a narcissistic rage of no equal. I could see she was waiting for me to say no…

I thought she said she had been on birth control all her life…no one mentioned anything about a terminal date on that issue by the way. Maybe the herculean nature of my erection that night defeated the chemicals in its way. It was a flesh diamond-tip chain saw.

So basically, we decided that our third date was going to be her gynecologist! This wasn't exactly the smooth transition to New York married life I'd been hoping for. Somers should have been my sister…what she could have taught me.

I was also supposed to be meeting a new client of Shearson's, a group called Waddell and Reed out of Kansas City, the same time of the ObGyn appointment. If I didn't show, that would simply be one more reason to can me…I don't think Somers cared much about that.

My mind was spinning. I could have sworn I'd pulled out well ahead of time, when millions of those little rambunctious Graham boys went seeking that precious little Gillette egg. I was sure I had. Well, kind of. OK, not exactly sure or even kind of, more like a prayerful of middling-to-nothing sure, perhaps all nothingness, guaranteed to come out in her favor.

What of Somers anyway? She had been with that other Tennessee guy the weekend before. She'd copped to that somewhat up in Millbrook. She said she needed the previous weekend to get rid of him. She treated the act of sex not as something deeply meaningful between two in-love persons, but rather as something that was a means to an end. Sex was only part of the deal, page 17 on her Life PowerPoint. She was Chairman, CEO, and CFO of Her Inc., and I was an hourly secretary. She's sexual harassment in reverse.

Why did she choose me? She could have had anyone. I wasn't a rockstar she could pry money out of, or even a Master of the Universe Taft young commie political apparatchik bonus snatcher, so she wasn't after that. I was a nobody... about the only thing I had were decent genes. My father's family had arrived on these shores from Hull, England on or about 1650. I was pure Church of England stuff. Was that what she wanted? Wasps were quickly going the way of the Edsel...cute, but useless.

No one likes to be alone, right? She wanted a companion, but someone who didn't give a flying frig about her family or her money. Mostly though, she wanted someone who didn't have more than her...well, she found the right guy! I was still busting down five loaves and two fish during the week...'I am the bread of life: he that cometh to me shall never hunger: and he that believeth in me shall never thirst.' I was going to keep you fed, just wasn't sure if we'd be on a G5 having the meal.

Was I ready for a family...not on your life. I wasn't ready to take care of two goldfish let alone a child. My sense of security was closing out trade positions at the market's close.

But, I don't turn my back on any friend, ever...never have and never will. She knew it, and she knew how different that was than anyone else she knew from the City of Museum soirees. She wasn't just some ordinary friend anymore, she was my {perhaps} dream girl with {perhaps} my baby inside of her, so you can imagine that there wasn't a snowball's chance in hell I would turn tail now. Let love open the doors…

"Look, we're in this together. Don't worry. I'll go with you of course."

I'll support you no matter what. She grabbed my hand with those perfectly elongated fingers of hers, and we just silently sat there at Melon's for half an hour while I sipped beer and she drank water. We stared at the other lonely summer souls on a Sunday evening. Her hands were cold to the touch while mine were sweating. We had collided, forever attached now at the heart and elsewhere.

No words were spoken, but a lifetime of thoughts went through our heads. We walked alone to our respective homes.

Dr. Schwartz and Central Park

Two are better than one.
-- Ecclesiastes 4:9

I partly blamed it on my roots. In Manhattan with the big boys, walking in boots, not loafers. The thing was my parents did the best they could so it was up to me anymore. Life's a mystery. I was contemplative of a kind I had never experienced.

I needed to man up in the morning and tell Rojek the full deal…I was going to need some understanding from him and talk plainly, which an investment banker would take away as 'now I get to fuck you even worse than yesterday'. With the way I was performing, he'd remove the Midwest mutual funds and assign me Haiti. I plucked a few chords and put my guitar back in its case. I wasn't sure I'd ever learn to play that twelve-string.

I took an early, empty subway to work.

When I saw Rojek later that morning, I stepped into his office and asked for some private time (which in the morning he hated, since he wanted to read the newspapers alone, quietly). I explained what had happened and told him I needed the rest of the day off. To his credit, he didn't fire me right then (I would have), but that's about the only thing he didn't do. He more or less laughed, smirking that he saw it coming, I had no discipline, and this is what happens to guys with no discipline, unlike the Buckley young communists (Rojek called them tigers)…they would have worn a rubber he said (those drugstore cowboys also couldn't get into her panties either Rojek…if they even liked girls…). I was on the one-way train to Shearson obscurity. This guy had no compassion. He was a mirthless member of the trading floor mafia.

I ran downstairs to catch a taxi to 72nd and Fifth, where Somers' gynecologist Dr. David Schwartz kept his offices. I wasn't born yesterday so I knew that rent in this part of town was kinda stratospheric, like it goes no higher in any other part of the world. Schwartz' clientele was Upper East Side heiresses and old Jewish ladies. If I was an ObGyn, this is where I'd set up shop.

By the time I arrived, Somers was in the waiting room reading a copy of Elle. If my heart ever started to wonder if she was the right woman for me, one look at her was all I needed…she was stupefyingly gorgeous. She called my name…I'd fallen so hard for her. She was wearing a summer dress of white Mexican cotton fabric, with an elastic blue and yellow waistband around her stomach…a baby bump already? Does it happen that quickly? If so, I'd need an advance on my paycheck to cover the meds for my burgeoning insanity.

The waiting room office had soft yellow lamp lighting, making us all feel warm and fuzzy. There was a pleasant looking receptionist with a gray nurse's smock behind the desk…she could have worn a t-shirt and jeans for all I cared, she only answered phones, didn't deliver babies. Everything in Manhattan is marketing.

As for me, since I only really had friends in fairly low places like music communes in upstate California, I hadn't been to any quasi gold-standard doctor's office. My previous girlfriends likely went to community clinics, not this…

The fact is I'd never been to any gynecologist's office, except when I was a fetus. I was so out of my comfort zone there as to be comical. I thought the doctor would check my penis to determine hereditary profiling and compatibility with Somers' private parts. Does it fit, is there enough mutual comfort kids, hey your erection is deflating son, etc…

We were led to an examination room by a real nurse. Somers floated like a Queen through the halls. When we got into the room, Somers hopped up onto the stirrup table like she knew the place cold. Which in some ways she did…she dropped big bucks there for the past ten years. I wondered if she had ever been pregnant before…The nurse hung around for the show, a semi-lesbian headfake for the stunted boy still in me. Somers was hot enough to cause fantasies at all the most inappropriate times.

Schwartz had been treating Somers' family for more than twenty years so he knew the girl, her psychosis, and her money. He was central-casting Jewish doctor: short, horseshoe hair bald on top, tortoise glasses, thick mustache, superb bedside manners, didn't live and never would in Locust Valley, owned her as much as she owned him. Schwartz must have been his own mother-in-law's nightly wet-dream…a Miracle Mile crowd pleaser.

He treated me like accidental roadkill, barely saying a direct word. I couldn't figure out why I was there anyway other than to verify that she was indeed pregnant or get asked for money, so he didn't really need to talk to me. He did ask how we met,

"You're a lucky man Sebastian…Somers is the finest young lady in New York. So, how long have you been dating? How did you meet?"

"Well Dr. Schwartz, we, uhh Paul and I, rolled into Hunter's the other night, a few months ago, and saw Somers. I guess you can see for yourself that eventually she and I did the 'wild thing' (said with nervous tone and inflection…)…I'm unsure if you could say we ever really dated though. That's cool though. She's great. We're sticking together."

Somers looked mortally embarrassed, as I couldn't elucidate my thoughts like how she wanted me to.

"Are you in love?"

Somers had to step in and end the banter before I hit the embarrassment TNT…she spoke,

"Love is hype David. We'll figure that one out with time…"

Just when you think she's yours…not.

Schwartz sat down on a stool in front of Somers splayed legs, shifting her panties to the side, and he probed her well-groomed business with his fingers, talking nonstop, clinically about pregnancy but humorously about family…He really knew the Gillette's and Kincaids, I could tell, which made me feel like I really didn't know them. The nurse kept staring at Somers' business, which unfortunately turned me on…I should have been more attuned to what was really happening, like my life unraveling.

"How's your Mom? I haven't seen her in a while. You know, she's got a lot of planning to do if you get married Somers (uhhh, Doc, over here, want to direct that comment to me…?)"

He would re-lube his finger inside some Vaseline-like jar and then re-penetrate my friend Somers. It was like I was witnessing some gross husband cuckolding porn film. I couldn't look. I bet Somers' business was prettier than most of Schwartz' patients though. There were two 80-year old women waiting in the reception area…that can't be well-groomed, that's hardship pay. This guy deserved his fees maybe.

Somers told him to slow down because he was getting her hot…They laughed together, as if this was a joke that had been told hundreds of times. I thought she was serious. In my head and delirium, the sensuous nurse moaned and massaged her breasts…

Schwartz was mentioning things like stages of pregnancy and foods to be cautious about. Somers was mostly interested in the dates, such as a due date, when she would begin to pop at the belly, those kinds of dates…dates I had never heard of and I was barely listening to anyway. It was as if I was in a business meeting taking notes but wasn't really a participant, more like a witness who didn't understand the terminology and frankly no one wanted him to. And for whatever stupid reason of modesty, embarrassment, or plain old yuckiness, I couldn't stare at Somers while Schwartz probed her. For all I know, he really was making her hot.

This was the weirdest meeting I'd ever been to. Part life planning, porn, comedy, and mostly overwhelming. I wanted to go back to the corner where I first kissed Somers, and reset the tape. This whole thing made no sense. My life was fast forwarding in real time, seeing thirty years get eclipsed without a thought.

After the probing, testing, and date settling, Schwartz proclaimed Somers 100% pregnant and announced a due date of April 1, 1995, April Fool's. April Fool's? Jesus Christ, will it ever end? Can't my baby at least have a normal birthdate? And how did he really know she was pregnant? I never saw a test taken. Were his fingers biblical divining rods? I was the one who walked out of there feeling like I had been probed.

Somers said this to Schwartz as we left,

"I hope you have the decency to send me flowers in the morning stud."

Again Schwartz howled even though he had heard this line a billion times before; he knew it was best to humor her…the check would arrive quicker.

Somers and I walked over to Central Park at the 72nd entrance. We sat down on a park bench. It was stiflingly hot with a broiling midday sun beating down on our heads…I thought one of us might pass out, me mostly. Gynecologist offices can waylay any man…a lesson for all women if you need to debilitate your hubby for the day.

Somers got serious quickly. Somers always knows where it's at…and I wasn't ready for it. She wanted to get it on, life that is. A shark has such a deep bite, and the teeth just keep growing back.

Our lives were changing violently and dramatically. Somers was committed to keeping this pregnancy. She was saying things like no abortion, I need this pregnancy, you'd be a good father I can tell, etc...Which of course is weird if you know Somers…she's a Margaret Sanger disciple. But her mind was set. She was asserting power, the entitlement narcissist poking her head out of the ground. I couldn't even see that far ahead. I was concerned about covering the Haitian National Bank …my concentration issues were debatable no doubt.

It was time to be a big boy. I rallied, I had to shine, no choice, ok Somers, I'm with you. You've got to know though, that I'm not the best catch so far as money goes. Where I come from isn't all that great really, so not sure you'll dig the Carolina homestead. My apartment is really small. I'll work my ass off, but I'm really just starting out, and I sense you are used to much more. My boss hates me and I hate my boss, or what he stands for anyway. So, I'm not likely to stick around Shearson much longer. I ski a ton and play ping pong. I want to be my own boss to be honest. I'm a good guy, and I know I'd be a really good father, but do you really want me? I mean, look at me. You could have anyone."

"We don't need money Sebastian (uh oh…). I have money. I've told you that. And we won't be living in your apartment; we'll live in mine, though you can start paying for it. What I don't have is a father for this baby; that's what I need the most. I need a man who will always be there, and never cheat on me. And I know you're that guy. No other guy has loved me like you love me. Are you going to marry me or what?"

Somers doesn't beat around the bush when she wants something. She lets the sentences hang. She was making life and death decisions, and she needed things to start moving in real time.

Again, I was fully unprepared. Marry her? I couldn't get by the fact that she was pregnant. Marriage was such a tidal wave of commitment. Wasn't I supposed to ask her father for her hand? Somers was a lady, not an elopement. And, that issue of having been married once before, for a day and a half. Now that would come back to haunt me! We hadn't quite discussed that issue yet. I assumed she already knew, since she had done her wholesale fact checking on me already (Christ, she even knew my fucking social security number by then…she put it on the doctor's visitation form and I never told her!), but I guessed we'd have to address it soon, as in the next few minutes. I could hear rumbles of thunder in the distance though I saw no clouds.

Babies and strollers and the summer crowds were walking by, and we sat there quietly, debating inside how to proceed from the question. Marriage? It took me ten minutes to recover.

I was being asked to dive into molten lava in exchange for my own spiritual sacrifice. I wasn't sure if heaven existed and I hadn't signed up for 72 Virgins, so diving in to the lava was a huge leap of faith. She was gorgeous though…I mean, if someone was going to hose me down the road, she may as well be gorgeous, may as well get something out of the trade. And she was great at sex, you know, the one time I had it with her…

"Of course. Is that what you want?"

"Yes. We could be married for a year just to make the baby legitimate. Don't worry about money Sebastian (there she goes again…)."

The length of our hypothetical marriage just leapt from a day to a year. When we spoke at Melon's the previous night, she said we could be married for a day and divorce right after. Now, a day later, and we're already up to a year. At this rate, I'd be married until the Gates of Hell opened…uhhh, bad analogy I guess.

Somerset Maugham used to say about love that it was only a dirty trick played on us to achieve continuation of the species. I was continuing the species alright.

Of course, money was all I was worried about…I didn't have enough to handle this, any of this. I'd have to stop complaining about Exeter political kingpins. Still, I always said if I married again, it would be my last time, so I really needed to be sure about this one. What did I have, like five minutes to make up my mind on that score? It was the perfect amount of time, for one of us…

"Somers, I'm not marrying anyone for a year. If you want to get married, we'll get married. But marriage is a lifetime…this isn't some warranty program where we trade each other when things don't work out. But we get married and that's it. I'll never marry again. We haven't exactly discussed this before, but I was married once. Not too proud about any of it, because I really loved that girl. I said I wouldn't get married again until I was 40, so I'm jump starting this ten years early. The thing is, I really like you. But I have to meet your dad…"

Somers burst out crying…it was a weird, tearless cry with bellowing sobs, almost a fake cry it had so much drama inside…it was a drama trap. She was gasping for air, her face contorted, her ridge lines bursting through skin. She hugged me really hard, completely beyond any expected strength, holding so tight so I could no longer breathe, but I could feel her body quiver. I hoped she wouldn't bite my neck. She was shaking.

Her emotions startled me. She was sobbing violently, uncontrollably even. People were staring at us as if one of our parents had been murdered. Her mouth was drooling uncontrollably, and mucus was raining down my business shirt.

Marriage was supposed to be a happy thing…

"It's OK, it's OK."

I was trying to calm her, but something had touched off a decade's pent up supply of emotions. Somers was not the emotional type, so when you got it, you really got it. My left shoulder was soaking from her drool. Eventually she calmed down enough to speak, but her eyes were bloodshot, really bloodshot…honestly, they were fully red, you couldn't even see her pupils. What's that all about?

"I think I love you Sebastian, and I haven't loved anyone in a long time. I don't trust anyone. And I don't even know if I trust you, but you came clean about your previous marriage and I was waiting for that (what was this, a test?…). And I can't guarantee what kind of wife I'll be. I'll try. But we're going to do this, for the pregnancy. And we're going to make it work. I'll never shut you out. Marriage is something I don't quite believe in, and religion definitely isn't my bag. But I'll give it a go and I don't lose at anything. I'll never desert you."

You know, in the heat of it, you'll believe the one you think you're in love with, and she in turn believes in you. She made me think I was a star… I wondered if this fairy tale would have a happy ending…Everyone has to stand alone at some point, but only marriage can make your dreams come true.

"Somers Gillette, you'll never be on your own. I swear. Would you marry me?"

"Yes."

Now that the smokes gone,
and the air is all clear:
those who were right there
had a new kind of fear.

(v. Filter)

"Jesus H Christ…Get Me a Glass of Water!!"

Nick's mother Granny Gillette (Somers' grandmother) was the Grande dame of the paternal Gillette family: 92 years of seen-it-all and done-it-all decency. She was the most likeable person in the world, eminently kind, direct, and honest. When I met her with Somers for the first time at her Long Island estate, after some idle get-to-know-you chitchat, she said to Somers that she wanted to speak with me alone. Granny Gillette took my hand and walked me out to her garden, while Somers stayed in the kitchen with the cook.

"Sebastian…I know why the two of you are marrying, there's no need to bullshit me; I don't have enough time left on this earth to be bullshitted. OK? It happens. I wish you had met Nick's father. He was a great man and I wish he was here for this. You'd like him and he'd like you. You don't really know your soon-to-be-bride, Somers, but I do. I love her dearly, she is my granddaughter after all, but I must tell you something: Somers has her mother's disease: she's mean-spirited. I didn't grow up rich, so I get to call it like it is, so sorry for hitting you like this, but like I said, I don't have much time left here on earth. I have to be efficient. You must be careful. This family has dark secrets and they can trip a man if he's not watching. I won't betray confidences and loyalties, but you must be careful around Gruella and Somers…they're not like you, or me (so I've heard…). This town is their kryptonite and yet it's their only goal. Which is odd; hell I'd just leave and never come back. When Nick and Gruella divorced, that was the best thing to happen to Nick and the worst thing to happen to Gruella. Gruella thinks she's important…as if! She wants to get back at Nick, but she doesn't have the courage to make it happen. Somers does. Together, they're dangerous."

I wasn't sure what Granny Gillette was trying to tell me…I felt like I was on acid, or she was. Her goal was to try to keep me from falling for Somers…but I already had. With this family I'd begun to expect that any response to their questions would be parsed until I was found guilty or criminally culpable. It was like everyone was an amateur lawyer with a trust fund. Granny Gillette wasn't cross-examining me like the others thank god…she was just trying to give me a heads-up. She seemed prescient about matters…she'd be the kind who'd warn the fortune-teller…

The fire in my heart wasn't out necessarily, but everyone kept throwing water on it as it tried to catch…Sometimes it's only in our own heads when we feel so left out and other times, it's all too real.

Somers had two sisters, Morgan and Ariane. The three sisters together were ravishingly beautiful, one topping the next on any given night. Gruella might be demonic but her eggs certainly knew how to pass off certain parts of the genetic pool to her husband. The sisters shared a visceral wariness around Somers, as if even they might get bitten by the snake. The tension was always thick. Neither sister desired press and society like Somers…I got the sense they could take it or leave it. Somers gave oral to the press...

Gruella and Ed Kincaid, Somers' birth mother and stepfather, were coming to Manhattan from San Francisco for a week. The dreamer was about to meet cold reality head on, I was gonna be flattened by the hurricane of the Slanderer. No one told them why Somers wanted to meet…Somers had only said to them she wanted to introduce a boy, like a Broadway play not yet reviewed, hardly an SRO recommendation. I was nervous without being asked, *Je suis nerveux à l'idée de les voir.*

The bassist set a progression mood with the D2 fret 8-3-0 popping, slowly at first, low rollers, gradually louder, like a slasher movie setup scene. The drummer warms up, slowly beating his muffled bass like a death camp's march, joined with a floor tom in arranged staccato. You can feel the music in your bones. Rhythm guitar waits for its open….he's got a D-Tuna smoking, ready for ripped action, dropping E to D. It was as dark a lead-in to a song I'd ever heard, in my head only. A mosh pit of another sort was brewing.

I was unsure what Somers was going to say to them when we all met, because among other things she kept the meeting a secret even from me…all week she was telling me we were just going to meet a friend. Ten minutes before meeting her parents, she sat me down at the Regency to go over what was about to go down, in other words, meeting her mom. When we walked over to meet the Kincaid's, it was like the Bataan Death March…I was being fed to my captors.

We were ushered up to their apartment by one of their five doormen and a man answered the door. Some little white mongrel dog was gnashing its yellow teeth at us from foot level. I'm a dog guy, so just go with me on this one: it's an ugly little fucker.

Ed Kincaid was an effete medium height man of 65, metrosexual business Saville Row…his face is a weak Irish sot. He had gray hair, average build, and looked to be extraordinarily un-athletic…you could just tell. I'd heard enough about him prior to meeting, how he'd made a fortune in farming and how he had children of his own. Ed was a member of the Bohemian Grove, another {supposedly} secretive fraternity-like club in California, whose motto is "Weaving Spiders Come Not Here", though that's all they do while they gossip over global intrigue and campfires, listen to Jimmy Buffet (ugh..), and smoke weed totally bone naked. OK, OK…they don't really smoke weed, the rest is spot on.   The Grove is like the Social Register in its patently disingenuous exclusivity factor.   It's full of anything but Protestants these days and the mechanism to get in is bold-faced shamelessness.

Ed loved the Republican Party…he got election erection every four years. Ed was also a member of Opus Dei, a secretive catholic fraternity of {supposedly} rigidly adherent practitioners. But Jesus was neither Democrat nor Republican. Romans 13:1, "Render to

Caesar the things that are Caesar's; and to God the things that are God's." I don't think he quite got that sermon…

Gruella at first glance (from say a couple thousand yards, through a periscope maybe) is pleasing to the eye…on second glance and up close, she's monstrous. Her fake blond locks didn't come cheap I suspected, as few women of 65 with morbidly black eyebrows (plucked to within a fraction of their original intent) do. She had an almost babushka-like, heavy-weighted hip displacement, making her ass appear square as a lead box and about as nimble as one too.

Her face was shaped by decades of intense bitterness, like the Wicked Witch of the West, except the Witch was much nicer. With some people, their frowns become their face…with Gruella, I wasn't certain where the face started and the frown ended.

You know how they say that horse people eventually have horse faces…Gruella had the face of a rat: nasty, gnarly, pointy, gruesome, malicious, impervious to extinction, adaptable to nuclear war…That's how I felt anyway. She's the queen earth rat snarling in the dark basement of death. I guess she must have been nice once in her life…maybe, probably at the age of four. After that, it was all downhill. Gruella must have vertigo from trading her soul so often.

She did dress nicely, that could be said, all haute couture and never worn twice, the ultimate tag-hag. Nothing came cheap on this woman. You could see that Ed shelled out huge sums on the wardrobe.

Every year he bought her the most insanely priced and remarkably gaudy gems that money could buy. Gruella's daughters (and sons-in-law…ahem) would end up enslaved to this preposterous annual gift-giving. After receiving a $200,000 brooch necklace say, Gruella couldn't even summon a feigned surprise or quasi-natural emotion…she'd look at the gift as nothing more than a steaming turd to stick in the noses of her social climbing phony frenemies in San Francisco.

Gruella Kincaid had to be the world's least-humanistic human being ever. There was nothing in her that spoke of a hint of decency. No friends. She was Michael Corleone in the San Francisco society social climbing nausea…keep your friends close, but your enemies closer. Therefore, everyone was close to Gruella. The world was all about her. Read any email from her…it's all about her, always. She's a communication narcissist among a billion other sub-categories of narcissism. She's uninhibited in response to anything, especially perceived slights. Revenge to Gruella is a holy cause.

Only her mongrel dog elicited any kindness out of her pestiferous pores, and even then, that sentiment had the air of plaintive selfishness, as the dog was the only thing that couldn't say fuck-you back…it likely wanted to. She protected that dog in the most outrageously pedantic manner, like a truculent child spoiled beyond human recognition protecting her favorite doll.

How did Nick Gillette, Somers' birth father and the greatest man in the history of the world, ever marry Gruella Kincaid? They had three beautiful daughters together, but wow…the Seven Wonders need to make room for that long-ago marriage.

She's everything I wished I never knew.

Somers, Ed, Gruella, and I gathered in the Kincaid's foreboding Manhattan co-op for the big meet and greet. They had no idea what was about to hit them, nor I.

The pre-war apartment smelled like death, a rat cage of fecal despair. Everything in the apartment was straight out of a Sotheby's pre-1700's antique catalogue, no color, light, or life. The Old Scratch himself had been the decorator. Even the windows were bathed in black cloth and the carpets were blood red. It was a perfect place to commit a murder...the trace DNA would be lost in the macabre schemes...

Gruella bought dark cubist art because no one could make fun of her for doing so. Minimalist art is disingenuous enough and so is never taken seriously by anyone...the joke's always on the buyer, the grateful galleries call these buyers musical chair arrivistes. As Oscar Wilde said, 'Bad artists always admire each other's work', and similarly, ignorant modern art buyers fool themselves the same.

After a one second split and for the first time in her life, Somers handed off the communication baton, to me, a verbal savant if there ever was one... Somers had an intense, primitive fear of her mother, like a child shirking from the ogre werewolf on the Scottish midnight moors. And yet, the two of them are eternal co-conspirators, joined at the displaced hip of Mephistopheles.

"Ed, Mom...This is Sebastian. Sebastian wants to tell you about himself and when we want to do some things ('Things'? Like get married Somers? Thanks for the flipping lead-in...not)."

Somers hadn't prepared me for this at all. This was the start of my fall. She was supposed to be talking, but her own jihadist mom made her puke.

It was like I was sitting at a sold-out Yankee Stadium being carried live on prime time television, an usher walks up behind me, hands me a microphone, and says, Sing... I don't sing (and I don't dance). If I'd been unprepared to say anything the night Somers and I met at

Hunter's, you can only imagine how blank I was now, when Somers essentially handed me total responsibility to tell these two hellish Mephistopheles what was about to go down. You just can't pick your enemies too carefully.

And mind you, Nick and Deezy Gillette (Somers' other, nice set of parents, birth father and stepmother) couldn't have been warmer about the exact same news…the complete opposite of what was to happen next. Gruella was itching her global rash to tell anyone, let alone me, what she considered wrong about anything and everything, forget the nuclear news I was about to unload on her. I don't enjoy listening to negative nabobs…so we had about a good a lead in as any two mortal mother-son-in-law enemies.

"Mmmm. Well, yes, that's right Somers, thanks (not…)…Nice to meet you sir and ma'am (Gruella doesn't like to be called ma'am; she fancies herself thirty years younger, or my age…). This may come out a little faster than I thought (or, faster than what I actually need…like never and forever…). So, I'm sorry about this (Somers was hyperventilating…), but I don't know how to say it any other way. And look, uhhh, why beat around the bush…(fake smile…crickets and clocks…). We're going to be family after all, and I think honesty is the best policy (except with you two, then abject deception is best…). Somers is pregnant and we need to be married, soon (and I'd like to get the hell out of this apartment, thanks everyone for coming…Allah Akbar!!…)."

A ta-ta-dum drum roll would have been perfect… This apartment had never heard a plucked guitar string, a piano's soft tune, or a drum's steady beat. It was sheer auditory death. I must have seemed like very urban-Amish to this crowd.

I pulled a Somers…I just let the sentences hang. I didn't think I had much of a choice. If I'd kept talking, I was going to hurl all over their hellish carpet. The oratorical choice of letting it all hang out there ended up being such a great choice…not! You probably never want to tell Genghis Kahn you just knocked up his daughter.

The stare back to me from the both of them was epic, a Bheliar brew of such intense hatred that trees in Central Park split and snapped. The psycho evil mother-in-law caricature had just hit the jackpot of eternal raison d'être…she now had a reason to live, she could hate again!

Gruella – "Jesus H. Christ!! Ed…get me a f.u.c.k.i.n.g. glass of water!!!!! Can you fucking repeat what you just said young man?!!"

This family takes the Lord's name in vain a ton…no one ever taught me that at an Episcopalian school. And they curse…whoof (that's just the mom by the way, soon to be grandmother…that had to hurt). Gruella's too-tight Dior top was all that held her soul from exploding and wrecking me that very minute. At the same time, you could see she was excited, an animal getting in touch with her killing instincts again.

"We don't have to get married really…she could just be my girlfriend! "

I was kidding, hoping a joke would lighten the mood…it worked as well as a mortar fart during a state funeral moment of silence. I only had three lower scales on the bar to go with my future in-laws, and that would have been to inform them that I spoke Spanglish, owned a double-wide in West Virginia, and happily voted for Bill Clinton.

Now that I know Gruella, I can say that it would never have been her to ask how Somers was feeling, or to say how happy she was that her daughter was pregnant, or that she was elated she'd be a grandmother again. Big laugh there. She doesn't like anyone, especially children…she hates children.

Gruella was sure to cause Somers a miscarriage. All she could think of was herself and she was cursing like Billy Martin and Earl Weaver over the worst blown call ever by an ump. Something at stake far greater than what I could guess was at risk for Gruella. I swear you'd be scared of that witch if you didn't know her, which I didn't, so I was peeing in my flipping pants. She wanted water damnit, fuck you very much, and she desperately wanted to know how this little indiscretion would reflect on her. Who asks for water by the way? Wouldn't you want liquor, like an actual human? Her head was shape-shifting into society's Beast, a comedic sunglasses and horns, steam and bile, Valentino and death guise.

Somers was half-conscious and I desperately needed her mental bearings to deal with this shape-shifter mom of hers. That woman was now a steaming pile of gnashing wharf rats…

"Do you even fucking care what New York will say about my daughter you fuckwit (why you directing this at me, woman? Why does everyone keep blaming me for Somers' birth control? Stop cursing by the way, my child might hear…)? Somers was the top girl in this town…until this (still the top to me…that was the best sex I've ever had, hands down, I mean excepting the neck wound…). Now look at her (still hot from what I can see, if not a little frightened, but then again, look at you Gruella, who wouldn't be?!...). Where are you from? What do you even fucking do (I don't think I should even get into that right now…)? Jesus. This is going to look real fucking great tonight…I'm supposed to tell the whole crowd what my daughter has done (tell 'em, It was Awesome, capital A...your daughter is a masochistic sex freak, that crowd would eat that shite up! They're bored listening to you complain all the time…)? How could you Somers (yes! back to her! off my back!…)? Jesus Fucking Christ does this shit a storm."

She said that! "Shit a storm". I'd never heard anyone say that before, especially not a 65 year old society woman supposedly at the top of the San Francisco heap of plaintive insecurities…and yet, it made sense in a weird way. You know when Lou Gehrig proclaimed that he *felt like the luckiest man on the face of the earth…?'* Gruella made me feel whatever the opposite of that was, *today I feel like the unluckiest man on the face of the earth.*

Gruella had a big MoMa party for profit that night…that's why they were here. God I hate large parties for profit. Gruella had engineered Somers' climb up the New York society ladder, a fanatic social climber, and an unplanned pregnancy was a huge issue if social climbing had been your only life goal. Quest didn't photograph out-of-wedlock pregnant brides…and Gruella wanted a Quest tattoo on her inner thigh so the last thing you'd see before entering was the Quest logo, to let you know what got you there.

According to Gruella, getting knocked up pre-massive wedding ceremony only happened north of 96th Street and only if you spoke Ebonics. Gruella spent an hour interrogating, planning, and scheming, the inquisition of the innocent by the oppressor. This was a holy cause from the moment we said hello. She had me at hello? She ruined me at hello…

"Somers has me wrapped around her finger. I really love her. I think this will work out great. We'll be great parents."

"You don't know the first fucking thing about being a parent you turd! You could have used a condom! Give me one reason why I should support you."

"I love her?"

She hulked out like a nutcase,

"Fuck love, Sebastian!!! Love doesn't pay the rent, and love dies after you fuck a few more times!! And you two have really fucked up, especially you Sebastian!! I'll do what I can to straighten this out (what needs to be straightened?...). I need a few days. In the meantime, get a fucking job. Musician…ha! Give me a fucking break you loser!"

What she really said to me was "I'll get you, my pretty, and your little dog too!!!!!!" I felt like Dorothy without Toto.

That hour was about as happy an hour as a man could ever have, if you're happy being sentenced to the death chamber with no last rites. Actually, the death chamber would have been more pleasurable, as at least you'd know the end was near….this was only the beginning. I'm sure in the last minute of her invective, Gruella concocted the long-term strategy to do me in…you could just see the scheme in 3D. She wasn't human. She was wicked, but naturally so, there was no posing to her Lake of Fire genesis. Scary. She wanted me to head back to whatever shithole I came from and I wanted to go there too!

All I could really think of was Somers, the baby, and getting the heck out of that dark apartment. I felt like I was in the lair of Beelzebub and only a scrubbing with holy water would do. Actually, I needed an ocean of holy water, and even then, I could see that Gruella was up for the battle, licking her bloody chops over the invitation to wage war with Good and God.

Here's my mother-in-law jihadist in a nutshell: she hates all humanity, or more accurately she hates creation, she opposes God, she spreads lies and she wreaks havoc on the souls of mankind. Pretty much has it all covered I'd say!

The meeting ended. I expected a dragon's fire blast would nail me in the butt as I walked out the door. That was an interesting meeting to say the least...for two reasons:

- I'm the least hateful man you could ever meet, barely have a hate bone in my body, but I finally met someone I hate.
- I'm the ultimate dog person, the dog whisperer before there was a dog whisperer, and that was the first dog that ever snarled at me.

Somers and I finally left the apartment, feeling our bodies for the bullet holes. There wasn't a single gesture of encouragement or sign of emotional thaw. Ed and Gruella leered at us as if we had committed the most defiling sin of all time, as if their own evil should never be trod upon by others...they owned the well of demonic despair and wished for no one to measure up. It was as if I had deliberately attacked them. They were hypersensitive to all things potentially unwieldy. They weren't narcissism so much as a felony murder.

My baby was coming, with and through the clouds amidst trumpets, angelic activity, heavenly signs, a resurrection, a gathering of saints. And Gruella needed to fuck that up. Her task was clear...only Armageddon would suffice. Game on...

"She goes first class, not steerage! She's the best young woman in all of Manhattan. Caviar, not fucking catfish! You better fucking come through Sebastian. Jesus, this is a mess! I need to lie down Ed."

Married couples are supposed to be really happy. Instead, I was depressed about the Botoxed Beelzebub, aka Gruella Kincaid. Even

Somers' freak sex pool act now had a bad stain. It was a nice shot by Gruella…right on the head of my mental happiness. This was a new fear for mankind.

This family was crazy. I couldn't wait for Christmas…they likely had Jesus morphed into a satanic voodoo doll. Jesus and Sebastian...the two men Gruella hated the most. This was the start of a really bad society trip. All I could think was: 'I gotta marry into this?'

A Quest Wedding

She'd take my money when I was most in need, and that was just Gruella, my personal Artful Dodger. My world was out of sync starting the day I met the mother-in-law. Gruella planted her flag in my town, my home, my life, and right on top of my testicles…my scrotum would be her moon until she could figure out how to nuke it.

"What was that all about Somers?!! I mean Jesus…Your mom isn't even human. She never once asked about you or the baby…It's all about her. Do you know what narcissism is? I can't even give her credit for that…she isn't human enough to deserve a sociological assessment. She needs a flipping exorcist. No kidding. You're shaking."

"Oh, stop being a pussy (I wasn't shaking, she was!...). She does that to test people. She'll be fine soon. Let her simmer down and she'll come around (what, in the next millennium…?). We're going to go buy a baby crib now…let's just forget it."

"And what's up with that dog? You've got to be kidding me…she was feeding it Evian! Not that I give a crap, but excuse me, isn't that somewhat weird? Did I see the number 666 tattooed on it? Is that a male or female, you can't even tell, it looks like a paramecium with hair."

Somers was throwing punches in the air as we spoke, almost mentally unbalanced, as if her Mom's beatdown had given her a bizarre energy shot…she just came out of nowhere with the next fusillade of craziness,

"If you lie to me, I will kill you Sebastian! I swear! I can take a lot, but I cannot take lying. Cheat on me, don't lie. Otherwise, I promise I will ruin you like no woman has ever ruined any man. You think my Mom was bad? You just wait…"

ET? I could cheat on her but not lie? Weren't they one and the same? And how did lying just come up? Weren't we just discussing Gruella? Why was I now on the defensive?

This was my very first instance of seeing and hearing Somers' Magical Narcissism. Magical Narcissists see themselves as perfect, using distortion and illusion to dump shame onto others. This Kincaid side of her family was certifiably institutionally wacky. I'm not kidding.

The meeting with Gruella was more than just ominous and dreadful, you'll never experience anything like it in your life. Nothing is remotely similar to Gruella unless you've been to hell. Ask anyone who knows her what the least impressive start to a relationship with her could possibly be and they'd all say the same thing, 'just don't get her daughter pregnant'… So I had that going for me… I'd have to learn Taps.

Gruella's neurotic but not in a classically zonked-out way…she's neurotic and aware… That's the worst of all psychotic combinations. I could have bailed, but the unborn child needed to be protected at all costs, especially now, by this dad. I felt like I had to protect humanity in some way. I was uncertain about everything else.

"Somers I think I love you, but I need to know what's going on here."

"Sebastian, we're getting married whether you want to or not. Let's stop talking."

She laughed it off, there was no time for such idle matters as love…our bed would never catch on fire. We hadn't begun, but the end was already near.

Somers went big pimpin' for the next few months. She had ninety days to arrange a wedding, HERS not mine, the most important day of her life (outside her 50th Birthday party), and she wasn't going to fail.

I heard Somers and her mother Gruella speak on the phone every night…they were as good a Chairman/CEO team as you could ever expect that is, if you consider pregnancy and business one and the same. Our sex life was canceled for the rest of the pregnancy if not life. It would take a lot of dough to touch Somers again. All the dreams I never thought I'd lose got tossed before we went to sleep.

Somers could organize, so organize she did. She got the church (St. Thomas' on 5th Avenue), the rehearsal dinner (The Racquet on Park Avenue), the band (Bob Hardwick), the honeymoon (Jumby Bay Antigua), the invitations (The Printery, Oyster Bay), and so on. We registered at Tiffany's, Crate and Barrel, Scully and Scully, and G Williker's.

There were to be Four Hundred guests, as if the number 400 had some magical connotation (witchcraft in hindsight I guess…or the Quest 400). Her family would be 85 of the 400, or nearly 25%…my family was 15 or not quite 4%. The cost of the reception was illogical, no need to split five loaves and two fish in this crew. We could have fed half of Haiti for a decade, or for the same price, Gruella could buy voodoo dolls for ten years…

Somers even organized me….everything about me. New wardrobe, new shoes, new ties, new clubs, new everything. I paid for it of course, so my nest egg kept disappearing, but it felt good to be looked after. I was a side project, secondary to the wedding, but an important accessory. I really dug her, if not being slightly fearful of her.

I moved in with Somers to the East 79th Apartment, six weeks after the ObGyn visit. The doorman was still hostile if not more so…I figured he would never give that up.

I ate about $5,000 on the remainder of the old apartment lease I'd just signed…more money washed down the drain because of this unplanned change of life, but don't worry about money Sebastian. I now paid for two apartments, a soon-to-be-baby, a soon-to-be-wife, a baby nurse, and so on…biting off more than I could chew. I ate it up, and then vomited. My nervous system began to shut down. There was no music.

During the entire phase of wedding planning, only Granny Gillette and I mentioned anything about the baby… I was psyched more and more each day. Granny Gillette always asked about the baby, what we would call it, how Somers was feeling. I really loved that old woman. I should have married her.

I had a dreamer's disease, ignoring reality…lost in some vision of glory and eternal feel-good illusions…

Occasionally when I had some down time, I felt maybe the pregnancy was a ruse, a concoction by Somers to simply get a new New York Times Sunday Styles photo layout. She loved to be seen by others. She ended up speaking with Quest, Anna Brady of the Times, Avenue, Town and Country (still acceptable back then), and

Tattler. They wanted her and she them. I begged her to decline, but that was like telling a monkey at the zoo to not eat the banana you just handed him while he laughs at you from behind the steel bars. Shyness did not become her.

We never had sex during the engagement, all the way until our wedding night, and then, Somers simply said, with not one ounce of emotion,

"We're going to have sex tonight, I don't care if you don't want to. Everyone does on their wedding night. I know you think I'm fat, but we have to have sex on our wedding night. Everyone does."

I didn't think she was fat and had never said anything remotely like that. I thought she was smoking hot, but never fat. Somers has a weird way of inserting words into your mouth as if you said them and that's that. And people tend to believe her, remarkably. I don't anymore, but then again, she royally hosed me as you'll see, so I don't believe her if she tells me it's raining during a hurricane. She ate a BLT while we made love on our wedding night...no shite! Turn-on...not. I think there was a message embedded in that move...

She laid another oratorical gem on me during our wedding night, a line that she would repeat, mantra-like, over and over for fifteen years...

"Can you believe we're still married?"

The first time she said that, we had been married for less than six hours. The last time she said it, we had six hours of marriage left. In between, she said it a billion times. I swear she and Gruella laid money in Vegas on us. At the end, she'd leave with way more than half…she'd want it all. I never bought the your penis is too big dick compliment…every woman says it to flatter their husbands.

We were so far at the low end of normalcy for sex, that we'd be ignored in any statistical modeling…We were the number you discarded because it skews the mean. The box lock almost never came off for me.

Of course, she was still having sex… After all, she had needs, just as her mother had many years before. More on that later…I should have known…hot society women don't go quietly into that good night. If they do, watch out.

St. Thomas' Church and Atheism

Before all that, she needed a church and she was on point. We were to be co-signers for life…ha.

Three Episcopalian church's in New York City are considered society top-shelf (so far as the New York Times Sunday Styles Section goes; Town and Country Magazine weddings are low-rent anymore, not then, but certainly now). St. Bart's on Park Avenue, which is rarely used by Society more by celebrities; St. James' on Madison, which is famously located next to Ralph Lauren's global flagship, natch…only Ralph Lauren could be that brilliant…St. James' is nouveau Episcopalian and full of UES social strivers who think it's high Episcopalian when it's anything but; and St. Thomas' on Fifth Avenue.

St. Thomas' is the most imposing from the inside and outside and certainly holds the largest congregation. Not incidentally, it happens to be the oldest in the city north of Wall Street, and the last remaining high Episcopalian in all of New York. The boy's choir of St. Thomas' is world famous with their signature upright collar vestments and beautiful Christmas choral music. Chances are strong that lesbian ministers will not be passing the bread and wine soon at St. Thomas'.

You don't just get your wedding day of choice at St. Thomas'. Extreme effort and even more extreme pull help. Somers Gillette herself could not get her preferred date without some genuflecting, and we didn't have the luxury of time for most engaged couples.

Both of us were asked to attend a meeting with The Reverend Christopher Warren, an Anglican transplant to America, and the highest of the high priests tending the St. Thomas flock. The few high Episcopalian churches left in the United States like to recruit

English ministers to take over their ministry, as the English accents lend an air of formality and doctrinaire devotion, as if hearing the accent will cause the parishioners to get in touch with their roots…If anyone really understood Episcopalians anymore, it's basically a quasi-hippie commune, attracting the kooks of American society looking for the most liberal of Christianity. The tent's wide, come on in…

We arrived to St. Thomas' on August 20. Rev. Warren's office was so large it would make the Pope blush. The inside was full of historical papers, globes, and paintings. There must have been five partners' desks as well. Somers came with her organizational skills down cold…she practically gave him a Lotus 1-2-3 presentation, just another metaphor for the corporate narcissist in her….everything, including weddings, was a deal.

Rev. Warren was a patrician-looking man of perhaps sixty with grey swept hair (think Baron von Trapp in The Sound of Music). When we were led into his office by the church secretary, Somers and Rev. Warren acted as if they had known each other for quite some time. Which as it turned out, they had! Not that she gave me any advance warning on that of course. She was dressed in a business suit, still sexy as shite, even in this muted form, like you simply wanted to tear it off…she didn't look pregnant, just ravishing.

"Somers, pleasure to see you again. I hope you've been well."

He had the toff accent.

"Well enough Christopher (no surnames used by this girl!...). This is Sebastian Graham, my fiancé. We want to get married."

Rev. Warren grinned like the cat that ate the canary.

Did he just say nice to see you again? This chick doesn't go to church sir. She told me she was an atheist doing the church thing today because we had to.

Somers worked Rev. Warren like a charm, easily maneuvering the conversation along. Obviously we had to provide our bona fides but I noticed that Somers was vague on the conditions of her church confirmation…That wasn't on her 1-2-3 presentation by the way. For me, I can't forget Sunday School: six years of school-fed scripture taught by rather unhappy and overweight Christian women every Sunday morning between my 6th and 12th birthday, me daydreaming about them naked in their blubber, and still I got confirmed.

Somers was an avowed atheist now, no butterfaith she….

When she initially told me she was an atheist, I wasn't initially thrown off by the hostile stance, as it seemed more of a reaction to her old boyfriend, Richard. You know, come to think of it, his last name was Warren…someone mentioned that to me. What bothered me more about her atheism was that she liked to stoke dinner conversation with other guests on the topic…she relished the idea that she was the designated dark shadow on an otherwise sunny subject. It inflated her self-importance.

Somers' atheism reminded me of Jezebel of Phoenicia, an historical woman ultimately eaten by dogs for her evil ways. Jezebel introduced false idol worship into Israel and then enlisted her husband to worship alongside the blasphemers. He was killed eventually for betraying his people and removing religion from their lives. Jezebel attempted to sleep with the new king to avoid the same. The Prophet Elijah stated that wild dogs would eat Jezebel with the exception of her face, feet, and hands, all because she had cast religion out of her people's lives, and the remainder of Jezebel would serve as a lesson for all the non-believers. That's what happens to you kids…tsk, tsk.

Somers answered his questions as perfectly as any bride-to-be could. Remember: we only had a little more than a month to go and the pressure was on for Somers to execute contracts. After fifteen minutes of beating around the bush, I could see Somers' chin and jaw tense up, as if this man was wasting her precious time.

She walked the Reverend over to a side alcove to talk mano a mano (I mean that), The Beauty (the Father) and the Beast (Somers), while I stared at his multi-million dollar collection of globes and atlases. I could only guess at what they were discussing. A crime was taking place before my eyes…I was simply an accessory, literally. They rejoined. Rev. Warren looked like a beaten-down salesperson and she his most ruthless customer who pays cash. We had troubles with God already…

Somers and Rev. Warren settled on a date, almost a month from the day, a Friday (which was not a normal wedding day for your average Episcopalian…). Somers' stomach and the little baby growing inside would not wait a year so Friday it was. That date ultimately worked out fine, as it was Columbus Day weekend. Out-of-towners could make a full New York weekend of it, while Manhattanites could get out for the weekend. A win-win for all, except the groom…I was on lose-lose.

Rev. Warren asked me only one question really,

"I hear you're a bit of a musician Sebastian. What songs would you like to hear during the wedding?"

"Well, Father, I love Ode to Joy and also…"

"Christopher, I'll be dealing with the music, not my husband. We need to leave."

Somers wanted none of that. He bid us farewell, but he eyed me as I left with a look of deep concern.

We walked down the stairs and through the center aisle of the church, to Fifth Avenue. Somers laid this gem of a line,

"What a cheapskate bastard Jew. He wanted $50,000 for one hour, for him to dribble his religious nonsense at me; I countered with twenty. We settled on $30,000. What a loser. If he only knew I have six weeks before my wedding dress won't be able to fit me anymore! He could have leveraged that. No wonder he's a fucking minister!! "

I guessed that was what the alcove negotiations were all about: money. She could be extraordinarily mean when she wanted to be, you had to give her that. And, vicious to a human she supposedly didn't know well, who was supposed to marry us.

This was merely Exploitative Narcissism, which involves the exploitation of others without regard for their feelings or interests. Often the other is in a subservient position where resistance would be difficult or even impossible. Sometimes the subservience is not so much real as assumed, like here. Somers assume anyone working for her was below her…

I probably should have reflected more at this point, that a woman I was due to marry was telling a high Episcopalian priest to go fuck himself...calling him a Jew...dribbling nonsense...leveraging a baby? What was that all about? Those piercing sounds were filling me with all kinds of doubt. $30K...? I didn't have that kind of dosh... The money worries eclipsed the character worries as they often do.

"Uhhh, Somers, we may need to rethink this. I don't have $30,000 lying around to splurge on a church (technically that wasn't true, but after the wedding rings and gifts, it would have sucked me nearly dry...). I thought churches were free for weddings?"

"Churches are businesses Sebastian (they are?...). You're such a fucking moron. Don't worry about the money. My dad's handling that. You just need to get me a ring."

I had already bought the ring...70% of my liquid net worth had. Somers reached for her cell phone (she had gotten one by then, her first sign of technolust) and dialed her Manhattan money management office,

"Alan, it's Somers, can you send a check immediately to St. Thomas' Church on 5th. Thirty Thousand Dollars. To the attention of Rev. Christopher Warren. Please notate "Graham Wedding...Ask more next time CW". This should come out of the Gillette Master Trust II."

Click. No good bye. No thanks. Testosterphone, Hollywood hangup. And who plays games with check notations to churches?

I couldn't fight it anymore.

"Somers, do we really need this huge wedding thing? I mean seriously, this is out of control. Thirty Thousand for a church? That's insane…"

Somers' speaking with Alan was a shot in the gut to me, much more than her negotiating with Rev. Warren. Any groom wants to be able to handle his own financial affairs. The dollar figures, not significant to Somers, simply represented down-the road markers for me…I knew I'd need to pay the house back eventually, you could just sense it. She was a casino lending cash at a very high interest rate, and I could never walk away from the table. Somers doesn't forget many things, but at the top of the list, perhaps numbers 1 through 100, she really doesn't forget money.

Her mother and she were charging their Amex's like ghetto lottery winners. They were gleeful to the point of perversion, squandering money for different reasons by the way. Gruella wanted to spend Nick Gillette's money as fast as she could, to get back at him. Somers liked spending both Nick and Ed's money…Nick's because she wanted to subtly avenge her mother's wrongful divorce, and Ed's because Ed was a national player, and she wanted affiliate points.

"Sebastian, are you down with this wedding? Don't get weak-kneed on me now big boy!"

""I'm good Somers. I'd just rather pay my own freight."

"Don't worry, you will. For now, just follow my marching orders."

ET, phone home. She was weird and possibly deranged, and better yet, I was marrying her! Betrayal had never had roots so deep. She was blowing my mind. My eyes were off the grid.   This was a bestial hagiographical tale with me as the meal.

We were locked in, October 7th, 1992. No turning back. You're gonna need a bigger boat Captain…

The Ambassador and Campagnola

I was still lost, possibly even more so, searching for signs of life that I could call my own…It would have been all too easy for anyone to shoot the dreamer that night.

Nothing could have prepared me for what was about to go down. Some people (like me) are born to be screwed, and worse, haven't done much to deserve it…we're just easy marks for the likes of them. Diablo-like Furies enjoy an easy shot from time to time and tonight was the ultimate trap. A trip of another dimension.

Here it is: I'm walking into a firefight without any ammo, no flak jacket, no warning, only my gal Moll by my side…unfortunately she's playing for the other team. She was the setup… I open the front door and see a distinguished maitre de. The whole staff is on the caper. It's a universal shit-storm, and I'm the only one who isn't clued in, because I'm the perp.

About thirty of Ed and Gruella's side of Somers' family and five of mine had gathered at Campagnola on the UES. This restaurant was all crystal, china, clinks, and a hidden piano….the cocktail calm before the storm. Somers' stepfather and mother wanted to have dinner in Somers' honor without the prying eyes and ears of Somers' real father and stepmother. No one got along in this crowd. No one spoke to each other. It had everything to do with deceit and cheating, but the story's too long for me to get into now.

Somers and I were the last to arrive to Campagnola at 8PM. Somers looked simply ravishing in a slightly too-short for fall skirt and her legs were on loan from God himself. I felt honored staring at them… I was so proud to be by her side, improbably fantasizing about her panties at as illogical a time as can be imagined. I was about to be caught in an undertow whose strength let alone presence you could not imagine.

Before I could even gather my bearings, Ed Kincaid came at me from stage left and demanded to speak privately before we sat down. He and his tag-hag Chanel-clad wife Zozar had been there for a while from what I was told later. I could see Gruella smirking in the corner of my eye, as if she knew what was about to go down. Her serpent eyes were backlit neon-red like a bad Polaroid. You just had the sense Gruella truly came from the gates of hell, a true Draculan pest: "Listen to them. Children of the night. What music they make."

Ed looked like he was about to blow a gasket…his aorta was pulsating in a comically science fiction movie gone bad way. He never said welcome, he would never bother to explain why, natch. That wasn't the point. He had a show to put on, just Upper Case Voice attack,

"You ever disappoint my daughter, EVER, I will fucking bury you, you fucking dirtbag! I know people who take care of people like you!"

Bang!

Hello! Welcome to the family…not! Who the hell are you, you drunk sot? Didn't I meet you a month ago? What's your name again? Oh yeah, Ed Kincaid. Somers ain't your daughter, she's your stepdaughter, and she told me she only puts up with you because you've got more dosh than her old man (I didn't actually say this, but goddamnit, I should have!).

The English and Irish hate each other already…this wouldn't help relations at all. I wanted to get the Queen on the line and take this

IRA bastard out! I needed Scotland Yard. What a rear echelon motherfucker…I hate the rear echelon guys. I needed to let Ed know that Danny Boy was written by an Englishman?

Ed had been drinking vodka like a fire hose draws from the hydrant, getting Irish-angrier by the second. He looked like the Devil's tired uncle. I'm a southern boy, used to southern drinking… you get drunk, happy, horny, tired: precisely in that order. What you never get is angry. I hadn't encountered this tragic version of inebriation…he was a venomous creature from County Cork. Liquor always reveals the real man…

I responded like the country rube I am…

"Huh?"

Intelligent. What a witty, remarkably adept debater I must have been! I'm sure my college debate team suffered greatly without me…

I was losing Somers before I even had her…The vitriol pouring out of his thin-lipped mouth was charged volcanic ash: Sunni-Shiite, Choate-Deerfield, dog-cat, Wachtel-Truth, Israel-the world.

This was indelible shite, meant to place markers on any future calamity, even if the calamity was of his own and Somers' doings {spoiler alert…}. I was supposed to give a toast later on that night… I couldn't even remember my own name now. I'd been expecting tipsy convivial euphoria, not character assassination anesthetization.

I needed Ed's disturbed intoxication like a hole in my empty head. I was already scared shiteless about marriage and hadn't had sex in three months, so I was dancing on the razor's edge of lunacy already. Hey, it wasn't I who controlled Somers' birth control (kinda assumed she knew she what she was doing at age 29…and let me tell you, she did mate!… a great memory until I draw my last breath…). Anyway, his bulldust was a fake…I just didn't know it then.

So, here were the Ambassador and I, standing mano a mano in front of a table for thirty. The third man in the battle, a male cross dresser named Gruella, was itching for sloppy seconds, waiting for me to pass out from Ed's phlegmatic psychopathic ravings.

"I swear you cocksucker, I will spend everything I have to bury you and anything you stand for; I will ruin you beyond anyone's imagination, if you so much as do one thing that causes her any pain…Do you hear me?!"

Bang!

He wasn't whispering like a good Anglican…This was obviously meant for public consumption, which pissed me off even more. I wasn't expecting a public slaughter, a near total fistfight in a nice restaurant with a weaker-than-shite old Irish sot. I think in the future, Episcopalians need to stick with Episcopalians. This intermarrying thing wasn't working out…

It was a certainty now I wouldn't be getting sex from Somers any day soon, not after this assassination. And blowjob duty for her just got extended out another decade, if not for life (thanks a ton there too, Ed). Somers was ecstatic in an emotionless way. I couldn't feel Somers anywhere near me anymore….her heat had jumped the table to the other side. She was all down with the setup, sticking my face in it over and over, shoving it up my nostrils. The night was as happy as a campfire mujahedeen sing-along of God Bless America.

And what the hell did he mean by what I stand for? I didn't even know what I stood for other than trying to climb Mt. McKinley one day…Was he going to dynamite McKinley? Did he have that kind of pull? Things had to get easier from this point forward, right?

Wrong.

This fake Catholic choirboy soon-to-be-US Ambassador vomited more obscenities than a bad night at the Friars. My ears were ringing with embarrassment for Somers, not for me, even though she stood there mute and was in on the act…I should have flipping known!

I was hazy as to why I was even in the room let alone caring what anyone thought of me, especially this inebriated blowhard. The preceding three months felt like one long strange LSD trip. Little did I know, Ed and I would share the same ugly misfortune eventually, a virulent strain of genetic and societal perversion, a black plague of revenge, deceit, and adultery.

I wanted to smash Ed's chinless face in and break his manicured fingers, but I just couldn't bring myself to snap. I needed more loco ammo, something to really push me over the edge. An Episcopalian needs the most awful and debilitating event to occur first. He needs to have nothing left to lose…he needs freedom of the total order…he needs Somers Gillette!

Anyway, Ed that night…he was just part of Somers' long-term play. I just didn't know the acts.

"I heard about your previous marriage you low-life jackass…Why didn't you say something to Somers first (well Ed…we have discussed it, but if you are referring to the pool night… sorry it wasn't on my checklist while she gouged my neck with her incisors and caused permanent kidney damage with her legs…should I have like taken a time out while we were thrashing the water? And while we're at it, may I point out a little family secret that Somers just told me, about infidelity at this very table? Want to hear that story brought up? Should I yell the particulars for everyone to hear and embarrass that wife of yours?! Or will I keep that a secret like I keep everything quiet, because I'm a straight shooter and don't play bulldust mind-games all day long like you?... NO?...Thought so…Fuck you, you hypocrite!…)? Were you too scared to admit the truth Sebastian? Well, here's the truth…I will destroy you in a way that you will not recover from…I've done it before to people who ignored me and I will do it again (he sounded like he had nothing better to do…). You're dead starting now…you can only try to live is my advice (til Friday cause we're getting married that day you know?…)…I'm connected at the highest levels and I will use those connections to bury you, and I will sleep soundly after I do it (I bet you will, you pestiferous dick…)."

Bang!

I was married once, for about 24 hours. Sorry I didn't discuss that ad nauseum…Married at 24, divorced at 24 and a day. I also masturbated a few times; should we discuss that? Oh yeah…my first wife/girlfriend, she tried to hijack the wedding as well, for $50,000 to be exact, saying she'd interfere with the wedding and the reason for it (the baby), unless… I hadn't spoken with her in years, but she surfaced when the timing was fortuitous for a little cash leverage. But, hey, believe her…How did I surround myself with all these she-satans?

I thought Catholics were all full of redemption and forgiveness, no? Was he first going to kill me and then perform a Sacrament of Penance?

The whole restaurant heard as if EFHutton was intoning the next day's market, the people cupped their ears. No one could tell if I had sodomized a dead boy or a live goat, or I was the de facto head of La Cosa Nostra. I wished I'd been any of those, because at least I could then know what the heck I was defending. Ed had confused whom to prosecute, he mixed up his defendants. I needed a lifeline…

Did I really do something wrong? All I'd done is had sex, man. I still don't know how an EPT works.

I couldn't verbalize what was raging in my head, the worst at confrontation… I won't admit any level of pain, no matter how deep. I won't go to a doctor unless the cut is ten stitches and I've lost two quarts…everything is a flesh wound when it doesn't kill. Ed would go to a doctor if he had a cuticle, he'd need a psychologist if his toast burned. Most men I know are like that…just god-awful modern-day metrosexual's, and ironically, full of tipped-over false confidence. Facebook pussies.

I was praying Ed would have a heart attack right there but maybe God had decided to punish him with many more years of Gruella's company, a horrific fate of whose equal mankind has not yet remotely approached. Being trapped in her presence was an anal rape and no lube executed by a five-ton scorpion wielding a twenty-inch barbed penis, the coup de grace dirty sanchez. I could only pray.

"I don't want you marrying Somers. I don't know anything about you, you fucking cocksucker. What's this joke of a career you have (not any worse than yours from what I hear…you stole government farmland and destroyed it…)? Get a real job at a respectable bank, fucker (Shearson doesn't suck…but I agree, I need another job…you hiring?…). You think a Somers Gillette would marry you if you hadn't gotten her pregnant (yes sir, I do actually…her other boyfriends were short and stout, and had small penises and are horrible athletes; that's what she says, I swear!…)?"

Bang!

Yup, she's pregnant restaurant folks, sorry about that. Thanks for letting everyone know Ed. Classy.

And, hey, not like we're picking straws, but can you concede that Somers might know her biological clock slightly better than me…I barely knew her. I never even took sex ed and she keeps saying I'm not great in bed anyway. Maybe society princess isn't such a vision of rectitude after all. I certainly wasn't #1 . Throw your hands up in the air and party like you just don't care…Whooof Whooof!

God, I wish I had said all of that. I just stood there in a groggy and drugged frame of mind. My mindset that night had been, well Somers, why don't we have a few drinks and laugh? That fleeting fantasy was now erased by my gang rape at the hands of Ed, Gruella, and Somers. I thought I'd found something true in her and yet he was already trying to pull her away from me like so many others. Maybe he was trying to help me in his own unintended venal ways?

He kept up his raging mental retard distress for twenty minutes. He was sticking it in my face and making me smell it like the turd it was. Where was the maitre-de? Honestly, the whole restaurant stopped… waiting for my never-coming rebuttal.

I despise rear echelon hypocrites like Ed... Many years before, he'd suffered a greater ignominious fate than I, though it never occurred to me that I should let the restaurant know about his current wife's wondering garden. I was trying to stop the conversation in my head to see why he was doing this, but I couldn't even hear myself think let alone plot revenge.

"Sit down you fucking retard. I'm paying tonight, like I pay all the time. And this family respects me because I pay them (you buy their loyalty?…)? And you will respect me too. So help me God, I promise, the last day you live will be the day you disappoint her, or disrespect me. If you want to say no, fucking say it now, and we will cancel this wedding (I'm almost down with that, except for the small matter of my never disappointing that unborn child of mine; I won't allow jerk-offs like you to be involved, so no, we're on, thanks anyway, go toss off and die…by the way, you're not Somers' Dad…)."

Bang!

Ed's oral exhaustion and drunken senility eventually shut him up…definitely an armchair general. The guy's breath stunk….his spit had hit my lips about thirty times. I hoped he wasn't HIV. My head felt like the initial stages of a metal thrasher concert, guitars slashing the air in a cacophonous orgy of unrestrained violence.

He wanted me to respect him... Respect me! I'd revisit that line and understand why it was so important to him later on. Ed had been emotionally iced by that matronly masochistic mess of a mother-in-law evil sitting to his right. Her own philandering ways would eventually mutate to her daughter.

I felt like I was on the edge of the universe, unsteady, trying to grasp hands with a young woman who was still dreaming of her other flirtations. She was supposed to pull me back from that ledge?

She'd release me when I needed her most. This was no time for a boy to not be a man. I'd stay.

The rest of night was as tense as a cat staring at the mouse through the peephole and vice versa. No one moved. No one talked. No one smiled. No one ate. We all ran for the door when the check was paid. The damage was done. Gruella glared…she must have been the first person born in her family without a tail.

Cue guitars: it's a hard tail…no need for a sissy bar here. Let the Low E fucking roll and rip…Lead and rhythm guitar humbucker max amp chaos cutting and slashing the night. Let the drummer pound his toms and snares mercilessly, double kick the bass, and psycho-slam the crash cymbals. Wail the lead vocal, a primal scream of unmatched pain, veins bursting through skin agony. This was all too real.

The angry mosh pit of high society: I wish I'd never met you.

The Rectory and John 14:2-3

I didn't know what was right anymore, there was too much anxiety floating around inside my head. Somers could be so great one minute and so wretched the next. I didn't know what she was expecting of me and you just never knew what you'd get from her. Judgment Day was approaching and already I had no musical notes left.

I got frightfully drunk after the rehearsal dinner, otherwise known to me as The Last Supper, going out afterward with some of my friends like raging twenty-one year olds. Smooth and wise…not. I was still rattled by Ed's dinner the night before. There wasn't enough Jesus juice in all of Manhattan that night to erase his odor from my clothes, so I got knocking over tables drunk.

The original American milf, a 44-year old married mother of two visiting New York from Akron Ohio, was sitting on my lap at the Monkey Bar on East 54th at midnight. Why we were at the Monkey Bar was beyond me…why mrs. milf was there was further beyond me…why she was on my lap…forget about it….too long of a story and squeamishly embarrassing. Possibly not even Christian.

The mrs. milf thing was working out great (in an innocent way) until Ed and Gruella Kincaid walked into the Monkey Bar. Were these guys shadowing me? They saw mrs. milf Ohio 1992 straddling my thighs… I'd found a new low, unbelievably. They glowered from the door, blew smoke, wheeled, and left, the door slamming behind them. That was a major buzzkill to say the least. See ya, mrs. milf, gotta be running!

Every step I took was becoming a massive unresolvable mistake. The guys and I went looking for a new bar, considering the potential of Ed returning with a gun and my not being able to resurrect myself like other, more moral Christians.

We ended up pounding drinks with California Governor Wilson's staff at the Plaza Hotel's Oak Bar until 4 AM…the Guv was there for the wedding and not missing an opportunity, to raise money as well. We talked about Ed and what a dick he was for three hours. Even those guys hated him. I hadn't gotten over the verbal beatdown from the night before…no amount of liquor would help ease the sting. It probably wasn't such a great idea, not the ranking of Ed, because that part was fun, but the excessive drinking.

The last memory I have of the evening was catatonically pushing a Heineken away from me, toward some other indistinguishable human opposite the table, staring as the bottle tipped over. Someone must have slipped me something because the bottle took five minutes to hit the table, not a likely physical time possibility. It was the video moment when the cameraman slows the action down and the voices become disemboweled. Someone had laced my beer with downers.

I took a beer taxi home, sleeping in my rehearsal dinner suit on my living room floor, alone. When I woke up at noon the next day (the BIG day), I needed oxygen and brain glue, so I walked over to Central Park to beach myself in the sun. I wanted alone time to detox. My tux was still on. It's probably not the brightest science test to be alone on your wedding day, hungover, in a tuxedo, in the warm fall sun, lying out, because…

I woke up three hours later at 4 PM and had a 6 PM wedding… I hadn't eaten, showered, shaved, or brushed my teeth. I'm not even sure I had the right morning coat. My head was aching like a champ. I had two hours to prepare for the biggest day of my life and I was sure to forget something if not everything.

I ran back to our empty apartment (Somers had left two days before to go to The Colony Club, a women's-only redoubt on 63rd and Park, so we wouldn't see each other the night before the wedding…fat chance of that as I couldn't see anything at 4 AM). My head was in a near-unresponsive state. Every second I wasted put me that much closer to missing my own wedding…

I took a cab to the church in my morning coat. My neck was bleeding from shaving and I was sweating profusely. I threw the cabdriver a twenty, jumped out and ran into the church. Someone on the street snapped a picture of me...FBI? I not only don't have Kodak courage, I have Kodak allergies.

Guests had already started to arrive and tourists on the street were milling, like when fans hear a rock star is staying at a hotel but don't quite know which rock star, still they congregate. Japanese camera maniacs were snapping away.

I saw my tuxedoed brothers and they could just tell I looked like shite. They said so. They also had the look of hopeless despair, a look I'd seen before mostly as they were about to tell me that I had screwed up again. They were disappointed,

"Where were you for lunch Seb? Brilliant. People have been calling your home all day!"

Unlike Somers, I didn't have what they called a cell phone by then, so if you wanted to reach me, my home answering machine was as good as it got…forget the work phone, I never answered that and nor did Erica. When I rushed home after passing out in the Park, I forgot to check my messages, so I had no idea anyone had been trying to reach me, not that it would have mattered by then anyway.

They wanted to know why I hadn't come to Ed's wedding day lunch at The Links (a men's only club), and I went blank.

What lunch? I couldn't recall an invitation...

Ed had invited all the wedding party for profit men to lunch at the Links but he never told me...Or at least I didn't think he had. It was like Jesus not making The Last Supper. Can you imagine Michelangelo needing to Photoshop the Sistine Chapel fresco with Jesus' face? My head was somewhere on Pluto.

Today was going to be the day when they would frame me, you could sense it.

Rev. Warren saw my look and asked if I needed privacy. I really did. I was dry-heaving and mildly logy. He showed me into his rectory office, somewhere near the apse of the church, but secluded enough so no one could hear or see me. I was shaking and coughing.

He wanted to ask a few questions. He looked into my eyes and didn't like what he saw. God was weighing in on Judgment Day...it was that important. I'd either be first or last, there'd be no silver given out today. He came at me in his toff accent,

"You don't look so well Sebastian. Every groom goes through this. I must say, Somers is a unique woman. I haven't had the pleasure of meeting anyone like her in my forty years of ministering. She is, how do I say this politely, not very warm and fuzzy like most brides; she seems almost urgent, compulsive, as if she has got to get things done yesterday. And that's quite OK. I'm sure you know what you are doing. You.do.know.what.you.are.doing?"

Rev. Warren asked me the last question, pausing deliberately between his words, with the air of a judge saying to a convicted felon, are you truly aware of your plea, because you can't take it back after you agree? Or more accurately, it was as if a man of the cloth was asking me if I knew I was lying down with the devil.

My head really began to spin, like my brain had turned into a fluid eddy of incurable vertigo. I couldn't answer the man. I grabbed a vase, likely Ming Dynasty, and threw up directly into the bottom of the well. Rev. Warren came around to me with a cold cloth and pressed it against my forehead. It felt good, like the first holy water that had touched me in the preceding three months. I think steam rose off me...the demons were being excised, milf demons at least.

"Don't worry about that. We'll clean it up. Are you finished?"

I didn't know if I was, but I wanted to crawl in after the vomit and disappear. I nodded.

"Son, if there's one thing I have learned in my life as a minister, it's that when a person is in a rush, which is when they make their biggest mistake. You need to be certain in this House what you are doing. God doesn't punish a man for making the right decision when it's not popular; God only punishes the wrong decision even if it's popular (I got a bad feeling where this conversation was headed…). You strike me as being a bit player in something else larger going on around you, and yet you are the most impacted of all. I am deeply worried for you. You need to think things over; you have twenty minutes until this show must go on. If you do go out there in God's House, in front of your family and friends, and you do say 'yes' to Somers Gillette, there's no turning back from those words, not in God's eyes, only the State's. And we do not care what the State says; we only care what the Lord says. The State, however, does not forgive; only God forgives. And the State has the power to enslave you and shall. Somers is a statist, I see that. I smell it in her. I see it in her eyes. Those are not the eyes of a person of this Church (I know what you're saying dude...you ever seen that color: steely grey, like a battleship?...). You must be very careful Sebastian."

Ralph Waldo Emerson must have had Somers Gillette in mind when he said that a man's wife has more power over him than the state…

"Thank you Rev. Warren. I'm not so sure what you're saying, but I appreciate it. I think I may have eaten something bad last night, that's all. I'll be fine. Definitely on for this wedding."

"Sebastian, I met Somers before the two of you came to see me. I don't suspect that she told you that. She came to me with a proposition. I'd never met her before, but I knew of her. She told me that she would donate a substantial sum of money to this church if we would block a certain parishioner's wedding (hmmm…). She did not want this young man to be married. We of course refused and instead invited her to meet with the senior clergy to understand her bitterness and hatred. I would never betray confidences of the clergy, but what I can say is this. Of my staff at the time, half quit after meeting with Somers Gillette, because she had done some investigative work on them, and she let them know that she was prepared to ruin their lives as clergymen if they did not stop that wedding (major trickster!!…). You see Sebastian, Somers Gillette is a moral fraud masquerading as a human. You must understand why someone wants so much and yet gives so little. She will destroy those she says she loves the most. And yet she demands to be married in the church she hates. She will not destroy the church though. I'm powerless to change your world; I can't stop the hurt if you go through with this. God help you."

The Rev. began to walk back out through the door, to leave me alone again with my hangover, my nerves, my vomit, and my dry-heaving, but before he left, he turned to say one last thing,

"Sebastian…I know why you and Somers are here. You see, I've been in this business for forty years. I've seen it all, a hundred times over my friend. I know a pregnancy a mile away (uh oh…good thing we aren't Catholic I suppose…). Yes, I know about you and Somers; I did when she demanded a wedding in four weeks; that part wasn't too hard. What I've never seen is a woman like Somers. I cannot guess how this will end for you…I hope well, but I fear tragically. Just remember this young man: in your darkest days, the Lord is your Sheppard, and He will be there for you. The Lord is not Somers' Sheppard…her Sheppard is not someone I wish to know (I think it's Gruella…). Incidentally, that young man whose wedding Somers wished to deny…? That young man was my nephew, Richard Warren (holy fucking shite, no offense God…). Somers dated him for a long time, but we had never met. Richard told me that she was unstable and it would never last. He knew he would never marry her even after seven years of dating. It helps to have a Minister in the family as you can see. You've had no father for some time. Please consider your decision wisely; time is of the essence (uhhh, I have less than twelve minutes now…and you're telling me now that time is of the essence?!...). I'll see you at the altar no matter what, and I will guide you."

I was frozen. This guy was intoning the end-of-days King James Deuteronomy speech, Somers was a psycho, and I'm about to marry her. Even my blood was sweating. I was here to stay for the child.

"Sebastian, may I read a small verse from the Bible to you?"

"Uhhh, yeah, sure."

"John 14:2–3, "In my Father's house are many mansions: if it were not so, I would have told you. I go to prepare a place for you. And if I go and prepare a place for you, I will come again, and receive you unto myself; that where I am, there ye may be also."

"Uhhh, okay. I understand, I think."

"No, Sebastian, you don't understand…that's precisely the point. A prophet asked that I read that to you. I've done my job. You will need those words many years from now, just don't forget them. Here, here's a slip of paper. I took the liberty of printing the passage for you. Don't lose it, because years from now, an angel called Dymphna will ask you to explain what they mean. And you better know by then, because Armageddon will be close."

I slipped John 14:2-3 in my pocket. There was still time to change the road I was headed down, but the atmosphere isn't kind to grooms who blow out of weddings with ten minutes to go, especially hungover ones.

Beaver Creek had just gotten their first dump of the year…

Epidurals and Last Names

"I was married by a Priest, I should have asked for a jury", compliments of Groucho Marx and about as relevant to me as you could get.

I said yes, I offered my heart on a silver platter and she stabbed it with her samurai sword. It was an easy yes, kind of, in my mental infanticide. A child was on the way and I was powerless to the power of that grace. Somers' walls not only remained up, they'd only grow from that day on. I'm not certain I was ever going to die by her side…more by her hands.

Ed and Gruella glared the entire service. It was death, judgment, heaven, and hell wrapped up in one tidy matrimonial package. In other words, love is one long sweet dream, and marriage is the alarm clock or something like that.

You know how they say the most amazing moment of any wedding is when the bride walks down the aisle and the groom finally sees his intended in all her glory, that's when your bride is at her most glorious…. I didn't feel that way. Somers came sprinting down the church aisle like a jihadist terrorist dressed in ninja garb, scepters swinging from both hands. She was sheer marital horror with unquenchable bloodlust. I stood there simply with a pacifist Anglican minister at my side, defenseless against the pernicious assault. Rev. Warren would read me my last rites just after he married me.

There is no fear in love; but perfect love casteth out fear ...
-- 1 John 4:18

By that point in my life, I'd truly confused sexy with beauty…and wedding dresses just aren't sexy, trust me. Somers had so much makeup on she looked like a Japanese geisha, mascary… When they say that women dress for other women, I think that's especially true at weddings. Men prefer to see women naked, not in haute couture…still, I said yes. She was the best part of me, which might tell you all that you need to know about me.

I looked over at Gruella during the proceedings, whose demonic nature couldn't have been more ill at ease within the walls of an Episcopalian church. Her pores hissed with putrid displeasure, her tag-hag pestilence and Chanel suit crying for attention. She was fighting over the souls of humans, but those demons were temporarily kept at bay by the church walls that day. When the Lord's Prayer was read by the congregation, she sat slack-jawed, silently ridiculing the huddle masses and their collective rote idiocy.

There wasn't any question that the overall tenor of the event was jacked up to absurd levels of tension. My own near comatose state seemed to osmotically transpose each guest. My friends sat agape in the aisles, hoping I knew what the heck I was doing…I didn't. All of society had heard by now how unhinged Somers could become at the slightest provocation, beasting at the smallest of worries. I was hoping that the bartenders at the Union Club would be ready for the mad-rush assault on what surely would be an inadequate stash of liquor…they needed semi-trailers at the ready. Like Bogart said, this was no time for wimpy fruity drinks like martini's…only pure scotch would suffice.

I never wanted an extravagant gala. I was there solely for an unborn child not another society fornication. Why we couldn't have simply walked down to Centre Street and had a justice of the peace marry us was beyond me. Not that my opinion counted much for that day, but still…did we really need this? I felt like she was forever leaving pieces of glass on the beach for me to step on, including that day. We were wed, forever, til sickness or death….something like that…bad call.

Her wedding gala was Acquired Situational Narcissism, a stage that develops in late adolescence or adulthood and is brought on by wealth or fame. Generally the person will suffer from unstable relationships and erratic behavior…great {sarcasm…}.

As we rode out of the Union Club that evening, me on the forgotten south side of the car and Somers on the Club entrance north side, through the window I was handed a sealed envelope by a man in white. He looked he had gotten lost from one of those Oriental weddings where the entire wedding party is in all white and yet his face would not have been out of place at Maidstone. I'd never seen him before and he just seemed to appear out of nowhere. I could hear the faint traces of a dark low chord in the distance. Somers was too busy waving to her subjects, so I opened the seal. Inside was our marital certificate, a religious conquest by my now wife. I turned to ask the man how he'd gotten this, but he'd already disappeared.

"Somers, did you just see that guy hand me the marriage certificate?"

"Sebastian, what are you talking about? The certificate won't arrive in the mail for a few months. Say good bye to everyone!"

We went away on our moneymoon, and returned weeks later to a new life. I assumed she didn't want to have buyer's remorse at that early stage.

Somers set a world record for morning sickness after the wedding. Every morning at 6 AM like clockwork, she'd sprint from the bed to her bathroom (the larger one) and heave so violently I was sure she'd miscarry. Her sickness was of such pain, it was beyond troubling. Somers would hug the toilet lying down and the pain was just infernally primeval, as if her body was not meant to carry the grace of child. She'd groan like an animal and her ribs cracked with pain. I'd run in after her,

"You alright? Do you need anything? Can I get some water?"

"Sebastian, get the fuck outta here!!! This is your entire fault, you fucker! Go to work and die!"

You've never met someone quite like Somers Gillette... She has satanic nastiness even in her deepest need. It was so much better for her now though that she had someone to blame every day. She delighted in projected, dramatized anger, a dramarama debutante. No one ever got to see it except for me, if you can call that love. Where was Billy Cunningham when I needed him most?

Six months after the wedding, Somers went into labor. We wouldn't have normal contractions of course. These would need to be the most gut-wrenching contractions globally possible, where you could actually see otherworldly stomach muscles rip a rib cage apart, in and then out, wrenching them violently, twisting their contorted bones around a spine, crackling them like tinder... Baby did not want to come out easily. Somers was in labor for 48-hours, with zero dilation....none. That's hard to pull off and possibly un-human...The doctors decided to perform a C-section.

Her eyes by then were absolute circles of fire.

When the anesthetist came to insert the catheter into Somers' spine, Somers nearly broke the doctor's wrist. She told him that she would not have any needle shoved up her spine and that he could just go fuck himself (her words) if he attempted it one more time. I was on the outside of the room watching, mortally embarrassed that she'd tear into staff like this. She was pure Upper Case Voice,

"Get the FUCK away from me you fucking Gook!! I swear if you touch me again, I will fucking shove that goddamn needle in your DICK!! Fuck off!"

Somers was shape-shifting in front of our eyes…the hottest most impossibly perfect swan heiress you've ever laid eyes on, had become the Exorcist leprosy girl, hair wildly askew, eyes backlit fire, hospital gown covered in mucus, blood, and bile, and mouth and jaw twisted into some evil version of human, shouting obscenities like you might hear at a Salem stoning. And still we had miles to go…

I felt for the doctor. He rushed out to speak with me, looking shell-shocked from the jungles of a surprise war. And doctors don't shock easy mind you,

"Mr. Graham, I'm not sure your wife understands; she will be in excruciating pain with no epidural for a C (yeah Mate…I don't think she will be the one in pain…it will be you after she kicks you…). You must convince her. This is urgent. This is my job. She is preventing me from doing my job. And she's calling me names which are vile which I also object to."

I felt like goat rope…what could I do, he was the pro…

"I get it. I ain't going in there though bro. She's going to kill someone and I think she blames me for the pain…OH, okay, I guess I have to…Let me have a whack at this…"

I walked in to the room where Somers lay, contracting and moaning like a dying animal. Her eyes were not the eyes of a human…she was crazed, paranormal, a monster lying on its side.

I tried talking to her gently, which is fairly stupid advice when you speak with Somers about anything let alone at the moment of the Rapture. Somers likes it hard and direct. And at shape-shifting times, she wants it even harder and more direct than ever.

Not what I chose of course…I always seem to make matters worse. It was as if they had sent a child (me) to negotiate with the rabid Kong (Somers),

"Look…how are you feeling? You OK? You look great (uhhh, for a monster…). The doctors really need to get this epidural going (and are scared shitless of you…). You're gonna pass out from pain if you try to have your stomach opened with no anesthesia (though I'm betting you could handle it…). Time is wasting (48 hours have never flown by so quickly…). C'mon. You can't do this to the baby (which I wish you might consider from time to time…)."

"Sebastian, so help me god, if that fucking gook (she often resorted to facile, racial epithets when worked up…) does anything to hurt this baby, I swear I'll kill him. Just stick it in (she always says that…)."

Somers was drop-dead serious. I believed her. He believed her. If this poor doctor somehow butchered the epidural, she would hunt him down, kill him, and happily serve the rest of her days in prison (you cannot imagine this woman unless you really know her). In the moment of birth, she was plotting another human's murder. The nurses stared agape…they had never seen such mentally ill torpidity.

Nuclear war hanging over everyone's head. It was the most pins and needle moment in the history of maternity hospitals…The doctor's hands were shaking as he searched for the right entry point. When he got the needle in, Somers passed out like a gorilla from a tranquilizer dart…Poof.

The animal was sedated. Why was she so nice to Dr. Schwartz but so vicious to other staff? Champagne corks popped with her temporarily sidelined. Everyone got down to delivering a baby with the ape knocked out.

This was all trumpets, angels, and heavens time. The baby was a mini-me. You could simply have stuck my face on a copier and plastered the page onto the baby's head. His eyes were open for the first 24-hours of his life…he probably was just so elated to get out, telling us how difficult life had been inside, he was so sweet. Somers slept it off for twelve hours.

It was simply wonderful now to have a third party in the marriage…especially while she was passed out. I loved that kid for life the second I saw him, I swore I'd be the best father ever. It was a beautiful day…I wondered if I could relax and revel in this child's greatness for a while…not.

My tag-hag Poltergeist in-law's arrived…"They're heeeeeeeeeere…"

Gruella and Ed showed up six hours after the birth, dark clouds, black flies, and plumes of dust in their wake, Ed in his Ascot Chang best, Gruella crop dusting the halls in macabre Givenchy.

Managing their arrival and the Gillette's departure was like being the White House Social Secretary when the Israeli's and Iranians are in town. God forbid that Gruella Kincaid actually ran into Nick Gillette…war would have broken out on the 8th Floor of NYU Hospital. Somers had been more worried about that possibility than the actual birth of our baby, but since the gorilla was sleeping away the narcotics, it was left to me to deal with the Kincaid's.

The Kincaid's had not taken a shine to me yet, forever and clearly. They barely said a word upon entering the maternity area….more like Madison Avenue grizzlies grunting. They looked miserable, like they had been forced to eat rancid sardines. Not the feeling that most grandparents have when they see a new grandson…

Gruella acted as if the hospital owed her, for reasons unknown to me or anyone else in the free world. She clod-hopped through the hallway, pretending to be Chief OB, with her square ass banging the walls and her mannish square-toe shoes stomping indents of darkness in her wake. She was by far the nastiest billionaire in the universe, worse even than Somers, not an ounce of goodness in one cell of her arctic/hellish body.

I think Gruella had made her mind up that her son-in-law (me…) had two primary faults: what I did and what I said. That covered pretty much all of me, leaving zero hope. And she loves those large parties for profit where she gets to shoulder surf all night…whereas I….

Here's what went down. Simply, without any setup, I called Dr. Schwartz Dr. Kaplan.

In a vacuum of the full set of facts, I guess your average Anti-Defamation League donor might possibly label that faux-pas a very tepid anti-Semitic moment, or charitably just one small semantic fuckup. The facts however were,

- I'd been awake for forty-eight hours
- I was apologizing to staff for Somers' language
- I was scrambling for the only private NYU Hospital room for Somers just as the Kincaid's came in
- the Kincaid's and their omnipresent doom were destabilizing me each second
- Gruella was gnashing her fangs in my face
- I'd only met Dr. Schwartz once before, nine months ago…we weren't exactly poker buddies.

I could barely remember my own name let alone his. And I'm mildly logy to start with…You could hardly call me an anti-Semite. When I screwed up the Jewish surname, Gruella fixed me with a stare I hadn't caught before. It was a Mastema glower, a Bheliar hiss, a Gehenna flame through the nose…she wanted to kill but only if she could do it inhumanely. She lasered in on the fuckup like she'd discovered the central evidence to the crime, mentally masturbating my death. The fact that her daughter had just had a baby and was recovering in post-op wouldn't register once in her diseased head.

All she could think of was the fuckup. Not as if I wasn't thinking about it even more, since Schwartz stood there next to me, a little embarrassed, a tad uneasy. Why did Gruella come to the hospital other than to make me uncomfortable, unless that is precisely why Somers wanted her to be there. Gruella hates babies, hates them, and has zero time for grandchildren. She'd prefer stabbing her hand with a pencil than spending a second in any maternity hospital. She wants to overpay gay fashion designers to listen to her bitch rather than anything else.

I needed God to come in all of His Glory, to end this now...take the Witch and dump her dude...

Gruella is bested by only one other vicious slug of a human in history who despised children worse than she. Countess Erzebet Bathory of Hungary was a noblewoman who lived from 1560 to 1614. She liked to bathe in the blood of young girls to maintain her own youthful appearance. She acquired a taste for young blood after she brutally beat a young servant whose blood ended up on Erzebet's face. Ultimately, she and her friends kidnapped, killed, and drained over 600 young girls. Gruella would be so lucky...

Gruella forcefully grabbed my wrist and lurched me away. I guessed she wasn't going to tell me how wonderful it was to have another grandchild...

"That was brilliant Sebastian. Kaplan!! Can you even fucking believe it?! Jesus Fucking Christ (I didn't know 'Fucking' was Jesus' middle name!...). Do you know that he probably thinks Somers hates Jews now (you think he's gonna make a sweeping generalization like that, about my sleeping wife, when all I did was screw up his last name?...)? Do you know that Dr. Schwartz is one of the pre-eminent doctors in all of New York, and he will likely besmirch you after this kind of thing (ugh...besmirch...)? He could be very important for Somers. Real fucking stupid!! I hope you don't get any worse than this, or the marriage will be over quicker than we gave it hope for (aren't you pulling for us? was my name floating on a Vegas sports-book somewhere? ...). So fucking stupid. Right Ed?"

Ed had silently slithered up behind her. These two had evil telepathy. Where were the Saints and the Prophets? I was fast losing this battle. I guessed this one wasn't going to slide easily...no encouragement from the in-laws to shake it off! *C'est en faisant des erreurs que vous progresserez. Pas!*

By the way, I hate that word besmirch. Add that one as well to the list of forbidden daily words: come, moist, sperm, and besmirch. Naturally Gruella would say it…she probably says all three in the same sentence every day.

What did I do anyway…I misnamed Dr. Schwartz? Sue me. I didn't realize that forgetting a doctor's last name was the end of the century screw-up. It was more than that obviously. Schwartz…Kaplan. Glad I didn't say something incredibly offensive, like Mohammed.

Everything in my head was spinning fast. She was sticking it in my face, making me smell it real good. I was transfixed by this Draculan invader, and in turn she was interested in my soul. She had tasted me and was chewing on a shank with feverish abandon. I couldn't stand the woman, whatever fucking religion she was. Where was the Pope? In Rome? I needed his number.

What I couldn't know then was that I had cut way too close to a bone of hers. Somers doesn't forget cash, but Gruella doesn't forget slights, perceived or real, especially religion. And she wouldn't forget this.

I was, how you say this nicely...royally fucked…from then on. Gruella would be on an eternal lookout for the perfect Judas and she likely knew that even Jesus forgave Judas by calling him "friend" at the very moment Judas betrayed Jesus. It was a little late though for me to learn about her underlying Furies, or even my forgiveness.

Board Dreams

Norma Desmond was primed, 'All right Mr. DeMille, I'm ready for my close-up.' Somers was off and running and I tried to keep up. She wanted to get out of her buffet pants and back in the catsuit. And she wanted to get artificially busy.

'...Everything has chains, Absolutely nothing's changed, Take my hand, not my picture,'...*{All song quotes in next six chapters are from multiple Pearl Jam songs and noted by a *}

I could hear this phase of my life before it began. It was new, straightforward, high energy, and raw. Stripped down basics, distorted guitar, zero synthesizer, and no glam, a Seattle-based guitar revolution with names like Sonic Youth, Pixies, Pearl Jam, Mudhoney, Salamander Jim, Soundgarden, Nirvana. The lyrics were focused on existential angst and apathy, and the meaning behind the tunes was real, an authentic fountain of facts and truth, culturally relevant to today, something sorely missing from the streets of Manhattan.

'...The lights of this city, They only look good when I'm speeding'...*

Things seemed okay between Somers and me for the first few years, with some notable exceptions, almost all of which had to do with museums and my underwriting them....The Museum of the City of New York, The American Museum of Natural History, the Metropolitan Museum of Art, and MOMA. She had me spend more time at monstrous cocktail party for profit fundraisers at these places than working out at a gym. I couldn't figure out what her fascination was...the Executive Directors of these non-profits made more money than fund managers and their multi-million dollar apartments were rent-free among a billion other questionable accounting tricks. Why did we have to raise money for them again? Why were they so exalted? And why did I have to spend my nighttime with all those aviation blondes (errr, black boxes…)? It was dreadful.

The lack of sex between us was somewhat worrying, we were down to ABC sex quickly…anniversary, birthday, and Christmas. It was hard to rail on that when babies were being made, born, and cared for. I was in my own dream state with the kids, my little Joseph of Arimathea and Nicodemus. I knew how to swaddle the babies and even she'd have to admit this, they preferred that I change their nappies. To say I loved them would be the greatest understatement in the history of the world. The vacuum in my heart filled and overflowed with the grace of two boys. Somers had a strange detachment to all things baby…it wasn't post-partum depression so much as a pre-occupation with schemes and ambitions that lay squarely outside the circle of family. She just could never slow down, it was all artificial business.

Somers hired teams of nannies to help with the overnight duties. Somers fired nannies as quickly as she hired them, just when the nanny got to know the kids well… Something about nannies never sat well with her, like she was jealous of their innate love and decency. That would become very clear to me later in our lives…

Where Somers and I drifted apart lay generally with her social parties for profit. Outside of work, I wanted little more than my kids, whereas she'd kill herself for any recognition, so the social calendar was a purposeful frenzy of activity…no kidding, five nights a week, all party promise types and such, the kind of people who say one thing but never really follow up. I'd never seen the society side of Somers Gillette, because we got married after our second date practically. So, to say I was blindsided later on might either be an understatement, self-serving, or just true. That would depend on how well you know us.

Yet, she evidenced even stranger behavior than simply the parties for profit. Her anger had other-worldly scale… Joan Crawford had nothing on Somers, "No wire hangers, ever!!!!!" She was Manhattan's Mommie Dearest, a combustible life force always set to explode. And like Joan Crawford, Somers signed up to the maxim, "Love is a fire. But whether it is going to warm your heart or burn down your house, you can never tell."

Somewhere in 1997, Somers decided that she needed to join a board in New York, but only a reputable charity would suffice for her. She was an ego searcher before Google and she was simply doing spade work for later conquering. She did not do society acoustic, it was all grandly staged.

The thing with Somers and boards is that although she joined them frequently during our marriage, they meant nothing to her emotionally. Nothing. Zero. Nada. She had no emotional connection to any charitable endeavor, other than her own self-interest and promotion. And the most reliable way to determine how much a charity really means to a society person is to ask for the checks they write from their personal cash accounts…unrestricted cash grants…Our checks, even for her boards, always came from me. What she asked of me would make the Catholic Church blush.

All Graham/Gillette donations to the NYSARC over fifteen years were made by the author, Sebastian Graham, with Somers Gillette getting sole credit on annual statements and Gala Dinner Programs. Natch! She shoots, she scores…

For the city board, Somers leaned on Nick Gillette to ask Pendleton Pierrepont to see if she might join the board of a charity that the Pierrepont family had begun in 1887, The New York Society for the Advancement of At Risk Children (NYSARC). The NYSARC endowment wasn't any more than $100 Million, but the money was secondary to the board's social pedigree. Mr. Pierrepont and his family actually care about at-risk kids. There ought to be a law that forces charity board members to spend at least a few hours every month working alongside the people doing the real work. We talked it over one night.

"Somers, I think it's great you're joining the NYSARC. I have some friends down in North Carolina who spend their Thanksgivings with the needy…always seemed right. And it isn't as if they are exactly rolling in money. They do it because they really think it's the right thing to do. I have a few more years of making money before I can get out and do that kind of work."

So it wasn't as if I was as selfless as I wished either, but I knew one day I'd be there doing the work, not simply cutting checks.

"You know honestly Sebastian, I think you're the stupidest fucking man I could have ever married, but then again, that's why I love you. I'm not actually going to volunteer my time there, for god's sake; like I have time for that. We (the spousal 'we'…) are just writing checks and organizing gala dinners. They have the best Christmas dinner of any board in the city at "21". And the guys on the board are really handsome."

I never thought that anyone considered how handsome the men were on the Boards they aspired to, but then again, I was a man and I definitely wouldn't sleep with a guy.

"Well, I guess that's great. And how much will "we" be writing to this handsome board?"

"Depends on how much you make, but I'd say $10,000 a year for a table would be great. Your company can do it."

I, or my company, was stuck with the bill six years running, the beginning of her attempts to reverse Midas me.

The NYSARC might be the most Anglo, most Saxon, and most handsome charitable board in all of New York, and it's been that way for over 100 years, so no one's catching up any day soon. Affiliating yourself is a great way to keep your wasp social lights on, even if, like many, you are trading on the Pierrepont's name. And she was...not that I knew it at the time. I couldn't believe that Mr. Gillette would make that call, but he did. Somers wanted it that badly, and the reality is even Pontius Pilate had a caring dad.

The only at-risk people she helped when I knew her were society social climbers falling a notch.

But, she got on the board and she did two things...she started in on the flirtationships that would be her calling card, and she made certain everyone knew about her board postings. Mostly in a discreet fashion so as not to seem to boastful or transparent, but without hesitation and not an ounce of self-promoting embarrassment. A calculated, discreet resume fluffer, an email promoter. She was transforming herself in front of my very eyes. I couldn't believe what she'd become. She had a healthy dose of narcissism for sure, perhaps a bit too much. Her shamelessness on bald-faced self-dealing was striking to a guy like me, but again, that ass...Maybe those big-hair glam rockers weren't as bad as I thought, all they did was make video's with smokers like Somers.

Her shift wasn't so much gradual as sudden, so there was no time to reflect. And we had never really dated to start anyway. Still, I was happy in the haze of my children, somewhat oblivious to her machinations and schemes.

'...To this day she's glided on, Always home but so far away, Like a word misplaced, Nothing said, what a waste,'... *

A friend's wife opened her new townhouse on East 80th one afternoon to her frenemies, including Somers. Manhattan apartments are great, but townhouses are 'eff'-you envy statements. The thing was, Somers Gillette did envy and she did revenge but she did not do petty...she went yard.

When she came home that night at about 10 PM (where had she gone after the afternoon party for profit?), she wasn't happy, she was pissed. I'm never jealous of anyone else's success and Somers is the opposite of that. If she succeeds, you better not succeed more. And if you fail, she wins. She looked crazy good though...in a short black mini-skirt and tight tee, accentuating those legs and shoulders again. Trying to separate the evil from the body was impossible for me...I was always dumbfounded.

"I need to go up to Newport tonight Sebastian. Something came up at St. George's. I'll be back the day after tomorrow."

And then she left, at 10 PM, in a mini-skirt. On a Wednesday night, leaving two babies, a nanny, and a faithful husband behind. The conversation was that short, I swear. She returned two days later, no calls, no checking in, as if nothing was askew. She was wearing a new outfit. She was rested and re-energized.

"Where were you Somers? Don't you think you owe it to me to let me know where you are going? I thought you might come home.... I mean, love has rules."

"There are no rules in love, Sebastian. Grow the fuck up."

I wasn't sure how to react to that. She was sexual carpe diem with a wedding ring.

'...I know I was born and I know that I'll die, The in-between is mine'... *

I was angry but incapable of expressing it. She was bringing out a side of me I didn't even know existed. I had to let it slide, more out of necessity than willful disregard. We had children and she'd always raise tense subjects right in front of them. She'd been pretty busy lately with all her stuff, so maybe her common decency was taking a temporary backseat…

Somers' talk of a bigger apartment became a nightly stew of rage. It was eating at her and there wasn't much I could do. Shearson had basically exiled me to the South Pacific clients in that first year of my marriage, so I quit and joined a new firm in Russia. Because this company was new, they didn't offer much in the way of a base salary but you did get stock (if you could just trust the other partners, no small leap of faith in Russia…). Equity meant retirement someday, just not today. I worked out of the New York office, but traveled to Russia often and everywhere. I went to Sakhalin Island in the East, Yakutsk in Siberia, Norilsk in the Arctic, Rostov in the southwest, and Moscow and St. Pete. I did well. The salary and income really picked up.

'...So this life is sacrificed, to a stranger's bottom line, I've seen the light, I'm scared alive'... *

Money can make your troubles seem so far away and yet it constrains you.

The ironic part was that whenever I got a raise or made a decent bonus, Somers' hands were outstretched waiting to snatch it. It was nannies, furniture, lavish events at our apartment catered and tended, vacations, etc… Or it was country clubs. Or whatever, there was no overcoming it, short of the lottery. Okay, no problem though, because I'd found a groove of sorts professionally.

I became a walking ATM. James McGavran said that "There's a way of transferring funds that is quicker than electronic banking. It's called marriage."

I was earning more than two times what I had been making when we married, but liquidity-wise I was no better. Every second with Somers was a step back, and yet the numbers seemed implausible…but, don't worry about money Sebastian, I've got money. I didn't feel like I was dancing on the edge of financial madness though, because it felt like love….the boys made it feel so and unfortunately I confused my love for them with my love for her.

After a unilateral negotiation between Somers and herself, she decided we were moving to the suburbs. She could tell I wasn't making the Forbes 400 any day soon. She really wanted a townhouse in the city, but she was nothing if not realistic. And not just to any suburb, but to Locust Valley (LV) in Long Island, New York. There was never a question where we would go. Locust Valley to Somers was a social Mecca and Holy Grail, a Jay Gatsby utopia, cleansed and purified of all unattractive genetic variants, the shoulder surfing capital of the world. Not much paparazzi in LV, but she could figure that part out later. A great place to get high on gossip.

Somers wasn't moving out to a smaller pond to be a small fish. She had reined over Manhattan during the roaring 80's…that's a big fish in a big pond. Locust Valley would be an easy mark to a woman of

Somers' means. Nothing, husbands included, would get in the way. I wanted to be her tower of strength, I must have looked like a chump. And she would never be a supporting actor….Norma Desmond was on the way with four Moishe's Moving vans trailing her…

*'…Hold me and make it the truth, I turned my back, now there's no turning back,'… ***

The Asparagus Plate Toss

Find yourself a girl and settle down, live a simple life in a quiet town.

Not Somers Gillette, and not where we were headed… Locust Valley on Long Island in New York goes yard and so does she. Locust Valley is really not that much different than any other community in America except you need to multiply whatever you're thinking by ten…income, median house price, shoulder surfing, and number of rounds of golf you play every year. LV is where Jock Whitney, Laddie Sanford, and CZ Guest made their homes of genteel pleasantry. With all due respect to Marilyn Monroe, Locust Valley is a place where they'll pay you a thousand dollars for an air kiss…and fifty cents for your soul. It was civilized and the thing was, I loved my semi-detached life there.

'…So this is what it's like to be an adult,'… *

The area ain't diverse. You won't find a mosque or a synagogue. You will find Episcopal St. John's of Lattingtown where members of Stoney and Creek wage war to become Sunday ushers, seen by some as an exalted position of neighborhood primacy, others as patently false worship of themselves over God. Somers was dispassionate about all matters religion (outside of talking up her atheism)…she only liked choral music at Christmas-time… Other than that, church was the birds to her.

Locust Valley is best defined as a dense vortex of waspy gossip, nighttime cocktail intrigue, and multi-generational inbreeding, unique in its people's wholesale familiarity of clubs, children, schools, and backgrounds. There's some male Brokeback, female box-lock, and know-it-all Dr. Google's, and you don't get away from the tornado once you've moved there… *La débutante fut présentée à la haute société lors de son seizième anniversaire.* Just think debutants and faux-pas.

*'…Little secrets, tremors, turn to quakes, The smallest oceans still get big waves, '… * *

The cocktail circuit may as well have its own cheat-sheet for newbies (who would be so unaccustomed to the fact that everyone knows everything about everybody to start). Stepping out of line will cause eternal ruin, you'll be cut to pieces. At the cocktail party dog parks, you sniff a lot, making sure they're pure bred and fit.

My favorite women in LV were Ariane (Somers' sister, classy, hated gossip, stunningly beautiful); Katie (Somers' sister-in-law, least bulldust person of all time, a great mom); Isobel (serious writer, intellectual but not obnoxious about it, hypnotically blue eyes, married to a great guy); Phoebe (discreet heiress, no bulldust, great husband); and Jenny (totally normal heiress, understood Somers' pathology best, funny as shite golf fanatic husband).

The annual highlight of the year is the gigabucks Christmas party thrown by the Cobbs (Phoebe's dad) at their house on the edge of the 6th fairway at Stoney. Cobb used to be part-owner of the Mets but he sold. If you don't get the nod to attend his party, you're a nobody in this town….and Somers knew it. Celebutante's make sure they aren't overlooked.

This isn't a Christmas party where when you ask someone how they're doing and they honestly reply: not too well mate, my back hurts, my wife doesn't blow me, she spends like she's the Federal Reserve, we were outside getting high, etc...The Cobbs' Christmas party is the opposite of that…everything is great, every day is swell, you look fabulous. The night belongs to shoulder surfing and rubbernecking. By the time you leave, you can't wait to get out of there…you need a drink!

*'…All the rusted signs we ignored throughout our lives, Choosing the shiny ones instead,'… **

The central nexus of Locust Valley, physically as well as temperamentally, is the Stoney Rock Club, the most attractive club in the United States and likely the most desirous, whose trademark is a Charles Blair Macdonald 18-hole masterpiece. Stoney has a thousand members, a third of whom live in New York City, a third of whom live in LV, and a third of whom live in Hobe Sound... It's not tough to guess which club we joined (let me be clear about this issue: Stoney is the club that Somers joined in her name, though I paid her initiation fee and for that matter, all club bills for fifteen years).

"Sebastian, we are going to put my name forward, because frankly you don't know anyone out here, and I do. And you know, hey, I'm not trying to be morbid, but honestly, if we ever break up, you realize I stay here and you don't? Send them the fucking check…"

The sell was it would be easier to get in since her father knew everyone. In reality, she wanted to be the member because she needed paid markers down the road. She's a freaking genius table queen and I'm a complete moronic urban Amish. But hayzeus if I don't love that golf course…god I miss it.

Somers, in an effort to put a scare into her father and help her own mother avenge her father's affairs, publicly faked an interest in joining Creek (which had the salubrious effect of painting me as the villain, since she wanted my name out front for Creek…though she was always driving the train). I had no clue what was what…I was along for the ride it seemed, but I noted how incredibly aggressive some of the club members were to get Somers and me to join. We'd show at one of the new members' teas, and Somers was the hottest woman in the room by a factor of a billion, the urban cougar now in the burbs.

'...Model role model, roll some models in blood, Get some flesh to stick so they look like us, I stink I'm real join the club, I'd stop and talk but I'm already in love.'... *

My inability to remember anyone's last name drove Somers to distraction. She used to ask me, how come you can't remember anyone's names? The implication being that I didn't belong if I couldn't remember who the players were, so work on it...The reality is I couldn't have cared less who was who. I didn't micro-focus on other people and what they thought. I did care if you could play ping-pong... I miss playing so badly...

'...It's out of my hands making all hands meet, Stumbling as it's crumbling out of reach,'... *

We took a drive to Locust Valley one summer Saturday to look at houses with a local broker, a family friend of the Gillette's (this would be the first of dozens of locals whom Somers knew, and whom I would be forced to hire for their services). We left the kids behind in the city with the weekend nanny (weekday nannies have weekends off, but my wallet didn't apparently). Somers was in a pink paisley summer dress which barely hung onto her skin...the dress was so flimsy, you could have torn it off with a feather and I wanted to....Screw the house, let's screw...not. The box-lock was on. We were pretty incompatible when you think about it. It's all I thought about on the drive out and it never crossed her mind.

The broker, Vicky Bancroft, hadn't even showed us the second floor when Somers dramarama'd up,

"We'll take it Vicky. How soon can you have contracts drawn up?"

I guess we wouldn't be putting on our poker face…I was furious,

"Whoah Somers. Can we speak privately?"

In a sign of Somers' megalomaniac need to act impulsively and strike without considering the consequences (the most emotional of emotional decision makers the world has ever seen), she was ready with the pen signing my check…apparently, she hadn't bought a house before.

The house was in Glen Cove, technically not Locust Valley, but Somers thought everything out there was Locust Valley. Fair enough. The Internet had just taken off…so she had done some quiet legwork. The Internet to her was real estate target practice. But she had worse spending habits than an addict who finds a c-note inside an opium den…gone.

Somers was on a Fanatic Narcissist's path, determined to come home with a trophy damn the torpedos. Fanatic Narcissists fight the reality of their insignificance and lost value, and attempt to re-establish their self-esteem through grandiose fantasies and self-reinforcement. Buying a house without a second's debate would qualify.

I ain't the sharpest tool in the shed, but I know that you never tell your broker that you simply want the first house they show you. You also don't tell your broker that you'll pay full ask, unless money is no problem…Which it was, for me anyway, since I was the one shelling out the dough.   In any event, like Bette Davis, "What a dump."…the house was atrocious.

Somers had gotten clinically impetuous since the marriage. Everything had to be yesterday. For example, and not to beat a dead horse since the horse was dying already, if she was willing to have sex, if anything (say a wayward sneeze) got in the way of having sex, the whole deal was off…for weeks, like that. No arguing. She played by different rules about everything because she had so many rules, and whenever there are too many rules, the people eventually rebel.

Ridiculously, I was still smitten with her, even without the sex, or maybe because I wasn't getting any (maybe my mind had begun to warp from back-up), who knows. Eventually we might recapture the Millbrook pool moment.

'…It echoes nobody hears it goes it goes it goes, We're faithful we all believe we all believe.'… *

So guess what? We had our first huge argument…not discreetly by ourselves though. No, Somers figures it's best to beast in front of others, so she can co-opt them to twist history. She'll bribe them with gifts and parties, and they cooperate. She can be a million different people…but then again, perhaps that's what's real. I am's who I am's.

I asked to speak with Somers alone in the kitchen. Vicky didn't exactly take the hint, as she walked behind us by ten or so paces, always in earshot and eyesight. And Vicky knows everyone in LV.

"Look, it's a nice house Somers, but the fact is, it's Glen Cove, and the property taxes here are insane. Also, the back yard is too small and I think we could practically whisper to the neighbor and he could hear us when he's having a barbecue. Finally, this is the best house on the block; never buy the best house on the block, because you will never get more than what you paid for."

"You just don't want it because I fucking want it!!"

How are you supposed to argue with that logic? I didn't want to buy it because she didn't want to buy it? Huh? I wanted to make her happy and a house is a long-term commitment, not some perishable item. I never said anything to make her question my motive, as in I wouldn't want something simply because she did want it. Unfortunately, if you even thought of disrespecting her convictions, she saw it as blasphemy. Her revenge would only involve overwhelming force and lunacy. She wants to weaken you so she can win, even her co-signer for life.

"Somers, I don't know what you're saying. I just don't want to waste Victoria's time; there's no way I will buy this house, for the reasons I spelled out. Let's just tell Victoria and go see the next one."

"No. I want this house. It's perfect and the boys would love it. Who cares about the back yard Sebastian! What do you know anyway?! What are you, Mr. Warren fucking Buffett anyway?!! Fuck you!!"

Her voice was rising at an almost perfect linear pitch upward. Something had begun to excite her lunacy anodes, and unless I could locate a tranquilizer, this monster was coming out of her cage quick....

I thought to myself, well the kids will care Somers, since they'll live in the backyard practically, because that's what boys do…they play outside. Somers only cared about the inside…we could be living on top of a Crip shooting den so long as the upstairs house looked nice inside. She had Restless Lip Syndrome, I could hear it coming,

"And by the way, my trust is making the down payment! You can pay the mortgage and all the other bills. I want this house! So we're doing it, and that's that!"

'…for every tool they lend us, a loss of independence,'… *

She was definite sounding again. Uh-oh…That always got me down, if not prepared for a new battle.

I don't know what made me snap with that last statement. She just seemed so dismissive of my ability to pay for anything, even though I paid for everything, and she said it in front of others all the time. I would never discuss money in front of anyone…I was timid speaking about money in front of my banker. Somers would debate money in front of the town crier.

Her trust was always there (in her head) to take care of things, as if she had an insurance policy against all of her other hallucinogenic behavior. Don't worry about money, I have money. But she would spend her money only after she'd exhausted yours, and then only if she could then use the trust to sledgehammer you. I must have looked like a lonely clown.

"We're not buying it Somers. That's it. I'm frustrated with you always wanting your way, with no thought or deliberation. No is my answer. No. Do you ever listen to anyone? I mean, this is insane."

Somers stared at me, silently building up a volcano of anger. I could see something rushing to her head. I could sense the eschatological bombing within seconds. Uhh, Saints, Prophets, Pope, Rev. Warren…anyone? I needed backup.

She stared at me with the look of a person avenging the death of a loved one. I had struck something deep down, likely her money bone. My words seemed so unthreatening (in my head anyway). The ticket price of the house was something I had to chime in on. I was spinning wheels financially, she was driving me into the ground, and she wasn't even paying with the occasional pity sex. The social eschatology was mine already without this impending blowup.

She was about to hulk out beast. Somers reached inside a Sub-Zero refrigerator door, hurriedly, grabbed something large, and came out holding an oversized yellow ceramic serving plate wrapped in saran covering dark stemmed vegetables. By the looks of it, the plate was five pounds, with nearly four full sprigs of asparagus piled on, fit for a party for profit. I didn't know she was hungry, but then again, she didn't hold it like she was going to sample the veggies…she looked more like an Olympic shot-putter.

'…once divided nothing left to subtract, some words when spoken can't be taken back.'… *

She turned around and threw it right at my head, the athlete unloading his package. She missed me by no more than an inch, close enough so I could taste the balsamic vinaigrette as the plate frisbeed by…this guy was a good chef. The plate smashed onto the wall behind me, the red wine staining the olive-green wallpaper and making my shirt look like a 70's disco heliography special. The ceramic exploded into a thousand pieces. I wondered how much that would cost me. The asparagus sprigs scattered into every nook of the room, like a thousand flaccid penises. Here was Upper Case Voice in hysterics,

"Fuck you Sebastian!! Just Fuck you!! You go buy a house without my trust!! FUCKER!! LOSER!!"

"Whatcha yelling for? Why did you just throw that guy's plate? Chill!"

If this was going to be our new house, we were christening it with really bad vibes…

Since she missed me with the first toss, I guess she thought she needed a reload. She found a heavy steel whisk in the sink and launched that as well at me, in the direction of the patio doors this time. It slammed into a glass door, sending a crack down the entire length…I was sure it was going to explode into a million glass bits. I was staring at this lunacy like an adult allowing a kindergartener to vent hyperventilating steam.

"Ahhhhhhhhhhhhhhh!!!!"

With the second throw out of her system, a primal scream, and her hands having exhausted all readily identifiable objects, Somers ran out the kitchen door to the garage, slammed the door and broke the jamb in the process. The heiress opened the driver's side of my new Jeep Cherokee, slammed that door, and peeled out of the driveway like you only see in a movie, wheels spitting gravel like a rooster tail. A Glen Cove psycho crisis in the making. She left her pocket book in the kitchen, but she had her cell phone. The last I saw, her face was a mess.

A social lunatic was on the loose. She was certifiably, clinically, mercury-retrograde, bazooka nuts. And she was the mother of my kids. She was uninhibited.

Words to live by…never argue with a spouse who is packing your parachute.

Vicky didn't seem fazed, as if she knew Somers' past much better than I. How come everyone knew her except me?! I just wasn't used to lunacy. Vicky calmly walked into the kitchen and put her arm around me. I didn't know what to say, I felt like my marriage had just dissolved in front of my eyes, not to mention even more of my net worth. This blowup would be the front story of the Locust Valley Leader for sure, if not the Post. Vicky said in a soothing, mellifluous, salesperson voice:

"You know Seb, buying a house can be terribly difficult for any young couple. I understand. Look, don't worry about the wall or the glass. The agency will cover that. She's stressed about everything (Vicky, Somers has the single best life of any human being in the world…I swear…she has no basis to be a nutter…)."

And, do we really need to be excusing Somers for some decidedly amateurish and boorish behavior? I wasn't the one who tossed a plate of asparagus at her head. If that was me, I'm not so certain that she wouldn't have called the Old Brookville Police by now.

"That's nice of you Victoria. But we can pay for it. I'm not sure what got into her. All I said is perhaps we should look at other houses."

I guess technically that wasn't true. I actually said we would not buy this house. Still…it was just a house, there's more to life than a house that wasn't even yet a home…

"It's OK. I have some other great houses to show you guys. There are always more houses."

That I know Vicky, you're a real estate broker (I did not say this).

"Hey look Victoria, I'm going to let her simmer down. Why don't you and I go drive to the other houses and hopefully she'll meet us at one. She left her purse. I wouldn't mind seeing what else is out there."

God knows where Somers had gone to…I wouldn't see Somers again that night. She simply never came home. She had no credit card on her. Likely she was sustaining her bloodlust, planting her freak flag in someone else's bedroom. I wonder who she spent the night with…I'd willingly ignore more facts like this when they stared me in the face, daring me to call them out…

 '…don't need a helmet got a hard hard head, don't need a raincoat I'm already wet, don't need a bandage cause there's too much blood, after a while seems to roll right off,'…*

I had a habit called Somers Gillette and I still had to have it. Like any junkie, you don't have the power to consider the downside, not until you reach rock bottom.

"No Tats, Gats, or Fats"

She was a marital rebel and I was already feeling the first shots of divorce.

'...here's a selfless confession, leading me back to war, can we help that our destinations, are the ones we've been before?'... *

The next morning, Somers returned to our E. 71st Street apartment at 9 AM, opening the door dramatically and pretending as if nothing had happened...but looking very, very guilty, and of course divine, as always, her sleep slut record intact. Even in guilt she could make the front page with those looks. Ink stains on hands guilty by the way...with a new outfit and I hadn't a clue where she could have gotten that overnight.

The kids were on the floor with me. I had stayed up most of the night after getting back to the city, waiting for Somers, faithfully waiting for Somers. The nanny was up early the next day, sensing a traitor in our midst. God, nannies are brilliant...they see and hear it all even when they don't speak English.

Somers had been nowhere to be seen all night. She had so much sex appeal but she was a moral butterfly, easily jumping from one situation to the next. I simply ignored or excused all of her reprehensible behavior and never discussed it with a soul. The nanny was watching...

I asked where she'd been, but her answer was as mysterious, as it was brutal, as it was final. She began to cut me then.

"None of your fucking business! Where's my pocket book?"

"Look Somers, when I met you, the fact is I didn't know what to do, didn't know you. You can't just leave at night by walking out. We have got to work things out like adults, not two teenagers. We have children if you haven't noticed."

The technosexual had kept her cell phone and unless she was somehow stuck on the Death Star, I assumed she could have gotten a connection and let us know she was alright, but she never made base contact.

"I spent the night at my mother's apartment. OK? Fuck!!"

Somers is a real good liar. I swear her split personality would cause any man to crack. This would not be a quick and easy Sunday. Year five of marriage, and happy as two lovers can be…not. Headed to Armageddon and I didn't have a clue.

If you're thinking how could you stay married to a woman who swore that much, I don't have a good answer other than lust…Weak.

After a significant cooling off of Somers' gaga, the Graham family and Ms. Gillette (she never changed her last name…I wasn't hung up on this at all) made the move to Locust Valley, out of Manhattan, and away from whatever it was that caused so much of Somers' angst. To be replaced by a whole new level of angst. Somers had a plan to be queen again, a celebutante in little old Locust Valley. Though queens are never what they seem…

We ended up renting a four-bedroom colonial from William Cobb.

Somers insisted that I pay her the monthly rent nut, so she could in turn then send Mr. Cobb a check in her own name for the same amount. We did this for a year, me writing a check at the end of the month to "Somers Gillette" for $5,500, and then Somers writing a check to Mr. William Cobb for same. I could never figure out why she insisted on being the name on the check, or for that matter the lease. It was as if she wanted to be the man in our marriage to everyone outside our marriage…but inside I was the one paying the bills. What she was up to in hindsight, was gaming appearances.

I was all Bette Davis, imploring, "Oh Somers, don't let's ask for the moon, we have the stars". Nothing doing with that. She wanted it all and then some. Her attitude only got more vicious…I don't know what happened other than I never really knew her to start. The change was always immediate.

We moved in May of 1997. Less than two weeks after moving, Somers Gillette hosted her first large party for Two Hundred and Fifty of our closest friends…250! I kid you not. I didn't know a soul out there yet, a total stranger in my own house. I was the pink poodle at the Quest dog park, the navy blazer army came and sniffed to be sure I wasn't a threat. A Memorial Day blowout, enough food to feed ten countries….we even had my favorite, guacamole, but every time I went for some, I got guac-blocked by one of the drunk guests I didn't know. I'm probably being harsh, but it seemed all Omega Mu and sausage jockeys to my eyes. Somers was a table queen, taking pinpoint precision with who sat where, especially her.

Somers didn't want any music because that would interfere with the talking apparently, so she told me to go get money from a local ATM so I could tip the staff. Before I got back, Somers had gone off to an after party reception at the club because she was having her own Post-Party Depression. A bartender, a nice black man who worked at one of the other clubs, saw a look of confusion on my face, so he handed me a beer and said,

"Hey, Mr. Graham (I hated them calling me by my last name…), thanks for the job tonight. We really like working for you. "

"No problem Paul. Hope your guys are happy with the tip. I'm not really sure how much I'm supposed to pay them."

"Hey any amount is fine. Ms. Gillette (even he knew she hadn't changed her name…) already gave us a tip as well (she took the money out of my safe, because I always kept $5,000 cash…but never told me she tipped anyone…). I hope you don't mind, but you didn't seem like you were enjoying yourself too much tonight. You don't have to worry about these people, they find their own good time."

"I know. I wasn't worried so much. I just don't like large parties."

"Well, it will be interesting to see if you like it. There's 'no tats, gats, or fats' out here. It's all good, all pure, all clean. Know what I mean?"

I laughed. I loved that line. No tats, gats, or fats. LV.

Of course I could have said no to everything, though I'm not sure how far that would have taken me. I could have killed the party, but I think she would have killed me first. So go ahead and lay me out that I didn't have the balls to stop this growing cancer when I had my shot. Guilty. I caved, and again, in my pea-brain head but ocean sized heart, I thought a happy wife meant happy children.

'...fuck me if I say something you don't wanna hear, Fuck me if you hear only what you wanna hear, Fuck me if I care but I'm not leaving here,'... *

Why Somers felt this constant need to be affirmed by the Locust Valley A-list crowd was so beyond me and others. She made decisions based solely on what others would think of her, or how they would react to her decisions. How she was perceived was paramount, never about whether the decision was right. Somers to me was already the Queen of anything she wanted to be…I was in love beyond any justification.

We bought a house in 1998.

There were six people at the attorney's offices for this, or about four more than necessary. An assistant to the lawyer for the seller arrived in a red jacket, which made him stand out like a hijab at a Creek new member's party for profit. He handed me a sealed manila folder, and inside was the contract for a secondary item listed in the sale. Houses are nothing but conflict and war when a marriage isn't strong, and ours would prove no different in the end. That strange low bass chord, a haunting progression of scale and arpeggios, was playing somewhere in that office, but I had no idea where. I signed the document and handed it back to the assistant but he'd already stepped away. I handed it to the primary lawyer, but he had no idea what I had just signed.

"Your colleague gave it to me to sign."

"Mr. Graham, I came here alone. I don't have a colleague."

I didn't want to look any more delusional than I am, so I dropped the subject and tucked the document back into my pocket, sealing it up again. We were now house owners in Manhattan's Promised Land, Locust Valley, the Gold Coast.

The parties for profit were crazy quilts of angst, fury, and speed, the party for profit promisers at full tilt. She was all Elitist Narcissism now, glibness, superficial charms, pathological lying, cunning, and lack of remorse.   And I had ten more years of that left… Jealous?

"My wallpaper and I are fighting a duel to the death. One or the other of us has to go." Oscar Wilde…

When we moved out to Locust Valley, my expenses (not including property taxes, construction projects, vacations, and gifts), instead of going down as I'd hoped and been led to believe, jumped up dramatically, from $6,000/month to nearly $15,000/month. That came out of my net income obviously. In other words, I needed a salary of $360,000 just to break even. I couldn't figure out where it all went…all I knew is that when I got it, Somers heisted it. What I wanted to do was play with my kids and get back to my guitar. What happened is she wanted to decorate.

Somers Gillette became The Barbie Bandit of Locust Valley.

Granny Gillette passed away. I was really going to miss her. All class.

'…Hold tight the thread, The current will shift, Glide me toward you,'… *

Mildred Ackerman (Gruella's mother) was the other surviving great-grandparent of Gruella but we never really saw much of her. She was kept isolated at an old-folks home in northern Westchester

County. She hated the place and desperately wanted to have her own, closer to her grandchildren but Gruella wanted her far from prying eyes. As Schwartz was central casting Jewish doctor, Mildred was central casting eastern European Ashkenazi. No one ever wanted to admit that.

Once ensconced in Locust Valley, Somers began to establish her position on the social pecking ladder. The process wasn't pretty, but she was determined and calculating, and only number one would suffice for the suburban Cougar. She was momentarily making her way back to Planet Earth from Mars. She wouldn't sell her body to the night, but there was no doubt the night was what she aspired to. And the men in LV loved her arrival…a new beauty queen had graced the shores. I was still proud to be her arm candy.

'…like weeds with big leaves, Stealing light from what's beneath, Where they have more, still they take more,'… *

Thongs for Sale at the Fall Fair

Our lives lost their color quickly and most things outside my kids became black and white. What had been wide open became narrow. I couldn't pinpoint the causes or condition. I simply misread everything. I stood by the kids, taking them to games and events, and Somers made social plans. That's the best way to define our existence.

'...I'll ride the wave where it takes me.'... *

Somers would identify and methodically pick off persons in the community she needed to wreck, to vault past them in the social ladder. Being inside any marriage, it's hard to understand what your spouse's calculations are really all about, and I didn't bother to examine Somers'. She hated nearly everyone, but acted duplicitously and shamelessly sweet to all. She needlessly engaged everyone every night about anything, mentally filing away rolodex cards of useful information.

"Somers, you've been busy lately, how about a little time for just us."

"Sebastian, 'us' will have to wait. Seriously, I have things I need to get done. We will need to come back to us after the kids are gone. OK?"

We were out of time before we even started. We didn't celebrate Christmas, we celebrated Cashmas. This was a no-win situation. On top of the money spigot, she had a need for public admiration and flirtation that you just cannot imagine, even with something like a 7 AM mini-mite hockey practice, Somers was nothing but a puck bunny in the stands.

Everything became calculated within a fraction of the intended target and she would not take the foot off the gas. She morphed so rapidly upon moving to Locust Valley, it was if I was in a rent-stabilized apartment one minute and a judge changed it overnight to market rate…you simply had no time to adjust.

Her LV approval ratings were sky high…the focus groups knew she was married, a hyphenated situation still, so they encouraged her to get more aggressive.

Somers was desperate to get on the board of the kids' school, Brook Dale. Brook Dale was part of the historical Wasp Establishment (though in actuality it had changed with the times as well), and being a board member was a reliable means for further social ambitions. Somers would never be so crass as to demand to be on the board…she simply wanted to make it such that the board felt it would be in their best interest to have her. She would be enough of an enigma so no one could pin her down...

Somers always had a bit of a Corporate Narcissist's guiding hand. This psychosis goes hand in glove with money, but it's most easily seen when someone runs a company or an event for profit. Corporate narcissists literally have only one thing on their minds: profit. Such thinking yields near term goals, but the problem becomes when such behavior drags down the performance of the organization as well as individual employees, or families…

In order for Somers to affect her plan, she first needed to prove herself and running the school's Annual Fall Fair was a good start. The Fair position wasn't hard to come by. The idea there is that if you're willing to commit huge blocks of time and have a modicum of organizational skills, a highway saluter when necessary, the school is ecstatic to let you run the Fair. She was given the role quickly.

"Sebastian, I hope you know this is nothing to do with you…but I am going to really focus on this job. I've got to get a move on. So do you. I can help you, but only so far. It's the only way to be out here."

'…seek my part devote myself, my small self, Like a book among the many on a shelf,'… *

Somers quickly ran into or up against parents who had been working the Fair booths for years with their kitschy products: smoked salmon, scented candles, preppy ties and belts, etc... I had to hear the late night phone calls to the house, with the aggrieved parents yelling at her and she at them. One parent called her a "fucking asshole". You'd think Somers would have been pissed, but she wasn't…it strangely energized her. She was turned on by it. Here's what she said back to that parent in Upper Case Voice,

"FUCK ME? You know what, FUCK YOU!! You are not invited to the Fair this year. Stick it motherfucker!"

Verbatim. She was cray-cray, crazier than a simple crazy. In case you're wondering, Somers didn't have the right to deny anyone entrance to a school fair, similar to many years down the road when she said I could no longer go to restaurants in Locust Valley. Somers was an accident waiting to happen, but damn if she didn't control the cleanup all the time. She effortlessly changed selves every day.

In most small school communities where everyone knows each other, those words would have ended all hopes of a relationship.

Episcopalians don't come back from that kind of bridge burning. But you know what? Somers and that man eventually agreed to meet for coffee and came away good friends…The last time I saw them together, they were laughing. She was confusing, fifty percent great and fifty percent narcissistic destruction.

'…walking tightrope over high over moral ground, Walk the bridges before you burn them down,'… *

Somers relished confrontation. It wasn't a side of her character I had seen much of before we moved to Locust Valley. Until then, she merely berated faceless service people in the City. In LV, she'd get into it with anyone…it elevated her social confidence, she always came out popping fresh. I liked the girl of Millbrook, but she'd become someone else now obviously, and like I said, there simply was no time to adjust. She was watching her back, asking others what their impressions were of her,

"I don't know what you've heard about me, but it isn't true."

If she didn't like the response, she'd Tony Montana the place, leaving behind any pretense of decorum and nicety, "Say 'hello' to my little friend!" I mean euphemistically of course, because she didn't actually own a handgun at the time…But still, she was Tony Montana in society drag, walking through the school in the morning yelling 'say hello to my little friend you fucker school mom idiots'….She should have been in the mafia.

The selfish benefit for me was that she often wanted to have sex after the verbal fisticuffs…the arguments seemed to be a weird sexual hot flash for her. Whenever she was done yelling into the receiver at some parent who was complaining about where his booth was located that year, she was fired up and ready to go. I had the most sex ever the year she ran the school fair. Stupid. The headlines proclaiming her demons were in three inch black lettering…I simply ignored the news.

It probably would have been helpful if I could have simply recognized her abnormal psychosis for what it was: social pathology. One probably shouldn't be turned on sexually by argumentation, but who was I to say? Sexual narcissism has been described as an egocentric pattern of sexual behavior that involves both low self-esteem and an inflated sense of sexual entitlement. It isn't always bad being married to a sexual narcissist…

'…Everyone's practicing, But this world's an accident, I was a fool because I thought the world, Turns out the world thought me,'… *

Sometime around then, Somers caved on one of our smaller but constant debates. Okay, perhaps not so small to me. I always wanted that woman to wear a thong…she has a world-class ass, really the best you'll ever see. Up until then, she'd been purely a white cotton panty girl, nothing else. She didn't even have another color. They weren't granny panties per se, but they definitely weren't tiny en fuego come-ons. Around the Parent's Association era, she began buying different, and better, lingerie…and thongs. I assumed it was all for me...

She showed one off to me one day in our bedroom at home, she in her long long legs, with a thong attached at the hip…I was combustible.

"Sebastian, these things hurt so much when I wear them all day, and I can't understand why you men like them so much. I'm thinking of selling some school logo thongs at the Fair. Thoughts?"

My thoughts are unprintable. They involved sex and tons of it, catching up for lost time. Apparently the narcissist and I weren't syncing our dreams too well. She had other thoughts…like how to make money off thongs.

The world was already strapped to my back.

Parent's Association Schemes

After she successfully completed the Fall Fair, having banked a cool $300,000 for the school (the corporate narcissist loves money…), a record by the way, Somers was asked to compete for the role of Parent's Association Head. I was proud that she'd made the school so much money, though the school never knew about the nightly internecine yelling. I could never understand why the PA head job is so important, but damn if the mom's at school don't treat it as second-in-command to the Headmaster. I still don't understand what the PA even does, after 15 years. No dad does.

Anyway, Somers represented the waspy Locust Valley crowd in the election, and she was pitted against Siobhan Ferguson, who represented the south of 25A crowd. It's similar to Palm Beach versus W. Palm Beach in many regards. The wasps had been feeling down and out for some time, and they were desperate to regain the upper hand. The problem was that wasps don't fight, so no one had stood up in years. Somers was not your usual wasp…and that's a huge understatement as I found out too late.

Somers would cut adrift Siobhan's crowd like third-class passengers on a sinking ship. Not one ounce of remorse either. Somers was a total baller, a thug who'd made it to the big time.

'…You're always saying that there's something wrong, I'm starting to believe it's your plan all along,'… *

The vote split down party lines and it got ugly fast. Somehow a rumor swept the other mom's that Somers was sleeping with the assistant Stoney squash pro up in Newport on her weekend trips…Somers had no idea who started the rumor, but she quietly said it was Siobhan. Now I think that maybe Somers herself slipped the rumor out to some people, so she could brutalize Siobhan as an uncaring woman and double dip the line that she was the ultimate cougar. The weird thing was, if Somers did do the leaking, the story ended up being true…she really was sleeping with the assistant Stoney squash pro. Not that I knew it at the time. Her boundaries were getting worse by the minute.

Somers decided to let me know about the rumor one evening, since people were talking, and in her unique estimable way she was able to convey it so I didn't quite absorb the full truth. No one out there besides Somers would have had the courage to say anything to me about it…that would have incurred her wrath. And frankly I still didn't know anyone well enough for them to have the confidence in me…I was leery of everyone as they were probably of me. She hit me with it while we were in bed,

"Look, Siobhan is a bitch, and she is doing anything she can to win this election. I just want you to know I love you, and we seem to have defied the odds staying together this long. Who would have ever thought we'd still be together Sebastian. I know my Mom didn't. I would never do anything to jeopardize our marriage. Here's the deal: Siobhan told some people that I was having an affair. I'm not. OK?"

Again, that was Somers' way of dropping a bomb and letting it hang. Here's your heartache, take it or leave it… You can't handle the truth, Col. Sebastian Jessup! And what if I had demanded to know more then? Would I be here today? Doubtful. She laid the challenge at my feet and I stepped back. My bad.

*…Is there room for both of us? Both of us apart? Are we bound out of obligation? Is that all we got?'… **

I didn't really know what to say. When you're first confronted with the idea that your spouse might be having sex with someone other than yourself, your first instinct is to not believe. Then, you blame yourself, thinking maybe you had failed to tend to some need of theirs. I also thought about my extended travel, flying back and forth to Russia all the time, leaving Somers alone. Had she gotten bored? Had her relentless flirting escalated into something more?

The nights were cutting me bit by bit. She said there was no other but I didn't sense conviction. I had some problems, but I didn't think that Somers was one of them…. I also knew sex was insignificant to her on some deeper level. In addition to always asking me who I would sleep with if she gave me a marital pass, Somers had a second line of astonishing filial indifference that she repeated to everyone, but specifically to me.

"You know, if you ever slept around with someone else Sebastian, I wouldn't break up with you. It's not the end of a relationship. I'd understand. I'm not that great in bed and I know what men need. The fact is I just don't have time for sex and it's just not that interesting. Just do me a favor: don't bring the affair home. Otherwise, go screw around. I really don't care."

I just didn't know if she was being perfectly truthful about this, as if my having an affair would mean less to her than a squished ant. I never pierced the veil. But she would say it to me so often and so dispassionately, you had to believe her: it wouldn't matter. Sex to Somers was just not a sacred trust…it was business, part of the marital compact so long as it suited and the conditions were favorable and that was all.

"OK. I trust you. Why would Siobhan say that though?"

I did trust Somers, but not for the reasons that you might think. That plate toss many years prior had never really left my memory. I was scarred from it not because she almost hit me (I can take pain…I can take more pain than anyone I know frankly), but rather I was bothered by her lack of self-control and I never really got over that. If Somers could come unhinged over such a mundane subject as our first-ever house visit, who knew if she would lose control in a situation that had all the right elements.

Again, my head said Somers was the closest to heaven I'd likely get, the best part of me still, even though the kids had quickly closed the gap. I had to stay close, regardless of warnings. She and my kids would always get my waffles.

'…We all walk the long road,'… *

Bottom line, I trusted her to not have an affair because she just did not like sex. She didn't. Look, I'm a fairly insecure guy. You could likely make mincemeat of my lovemaking skills and unfortunately I'd believe it… Sex to Somers was a means to some end. Somers would want way more out of that trade…she'd want massive material rewards.

It was a mutual assured destruction view I had of Somers' cheating… if she ever wanted to have extramarital sex, she'd blow up the marriage first, because she couldn't get the end out of that trade with me still in the picture…That thought would come back to haunt me later boy! And this kid wanted to be in the picture.

We dropped the conversation…she wouldn't discuss why Siobhan had been such a bitch or had started the rumor. She knew I was an easy mark to slide this issue right on by.

Once you get Somers going though, even if she self-creates the fantasy, she's always going to hit you back with much more than what was now in her way, so if Siobhan had started the rumor, she was dead before she knew what hit her. Somers' self-worth had been threatened. And since Somers needed the swing vote, Siobhan would be pulverized.

Somers had pure Destructive Narcissism, exaggerating any fact to suit her absurdist levels of improbability, and yet she was content with that self-made world. She would resort to extreme forms of retaliation, against falsely conceived excessive stimuli.

'...Tamper if you like between the doors, Can't expect to go out with anything, With anything more,'... *

Quickly and effortlessly, with the seasoned cool of a character assassin, Somers targeted Siobhan's reputation in the most vicious manner possible. I got to hear all of her rapscallion scheming, because she 'brought me over the wall' occasionally at night, to let me know that she would not allow Siobhan to hijack this great school, because after all, look at her. I would tell you what she concocted, but my lawyers say she could sue me until I'm six feet under, so let's let it lie for now. Ask me in person...

She was heartless. It was astonishing. Not what I had signed up for. She was changing, becoming less real, looking less real, tasting less real. I was crumbling inside but I didn't realize it yet. The vote came and went, and the Headmaster sat on the results for days. I thought this little private day school in Long Island was going to erupt in social riots.

On a Friday before the school's two-week Spring break, Jackson Stephens the Headmaster announced the results. Somers had won. Jackson, a tall, lanky, bearded Williams graduate, who had been leading the school for nearly two decades, knew better than to announce the precise voting tallies. He simply allowed the win-loss to speak for itself. Siobhan asked to sit down with Jackson so she could tally up the votes herself, as a check, but Jackson wisely declined. We never saw nor heard from Siobhan again.

Somers was smug in victory, not letting on that this was the most important day of her life so far, more important than even the birth of the two boys. We were headed to Hobe Sound Florida for the break, and Somers knew she had gamed the system, again.

The school board was in her sights. By then, I was passing right through her.

Hobe Sound: The End of Sex

Hobe Sound is where Locust Valley goes in the winter. That's what it seems like anyway.

The British had made a huge revisit on the musical scene. This was England's answer to grunge, an Alternative Rock invasion of incredible, thought-provoking lyrics, wrapped in some of the best chord processions we had heard. Bands like Radiohead, Blur, The Verve, Oasis... guitar tab websites helped us quickly learn the newer songs. The lyrics were universal in nature, so you wouldn't wince when you tried to capture the impossibly high falsettos of a Thom Yorke. Somers hated my music. She was all CSN and Dead, except she wouldn't even play that. I think our only common friend was Neil Young, but she hated his new stuff whereas I thought it was balls to the wall.

When we got to Hobe Sound for the '99 Spring break, Somers wanted to have sex, a lot of sex... The celebutante was charged up over her Parent's Association victory and the bloodlust was her aphrodisiac. Usually on vacations, wherever we would end up, she would use the pretext of the rooms being too close as the go-to defense for avoiding any sex. She had slightly more wine than usual each night of this vacation, and after we put the boys to sleep, she would crawl over to my bed (twin-beds), we would do our thing.

"Hey Sebastian, me love you long time...wanna rock charlie?"

It wasn't crazy sex, but it was consistent, seven nights in a row. She'd hop right back in her bed afterward, Asian masseuse accent recoiled, and fall asleep quickly, the sleep slut maintaining a perfect record. I was on a misleading romantic high, still slightly confused because of the after-shocks of sex. It didn't feel like it should, like waiting for an encore that never comes and then wondering if what you thought of the artist was ever honest. We had one-way chemistry.

Nine months after that trip, our third and last child was born, September 9th, a girl.

This was love of a different nature. *1 Thessalonians 4:15-17, "Then we which are alive and remain shall be caught up together with them in the clouds, to meet the lord in the air."* The staff and I were suddenly caught up in this child's preternatural calm and angelic face. She had no cries, just a soft coo. Her eyes were of the most vibrant blue you've ever seen, and her hair was soft as blond cashmere. Great things would happen for this little child and she even had two soldiers to protect her. This was a premillennial rapture for New York, a thing of beauty and forever joy. A Lamb of God straight from the Mountain of Megiddo, as perfect a baby as you shall ever lay eyes on.

When Somers came to, she and I were on polar opposites as to happiness that it was indeed a girl. Somers hadn't even considered a girl's name before we hit the midtown tunnel on our way to NYU, so she casually passed off the naming rights to me. I was so excited when our daughter was born, but to Somers it was simply an oil change…I mean, this woman had the emotions of cold steel pipe.

She was happy about one thing. Her reproduction job was done, and for the next ten years, I'd take a number and wait.

For Somers, it was now on to more maleficent schemes, and my marital role, outside of making money, evaporated… I think whoever said that marriage changes passion because suddenly you're in bed with a relative had it nailed. Somers wanted to rule now, and she got her society face on immediately after baby #3. She wanted to be the Mack Mama of Locust Valley.

She would only be looking for herself anymore. I never realized that the days turned dark as they did, they just did. She reached into the recesses of her character, elevating her mother's blood over her father's, seeking larger and larger parties for profit. I didn't recognize the shifting sands. She always told me she hated society and all that, but she was only gearing up. She was cruel in her machinations, relentless in her pursuits. She became morally righteous about some things and shockingly diffident to others.

As for me, I didn't think she was fooling anyone with what she'd become, but then again, I never really paused to think things through. I had my kids and loved being with them with every fiber of my being. We did the dad thing every day. Somers noted my love for the kids and began to take offense, as if I was deliberately attacking her for my time with them…I felt like I was on Planet Nutcase. She never knew how lovely she was and it's all I ever thought of her.

Somers had extreme Envy Narcissism, securing some sense of superiority in the face of another person's ability by using contempt to minimize the other person. For example, if the children and I decided to go play golf on a Saturday, Somers would schedule them for a professional lesson that Friday. She would say to the kids, "This way you can be taught by someone who knows what he's doing…" My handicap has been hovering around 10 for many years, which makes me adequate, adequate enough to teach my kids anyway.

She became completely unrelaxed, a complete faker. Dressed for show, she wanted to be where it was at. And I definitely wasn't the best partner in that scheme….I hated being where it's at. She made our lives complicated without any need. Or maybe her wants became her needs. It was a constant craving of approval, logrolling, and backscratching on the society wheel. The magnet was pulling so hard, there was no way for her to resist. Her character shape-shifting would make me and her crazy, being drawn away to this party for profit or that, never a moment of relaxation ever.

She was turning into something she never was, or at least I'd never seen it. With marriage only, there were countless times when all I wanted to do was go back to the start. I felt like that joke that the happiest time in a man's life is between his first and second marriage, he just doesn't realize it until his second marriage.

A friend and member of the Brook Dale board, asked to have lunch with me while Somers' PA Chair reign was drawing to a close. His name was Robert Parsons. He was a tried and true member of the Locust Valley elite, as well as Southampton. Robert was a maniacal workout guy, and for two months every summer, he was able to live in his Locust Valley house during the week with no one else around, as he had sent his wife and kids to Southampton for the summer. He only joined his family on weekends. He had the best marriage of any man I knew.

Robert and I grabbed a bite at Buckram's, a local Locust Valley watering hole with the best hot wings in America.

"Seb, not sure where to start. So I'll just say it. The Brook Dale board is going to ask Somers to join. We would prefer to ask you, but given that she has the time (she does at that…) and the money (that would be my money Robert; she's never reached into her checkbook for any of 'our' donations…gawd…), and she's proven her commitment to the school (sort of…she faked being committed, so she can get on the board…), she really stepped it up with the Fair and the PA Head (by killing others along the way…), there isn't much choice. I wanted to tell you first, so you weren't offended (I'm not…)."

"Hey Robert…totally appreciate the heads up. But, really, I think Somers is the better pick anyway; no argument from me. She seems to really want this role."

Truth be told, Somers didn't give a shite about the school…I did. I was already on another school board at the time and I actually went to that school's events and met with the school children to see how they liked it…and my kids didn't even go to that school…imagine how I'd react if it was a school where my kids went! Brook Dale probably should have asked me, not her, but she was my wife and I had her back. Wonder if the Woman of Halves had mine in similar situations…ha.

"Yeah, I know. And that's why personally, I don't want to give it to her. You and I have talked about this before. She's the most transparent woman out here I've ever met. She's a disgusting social climber, and she doesn't really need to be. Why does she spend so much time on the society bullshit? Am I missing something? Her dad's a great guy and the family seems solid (you don't know Gruella do you…?). Also, and I'm not sure how to say this to you either, so again, I just will, and I hope you don't take offense (here it comes…). A lot of people out here seem to think she has been having affairs on you, and you seem oblivious to what's going on. You focus on the kids perhaps a bit too much, and you're never focused on what she's up to. Sorry to say this."

"Dude, you know, I just don't think so. And I'm not offended; I guess I ought to be. Somers told me about a rumor like that. Somers doesn't really like sex enough to have affairs. She hates blowjobs, like, really hates them (so far as I know…). Our marriage may not be perfect, but I just don't think she would. Have an affair that is, not give a blowjob. Everyone thinks I'm going crazy by not admitting this."

I had somehow confused having an affair with enjoying sex. My read on this failure of mine now, as I sit here all alone, is that when I first had sex with Somers in Millbrook, it was of such eternal ecstasy that she could do anything to me and I don't think I'd never notice. I was forever on relationship euthanasia with the Iblis. I could never pull apart the love puzzle and reset it…she always had me confused.

So here was Robert Parsons, a friend of mine, with no upside telling me that my wife was screwing around, commettre un adultère, laying out the story as a friend willing to die in the flames with me, and I ignored the facts. He was trying to keep me from falling. Another friend begging me to wake up. Duh. I ignored it.

"Who is she supposedly having an affair with Robert? She barely has time for the house let alone an affair. You don't really know the truth; seriously, I love her so much."

"They say a couple of guys, I'm sorry. The assistant squash guy at SRC up in Newport (heard that already…). There's a guy on the board up in Newport (know him too, but isn't he about 55…?). There's a divorced guy out here (a little too strivey for her tastes…). I don't know Sebastian, where there's smoke, there's fire. I'd just keep a tight watch on it. You know the crowd out here. The wives are chatting (that's what they do…). The gossips won't let up until someone is dead, and that person will not come back my friend. What I fear is that that person ends up being you. Somers is not a benevolent person (I already know that…). She's your wife, and I appreciate that, but Seb….you got to get your head out of your ass. She's from out here and you aren't. Something's going on with her, and it isn't right. And for what it's really worth, I knew her when she was younger…my friend, she will kill you if she leaves you. She doesn't know any other way."

"Then why are you inviting her onto the board?"

"Because she forced our hand."

"Robert with all due respect to Don Vito Corleone, did she make you an offer you couldn't refuse? I mean, you don't have to offer her a seat…"

Robert's face went blank. He looked defeated. He was speaking about Somers as if she was Mafioso, ready to lay waste to Brook Dale if it didn't invite Somers Gillette onto its board. Was that even possible? These people were Church of England types, not thugs. Right?

I stared at the bubbles in my beer. Robert was trying to put doubt in my head and I was bleeding. I had to finally give it some thought, because the thing was, it was possible she was having an affair, or five. People were talking so loudly now. I'd ask that we spend a night in the city and the answer was always an unequivocal no. {You should see her now; she spends every other night in the city! It will make sense in a bit…}.

On the rare occasion when we did have sex, the act itself had gotten progressively duller, like eventually an inbred coupling between uninterested slobs. The thing was: neither of us was a slob. Just uninterested. In some weird way, I felt like a stranger in my own house, as if I needed permission from corporate to sleep at the house.

She'd say, "Just stick it in…" Talk about a foreplay buzzkill. After marriage and babies, Somers wanted the business of sex to be just that: business. That line of hers totally deflated me sometimes…the words were loaded with complete detachment. Half the time I felt like a lawyer was sitting in our bedroom alcove with an indemnification form I needed to sign before touching her. Marriage is the only war where you sleep with the enemy.

You kiss my children with that mouth. Yes, yes I do, and I have no qualms about doing either to be frank. Needless to say, I didn't have a blowjob in fifteen years, and I sure as shite don't want one inside here! I think in hindsight that for most of our married life, she just stared at the clock while I did the dishes.

Maybe Robert was right. Fifteen years of practically no sex. Love is such an easy game to play when you're young and reckless. We weren't young or reckless anymore. Marriage definitely is the chief cause of divorce.

The Internet Crash and 9-11

The next few chapters depress even me, I hate reliving them to be honest…so skip them if you only want the fun juicy stuff.

I was in my home office mancave reading a book on Kurt Cobain when Somers stepped in, never a heads-up warning, praying she'd catch me whacking off to a spank bank, or have a pornstorm popup attack my computer.

She took a look at the book cover and said simply, "Loser." I wasn't sure if that was to me or about Cobain, but I would have been significantly more bummed if she was referring to him. She either hated my musical tastes, or she simply hated my tastes because they were mine. Or maybe she just hated me. This was getting perilously close to that point where a spouse can claim he has a nice quiet little house, because you don't speak to your wife, and she doesn't speak to you…We were having trouble figuring out what we had in common, and still, remarkably,…I dug her because I dug the kids.

I left the Russian bank and started my own consulting business (that takes some explaining, but the Letter to Somers at the end explains what you need to know). Russia had been good to me. I decided to open my own shop when a buyer laid his gun down on a conference room table at a meeting in Moscow and he was shocked I didn't carry my own. I figured if someone was going to pull a gun out during a business meeting, I may as well get paid for that kind of risk. From the beginning, we thrived, but my soul crumbled little by little and I forgot who I wanted to be.

Throughout the good times and bad, Somers treated the office staff and my partners like garbage. I pleaded with her to act friendly toward them, even if she didn't mean it. She never once set foot inside my office and never once came to any holiday party for profit….which makes her penultimate hose-job (see third to last chapter "Lucy Pulls the Ball Yet Again") so fascinating…she had nothing to do with the company except when it suited her at the end.

She called the office incessantly, often just to check that I was there, as if she were nervous that I might show up unexpectedly in Locust Valley. The truth was I wanted to sell my company practically the day I opened it and do something tangible with my life. That conversation never occurred at a dinner table between us, not that I didn't try. She would not allow business conversations at the table, or the living room, or the bedroom, etc…But if you owned a business and were a guy, she'd ask you a thousand questions over cocktails and dinner, and she was well-versed…Flirtationship 101.

For seven years, I had a very trusted English assistant who could not have been kinder to anyone...everyone adored Lorna. Lorna was genuine, bright, pretty, and young…her accent melted a thousand men's hearts. Somers was rude to the point of being fiendish to Lorna, and I can honestly say that in Lorna's entire life, I suspect Somers was the only person to ever be so toward her.

On more than one occasion, Lorna would have a private word with me about Somers.

"I don't mean to pry Sebastian, but Somers is very demanding, and very rude. I've never even met her. Why does she treat me like that?"

My stock answer, which I'm sure sounded fairly predictable after a while,

"You know, she's under a lot of pressure…She sits on three boards, the kids, the construction, her health. She's just going through a tough time."

"Well, you need to look out for yourself sometimes. I can always just quit, but you can't quit her anymore…you have three sweet children. I don't think she has your best interests in mind by speaking with me or Jenny (the receptionist) like that."

Lorna was filling me with even more doubts. I just couldn't admit what was happening, nor could I stop it. If I threatened Somers' greatness, she'd exact revenge like no wife ever. If I kept my mouth quiet, maybe there was a chance that her father's good blood would resurface. It was a no-win basically. Anyway, what was I supposed to do, turn on my wife, like Robert wanted me to? I actually trusted Lorna more, but I was married to Somers. Even my kids liked Lorna more than Somers and kids are the best bulldust-readers bar none.

The Internet crash didn't hurt my company…in fact, we seemed to benefit from it. But the market crash really damaged Somers' trusts. She was shaken by the experience, as her money managers had gotten swept up in the Internet/Tech mania, as most investment advisors did. Every month, Somers' trust valuations would arrive by mail, and she would ask me to explain what had happened. It wasn't pretty…many of her holdings had gotten wiped out. My corporate clients ended up being a good hedge against the Internet.

My fortunes rising while Somers' were plunging was not a universally good thing…it was just one more instance of the zero sum assessment by Somers against the world, including her own husband. What I made, Somers took to mean I took, from her especially, even though my company had nothing to do with her. The Magical Narcissist was at work.

In fact, Somers' single best performing investment was a zero coupon bond I had bought for her with the refund from one of our kids' medical bills (which was my money…). Why I never held on personally to any assets like this over the years is beyond me now…Everything (tax refunds, unexpected gifts, unexpected income, appreciated assets, art, etc…) went to Somers. Nothing to me. Ever. Even though I paid for it all.

She never quite got over losing half of her trusts. Seeing your trust drop in value by 50% in the span of a year can make any investor nervous. They ultimately rebounded, but the scars never left Somers. It simply launched her into new spheres of lunacy.

Doubling down her madness was the event of 9-11. Somers had a reaction to 9-11 that I simply couldn't understand…it wasn't so much sadness or fear, but more a projection of self-importance, an Iraqnophobia-like condition. She thought the terrorists were coming for her! The mania that she self-perpetuated was comical. As for me, I stayed at work that day and went back the next morning.

I could say more here regarding 9-11 but it gets too squeamishly close to sounding like I'm needlessly bashing her with irrelevant facts…. I should let the missiles loose but I just can't do it. She's a demonic lunatic, that's all I should say about that event…you'd laugh or cry if you knew.

The answers for 9-11 for Somers really came down to decorating and construction.

We embarked on our 7-year odyssey of construction of the house. Either I began to pull a lot of money out of my company, or we borrowed to fund the construction. We decided, together, to borrow against our assets (to help lower the interest rate), and at least we could write the interest charges off. I figured if worse came to worse, I could always just take some money out of the company, which at the time I still owned 100% of.

Borrowing seemed a win-win, and every year Somers was content to personally bank the tax refund we got with my overpayments and interest write-offs. Mind you, all borrowed moneys went into the house and property, and the house and property we kept in Somers' name (her demand…another Somers' nuclear explosion back in 2000 with an unraveling marriage as leverage forced me to capitulate on this matter…duh).

The decision to borrow may have been the worst bet I ever made. It allowed Somers to flip the switch at the end, when she needed to. Who would have thought of the end when we were supposedly just beginning? Hmmmm…

The construction ground on for years. There wasn't a day that went by when I didn't count at least five workers milling around our house. I hated their presence, but Somers shamelessly flirted with the workers, and she absolutely loved the leverage of money over their livelihoods. It was a wretched psychosis of despicable foundations. I could hear the growing talk but I couldn't snap out of it. I couldn't keep up with the drumbeat of rumors, to be honest.

"Sebastian, you won't believe what happened today! I was in my bathroom taking a shower and when I came out, completely naked, the gardener was staring inside my window! Can you believe it?!"

"No, I can't. Why didn't you simply close your window shades that Jaimie put in for ten thousand bucks?"

Somers laughed it off. She told everyone in Locust Valley about this chance encounter with the gardener…Meanwhile, my gardener, who one day would be given my wedding ring which I bought by my ex-wife, saw my wife fully naked at least one more time than I ever did…

So far as the social entanglements of a Locust Valley, it became unbearably worse. Somers was a ferocious social animal, never saying no to any party for profit. She was deathly afraid she'd lose her edge, and manically determined to avoid going backward socially. She had a pathological obsession with figuring out if this friend or that friend was slighting her. And yet, she was so lovely to look at…the physical/emotional conflict would cripple a normal man.

She had horrific things to say about any woman who even considered crossing her path…high society women were her mortal enemies, lockstep adversaries, all competing in a capture-the-flag game of no real importance except to them. In a euphemistic sense, she much preferred drinking beer with the guys. Like a rooster who has to kill young cocks who threaten his dominion over his hens, Somers was the female equivalent of that to women.

If you ever reviewed Somers' few close girlfriends, one common thread among them is that the husbands of these women are the most atrocious, overweight, and homely guys in the universe…ie: she would never be tempted to cheat with them, so therefore she can be friends with the wife. Otherwise, she couldn't stop herself.

She would have been a horrible queen, thoroughly corrupt. Somers was more like Queen Ranavalona I, the she-devil who ruled

Madagascar from 1828 until 1861. Her primary amusement was throwing Christians off cliffs. In order to become Queen though, Ranavalona first murdered her husband, the King. Then, to be certain there would be no competition from within, she had all of her relatives summarily murdered. I knew someone just like her.

Somers' most vicious comments though, and by far, were reserved for her stepmother. What she would say would just sound so unreal. Her stepmother admittedly had helped cause her own mom's lunacy, and Somers was deathly loyal to her Mom. It was the enemy of my enemy is my friend.

Deezy Gillette, Somers' stepmother, has an eternally sunny disposition and generally is nice to everyone…occasionally things put her on edge, but not often. When Somers wee-wee'd over nothing one day, that somehow begat a three-year war of no words with Deezy… It was a chick divorce.

Mostly because Somers wanted extreme dramarama…Deezy at least attempted to make up. Somers forbade any of the kids from seeing Deezy for three years, while Somers used the time to damage Deezy's reputation. If Deezy only knew what Somers said behind her back…Somers would talk on the sly with Deezy's Locust Valley friends telling them horrible things about Deezy, mostly made up or at the very least very exaggerated. Somers laid down a gauntlet that you couldn't pass. She was unholy in her determination to wreck Deezy.

"I swear we will never see that evil bitch ever again! NEVER! She manipulates my father, she's evil, pure evil!"

Somers was projecting again, not that I knew it at the time. This is a classic Magical Narcissistic tendency, to shift blame or insecurities elsewhere when it really rests right at your own feet. I simply thought she was having disastrous PMS. The discord never had any real basis, but her fury was very real (setting the stage for later…).

As always with Somers, she had the Captain's disease in Cool Hand Luke, "What we have here is a failure to communicate." She never made the first move to break ice…that burden always rested with the enemy, whoever it was. This was a society verbal high-noon standoff, splitting an entire family, half a town. Même s'ils incarnaient de très bons amis, les acteurs ne s'entendaient guère. The actors really don't get along no matter how they must perform.

And then one day, it was over. Just like that. Snap. As if three years of incredibly corruptive comments about her stepmother didn't matter for shite. You've never seen a woman do such a 180 degree turn. She never offered a plausible explanation, but I suspect it came down to money, as ever. My children got to see and witness the rottenness as well, and they too were curious how this matter could be resolved with not a word of address, remorse, or assessment.

Starting in 2005, my business didn't perform as well. Wait a sec: that's a bit of an understatement…my company began to really suck wind… I was inexorably drawn back in, doing one-handed flips trying to keep the business going. It seemed that my personal capital account had become the company's operating account, and since I had until then been the only owner, I guess that was fair enough. Whenever we needed cash to cover payroll or pay vendors and our operating account was insufficient to cover the shortfalls, the office manager had the right to draw down from my personal account. She began to tap it faster than Somers…it was a dead heat to see who could exhaust my reserves first.

I ended up selling 15% of the company to four investors and that was just a fatal mistake. I was thinking it might be nice to have others help me with the balance sheet, but all that ended up doing in the end was giving Somers people to game. My negligence was forgetting that I had partners now.

Somers recovered her Corporate Narcissist bravado as the market swung up in 2004, and once again she and I were trending in opposite directions (seemed to be a common pattern…). Her fortunes were soaring while mine stagnated. I didn't mind that though, because as opposed to Somers, I assumed we were in this together…co-signers for life. Little did I know how wrong that assessment was! We had sex again after a three year hiatus, cruel and unusual punishment, a reverse Pavlovian experiment.

Somers launched into absurd and obtuse hypothetical's at cocktail parties, since she thought most of these events needed oratorical aids, as if the excess Dom Perignon wasn't enough to loosen people up. She had a crazy obsession with finding out who I would sleep with if given a chance. I used to remark to Somers that there was only one woman in all of Locust Valley I wanted to have, and that was her…likely because I never had her. When she asked and she asked the question so often as if it was some weird obsessive-compulsive autodidactic disorder of hers, I'll give you a pass, one night, no restrictions, tell me who you'd bang…my answer was always 'only you (Somers)'. I meant it, I really dug her. She's demonic, but the good half is really great when you get it and it's whom I wanted to sleep with.

When we'd go to her parties, I became progressively more detached from the scrum, avoiding most conversations, seeking out ping-pong tables and challenges. I'd stand on the edge of the room and stare at the gossip infestation,

"Look at you all…"

If you saw the two of us return home from a party, I looked like I'd run a marathon, sweating, shirttail out, exhausted from Olympic-caliber ping-pong. Somers looked exquisite in the newest Tory Burch, but mentally she was angered with the uselessness of me. I get that now. I just don't like large parties for profit. I should have been man enough to say it to her, and I failed.

Flipping the hypothetical of who would you sleep with (one of us apparently thought this was only a hypothetical), you couldn't shut her up…she thought every guy was 'doable', with a tweak here or a tweak there. The better question was who she wouldn't sleep with. I mean, what low-life could be on that short short list? Ironically, tellingly, prophetically, sadly because it should have been setting off alarms (not that she'd sleep with the following guy, but that she'd use him for other ends…), the one and only guy from all of Locust Valley who was on that list year after year after year was Somers' go-to gossip mouthpiece during the divorce, the bombastic, blubbery, Fauxlex, porch dog-yapping polo player Chuck Standernly. She said he was "vile" and "smelled horrible". More on him later…

So many other guys saw Somers ass while we were married...I got to learn this during our separation, so I may as well list it here. People gave us documents, people who knew. The young Stoney Rock Club squash pro who met her in Newport during her winter board meetings (I guess she was a cougar…); the older New York fund-manager/school-board member, again in Newport; the New York City foreign investment-banker ex-motorcycle-riding bachelor; the English divorcee of a former friend; and the wannabe Manhattan society California-transplant banker. Three bankers, as if she hated herself for hating what they were. This was information I could have used yesterday. I wished she'd had a lesbian streak in her…my rage would have been confined to sexualized confusion. I still don't know when it really all came unglued.

Somers' profound sexual narcissism was executed in a compensatory, unprincipled, amorous, elitist, aggressive rage, with no boundaries or cautions. It came and went as she saw fit. Robert was right…I had my head in the ground. I stayed obliviously faithful to my woman.

Anyway, it wasn't her adultery that ultimately did me in. It was the dark side of her mental despair. Her vampire was only beginning its cruel walk down the valley of shadows, conspiring with forces unknown to me and unseen. I simply tried too hard at love and marriage. And that bored her. Hers would need to be a silent assassination, carried out by trained professionals.

The house construction continued unabated, and Somers' open flirtations with construction workers and society dinner partners amped up. I became mired in my company's demise and I just didn't have any interest in the nightly town gossip festivals. Somers wanted me to play golf with the other men, and she always asked that I travel more, to give her space…She told me if I quit my job, she'd have to kill me…

If only I could have worked this all out, I'd be spending my full days with my kids. I'd rather be outside anyday, not a clip-on…I wasn't one of those guys, and here I was shuffling alongside them, all wool suit fantasy.

I was the opposite of the man who says that his wife tells him that he never listens, or 'something like that'…On at least ten occasions, I sat her down and asked for what these new emotions were,

"Talk to me Somers. What's going on?"

"It is what it is, Sebastian. I have a lot of ground to cover, and we only live once."

"Whatever that means. You seem different."

"Don't push me Sebastian. I'm barely hanging on now to see if you can make it."

"What do you mean? What do you want?"

"I want nothing….just leave me the fuck alone. Make some money."

We definitely had a failure to communicate! Hard to argue with her logic, or lack of. Money does help, and it's also the only thing that binds those that have a ton of it and those who have none of it…it's the only thing those two groups think of.

Somers and I drifted apart little by a lot. I slowly lost my sense of humor, my musical talent or what little I had, my waist expanded, my GHIN score improved (natch), and I gave up on those Anthony Robbins self-empowerment courses…had I ever gone that is. I focused on my kids and getting some Libyan group to buy my company…Angels and demons were already screaming, wrestling for the outcome.

I could feel myself free-falling from my tree.

Interior Decorators: The Co-Conspirators of Divorce

Somers was now on three boards, she had three kids, three cars, three diamond rings, and a gorgeous house. And I still needed her like a drug regardless of the beatdowns…apparently, I'm sado-masochistic.

Ooops…that would be only one house. Her friends had traded up to multiple houses by now, and although we were holding our heads okay and my income had increased, the reality is that friends seemed to be leaping past her. I didn't mind at all, but Somers was furious.

She had a new, less pleasant attitude, looking for fights all the time (hitting her own lower lows…), retreating only as breaks in an ongoing battle. Our big debate then had been: should we buy a second house or simply do another renovation on the existing one. After months of discussion from Somers to herself (similar to when we moved out of the city…a unilateral decision tree), she elected to redo our house again. I approved for one reason and one reason only…I finally got a house-wide stereo system. More on the stereo later…

That newest renovation project extended the two-year renovation into the seven-year, five million dollar one. And as you can probably relate, seven years of construction catapulted our marriage into whole new orbits of arguments, going from petty and witty to all-out psychological warfare. Seven years of workers marching in and out of a house, three interior decorators charging the most obscene bills you can ever imagine, and the daily grind of life added up to an emotional hurricane. On top of it all, Somers soaked in flirtations as only a lunatic can, and I stood to the side.

Generally, Somers and I divided our labors into inside and outside…Somers dealt with the inside and I dealt with the outside. The outside of our house became fantastic. Learning soil proclivities and blooming times is an art and science, and it took the better part of five years to get it just so, but when it did, it clicked. I never hired others to do my work.

Our (or…her) property blooms for five months of the year, and that's saying something on Long Island where your growing time is only two months of the year. The property starts to bloom in late March with rows and rows of yellow forsythia, then fragrant pink wisteria in April, white azalea's in May, blue rhododendrons in June, and finally two months of purple and white hydrangea's. I planted it all, with my own two hands. I built the stone walls, created a raised-8-box garden, and affixed climbing lattice to chimneys for all-summer roses.

Everyone who visits appreciates the outside, even the new husband. Everyone likes it…except Somers. Ohh…she gets to claim it as her own now so she doesn't hate it as much anymore. And as previously mentioned, recall that when Somers says she hated something, she actually loves it…You can shake your head like I did in wonder and awe with that kind of mental flexibility…the world stands on its head.

Somers said she hated the outside. I couldn't figure out why. I tried to change her mind by working harder on it and even soliciting her advice and input. But Somers didn't want to talk trees, bushes, flowers, and blooms…that's a guy's job and just don't bother her. What Somers liked most was the inside of the house, and compliments on the outside to Somers meant one less compliment to the inside for Somers. It's the zero-sum game all over again. A narcissist's envy pressure point.

Either Somers or Jean Kerr came up with this line: Marrying a man is like buying something you've been admiring for a long time in a shop window. You may love it when you get it home, but it doesn't always go with everything else in the house.

Somers has great innate style, she truly does. She could just as easily have been an interior decorator if she hadn't been so perfectly demonic. In spite of her design abilities, Somers hired not one interior decorator, but three…argh. She hired a decorator from the city and two from Locust Valley. And you know, these aren't Wal Mart shoppers…they aren't even Pottery Barn shoppers. These guys charge whatever the buyer can bear, or in other words, until you choke or snap.

If you ever want to know why interior decorators have no friends except single women and divorced heiresses, it's because those are the only two human categories left that the decorator hasn't and won't screw. Interior decorators, by the way, have more gay relationship drama per inch of penis than any human category in the entire universe.

Decorator invoices that could make a defense contractor blush were like daily newspaper inserts for me. I swear I bought three Hampton houses with what I spent on designers and you wouldn't even know by visiting now, since Somers changes the interior every other year. So what I paid three times over is now but a distant, not-fond memory.

A major air and land battle between us came in 2005. It concerned a decorator's bill that I accidentally intercepted. Arguing over decorating expenses isn't an infrequent thing between couples, except when the weekly bills can buy space ships.

This was a 2005 design bill from the swish Manhattan decorator Jamie A. Mignano III, in the amount of $23,000. Doesn't sound like a huge amount, does it (if you live in LV that is)? I mean that was one tenth the largest one I ever paid, so the number didn't throw me for a loop. Until you realize that the bill was for four lamps... Four flipping lamps...Spell it out with me. f.u.c.k. Sorry, I meant f.o.u.r. My most expensive guitar was a $1,200 Fender that I actually liked...I wasn't sure I could marry a lamp for more than two hundred bucks, let alone pay for one for over $5,000.

Somers was in the city that day, and Jamie had never sent a bill to our Locust Valley residence. Jamie would always make gay-friendly exaggerated compliments to Somers and Somers outwardly lapped it up as if she cared...which she didn't. She ripped the guy behind his back when he'd leave the house.

Jamie hadn't been to our house in over a year, since Somers and he had an argument over something so trivial I couldn't recall, similar to Deezy, but like always with her arguments, once she figured out how to one-up him, the end was he was back in her life as if nothing had occurred (she still secretly hating him, he thinking that she loved him...).

I was maybe more than a little curious when I saw an invoice from Mignano Interiors. We'd already paid the guy well over $500,000 (for what, I had no idea). Somers would simply say to me that she needed money to pay Jamie and I never asked for any invoice. By then however, 2005, her spending was getting crazier by the second and I had started to review our budget more than ever (our budget meaning my checkbook). I was getting pissed that I couldn't save anything even though my business had done well. Our primary country club bill was approaching $7,000/month and that was just for kids' tennis lessons, or so I thought…

She had a rockstar life but played no instrument.

I hadn't seen a new lamp in our house in years and I certainly wouldn't pay $6,000 for one. If you had oligarch money and you really wanted to splurge (an antique or a ridiculously great new industrial design), then the price would be closer to $20,000 per lamp, not six grand. No lamp falls around $6,000. A good new lamp at Gracious Home might set you back $500 at most. Six grand was a number that suggested that the seller hoped the buyer wasn't paying attention…which I hadn't. Nor she until then.

I stared at the bill and wigged out. You might say I'm hyper-sensitive to interior decorating charges, and I am. Somers was on another trip of hers to the city without me. I called her cell.

"Somers, Jamie just sent me a bill…He's charging $23,000 for four lamps. What gives?"

Somers in turn wigged out, at me, not Jamie. Like a defendant yelling at the prosecutor for bringing the charges. I think most couples would resolve this normally and call the company and question what had happened. Not Somers. The magical narcissist was hard at work behind the curtain and the Wizard never wanted to be seen. I hope you can grasp the lunacy beginning to afflict my house… here, go Upper Case,

"Who the FUCK gave you permission to open my mail?! That bill is for me! If you can't pay it, I will! Maybe you could work a little HARDER! We will speak about this when I get home!"

Testosterphone! She was pummeling my manhood with verbal uppercuts and roundhouses, chewing my ear for good measure, stomping on me like a rag doll. I'd stirred up a hornet's nest of something. Hold on: I could pay, I just didn't' want to! Money kills and interior decorators are its most efficient co-conspirators. I was a little divided, happy to have escaped the bill, pissed Somers was hiding something behind my back.

"Uhh, not to layer in too much reality here Somers, but the invoice has my name on it…I didn't open your mail…I just think we should call Jamie and ask what's going on."

"Don't you do a fucking thing! I may stay in the city tonight I am so pissed!"

She stayed. When Somers got home the next day, looking more and more bedraggled as if she hadn't been sleeping normally, she was in no mood to discuss Jamie's bill. Her eyes were ringed in dark circles and her face was a mess. And yet, that figure was scintillating…I couldn't help stare. Her body was intoxicating to the puerile in me, like an inmate to a beautiful female guard.

Somers flung open the door dramatically, stomped to the table where we kept the bills, excitedly grabbed the bill, and attempted to flee the scene of the crime. A drama riot. I never saw that bill again, but I did have a question,

"Somers, if you want to pay an obscene bill like that, go ahead. I think you're crazy. I would hold the guy accountable. By the way, where are four new lamps in this house? I don't see any."

"Jamie must have made an error. As I said, I will pay it, so just don't worry about it. Next subject: did you get the kids to tennis?"

And that was that. She always moved awkward conversations immediately on, to put you on the defensive, as if she knew where your weakness was. Magical Narcissism. I'd threatened her hegemony, so the counterattack was coming and it was about to explode… I hadn't taken the kids to tennis yesterday…they and I had chilled out at home and played with the dog. But we still got charged for the tennis lessons… Ooops.

"No, we swam in the pool and just had a relaxing day. It doesn't hurt sometimes for them to just kick back with a parent and not be over-scheduled."

Somers' guitar face came on, all distorted and awkward and angry. She was quickly beasting, making a bigger deal out of nothing,

"Are you fucking kidding me Sebastian?!! Those lessons are very expensive!! Jesus H. Christ!!! That's fucking brilliant!! They ARE NOT OVER-SCHEDULED!! Fuck you!!"

I kind of knew the tennis lessons were expensive since I paid the club bills every month. She laid all the bills to be paid on my desk once a month, when I stroked thirty to forty checks. Like the President signing treaties, except a gun is being placed against his head: Sign or else sir…

"Well maybe you should lay off on the thousand hours of lessons we handle each year. It doesn't look like anyone of the kids is super motivated to play anyway. I mean, last month's Stoney bill was $8,300. We have to be setting billing records there, I don't think accounting can keep up with you. If you want to continue on this pace, why don't you get a job… And the kids enjoyed themselves yesterday, thanks for asking."

"Sebastian, I'll have you know that we use that club far less than any of our friends (at $8,300 a month…not a chance!...)! I hold off because I know you can't afford it! And if it's such a hardship, why don't you just ask me (I wouldn't ask you for a shekel…I mean, dime…)! I have money! I'm not getting a job."

There she went again Mr. Gorbachev, hitting me where it hurts the most. Tear that wall down please.

I felt somewhat proud I had started a company with 25 employees and that someone else wanted to buy in at a pre-money of $80 Million, but that didn't count for anything with this woman. I paid all of our household bills. I even stroked her a monthly check of $7,000, so she could pay the nanny and other staff in cash (she loved the envelope drop every Friday…narcissist self-importance).

I went outside to work on the property with my black lab who knew unconditional love. That dog always wags her tail and never seems to mind the rain… She's me, my black coat alter ego.

The Chimney

I was the house elf, doing whatever the boss told me to do.

This mini-era was really clean rock and roll, professionally recorded, digitally re-mastered to sound flawless on the new digitized players. It wasn't raw like grunge, and it wasn't post-grunge, but it had a grunge lyricist's purity to it. Bands like The Strokes, Snow Patrol, Green Day, and Heather Nova. This was all localized rock, clean chords and old style percussive beats.

On our fourth year of house renovations in 2005, having just started the western side complete tear down and rebuild, I suggested an idea to the contractor.

One of the oversights of the house was that it had no distinguishing architectural features. The house was a plain two story colonial, although we did have roofline quirks which I thought were appealing; Somers hated those. In redoing our entire house, we decided to add a huge 20' ceilinged room just off the kitchen. I thought it would look neat to have a look-through red-brick fireplace in the center, where the fireplace would be a natural divider of the room, walking around either side. The chimney fireplace would rise majestically through the beamed ceiling. Everyone, including Somers, agreed and it was built.

After we completed it, one of the unanticipated benefits of the new fireplace was that it had the best draft of any fireplace you could ever have…the logs would fire up like they had gasoline on them and heat up the entire room (which is no small feat considering the room measured 40' x 75'). Every guest who came over raved about the fireplace, saying it was the coolest thing, they had never seen anything like it, and who was the architect? You could seat about ten people on the raised hearth, and indeed that is where guests tended to sit whenever they came over, which in our world was about every weekend.

Each compliment seemed to sting Somers more. She never complained while we were designing it, she never complained once it was done, and she never complained when we first used it. But she complained the very first time anyone other than me said they loved it. She said:

"It's ok, but we (uh oh, the spousal 'we' again…never a good sign) just aren't sure."

Who is we? I loved it. So did the guests.

It's hard to remove a fireplace once it's built, as the support joists tie into the house's footprint, the copper flashing covers the extrusion through the ceiling, and we had meticulously sourced thousands of pounds of aged red bricks. These aren't simply idle construction efforts. Not to mention the sheer weight of the structure. This original construction of the center-room fireplace had set us back $100,000.

Someday she's going to wonder why she was never there for me. This one fantasized pimple ruined the entire scene for her.

After a year of her going apeshit over the fireplace, she insisted that it be removed and reset against the far wall, 'like normal fireplaces'. I patiently explained that we'd already paid for the first installation, that in order to do what she was suggesting would not cost just another $100,000, but likely double that, because now we had to tear the existing one down and repair that damage, and the proposed chimney had its own technical problems.

"Somers, do you seriously think I'm going to spend another $200,000 on a new chimney and fireplace? This is insane. That chimney's the best thing about this house…why in the world would you want to take that out? You should want to take out the second floor before you would take out that fireplace. The draft is perfect."

"It is not the "best" thing about this house Sebastian. It screws up that whole room so we can't have large parties inside. I want it out. I will pay for it. If you do it, I swear I will have mad sex with you."

She knew the currency I preferred. It was built.

Still, most things in our marriage had gone out the window by then. Threats of even less sex were thrown around like careless threats. I was caught in such a bad marriage. Complete diabolical meltdowns became nightly happenings, causing me to want to do anything to soothe her. I needed an Exorcist, not a new chimney.

Two years after the original installation and maybe one extra sex session for my troubles, the chimney was removed, the floors, ceiling, and roof repaired, and a new one rose up against the back wall. Total cost to install, remove, and re-install: $319,000. For one chimney and fireplace, the most expensive unexciting chimney in the whole United States. Guaranteed.

Architect: Somers Gillette. I was being sucked up in the new draft fast.

The draft on the new chimney by the way doesn't just fail to work well…it's actually a fire hazard. The first few fires in the fireplace caused the house alarm system to go off five times.

And no guest has ever commented on it.

A Board Resignation

Somers was still maniacally focused on how to advance her social case out in Locust Valley and no matter was too small for her attention. She became mental about image, society, Boards, and parties for profit. She became the anti-me…the queen cocktail party for profit playa.

I was trying to make ends meet, a slave to her ever increasing needs. I should mention something about the stereo system. I wanted to hire the guys at 6th Avenue Electronics to handle it. Somers insisted I hire a family friend, a Corning heir, who ended up installing the most worthless $15,000 stereo in the history of stereo's. The stereo only worked via the internet, so when our cable lines went down as they often did in wind gusts of anything over 2 miles an hour, bonus: no stereo for days on end! And I wasn't allowed to complain to Corning. He's a great guy and all, but even he suspected that the system wasn't so great after he installed it. He once offered to replace it, but Somers wouldn't allow that because of the optics of warranty. Somers boxed me in with him and so many service others. I paid.

We hired a landscaper for a small project….He was a descendent of the Carnegies. My original budget for the front courtyard was $25,000. Final bill? $51,000….for eight trees, twelve bushes, some pachysandra, and a little mulch. He simply doubled my budget estimate and submitted the bill, with no breakdown of cost. Somers told me to pay. I paid.

An architect for the house?   Descendant of John Jay Mortimer. Total bill? $287,000.   She charged me $50,000 for blueprint copies I never needed.   Somers told me to pay. I paid.

I couldn't tell any of them what they had done wrong, but I sure as shite had to pay the bills. Somers wanted social approval and I guess approval costs money, just like The Register and The Grove.

Somers resigned from the NYSARC unexpectedly.   Although she was impetuous about many things, social considerations were not something she trifled with loosely. Board seats were very important to her manic resume which she used to support her self-confidence. Normally when Somers would lie to me, she lied with such ease…lawyers have nothing on Somers Gillette. But with this sudden resignation, she was all over the place, unsure what to say to me or anyone. She loved going into the city alone, and often stayed overnight or at least out until the wee hours of the morning with the only single male member of the board.

She would lead me to the water over this issue, but I didn't have the courage to follow up with the obvious. Anyway, I thought better things would come our way shortly. All I needed was for that crummy job to pay off….

"Sebastian, Frederic and I had drinks at the Regency tonight. Do you think that's weird? A married woman and a single man having drinks? I mean, I'm an adult; aren't I allowed to have male friends?"

You know what, the funny thing was, Somers had no female friends. And yeah, I thought it was totally wrong, as if I would go to a dark bar with a single woman and stay out until after midnight…no way. I wanted to call my friends to have them wake me up from this nightmare. Somers and I were having dinner one night at Diane's in Roslyn when she just blurted out,

"I'm going to resign from the NYSARC Sebastian. I don't have the time anymore. I'm going to nominate a friend of mine to take my place; she'd really like to do it."

Somers had spent a year angling to get on this board and she had identified herself to many people as being on the board. I knew she couldn't have cared less about Dominican kids in Washington Heights, but this board was pure social affirmation for her. There must have been something deeper about the reasoning than simply time considerations and I knew it. She acted as if it was her right to nominate her successor, as if the Pierreponts wouldn't want any say in the matter. That was so like her, to assume it was about her only. Corporate Narcissism, Magical Narcissism, and Histrionic Narcissism wrapped up in a sexy package.

"I don't understand Somers. I thought this board meant so much to you. You've always enjoyed the Christmas party they throw (kind of the only thing you enjoy, but hey…that's life sometimes…). You definitely have the time. It doesn't make any sense. And I'm not sure you can simply pick your replacement, I think Boards do that on their own accord."

"I'm going to resign. It's time to move on to something else. I am telling Mr. Pierrepont tomorrow."

Her mind was set. It was one less check I didn't have to write that year I guessed.

What I didn't know was that she had resigned two months prior to telling me. And the reasons had everything to do with an affair coming unhinged. Years later, one of our lawyers would discover that awful truth.

That simple thing called love, it had long gone by and I wasn't even aware. I was still on the outside of the maelstrom. Our love had become a cruel test. I had made a logical error with my wife, I had treated her as if she was a perfectly normal human being. Even Oscar Wilde could understand my fix.

Lyford Cay Flirtations

You know the honeymoon is pretty much over when you start to go out with the boys on Wednesday night, and so does she…

I couldn't breathe with the nightly parties for profit, the moral vagaries, and the open flirtations. I couldn't even sleep. The lunatic crept into my head.

We were invited to a friend's 50th birthday party, to be held in Lyford Cay in the Bahamas. Lyford Cay is just another in the elite category of privileged waspy club enclaves. I wanted to get away, so did she. We had different motives unfortunately and this would be one for the books.

'…Oh please let it rain today, This city's so filthy, like my mind in ways,'… *

I really needed to get away. Lyford seemed like a hopeful place to rekindle what was slowly becoming a very stale marriage. Somers wouldn't even pretend to have sex anymore…I was hearing adultery rumors now from all corners. I ignored it for the most part…I had my kids to focus on. If I'd done the math in my head, I guess I could have figured it out. But I chose to be oblivious. Better for the kids, much better for me. What you don't know can't hurt you, right?

When we arrived in Lyford Cay, there was one single man among the 60 or so guests, a true drugstore cowboy, all show and no talent…which remarkably Somers found attractive. A party with 60 people was about 54 more than I'd been counting on…Somers was ecstatic, her conversational puma game face on. The single man was divorced and apparently was barely able to visit with his own kids. It had something to do with anger management and an obsession with pornography.

We were due to stay there for three nights. Somers and I had left the children to be looked after by my mother. I'd left her enough money to have a great weekend and the kids always enjoyed having her around (Somers has now cut her as well out of the kids' lives…class…). She liked to make them breakfast and watch their games…she was, putting it mildly, the anti-Gruella grandmother. Almost too nice, but in the darkness of Gruella's mien, any light seems really bright.

The first night was a welcome dinner, two long seated tables by the main pool under the Bahamian skies. The dinner table conversation was forced and perma-smile. The hostess had seated Somers next to the single guy, because by now, every LV wife knew that Somers liked to give as good as she got, and the single guy and Somers had reputations for good repartee. Somers was in her Little Black dress…the LBD and that was never a good sign, it's a penis magnet, no finer way to put it. She looked pure puma that night. Heck, I wanted her…

In hindsight, it was my mistake obviously…should have been a no-brainer. I just should have said no to going to Lyford, and taken her somewhere away from a high society mosh pit. What I hadn't counted on was Somers reverting to prepubescent times, when she could tell her boyfriend to go stick it and make out with a new guy in front of the old guy's face. The LBD gave her enormous confidence, it transformed her

Somers embarked on a no-holds barred flirtation of epic scale. She shamelessly, satanically flirted with the guy, touching each other in front of forty guests. One friend came over to me and he asked if I was going to stop it. Somers was oblivious to everyone watching her…it was as if her mind on our marriage was made up, and she just didn't care what anyone thought anymore. She was an ice woman instigating a test on mankind, a devil's baiting trickster.

I was speechless watching this unfold before my eyes and everyone else's. I didn't get the sense we'd be building any more dreams together. It was cuckoo land for the insane…this was a crisis of faith, individualism, free will, wisdom, and enlightenment… in a party dress no less, with a thong underneath there somewhere.

The dinner mercifully ended, and some of the guests were in the pool already. The rum bottles were piled high….Everyone was flat-out drunk, except Somers and me. Some women were getting into the pool in their underwear and bras, but they stayed close by their husbands. Everyone was mortified by Somers' Diavolos moment.

I walked over to Somers and practically had to crowbar the two apart. My heart was pounding. Their heads were so close and Somers' hair was enveloping him…you couldn't tell if they were making out or simply whispering lies and schemes. I did see their hands on each other's thighs. Another unhappy wife had gotten jealous that Somers apparently had such a liberal marriage (not…), so she too was trying to horn in on the action. If I hadn't been there with Somers, there's not a doubt where this was all going to lead. A threesome, and I wasn't invited….that hurt!

"Somers, do you want to go into the pool? C'mon.

"No. I'm staying here. You go."

That was a sexual market value bankruptcy petition right there…I was destroyed. She didn't say meet this guy or how was dinner or sure I'll go into the pool or in a little bit. She simply said no. And she continued to nuzzle him right in front of my eyes, as I stood there non compos mentis. The warm tropical breeze was so at odds with the unfolding icy humiliation.

Pardon my French, but I was fucking furieux…livid. I'd never felt such rage in my body…it was all I could do to restrain myself, from both of them. And the guy was a beak-nosed, homely, Napoleonic, egotistical, wife-beating banker (I give bonuses to my people…god, maybe I do hate bankers)…guaranteed he badly hummed along to Toto and Air Supply, or worse, Kansas and Journey!

"You know what Somers. I'm outta here. Have fun. I'm going home."

I'd had it. I was done. I'd have gotten out on a jet if I had one. No way could I hang with Air Supply fans. I was going mental and it scared me what my next move would be...I silently walked back to the room listening to the tree frogs and then stewed under a mosquito net for two hours, watching Bahamanian cricket on the 'telly'.

Somers finally appeared in the white wood-slatted doorway, coming in firing from both sides as only she could do. My magical narcissistic terrorist ninja wife in a tan thong….the verbal missiles and bombs raining down on me before one fact or ounce of reasoning would be considered… Here I thought that she might have come in with apologies…my bad. And here came Upper Case Voice number 3 billion,

"You ever fucking do that to me again, so help me god, I will RUIN you!! You hear me. I will FUCKING RUIN you!! You embarrassed me! What was I supposed to do, sit around and wait for you?! FUCK YOU!! You fucking loser! You could be a man and stand up for yourself, you dick!!"

She'd rung the bell…no taking this one back. It was a death shot.

Somers was screaming at the top of her lungs. She was berserk. Possessed. Unbalanced. Influenced by Satan, a serpent dragon in Diane von Furstenberg. Bahamanian crickets, tree frogs, Somers, and santaria spells were a screeching cacophony in the bandshell of my room, quivering under the mosquito net, which she tore off anyway.   The Knights of Templar were circling my soul, chanting, and Lady Baphomet was about to drain me of my blood for her enjoyment.

And here I thought I was the one being offended at dinner…

I don't think she needed me anymore, or I her. She was gorgeous though, I had to give her that. I mean, one careless finger pull of that DVF shoulder strap and the whole dress would crumble to the floor. How can anyone that freaky gorgeous be such a mental freak? She was sin and temptation, and my force field was weakened as it had never been.

"Is it against the law to have a little fucking fun Sebastian?! Christ, you acted like I was fucking the guy out there (you weren't, cause it sure looked that way to everyone there…)! You're a fucking embarrassment!!"

Sometimes when you say something, the words become indelible for all time. Somers had reached this point. There'd be no turning back. Her narcissism had tipped over. Her cockamamie pestilence is cute, in a tyrannical sort of way, until you start getting cut too deep.

The room phone rang. She answered. It was the night manager of the club and he wanted to know if everything was alright. She switched tack like a 360° lawnmower. She went from nuclear angry to over the top sweet in the blink of an eye…"Gentlemen, you can't fight in here. This is the War Room". I was in Dr. Strangelove's lair.

You have never seen such a bald faced display of spin-on-the-dot reverse wretched shamelessness. There were pools of blood on the tropical floor and bodies were piling up… No sign of a crime here folks, just move along…

"Everything's fine, sorry for the noise. We'll keep it down. Thanks for asking though. Rekindling the flame with the old man, you know how it goes! Sorry again. Ta-ta."

God she's good. Such a phony, such a total fake, such plastic deviancy….but good, a PHD of lunacy!!

I could never do that, never…I hated who she was. She was an ice woman of an order the world had never seen. Reference books would need to be written about Somers Gillette after she died, after the autopsies discovered rare and unusual carnal matter in her heart and brain.

And then just like that, she stopped talking. Mastema was considering the consequences of the kill. She stared at me for a minute, like she wanted to say something catastrophic (or do…), but just didn't have the scheme fully thought through yet. AOL Keyword: 'Yet'. It wasn't the right time. My business was still alive after all, I could still afford a fight. We stared at each other West Side Story like, as we often did in our relationship, no words, no music, just her thoughts of large parties for profit. She blinked,

"What is it about you Sebastian that makes me act like this? I'm out of control. Let's go to sleep."

"I'm a fool Somers...your fool unfortunately. You've been playing me for so long. I have to leave in the morning. "

I wanted to fly naked, just leave my gear behind. She could bring it back when she came home.

"Yeah, right (sarcasm). Sleep on it Sebastian…we're here to party for profit for three days, not ruin our marriage."

I was out of faith, torn without realizing. Ten years of beatdowns, flirtations, and no sex, watching your wife become something you never expected…I was done. The day of reckoning was at hand, my eschatological mini-Armageddon was here.

She hopped into the bathroom, shut the door, and stayed there for one hour. Whatever the hell she was doing, I'll never know. I'd hear noises like she was putting on makeup, or taking off makeup, for the whole hour. Perhaps she was crafting a home-made bomb? The terrorist was alive in Lyford Cay? It was 4 AM.

When she came out, she got into her nightie in the dark and crawled in bed. No touches. She fell asleep quicker than I can snap my fingers, her sleep slut nature taking over...beauty rest before reconciliation. I stared at the whole procession as if a new unmanageable circus animal had been introduced to the big-top, and I was fascinated but yet scared. How can she do what she does, fall asleep like that...I was more wide awake than ever. And she never slept better. I just stared at her, intrigued by my discovery. I wanted to call National Geographic, Psychology Today, and Science Quarterly to sell the story and pictures.

Somers reminded me of that woman in Arizona who purposely framed her husband for murder, a murder proven later he didn't commit. She kept repeating her lies every year for 35 years, getting more fanciful with conviction every day. DNA ultimately exonerated the poor guy and he was released, but his life had been ruined by an ex-wife. Her sole comment on the situation: 'he's lucky they didn't have capital punishment when he was found guilty'...fully neglecting, by the way, to account for his proven innocence, the unbelievable injustice, and her role in the setup (their only child no longer speaks with the mom...natch). The son's comment: "My reaction was that it didn't surprise me," he said. "She's my mother, and I love her. But I think she's capable of anything." Somers would trump that woman in spades. She wanted to compete with Thais...framing someone for murder was child's play to Somers (and Thais). They wanted mayhem of a more epochal order.

I couldn't live with her. She was making me loco. It was late to apologize that night, or in our marriage. Still, she was my wife. I hadn't had sex in so long, that was weighing down on me badly.

The last time I was inside a woman was when I went to the Statue of Liberty...Woody Allen.

In the morning, Somers got up at 6:30 AM and went for a run. I packed my suitcase while she was gone and checked out. I wasn't staying for the weekend and maybe not even in the marriage, who knows. I was too embarrassed to even show my face to all of the other guests. You'd think she'd have been as well, but when life's a stage and that's it, even bad news is good news. When she came back from her run, she saw me in the lobby, suitcases and all. I was waiting for a taxi to the Nassau airport.

"Where the fuck are you going?!"

"Look Somers, I think it's better if we just spend some time apart (like a year…). You seemed like you were having a great time last night (like, really having a great time…). I don't want to be the man who held his wife back. I really love you, but my heart is being torn to shreds. I've never said anything to you in ten years of marriage, but your flirting has gotten so ridiculous, it's crushing me. I don't know if you're having affairs and all that, but I'm out of strength. I'm done. You're beating me whether you know it or not (and I think you do…). I'm a great dad and I really only want to be with my kids (unlike you…). Stay and have fun and I'll see you when you get back. We can talk then. I'm getting tired and I need somewhere to rest my head for a while. If you want to talk about it when you get back, in a real way, and end the bulldust, then we'll talk. Otherwise, stay and do your stuff. I'm sorry. I think I'm done."

I was beaten. I didn't even have any humor left in me. No tunes. This was the end of everything as I knew it. I just wanted to be with my kids. She saw a look of utter defeat in my eyes and shoulders. I think she had seen it before in other men, but this time, her man had lasted ten full years, and the cumulative effect of ten years' of her shite was a crushing burden too great to accept even for her.

For the first time in ten years of marriage, I saw Somers Gillette shed a tear, as if she recognized what her pathology had accomplished, what she had intended it to do, and the results flat out scared her. She was trying to resist her mother's monstrous abominations, but in her actions she was incapable of doing so. She cried because I'd been too weak to win, and she'd wanted me to win, to beat back her pathology, even if she couldn't say so. Without me, she'd simply be reckless, she wouldn't trust her own worst instincts, the dad's silver spoon was okay, but her mom's pathology was dreadful. Her tear made me think for a moment that perhaps she was human.

I'd probably lasted as long as a man could with Somers. I'd softened her worst flagitious edges but they'd only grow back stronger, like a shark's teeth. Her malevolence had to persist, it had no natural enemy... and it would only be incented by my sticking it out. She was turned on by the beatdowns, she fed on the marital genocide.

The marriage by then was the only thing that bound us. We had nothing in common, and likely never had. The kids were left to me in the most real sense, the lying in bed with them to talk about fears and dreams stuff, the taking time to play ball or teach them to ride bikes stuff. She simply did the organizational thing for them to impress society, as if society's approval was her only need. I was beginning to see things the right way, the way they were. It wasn't pretty.

She convulsed onto the terra cotta floor. I thought she was having a heart attack. I thought her walls were crumbling fast and ferociously. I had never seen this move, a puzzle to be sure given her noise and sounds from all the years of destruction. She was heaving, sobbing, doubled over in primal pain like she was giving birth. This was Azazel's trick, The King of the Devils hoodwinking the shepherd so he would release the yoke on his lambs, the ultimate drama trap from the heiress of halves.

"I'm going home with you Sebastian. I'm sorry about last night…I swear nothing happened. I was out of control. I don't need this crowd Sebastian, believe me. We can get stronger; I promise I will get better. I've been a horrible wife to you Sebastian, and you've been good to me and I don't deserve it. I don't know what's wrong with me. I should see a shrink (ya think?…). I don't know why I keep cutting you down. I swear I will be better, starting today. You have to give us a second chance, for our children. Please. Take me away to somewhere besides Locust Valley. It's destroying me, it's destroying us. You'll never understand. Ahhhhh…."

She would tell me she wanted me, but then... Sheer impotence and empathy forced my hand, I took another chance. I'd regret it forever. Nothing new there…my regrets were piling up fast. The narcissist has no empathy, but I did.

There's no place like home Dorothy.

We flew back to New York together that morning, leaving the 50th birthday revelers in Lyford, and had the best sex since the pool. That night was a release of ten years of tension and hatred. She knew how to take men from the depths of agony to the heights of ecstasy like no other woman you'll ever know. It was the craziest ride a man can go on, to feel so thoroughly beaten one minute, and then to hold her in your arms the next, a woman of such pure beauty and radiance, a woman with no obvious physical flaws, who could smell and feel so rapturous…this was a mini-rapture of the sexual kind, and it was all a lie.

I wanted to be King and I wanted her to be my Queen. I needed her like my heart needed a beat, and I was too afraid to admit the obvious. Her schemes were practically slapping me in the face. Hers was a material society world of the worst order, not because of the nature of inanimate objects, but because of those who were animated. People were her currency, to be bought and sold, used like commodities. This was delaying the inevitable. Well, at least Lady Liberty was now in second place…I had that going for me.

Why did I want to be King again?

Une Bonne Speculation et Le Denouement

Nothing would keep us together. These were simply breaks in the battle falsely keeping my hopes alive, but I was slashed and torn. I played Ahab, looking fruitlessly for the white whale of love, but it never existed.

And then the GD2 arrived, the Great Depression #2 of 2007, and my business touch became the Inverse Midas.

I realize things happen for a reason, and maybe all this was meant to make the ultimate fall that much worse. I couldn't get out of my company, or Locust Valley. It was a universal trap. The betrayals on all sides seemed constant. Whatever they were showing, they were showing to someone else. I was holding on to nothing, caught in a horrific storm, the perfect storm of tragedy.

My company was really floundering and I simply had no one to talk with. That's my fault entirely.

I couldn't find the right combination for the company…maybe Somers would have gotten better had it survived. But the company just couldn't find its way and I'd long since checked out mentally. I performed a wholesale change of the company's executive ranks, which in hindsight was monumentally stupid. We brought in twelve new senior hotshot bankers to run the Manhattan office. As I said, I hate bankers, so why did I do it? I think I was delusional from the marriage but this time, I was the bank…and you can't turn your back on your own monster.

Somers paid lip service to the better wife thing. She was better…for a month….maybe. It was a sexual dead cat bounce was all. Her sister Ariane laughed when I confided in her that Somers promised to be a better wife, knowing full well that that song had been sung many times before.

"Sebastian, my sister says a lot of things…you will learn one day to ignore 90% of it. The 10% she's serious about, now that you better be listening to…we know Somers well, and trust me, you don't want to get on her bad side."

I'd been married for ten years to Somers, and this was the first good piece of advice anyone had ever given me about her.   Promises promises…Somers needed dramarama and parties for profit and I needed concentration and support. She was having trouble figuring out reality and fantasy, la séparation du réalisme et de l'imagination. We were passing each other fast.

It wasn't a secret in Locust Valley that we were having problems. Neither of us smiled at cocktail parties anymore (for different reasons of course). Somers didn't smile because she was scheming and too caught up in the game; I didn't smile because I hated being married to the devil and I especially hated the game of Locust Valley, the incessant talking and not doing things. I wanted to head out to Beaver Creek and do my thing there, but my company wouldn't let it happen, or Somers.

Some suburbs are reality wastelands, and reality is what I needed most, someone to kick me in the teeth and throw cold water on my face. No one fought over anything… The parties for profit echoed with deceitful laughter. When I move, you move…Somers attended them all. I wanted to go to just one party and say, they call me Mister Tibbs, to get a reaction. She would have shot me if I had. A man needs to say what he truly feels, no? I wanted just one Friday night to come home and stay home…That would never happen while she piloted the ship.

I just wasn't strong enough for the eternal hellish flames spitting around me.

Gruella began to harp on Somers for not having certain material things. That had to be annoying, if not cancerous. Gruella couldn't believe that we didn't have a second home, or a private jet, or that Somers didn't get the same god-awful gems every birthday that Ed got her. Gruella would often find the worst possible time to visit New York, and I would be asked to go with the two of them to dinner. I just stopped going after a while, which made them conspire even more. If you can keep your enemies closer, it probably does help. I came across rotting skunks that were less offensive than she was.

I needed a policy of honesty instituted inside our marriage, but asking for that seemed like shaking hands with molten lava. She would never be satisfied with anything. It was nearly time to pay the price for this family's schemes. They wanted me to become a missing person.…

I had also given up on ever liking Gruella, the Day Star, and she knew it. I could feel her disease days before she would arrive for her spontaneous visits.

She used to be quasi-civilized, you know, for a second or so, somewhere between my third and seventh year of marriage. All the son-in-laws had abandoned that futile quest of loving Gruella. Just when you thought you might have found a common interest to keep the relationship at least above an acceptable level, Gruella would do something chaotically obnoxious, reducing the foundations of your relationship to rubble again. She was in business to wreck spirits and destroy lives.

I swore I'd never allow her into my kids' lives in any meaningful way.

By the way, it might help to know how Ed got involved originally with private detectives, and the issue I desperately wanted to bring up at Campagnolo. Gruella couldn't contain her infernal vexatious nature after about five years of marriage with Ed, so she spiced things up by roaming off the reservation (I always come back to the same question: what the fuck do these men see in her?!). Ed became suspicious, and like Somers, Ed doesn't do petty, he goes yard. For Gruella, it's all Agentic, Special, and Inflated Narcissism, despising something about yourself which you then use to browbeat others with…More on that later.

She needed a yearly bogey man to focus her anger in on…and I was the lucky recipient in 2007.

I refused to go out to LV parties anymore, having decided in Lyford that I just simply had better things to do. Somers loved the parties no matter the occasion. I loved the LV guys and some of the women, but really, we all had better things to do than listen to some of these blowhards harp on about matters they had thin-ice knowledge of. It wasn't really Locust Valley that got me…I like the area and most of the people…it was Somers and her feverish Lord of the Underworld backstories that others never got to see that I was burdened down by.

Somers despised me for my choices and it only hardened her resolve. I had the blues, feeling like I didn't belong anywhere, especially at large parties for profit.

Somers got a blackberry addiction, an Obsessive Blackberry Disorder (o.b.d.). She would tuck it furtively into her pants or dress, never allowing it to be read by anyone. It was a huge and costly mistake….the Crackberry became her co-conspirator for adultery. Once, she lost her blackberry for a day, I thought she was going to have a heart attack. Whatever was on there was comically important. The Head of the UN wouldn't have been that concerned. She was maniacal about finding it, but she didn't want any help, she actually asked that I leave the house while she looked for it!

I had zero idea at the time of course, but I do now. Somers was a complete Sexual Narcissist behind the green door… This psychosis is an erotic preoccupation with oneself as a superb lover through a desire to merge sexually with a mirror image of oneself. Hurlbert says Sexual Narcissism is an intimacy dysfunction in which sexual exploits are pursued, generally in the form of extramarital affairs, to overcompensate for low self-esteem and an inability to experience true intimacy. Yup…that's her.

Her mom called one day and we picked up the phone simultaneously. I held on, eavesdropping, snooping, whatever you want to call it. I shouldn't have but I couldn't help myself. Among many other things that day, Gruella said this to Somers,

"I bet you two won't make it; none of my friends think you will either (Gruella doesn't have friends…). Maybe another year, then screw him. Do you know how much Jeff Weinberg makes here in San Francisco? Fifty Million a year. You can have that Somers. Who cares if Sebastian is a good dad. For god's sake, get a grip…"

These two weren't good friends obviously, true friends stab you in the front... I wanted to send her a text right away. What would Jesus text? WWJT...I backed off.

This ship was taking me farther away from anything I wanted. Somers was driving every boat, every car, and every train. I just wanted to have the woman I knew way back when. I wanted to hold her again but she was long gone. Her parties for profit became nightly tributes to useless junk chatter and black holes of society stupidity. She was hanging around people who didn't care about anything or anybody, and she couldn't begin to recognize how this was weighing down on me and the kids.

Somers became a single woman again without actually getting a divorce. We often slept in separate bedrooms, since she would come home at 2 AM or later, whereas I would go to sleep at around 10:30 with the kids. The thing was, I still got her humor and that's not easy...No one would ever know her real story like me.

The walls were closing in. Fortunately, I had engineered a sale of the company to a Libyan bank and this was going to net me $20 million (and my four co-investors solid returns on their capital). Twenty Million sounds like a lot, but it was a steep markdown from where I had been led to believe the company would be worth a few years prior. So yeah, it was a nice marker, but after taxes and after paying off the debt on the house, it still meant I had to work for a living.

The markets had other ideas for my Libyan salvation...the markets didn't think I belonged with Somers. It was more here comes the rain again...I kept thinking of all the chances I'd blown over the preceding last few years...

Starting in late 2006, you could see the global economy begin to sputter and the credit markets began to seize. My buyer was a Middle Eastern entity that wanted exposure to the United States, and they felt that purchasing us would be easier than building their own. When the markets fell in 2007, they backtracked from our deal, arguing over pricing, non-competes, retention bonuses, executive responsibilities.

Meanwhile, my organizational papers for the company, never great to start with ten years prior, were becoming a mess. I hadn't done an admirable job of keeping straight who owned what anymore. The fundamental truth was I disliked the company and I wasn't really a great business leader of bankers. These were guys who sat around and acted entitled all day long…sort of what makes a banker good I guess. As Oliver Hardy said, and I only had myself to blame, "Well, here's another fine mess you've gotten me into."

I don't blame it all on the marriage, but it certainly was of no help. I was playing blind man's bluff in our marriage, praying she was still the one…someone for me to rely on when the S hit the F. Again, big laugh for those keeping score.

The company began to snowball losses as the economy got worse, and each day brought another ignominy. The rush of bad news became laughable. Not a day went by when we didn't outperform yesterday's bad news. You name it, it happened, starting with Lorna's husband accepting a job in England.

It was elementary, my dear Sebastian. I would lose.

The whole situation became one large self-actualizing shit-storm. This wasn't easy. I hadn't smiled in a while. I couldn't sleep at night. When Lorna tearfully left to move back to London with her husband, she had a last sagacious piece of advice for me,

"Sebastian, you made two mistakes. You hired the wrong guys and you married the wrong girl. None of these people have your back, believe me, especially your wife. They're all talking amongst themselves. And she's leading it. You need to be so careful. They're all parasites, your wife mostly. I don't like what's going on, but only you can do anything about it. You have been so great to me…I really am concerned about you."

It was a little bit of this and little bit of that, coming from everyone. I was paralyzed and I needed a hand.

I didn't know what had gotten into me. Before then, I'd always had the strength to confront challenges, but I just folded like a tent in the face of what was so obvious. In hindsight, my fifteen years of marriage had simply decapitated me. It broke me. There's simply no worse feeling after you've given it all you got, and I had, and either you own the failure completely, or you crack.

"A dreamer is one who can easily find his way by moonlight, and his punishment is that he sees the dawn before the rest of the world," v. Oscar Wilde.

You can call it a cop-out…but I prefer to say that Somers was that powerful. When I ran out of money, by then that is precisely what she wanted.   She had waited for me for the past fourteen years, but I'd failed. And failure was not in her lexicon, not for husbands. I'd only come for fun when it all began in 1992, and it was about to end in a fireball. What Somers was now looking for, was right around the corner.

Ed and Gruella Kincaid had been taking notes. *Merde alors!*

The Saudi-London Web

Ed called me at my office that January. Ed had never called me about anything, he never asked me to get a manicure with him…. I didn't realize he even had my office phone number. He asked to meet. I said sure, whenever you're in town next. Ironically…

"I'm downstairs. I'll be up in a minute."

I guess I'd need to clear my calendar. I could smell the dawn of the Millenial Age, the Antichrist and his dark flies of death approaching.

My new secretary ushered Ed in to my office. I didn't know what to expect from him. He came in and sat, coat still squarely on and not coming off. No handshakes or pleasantries just all toxic business, this rear echelon motherfucker. This clearly was not a cuddle visit, shooting the shite with the old man about how loony was his stepdaughter….I could go on for days about that! Like I said, stranded in the wrong time…

"I'm troubled by something. Sebastian, there's a man in London I know who called me to say you have a very unhappy investor. Tell me about that."

My head did some furious calculus to figure out who he was talking about. If I did have an unhappy investor, I wasn't sure why they would tell Ed or why Ed would even have the right to barge in to my office and ask me. Was I five or fifty? Couldn't he have first sent me pink peonies with a heads up warning?

"Look Ed, I'm not sure what you're talking about to be honest. Generally I need at least a minute to figure things out when someone comes in and accuses me of something, least of all my wife's stepfather. So, do you think you could just tell me who it is you're talking about, and save us both the time (you complete dick…). The impression I'm getting is you're looking for information, not giving some."

I was kind of pissed with Ed's original malevolent statement. His stepdaughter had five known raging affairs on me, flirted with everyone else, and I never once asked my mother to call Somers to bitch about that (and the adultery was just for starters…there's so much more I didn't even realize…). I mean, give me a break, are we adults here or wannabe Interpol sleuths. I don't talk in code Danny Boy…I talk plain English.

He was getting all da Vinci on me, speaking of hidden conspiracies,

"My friend is Lord Althorp of Brook's Club (I know that club…just had lunch there the other day…). He's an advisor to Prince Turki bin Al Satrah of Kuwait (I know that guy too...). They say that you have screwed up your company (how would the Prince know…). There are rumors of a lawsuit."

My first response was who the heck are you to even know who my investor is, as if you have ever done anything but try to damage me, but I couldn't be so dismissive to the man while he sat in front of the firm's partners who could hear the whole conversation…I kept my doors open every day. Ed had no plans to help me work this out…he was digging for pollution on me, and from me. He wasn't here to help and never would because narcissists have no empathy. And he said the word lawsuit like it was dripping in raw fish guts….

I knew for a fact that Ed Kincaid had been named in well over a dozen lawsuits in his career, one even from a former partner, where Ed had to pay out millions to the guy to make him/it go away. That partner now enjoys Ed's money in retirement in Florida but still hates Ed Kincaid with a passion… He wanted to bring Ed down, but Ed's money bought his signature.

"Ed, I gather the man you're referring to is a minority investor here and hasn't attended one board meeting. I don't feel comfortable discussing a private business matter with someone like you who doesn't have skin in this game. I'm sorry, I don't mean to be disrespectful, but really, it's just none of your business (as you already know…and what is it you really want to know by the way, how I made my first money?...). So, if that's all that you have come here to tell me, all I can say is that I will call the investor immediately and ask him why he has broached his thirty page limited partnership agreement by talking to anyone outside the partnership and its lawyers."

"Sebastian, I once told you that I make it my business to know everything about anyone related to me (I recall that public rape well Ed…I'm still sore in the ass fourteen years later…). I told you I would destroy you if you hurt my daughter. Reputations are easy to damage and impossible to repair (as it seems you are about and want to do...). If investors are clamoring for you, my daughter (your 'stepdaughter' you asshole…) will be hurt, and then her mother will be hurt (Gruella doesn't know pain, Ed…). I told you then, I wouldn't allow it. Take care of this in five days or we will have a different conversation."

Ed walked out the office without saying another word. What a Homer.

He left his steaming pile of unobtainium right on my office floor. The little devil tornados of pestilence and roaches swept out with his force. Still, maybe I had him wrong…maybe he was a true friend…he'd stabbed me in the front. I was learning what his world was all about, and it wasn't pretty.

My ears were fire-red. You know when you just have a feeling that someone is fucking you…This was a blinking neon billboard hanging at 52nd and Park, with horns for good measure, a drive by shooting with your stepfather-in-law squeezing the trigger.

I always said I should have been born in the 19th Century, so I could have resolved matters by force. I wanted to have Ed come back in and allow us our twenty paces with our Colt pistols. Five days? I didn't know what I was supposed to accomplish in five days… Or, was he accomplishing something in those five days…?

I was the largest investor in my company by a factor of 10…he never knew that. If anyone lost anything, Sebastian Graham would be the biggest loser. If a minority partner was upset, multiply that by 10 to understand how upset I'd be… Ed never asked to see if I was being pinched by the company's troubles. But that's not why he came after all… He was simply gaming the end.

I called Somers to tell her about Ed's visit…but she'd already been fully informed, natch. And, she sounded like she'd picked sides, no surprise there.   Ed's checkbook guaranteed that. Somers' loyalty lay with the jackals picking over a carcass never the Resurrection. Resurrections aren't guaranteed, but Limited Partnerships are. It wasn't going to be a good night at the old homestead….

"Look, Ed is not kidding around. You have to fix this now, or he will bury you."

"Somers, the honest to god truth is until I sell this company, I can't take any money out. There's nothing I can fix by the way. The company's sucking wind…the economy stinks. The only cash I have is the remaining balance of our credit line, but I need that to finish the house. And why would your stepfather want to bury me by the way? What is wrong with your family? It's like everyone always wants to fuck everyone, you know, except in a biblical way naturally. Speaking of…"

"I once told you 'I have money'. I do. How much do you need?"

"Somers, very gracious of you, but I know how this ends. I borrow from you and you charge me my life! By the way, your trust and my assets are supporting our CL.   Why don't I just borrow some from the CL and I will refund it once the sale takes place. And if worse comes to worse, we can sell one of my paintings or two. I just need the Libyans to stop dicking around."

"Sebastian, we are not selling any paintings; remember, those are mine; I'll tell you if we are selling a painting. You signed everything over to me ten years ago (yup, simply to placate your volcanic outburst….smooth move in hindsight since I ended up buying everything…). Just take care of it, today. Borrow from the CL. Steal from the CL. You handle it. Whatever. You don't need to tell me how you do it. You're a big boy."

Click. Hollywood hang-up. I thought I heard her say it was fine to draw down on the line. You handle it. You don't need to tell me how you do it. Verbatim, I can see hear her say it today…what a load…I thought I got approval from corporate.

So I did. Not much mind you, $200,000. We were married, why would I even think someone was setting me up? This was the turning point….The inside of me was falling to pieces, but not because of business. They say that a man's downfall begins with the most innocuous event, and this was it. I asked, she said yes, I was a committed husband, she was a serial philanderer. This one act begat all of the real problems eventually.

I called the bank and they messengered over some papers. The documents arrived in a sealed package, a black seal with the bank's logo. I opened it and signed the papers. I called the banker to see her if she wanted the papers back that day,

"Hi Terry, thanks for the documents. I just got them from your messenger service. Would you like for us to sign these and return now, or tomorrow. Somers can't them til tonight obviously."

"Uhh, Seb, we didn't send any documents over. We emailed them. But you can just print the attachment, sign it yourself and send it back to me today. We don't need Somers' signature, you guys have been great clients for so long. I'll transfer the money now. Have a great day!"

This was the third sealed package that someone had delivered to me in the last few years where someone said they had never sent it, but they had…I knew it. I was there. I was a little unnerved by this newest phantom delivery. Still, I let it slide.

I didn't hear from Ed in those promised five days, but he was on my trail. I could feel his disease, Gruella was pushing him, breathing down his back. She wanted her sidekick back.

The company continued to flounder. I couldn't keep it going like it was. And guess what, I was the CEO. About as fun a position as being Gruella's lover. People knew where Locust Valley was, where I lived…Somers made sure they would.

Somers had a plan. That whole meeting was one big barnstorming screwjob. Ed had been talking to Lord Althorp for years, not just once innocently a few months ago. Gruella, Somers, and Ed had hatched the perfect plan: my insolvency. The clock had been ticking for years.

They weren't as bad as people said, they were much, much worse.

And the sun will set for you
The sun will set for you
And the shadow of the day
Will embrace the world in grey
And the sun will set for you

(v. Linkin Park)

The Cravath Meeting

I think when you are feeling low and down, there's no better art form than the Blues, but for whatever reason I've never been able to get into it. I've got southern blood in me, but to embrace the blues fully, it helps to have more Mississippi and Louisiana, less Carolina.

I've always preferred rock in whatever form. With my new turn of life events, I began to listen quite a bit to some deeply depressing lyrics like Adam's Song, Filter's One, Clapton's Tears in Heaven, and especially Linkin Park with Shadow of the Day. These are all clean, purposeful lyrics, basically stripped down musical arrangements (Shadow of the Day has some difficult extended-range guitar play, as well as crazy octave vocals). I would re-loop Shadow of the Day in my home office, remove the vocal tracks, and belt it out. Somers would look in on me sometimes and simply shake her head. I no longer had any time to keep up with my guitars.

A few months after Ed's sneak attack in my office, Somers called me there to speak. The Fallen Angel had been working overtime while I had just been working. The soul hunters had arrived.

The receptionist said it was urgent and Somers never called saying anything was urgent…she was always in control of the flagitious schemes unless she was on stage. We no longer had dinner time conversations, mostly because she was out at night while I tucked the kids into bed, so we reserved any important talks for the phones. She was clever by half, because among many other things, she had begun to tape record all of our marital conversations….a felony in New York State unless you can pay the DA to look the other way, you know, by claiming criminal mischief on the part of the receiver… I was still along for the ride, unaware of anyone doing anything to ruin me.

"Sebastian, I want you to go over to Jim Vander Hoorst's office at Cravath tomorrow and discuss our CL. They think they have a great plan to refinance our debt and allow us some breathing room. Also, they want to make sure my credit record is spotless, and I am sure you agree that that is important."

It was easy to know if Somers was lying…her lips moved. Anything that came out now was suspect.

Yet, I would still have taken a bullet for her, so of course I went along. Cravath had a saying, "Trust your husband, adore your husband, and get as much as you can in your own name."

I was willing to support the woman no matter what. I had a marital duty to do whatever I could for her, up to and including signing anything, to help us get to the other side… I was convinced the Libyans would come through, I just needed the time to get there. Every day though seemed tragically long and suspiciously bad, as if the window was inexorably narrowing, leaving me with scant breathing room.

This day would be a day for permanent scar tissue. The Slanderer, the Accuser, God's Poison was about to be released.

Somers wanted me to meet with Jim Vander Hoorst, our Cravath lawyer in Manhattan, to review our debt, or my debt. Cravath was the whitest of white shoe firms in New York and Vander Hoorst was the best Trusts and Estates lawyer in the city. He was a Round Hill guy from Greenwich and classically, lawyerly un-masculine, as if he spent more time getting manicures than tossing a ball. I always look at a guy's hands…not gay, just saying. Just more Facebook pussy drugstore cowboys.

"And, I won't be there. It will just be you and Jim. You know how I am with money and agreements. You two men can sort it out. Let me know how it goes."

Why didn't I universally feel good about this meeting? I wasn't looking for a noose, but a noose was being lowered anyway.

Wherefore they are no more twain, but one flesh. What therefore God hath joined together, let not man put asunder.
-- Matthew 19:6

A Cravath partner hadn't marked up the Bible yet. Those guys do nothing but put asunder.

I showed up alone at the Cravath offices on 7th Avenue at Worldwide Plaza at 10 AM February 16, 2007. AOL Keyword: "Alone". I was led down a long soft-carpeted hallway past rows and rows of dead partner oil portraits to a solid oak door. The young lady opened the door to a conference room where a fifteen foot-arc circular table sat surrounded by eight chairs. I could tell which chair was for me because it was set away from the others, like a condemned man's death row throne. I saw Jim first, who was walking toward me with his outstretched manicured hands.

Who else was at the table? You ask, I answer… none other than Ms. Somers Gillette, my wife, the Old Hob, Iblis, Kolski herself, surrounded by two young Cravath associates. She'd put me in the hospital for nerves with this kind of sneak attack. If this wasn't livin' the dream, I don't know what is.

Somers was dressed in funereal black, down to a strand of pearls hanging from her neck…I'd never seen pearls on that woman. I also spied a hint of a skylit blue bra with butterflies under her black top. I'd never seen a blue bra on that wife of mine as well, ever. What was up with that? That would definitely neutralize me. I was surreally turned on…like in Dr. Schwartz' office with the nurse. She'd only owned white bra's until today! Was this a new look? Who bought the blue one? How was I supposed to focus on the meeting now?

Somers wasn't feeling romantic with me though. She was feeling more Lt. Col. Bill Kilgore, she 'loved the smell of napalm in the morning fucker!' This was as close to marital genocide as you'll ever find in Manhattan, or at least Cravath Swaine Moore…Wachtel maybe it happens often…but not Cravath. Cravath is all happy smiles and trust fund quiet.

Outside of my incomprehensible feeling (stunned doesn't begin to describe me….), about the bra that is, skylit blue….Wow! That was a freak flag signaling a new life.

Oh, that other part, the part where she lied to me about not being there but shows up anyway… I half expected her there. She no longer failed to amaze with the depravity anymore. This was a setup and she knew I wouldn't walk away from a setup. Just not in my character, I don't feel pain.

I was also stunned that she never thinks of legal bills: did Somers even know what three Cravath lawyers charge? I did because I paid them. Seeing Somers ignited an internal LSD trip, as I was trying to figure out if I was supposed to kiss her on the cheek (as I'd always done), or ask her if she was lost…

Somers didn't rise, she just stared down at her legal pad embarrassed but ready to start the war…her demure posture was all award show, a total fake stage play. I guess I wouldn't be able to kiss her. Her face was drained of fluid, the hateful vampire suffering in daylight. One of the lawyers surrounding Somers was a woman, and she immediately placed an arm around Somers as if Somers was the one who needed comfort. Her blue bra slid out some more….

Lady, Somers Gillette doesn't need comfort; she's a snake in the grass, starting to feel like a snake in my ass. Look at me, 'nobody puts 'Baby' in a corner Johnny!'

The thing was she would never know how lovely she was…she could glide through life irrespective of her diabolical airs because most people would let her get away with the mayhem. She's too good looking for you to hate fully.

The room had the feel of an infectious inquisition, not a refinancing powwow. The hostage (me) sat on one side of the table, while the four of them sat on the other. It was like my mini-mite hockey squad of one playing three shifts of the Soviet Union Red Army. I wasn't really pissed, more confused and mentally dormant. I hate baring the family laundry, Somers thinks nothing of it. The 50% of her that was Gruella was crowding out the 50% of her that was Nick in a runaway…

For an hour, I was grilled about the loan and about me. They never even gave me hostage tea. Somers stared at her notepad, never saying a peep, never looking up. I think she was doodling devil cartoons.

Jim and I discussed the CL and what it had been used for: construction. Construction which had increased the value of Somers' house from $1 Million to $6 Million and counting. The loan certainly hadn't benefitted me. I affirmed that the impending sale of my company was going to be used to refi the debt, as Somers knew all too well, and I still wouldn't want any piece of the residence. She hadn't informed anyone in that room of that fact. No one cared anyway….they were coming for my soul, they just needed clues as to where to stab me…

What they seemed most interested in was the fact that Somers and I had not co-signed the extension of the CL, only I had. Somers had signed the original agreements but they were now superseded by the extensions. That was easy, as Somers had decided way back in 2002 that she didn't want to sign anything anymore and asked that I handle everything. You deal with it. How many times had she said that….a hundred, three hundred, a thousand? I bought into it because we were a team, so-signers for life. Ha!

Was the signature thing a problem? You could say that….To the Cravath cavalry, it was the only problem in the universe, cancer no longer even mattered….and it appeared like I was the only culprit. Harvard crimson fuckers…glad to see that their education wasn't getting in the way of their morals… Where Somers and I broke rules, I thought it was backstopped with love. Somers thought it was backstopped with my soul and she was here that day for my soul, nothing less. We'd never be together on any dance floor again, except perhaps the tango of divorce court.

Whoa. This thing went from hopeful refinancing to grand jury interview faster than prisoners scurry out of the shower when the soap hits the floor. I was royally steamed. I asked to speak with Somers outside alone, and Somers said that anything that is going to be said today will be said in this room. So that was us, gone, say good bye. I rose and said,

"Somers, first of all, you said you weren't coming here today. So, to say your presence is a little unnerving is a slight understatement. Secondly, are we trying to resolve something, or are you guys trying to fuck me? Everything, and I mean everything, has always been above board in my marriage and my financial dealings, and it sounds like you're trying to trip me up, nothing less, because no one else wants to share in the pain. I'm not used to this kind of bullshit. I like to say it like it is so if you're just going to keep screwing around with semantics, let's table this meeting for another day. I actually have real work to do".

I thought for a second that I should say what I really wanted to say, which was you are one evil manipulative bitch, tell the fucking truth and stop lying, but I had an ounce of reserve left. She and I were done. I officially despised her and I don't despise many people. Jim spoke up,

"Seb, no one's tripping anyone up (really? like I-bankers, don't listen to lawyers when they say nice things about you, especially if they went to Harvard...). We just want to make sure you two have a solid financial standing. That's all. We want Somers to have a clean credit score, and we know you share in that desire."

It occurred to me during this meeting, when I finally could see that Somers had initiated project kill, that if worse came to worse, I had nothing to show for my marriage. I'd abandoned my life to a life managed, controlled, and owned by my wife...worse, she knew that more than anyone. If I wasn't in her life, then I wouldn't be around at all.

Sitting at the Cravath table high above 8th Avenue, my head spun and spirits sank, as I absorbed the enormity of no longer being in partnership. And…she'd set me up in a way which is almost impossible to convey without spitting. Evil aberrant brilliance, passed down from the Mom to the daughter, as never before. A brilliant murder, chopping me into 13 pieces except my phallus, a trickster temptress, the Old Hob on full display. She really broke my crayons that day.

Vander Hoorst had this plastic Harvard lawyer smarmy way of ingratiating himself with the enemy, a classic trick to diffuse the tension and make the opponent feel that everything was going to be okey-dokey, A-1, OK, hunky-dory, fine, let's let bygones be bygones. The manicure men of Harvard Law. He's good, you have to give him credit for that. Like Rojek at Shearson, I was getting screwed and I hardly felt it.

My next fork in the road decision and no, nothing would be hunky dorey okay. Jim's secretary brought a two page pre-typed sheet into the room, as if she had just typed it up not a second before. Like no one had thought about it before that very minute. Voila!

"I think this will make the whole problem disappear Sebastian. And I know you want to help Somers."

He asked me to sign it on the spot. The letter essentially said that Somers had no knowledge of the CL, and that I would be responsible for the payments on it. Well, the first part was pure unadulterated bulldust since she had banked all the tax refunds which were made possible by the write-offs of the interest, but the second part I had no problem with. This letter had the easter-egg surprise, the Hot Coffee gotcha hidden trap of incrimination, a land mine they needed me to step on.

I didn't ask for my own lawyer to review the letter because I assumed these were my lawyers. So, yeah, of course I signed it. Who wouldn't? I'm not a Homer. If I piped up and said, boys I think an independent set of eyes might be useful for all of us (including Cravath for hosing one of their own clients and directly benefiting another), they would have turned to Somers and said,

"Run!!!!"

I hate the immorality of lawyers. No offense to the lawyers I like of course and there are some.

Jim was further fascinated with how I had started my company with $5 Million. I should restate that…someone else was fascinated with how I had funded my company with $5 Million of my own money, and Jim was simply doing her bidding. Up until that meeting, I'd been unaware that Somers was so interested. Who were these Cravath people, the FBI….? You should probably read this book in reverse to understand the black humor in that statement…Ha!

I told Jim that I'd made my money in Russia but that even I wouldn't get into what I'd done there. He didn't realize how close he got to a trip-wire asking me about this…that would have made life for everyone in that room, secretaries included, very dicey indeed. You don't mess with the Russians. Cardinal rule #1. More on that later at the end in My Letter to Somers…

Jim asked that I walk with him to the elevators, leaving Somers in the conference room, still seated at the circular table, still refusing to look up. They'd purposefully wedged themselves confidence-wise between Somers and me, a husband how without portfolio. It would be a lonely day. Jim was smooth as only an alley cat can. Although the elevator walk was only a physical gesture, it was an unmistakable message to all.

"Everything will be fine Sebastian (while you're fucking me?...). You and Somers love each other, and we just want to be sure we got everything out in the open (getting things out in the open is not the same as trying to implicate me Jim…). This way, we all win (I lose, she wins you mean…). Everything is in order…there's nothing to worry about. I'm actually really encouraged by today's meeting. The two of you will be married for a long time. We can sort this stuff out, and you can get back to the business of being in business. That's what you need, right?"

These Cravath folks now owned Somers. Lawyers always make me feel like Bud Abbott, my who's on first confusion stems from them smiling while they knife you in your back, front, and penis. You don't feel the pain until you're fifty blocks away from the office. A guy like me is so easily disarmed with one compliment. Was the goal here to keep me from falling or to push me while I stared over the ledge?

I didn't know what to do when I got to the ground floor. Should I go home? Did I have a home? Who was Somers Gillette? Who would do what she just did? Was Cravath representing us or her?

Depression begins to hit home when you start assuming the worst, and with all my questions, I only had the worst answers. Why would they target my reputation? Lawyers speak at cocktail parties…I didn't really know the other two in that room. I didn't even trust Jim to keep his mouth shut. Everything was blurry. This would be an all day funk for sure.

The meeting was a sham in hindsight. They'd essentially stroked my concern for my wife to get me to agree to say something that was untrue. A storm was threatening and I'd become her punching bag. This would turn out to be disastrous, and I knew from disaster. Oy vey.

The Libyans Pull Out; the Mini-Dachshund Pulls In

I was one bullet away from utter destruction, not that I appreciated that yet.

I walked back to my Park Avenue office through the frozen Manhattan landscape and plopped down at my desk, overcoat still on like a real nutter. I wanted to go back to the start or else I'd fade away fast. Jenny, the new secretary, sensed I was devastated about something, maybe because I looked like a bum with my overcoat on, sitting forlornly at my desk, alone and lost in thought.

She quietly shut my office doors, doors that hadn't been closed in ten years of business (talk about symbolism). Maybe she wanted me to commit suicide? I was almost there by now, so it wouldn't have taken much to get it done.

I felt as if the whole world was against me. I'd really withdrawn from all social engagements by that time and there were at least fifteen creditor lawsuits naming me personally even though I wasn't exactly on the hook for a company's debts…That's why they call it an LLC. Creditors don't care about that shite though and their persistence only amps up when they know you live in Locust Valley.

It would only take one more mind rape from Somers to push me over the edge. Losing your wife, or having your wife pull a surprise gang-rape on you in Cravath's office, was probably as good a trick as any, but I wasn't fully there just yet. I think I'd fooled her into believing I was stronger than I actually was. My defenses were down on every flank. I had no ammo left. My troops were demoralized and we were out of food and water. Somers was society's General William T. Sherman's "total war", her "March to the Sea" marital scorched earth policy was being waged from Locust Valley to Park Avenue.

I didn't have the strength to sit in on my daughter's first grade recital let alone work alongside tiger-bankers on Park Avenue let alone fend off Lucifer. I took the LIRR to Manhasset that night in cold silence, knowing celebutante piracy and barbarism was awaiting.

I wasn't sure what to expect when I got home, the home I lived in with my three precious children, and the property that I had carefully built with my own two hands. I purposefully didn't call Somers that day, I wasn't sure if I could restrain myself. She set me up in the most unimaginable way: two adults married to each other, parents to three children, with all of the shared experiences, triumphs and tribulations that fifteen years can produce, and she was playing lawyer ball finding ways to isolate me legally and reputationally. She was tossing the marriage out like last night's trash…the spousal we no longer had more meaningful significance to her than a used packet of Hunan Taste duck sauce.

Did I have one more good reason to stay, or did she? I'd find out soon.

When I walked in the front door (my key still worked…), exhausted, dizzy, unsettled, mentally comatose, Somers was there to greet me. She had switched out of her funeral office outfit into something more winter chic, sort of an après-ski fireside ensemble, hot enough to make me numb. I'd never seen it, that's for sure. It was tight black pants, blue cashmere sweater, and pumps. She looked good enough to kill…I mean love. I wondered if that blue bra was still on.

She was already so at odds with the day's events, I mean that was the end of life as we knew it so far as I was concerned, but she stood there looking like a supermodel. Her figure was fantastic, you had to give her that. Whenever she had me beat, I could always stare at that figure, as if it compensated for the emotional malignance.

The fire was lit in her new $300K fireplace, plumes of grey smoke pouring into the great room. She had disconnected the fire alarm. She had a speech in her hand and she asked me to sit down… I felt like I was being fattened for slaughter. She pulled out the sheet and began in a stilted way,

"I've sent the kids to Ariane's for dinner. I don't want to talk about things we've gone through today. I didn't want to meet you at Cravath like that, but Jim suggested that was the best way to do it. So, sorry about that (like that just completely ends that weirdness…!). We're both big boys (actually, only you are now Somers…I'm fried…), and sometimes you gotta do what you gotta do. We're going to forget today as if it never happened, and we will grow from it. We're married Seb (Seb….hmmmm…), and we will need to just make this work for the kids. Let's kiss and make up. Sweetie, there isn't any more to say."

This was a speech she had rehearsed; any speech that Somers needed to make that could possibly contain emotion, she always wrote out.

I was looking for the sniper. My heart was under arrest anyway, so maybe she could spare the bullet.

I didn't know what the hell was going on. She practically had me on the guillotine today but now she wanted to make it work. Her words came out stilted, as if there was a broader agenda behind this. I was buffeted by her demeanor and words, not sure where I stood. The pain I felt was real alright. Her glamorous life was being hijacked by my corporate meltdown and I knew she wasn't likely to hold on.

She wanted to know how sure I was that I could still sell my company. To be fair, I didn't really know anymore…this Libyan group had become difficult to track down, but I knew they wanted my company, so I thought it was about 50/50. If they didn't buy, I could always recover. I always had.

Because I was so universally weakened, I consented to her peace offering…we made up and had sex that night. She was getting the best of me, she was simply stealing time. I should have run but I had my kids to worry about. It's true…you can run from a marriage with no kids, but you will always be married to your spouse when you have children.

I needed those Libyans to come through with the wire. They had signed the acquisition papers finally, but they definitely had one very important out: they were Libyans and it's hard to sue Libyans in Libya when you're American. They had yet to acquire any assets here in the US, so suing them to get a worthless judgment seemed stupid, even if I had the money to hire a lawyer to do so. And I didn't.

I was trying to keep payrolls met, vendors paid, and my wife content, and I seemed to be striking out at all three. When you own the ship, you go down with it and people aren't so stupid to hop on board when they see that. Society gold-diggers are first to jump ship.

It was a gimme gimme gimme mob circling my head. More lawsuits were filed. I was personally named on everything, because no one could distinguish the company from me. Somers refused to make our house telephone number unlisted, as I'd asked a few hundred times. She ate it up…she was turned on by the mayhem.

We didn't have sex but she was emotionally energized by the beatdown of me. She worked out like a fiend. She was still having sex mind you…just not with me. Every lawsuit paper served at the house she scooped up and redirected to someone other than me…Somers never informed me. She kept me in the dark about anything, making an improbable situation even more dire.

I wasn't succeeding even with my best efforts. The sun was setting quickly.

Our marriage nose-dived. When I'd lain in her arms fifteen years before in the Millbrook countryside, I thought I belonged there…now we walked past each other like total strangers, marital ghosts, and there's no worse feeling in the universe to a guy like me.

I never said a word to anyone about anything, as I spent my time solely with the kids or at work. Somers was at lunch and dinner every day with friends and the subject was always me. She told everyone about Ed visiting me, about the Cravath meeting, about our sex life. She seemed to revel in my misery. The demons were calling her and she was responding.

Maybe I was too frightened to admit the obvious. It had been good living with her…but no one was home anymore. Dreamers and devils are not a good match. Somers would never fall for shooting stars…she'd blast the fuckers to smithereens first.

Somers began to load her Four Horsemen with infoporn, suicide bombers to my reputation. These were four people I particularly disliked (not necessarily hated, but let's say I just didn't wish to be with). But the really weird thing, Somers hated these three worse than anyone.

One of the persons she brought back into her fold in was a Manhattan party for profit promoter, Polly Pullay, her buzzkill friend, the Red Horseman. "A fiery red horseman, its rider was given power to take peace from the earth…"

Polly was a red-haired missing link of a woman, forever single at 50, forever bitter at her life. She had a demented face, distorted by years of iniquitous bile…she smelled like a nursing home. She had ex-communicated herself from Locust Valley when her dad had some issues and she simply resented anyone else's success. Somers lent her money from time to time, thereby gaining Polly's undying devotion (which you could argue was actually my money, since I gave Somers so much over 15 years…ironic).

Polly slept with any man who spent a dollar on a Hershey bar for her. She was about the most indiscreet, reckless, and twisted shoulder surfing gossip I'd ever met. There wasn't a soul on this earth that she would have a kind word for. My children despised her. Polly would be useful to spread the word in Manhattan when the time was right. I would never worry about her because I knew that no one liked her, but that wouldn't prevent her from gossiping, because she had nothing else in her bag to offer anyone anyway. She needed this role like a junkie needs a drug.

Mary Johnson was the childless Locust Valley wife, the White Horseman. "A white horse rider who held a bow and was given a crown, and he rode out as a conqueror bent on Conquest."

Her husband was a great guy, an all time best guy, so why he would ever marry her was beyond me and many others. Mary was as thornily spiteful a person as the world had ever seen, just another loathsome bitter shoulder surfer. Prior to 2007, I had asked Somers to stop asking the Johnsons over because of Mary's poisonous gossip… Even Somers agreed with that assessment and that's saying something! Mary had no career, no children, she despised her own husband's children (like Gruella…), and she feasted on other people's problems. Ariane, Somers' sister who didn't have a mean bone in her body, couldn't stand the indecorous insidiousness of this woman.

Mary could not be trusted with anything, so Somers cultivated her of course. Mary too would be useful later on, for Locust Valley, Palm Beach, and Hobe Sound. Mary reminded me of Axis Sally. Mary had a similarly detached view of life, she was a self hating Catholic who wanted to bury her religious past in favor of her husband's perceived better genes.

The last person was the overweight conversation-earjacking shoulder surfer Chuck Standernly, the Pale Horseman. "A pale horse and rider named Death, and hell was following close behind him…"

Chuck is a job douche, food douche, intellect douche, credit whore, air quoting social plagiarist who lived off of his father's money…he could slow down any group without a word, though fat chance of ever shutting him up. He acted as if he was the Chairman of the ten companies he'd ever been fired from. If you visited Cairo on a family vacation last month, he just had lunch with the President of Egypt, that kind of nauseating thing. Somers named him as the one and only man in all of Locust Valley that she would never sleep with…he was her list of one. To her, he was "vile" and "smelly". He was a person of no known sharpened skills except gossip, a party promise of the worst order. She befriended him when she needed him because he could help her with the Manhattan business community. He likes Styx and Foreigner of course!!! Argh….

Her fourth horseman had always been by her side, Gruella Kincaid, the Black Horseman. "The Black horse and rider, the Famine bearer, A quart of wheat for a day's wages…" Even more on her later…

'…the haves have not a clue,'… *

She carefully began to plant blind item ideas in their four diseased heads, mostly that she was leaving me six months before she actually left me. That's either exquisite brilliance or calculated evil. The geographic planting for Somers' future schemes was deft. It took a year of careful planning, but she had them trained like no one's business. And yet, she hated them and still does. And ironically, all four hate each other…of course.

You can't say anything about this other than Somers Gillette is an Approach Oriented Narcissist of the highest order. It's hard if not impossible to plan on someone's murder a year in advance and have the temerity to execute it. Most murders are murders of passion. The Fallen Angel had to be resolute in her scheme. Also, just to somehow keep the data flow secret, that takes control. Rats are very compromisable and yet she corralled them though the end (though not after the end, as you will soon learn…). Her deliberate apocalyptic schemes were of the highest order, so much that heretics, infidels, and other unbelievers will bestow upon Somers an award for the ages, a modern day Thais Achievement Award, a trophy for her Society mantle.

Somers for some unknown reason decided that we needed another house pet in addition to our perfectly agreeable black lab, my canine alter ego. She went out and bought the nastiest miniature dachshund in the universe, a pestiferous rat she called Foxy.

She never asked any of us if it was okay…she just ran out and bought it, the only thing she ever bought in our fifteen years together. Mini-dachshund's are fine for old women and gay decorators, but families? These dogs really don't enjoy kids….hmmm, like Gruella. Foxy was belligerent to everyone, ridiculously venomous to anyone, except one person…

On June 15th, the Libyans finally called and they weren't calling to tell me I won the Tripoli Mega-Millions from the King for Life, His Excellency Muammar Ghaddafi. I had harassed their point person, Mustafa, to the point where I was sure I was a bulbous irritation, but the company was desperate and so was my marriage. And that small issue of no sex…

"Seb, we must indefinitely postpone out investment into your company. We love you, but the global economy is such a mess. Our Leader has forbidden any further external investments until we know where we stand internally. Things do not look so good right now, but times change. Just hang in there, and I promise, we will be back. And you will be a rich person indeed. By the way, I hear you are related to Lord Althorp…we know him well (I'm not related to Lord Althorp, Mustafa, but how the hell does this guy's name keep coming up…?)"

Mustafa said they were pulling out. We were toast without their investment, I was toast. The markets were wobbly and there was no way I could begin to excite another buyer. I was floored, I guess I wouldn't succeed. I didn't know where to turn. Without the Libyan acquisition, we had weeks at best. I stared at my Bloomberg

terminal and watched stock prices on the ticker. Everything was red.
My mind was playing tricks on me. I needed a shoulder to lean on.
I couldn't lift this by myself anymore.   I needed a rebound investor.

"Uhhh, Mustafa, by the way, how do you know Lord Althorp?"

"Oh, he knows everyone in the Middle East. He knows a partner of
mine here, and between you and me, Lord Althorp tried to scuttle
your deal with us. Said you were having trouble with your wife.
We don't care about that though…wives are a pain in the ass in the
Middle East…We'll be back to you, I swear my friend!"

Althorp was Ed's friend. Had Ed interfered in my acquisition, à
mettre à mal la reputation? Had my wife? On the way to
insolvency…how did people in Libya know about my marriage? I
don't even talk to my brothers about her…

In addition to the ultimate destiny with my perfect destruction,
otherwise known as my private Armageddon, I had negotiated to
buy a house in the Adirondacks. Call me crazy, I was. I'd already
laid out a non-refundable deposit of $150,000 and another $150,000
was due. That wouldn't be happening now without Libyan petro-
dollars swimming in my checking account. I called the real estate
broker immediately and told her I was bailing…the owner could
keep the $150K. I figured that wasn't the worst outcome for the
seller. Wouldn't you like to be able be paid $150,000 for no work?

Unfortunately the broker then called my real estate lawyer who then
tried to reach me, to confirm I was indeed pulling out, but he
couldn't get through to my cell. So, continuing my unbroken string
of what can go wrong will, he called the Locust Valley house and
the Morning Star (daughter of the Day Star), Ms. Somers Gillette,
picked up. Then all hell broke loose, hell being an eruption of an

order Locust Valley can only imagine since there was no equivalent ever... She took the news about as well as anyone....Not!

Round 2 in the house wars had erupted and I couldn't hear the shots from inside my office. Cruise missiles were silently guiding their way down the Long Island Sound and the East River, about to turn toward Park Avenue, my office address in their guidance system.

Somers called…me….not very happy….uhhh, actually beyond livid….quite nuclear to be clear…demented murderess to be perfectly clear. Demanded that the secretary put her through to me. The office staff could hear the warm geyser of love…not.

"There is no FUCKING way we are bailing on this house! We have to have it! I told everyone…!!"

Implying of course that by telling everyone, she wouldn't be going back on the news to anyone, with or without me. But it was my house…I'd negotiated it, I set it up to be in the kids' names only (that takes explaining, but I sensed by now that I shouldn't be putting things in her name…). This was Special Narcissism, a profession of uniqueness from a human to oneself…only trailer trash bailed on house acquisitions.

"Somers, the Libyans pulled out. I'm cooked without them. I can't agree to anything right now. I need a few months to sort things out. I thought it was fair to the owner so she can remarket the property. And the house is in the kids' name, not yours."

If you can remember what you were doing that day and saw a small yellow cloud of atomic particles above Park and 52nd, that was Somers Gillette letting me know over the phone that she was disappointed in me for putting the house in the name of the kids…uhhh, let's rephrase that some: enraged, furious, incensed, fuming, explosive, mental, murderous…yeah, that's the ticket. I didn't think I'd be allowed back home that day. The Trickster now knew I didn't trust her completely.

She wanted me to feel more worthless than any bum on the street. That wasn't hard. You know how all of us end up in the gutter at some point but some of us still look up at the stars, even there. That's me. Bear Stearns and Lehman brothers were dragging my company's corpus down, and I had a hyena in Halston chewing on my leg already. Upper Case Voice, natch,

"No we aren't!!! I just wired $150,000 from my trust to the owner. I'll buy it on my own! I don't need you! I'm so FUCKING pissed!! But if you want to do anything to save this marriage, you better come up with a way to buy me that house…Or else fuck you!! And fuck your dreams!"

Her disease was in my bones now, a cancer in my marrow, the same feeling as Gruella but worse because I slept with Somers (infrequently…). She was so far gone, she was out of my universe let alone my planet. She slammed the phone down, likely breaking that as well. This felt like a funeral, mine, with cards and flowers being left for me on the window sills by grieving neighbors, buried alive by my wife. Experience is the name we give to our mistakes…call me overqualified, bagging groceries looked like a solid career move at that juncture.

She was pissed?! I lost $6 Million on my company and yet the buzzards were circling, I hadn't had sex in a year, blowjobs in fifteen, and she just unilaterally inserted herself into my house acquisition…and likely just pissed away another $150K because she didn't call me first! When you bluff in poker, always make sure you can walk away from the table and play the next day.

Time passes and the next thing you know, your life is over. I didn't have any easy outs. No answers leapt out at me. I wasn't even horny anymore, so of course I must have been delirious. I was at death's door and she was pushing me in.

From my office window I could see the summertime lunch crowd gathering on the steps of St. Bartholomew's Church. I walked out of the office, across the street, and sat in a rear pew, alone as ever. I wasn't there to analyze architecture. Tourists came and went. I spoke with God, like all crazy people in the back pews.

"God, seriously, what the fuck? I've been a good person, and I know the mantra about only a strong man being asked to shoulder a heavy burden, but this is getting kinda ridiculous. I haven't asked for much, but I need a break. Here's the story…can you find me another investor and have them me call at my office, like in the next hour or so?"

Of course God ignored me, my church protocol was woeful …you don't go to church to ask for money, it generally works the other way. At that point I hoped heaven was overrated. The shadows of Park Avenue on a late summer afternoon just got longer.

I'd only wanted to be King of my small nuclear family, and she my Queen. This fairy tale wouldn't have a happy ending.

<u>Sun Valley Revelations</u>

Regrets were piling up on regrets inside my conscience. I needed to confront them (I'm just shamed by my cowardice now). I was a dead man walking, a society zombie. My wife the Haute Heiress was in full plumage because I was reeling, and ironically I felt that the marriage was the only thing keeping me alive. Yes she sounds like a witch, but I'd long since made a big ball of marriage, kids, and house…it all seemed as one.

We headed to Sun Valley Idaho for a long-planned family trip in July. I should have never left.

We were joined by two of Somers' sisters and their families. I'm sure I didn't smile the entire time except when my children were with me. I was preoccupied with what was going on back in New York, twenty-five employees staring at each other with nothing to do and the payroll meter continuing to click inside my personal checking account.

Somers behaved like a coiled asp, ready to strike for the smallest reason. What I remember most about the trip was being asked to unclog a stuffed toilet, which I did characteristically no questions asked. I should have been a handyman in my life. I'm likely to be one soon.

I hiked Baldy Mountain with my oldest son on the second day, and by the time we reached the top, I made a decision to let everyone go from the company and just mothball it until the markets improved. There was no alternative. I didn't have the heart to restart a bank…ugh, that seemed cruel and unusual as well. I didn't know how tolerant everyone would be. I'd tried my best, but I hadn't really succeeded.

I couldn't tell Somers about any of this, mostly because I guessed at this stage she was doing significant unnecessary damage to me from multiple fronts: Ed, Mary, Phoebe, Chuck, Gruella, and god knows how many more. I sensed big trouble brewing. Somers also knew I had $20 Million in life insurance at Northwestern Life.

I maintained the policies for over ten years. The Cravath team of supposedly independent lawyers had crafted an insurance trust on my life, which had just one beneficiary, Ms. Somers Gillette. The Trust was written irrevocably, meaning no matter what ever happened to me (death, murder, checkout line bag grocer), she was entitled to the proceeds. So I had that going for me…I was worth more dead to Somers than alive.

Oh god…just giggle a little with me here. Can you imagine giving my smoldering Angra Mainyu that kind of incentive? It was like giving Satan a sales quota bonus…he's gonna make the number no matter what. Talk about no-win. Now she had a cash incentive, in addition to her own Sexual Narcissism. Taking me down never looked sweeter. I'd stepped way over the highest bar for what can go wrong will. We were now in cosmic lunacy territory. The policies were even tax free.

On the last day of vacation, my two brothers-in-law and I headed out to play a round of golf at the Sun Valley Trail Creek Golf Course. Trail Creek is a Robert Trent Jones masterpiece finished in 1980. The course is idyllic in the summer, with incredible majestic views of the surrounding mountains. The day was sunny and about 75 degrees, not a cloud in the sky or an ounce of moisture in the air: perfect Sun Valley weather.

We were walking down the par-5 first when Billy said something to me which ended up being the complete nail-in-the-coffin, tie-up-all-loose-strings, that-explains-it, fin-de-siècle how come I never thought of that in the first place moment. It made me feel like, hey I don't think you're a fool, but what's my opinion compared to thousands of others.

"Man, you and Somers seem fairly bummed. What's the deal?"

"Just a lot of stress dude. She's pushing me so hard on money these days and she won't let up on the throttle spending-wise. The economy sucks, and I'm going to mothball the company. She's spent about $40,000 at Stoney this year alone. Scott (the other brother in law hacking away in the sagebrush) tells me he only spends about $300 a month there; Somers spends that in ten minutes. She's going to bankrupt me before the company does. Nothing's right and she's up to something; it's like I'm living with fucking Gruella, not Somers. I can't concentrate on anything. My handicap by the way is now a 12, so I need two shots a side."

"Whoa. You didn't say that before we teed off. No worries. Do you need any money?"

"More than you've got! It's a mess."

"Look, for what's it worth, she calls my wife a ton these days. Somers and Gruella have been scheming on something, and I didn't catch it all, but I know one thing. And I hate like hell to tell you this. She's definitely seeing someone else. I don't care what she says, she's cheating on you… I think she may be done with you soon."

"Jesus."

"There's something else, and I know we've never discussed this, but it's something I knew about a long time ago. I just never could figure out how or when to tell you, or whether it was even important enough to mention. And it wouldn't even be interesting if not for the fact that Somers fancies herself such a queen fucking Wasp, which she's been throwing around a lot this week at dinner. Which I fucking hate, alright. She isn't so fucking waspy man. You know Gruella's Jewish? "

"What?"

"Look, her dad was a dentist in Erie Pennsylvania. Have you ever looked at Mildred's face? And have you ever wondered why they basically hide her in some upstate nursing home that no one ever wants to visit?"

"Uhhh…guess I've never thought about it."

My words were coming out slowly, as I was absorbing what was being told…Somers was a certified, stamped member of the Locust

Valley wasp elite. This wasn't computing as we walked up to our balls to hit our second shots.

"I hadn't thought about it either Sebastian, until my wife started spending ridiculous amounts of money on new fashion every year, and one day I kidded her by saying she was such a Jap. Well, guess what? She came clean. She told me that her grandmother had convinced her own daughters to disguise their identities, so they could move up in the world. You have to remember when Mildred was born…We're talking before 1900. Jews couldn't get into Stoney or National; they still can't for the most part. But back then, forget it; they couldn't even drive the roads let alone be members. They couldn't caddie.   So, Mildred wanted to guide her daughters to better lives than what she had. Mildred was brilliant. She saw a better life, but the only way to get there was by hiding her own. So they went to Erie to start over, changed their last name, did a few things surgery wise, and assumed a newer, less obvious last name. When Mildred's husband died, Mildred moved back east, and the girls, Gruella and Constance, looked like fucking Ralph Lauren models practically. Remember, David was a dentist; he knew other doctors. The rumor is they changed everything about themselves. You do that to a little girl like Gruella back then, that little girl comes back determined to be one of the wasps they were reconfigured to look like; how could they not. If your mom changed your appearance, you would assume she was doing it for a good reason. Gruella came east to be a wasp."

"Yeah, but how would Jack, or even Ed, marry her? Those guys are fairly hard core-Christian types."

"She fooled them all Sebastian. She's fucking evil. They never knew. Go try to find the birth or death records of David Miller of Erie PA….gone. Go ask the nursing home where Mildred lives for her records…Gone. Gruella wiped the slate….like a trained FBI agent. No one can know Gruella's past unless you connect the dots. Constance's first husband was Jewish…look at Mildred….Dentist in

Erie…First names of David all around…No church background and still no interest…Gruella doesn't even know the Lord's Prayer, and I only found that out when I watched her during one of our kid's baptisms (I did the same at my wedding!…). Somers' need to be Queen fucking wasp…take away Gruella's Peroxide blond hair….Don't you see? Like I said, who gives a shit, except you have to know your wife, and man, you've been misled by a lot of things about Somers, this just being one."

"Holy shit. You sure? I mean, she doesn't look Jewish (sorry, I said it…). Jesus. That explains that fucking miniature dachshund I guess."

"It explains more than that. Your wife, queen of New York Society and now LV, it's a lie. Your wife, my friend, is Jewish, no different than the people she pisses on. I wouldn't bring it up with her though…let her do it when she's ready, if ever."

Queen Mary I of England, daughter of King Henry VIII and Katherine of Aragon, was the ultimate self-hater and burned over 200 Protestants at the stake. She hated people like me. She was also prepared at one point to turn her kingdom over to the Spanish. The great thing is she's known forever as the breakfast of champions, not Wheaties, the "Bloody Mary", a fine wasp morning pick-me-up hangover remover. Was this Somers' vituperation, a self hater who took her anger out on her husband? More on this later…

We hit our balls...golf balls that is. They could have hit my other balls and I wouldn't have felt a thing. Billy drilled his to ten feet from the green, I ended up in a trap, and Scott was buried in a bush somewhere about a hundred yards up a mountain wrestling wolves.

When we both got to the green, I had an important question, one of such depth and scale, one so fascinating that centuries of social scientists might pursue the answer as to meaning and relevance, a possible game changer in the evolution of society, that no man, country, or golf ball should stand in its way, it had to be asked then and there, this was no time for weakness:

"Does your wife give you blow jobs?"

He howled.

Now, you're probably thinking, what's the big deal, so what, your wife's Jewish and she doesn't give head (to her husband anyway…). You wouldn't care unless your wife's entire existence was predicated on NOT being that. My castle had been built entirely on sand. Houston, we have a problem…I was reeling.

It's hard to capture into a coherent message what I was thinking. My head spun a thousand times. It was as if my center of gravity had lost its positioning. It was all fake, just one long flipping plastic back-story, our history together. I was a broken man looking at the 2nd Tee at Trail Creek. I could only think one thing.

"That mini-dachshund…damn."

Billy, Scott, and I were mostly silent for the rest of the round. I shot a 96, worst score in fifteen years. My eschatology was near.

"How Did Nick Ever Marry Her?"

The shite was about to hit the fan. Was it all amusing to her, or deadly serious? Did she want to decapitate me if I rose again, trapping me in a perpetual hell?

On the plane ride back to Kennedy, I kept thinking about Nick Gillette and how he could have married a Jewish girl in the sixties. I never said a word to Somers. Was it even legal then? Those times weren't favorable for a marriage between old wasp and new order, especially in a town like Locust Valley. Seriously, that would have been grounds to kick you out of most clubs. How did Gruella pull it off? I mean, Nick's the best, hands down, man you'll ever meet…I mean that for the entire world. He can say whatever he wants about me, but I'll love that guy until my last breath is drawn. And Gruella's the anti-that….the opposite of the best, the extreme worst, *Le Tag-Hag Voland du Monde s'il vous plait.*

As we flew over Erie Pennsylvania, I was determined to find out all I could.

And I always remembered Granny Gillette's admonition to me about Somers and her Mom: they are not like you and me. Maybe Count Dracula had a sister…"And after you deliver the message, you will remember nothing. I now say…Obey!"

Gruella looked like a shiksa. I'd have bet my life before I found out she was more like Ilsa Koch, the She-Wolf of the Nazi SS and not a target of the She-Wolf. Gruella likely never attended synagogue, spun the dreidel, or lit the menorah. She was her own She-Wolf.

Nick Gillette had two things in his favor when he divorced Gruella which I didn't…Locust Valley was his home and he had Gillette money to make her fuck off. She high-tailed it as far as she could get from Locust Valley, to San Francisco. She swore revenge on Nick and all of his friends and especially Deezy. Before you start thinking I have even an ounce of anti-Semitism in me, you can fast forward (though I wouldn't) to the Chapter called Dymphna's Corner…it's all explained there.

Somers Gillette would never get kicked out of Locust Valley. She'd make sure of that. She would learn from the master, and she would survive. Somers is always where it's at in LV, always big pimpin' at the society mixers…her sun rises in Oyster Bay and sets in Glen Cove. She had all the angles covered and wouldn't let any party for profit go on without her there to watch her back.

Just to capture the essential spirit of Gruella Kincaid, recall just one story from a billion, this one involving grandchildren while in France, grandchildren being the least favorite of all Gruella's creatures (I have so many of these, my editor wanted a second book). Somers and I came to Paris with our children…I had been fighting going there since Day One of Ed's nomination (as a family that is), but Somers prevailed and we left Kennedy for Charles de Gaulle.

When we arrived, one of our children was thirsty. I found a cold Coca Cola in one of the stateroom refrigerators and handed it to my daughter. I didn't keep my eyes on her while I unloaded the bags and helped Somers figure out how to survive a week with Herr Gruella. After fifteen minutes, my daughter appeared in the hallway and handed me the still-unopened can of Coke. I was surprised she hadn't opened it, but I didn't give it too much thought.

"Daddy, can you open my Coca Cola? I'm so thirsty."

"Of course Sweetie. I would have thought you'd already be on your third by now!"

"I couldn't open the tab…they're different here in France."

We were in the hallway of the fourth floor of the Residence where the Ambassador lives. The hallway is a regal setting, wide and long with beautifully appointed and massively expensive wallpaper. There are priceless art pieces on the walls and a long oriental runner covering the floor. I popped the top and what followed was a comedic explosion of fluid so great and so long lasting, I thought I'd been spoofed. The soda went in every direction, on every art piece, all over the rug, all over the wall, and all over ourselves. It wouldn't stop. When it was over, everything looked like a Jean Michel Basquiat painting…pure chaos. She had been running in the halls with the Coke in her hands.

Gruella thankfully was out walking her mongrel dog, and we figured we had at least an hour before she returned. So all five of us set about working to clean up the mess. We brought every cleaning item out of the closets we could find, and even the Residence staff chipped in. They sensed doom…the house Boss would not stand for imperfections no matter the intent or lack thereof. All in all, ten persons cleaned the hallway for an hour. We vacuum-dried the floor and wall, and by the time we were done, the place was cleaner than it had been prior to the soda exploding. Everyone exhaled and was satisfied we would not be caught by The Slanderer temporarily overseeing the Residence.

Security called up to the house staff when Gruella returned to the gate (even these people had wizened up to her nuttiness…security would warn everyone of her impending gloom), and we quickly hustled into our non-chalant poses as if nothing had happened. Gruella, like Somers, knows when there's too much of a good thing, she's wary and prone to investigate…which is exactly what she did. She came upstairs and barely said hello. The whiskers on her rat nose were excited, and something came up deuces.

She got on all fours and looked under every bed and chair and sofa. This comi-absurdity lasted for ten minutes, while the five of us were lined up in a criminal identification pose. Just when we thought we'd escaped…Gruella came in with it-runs-in-the-family Upper Case Voice

"What the FUCK is this?!?!"

If looks could kill….I was more than dead. I was being dragged behind a pickup truck on a dirt road. It was all Agentic Narcissism of the worst order, exaggeration and self importance. Does anyone ever give this woman any attention? She hijacks her family to be slaves to her preposterousness. And by the way, Somers is always so quiet around the mother Angra Mainyu…as if the cat has her tongue, in the presence of a greater evil.

Gruella had found the one and only (and I mean that!) spot of water, not even soda, that someone had failed to dry, on the floor, about twenty paces from the Vesuvian explosion of soda. In the dimly lit hallway, we assumed it was the Coca Cola so I copped to the crime immediately, not wanting to emotionally damage the children any more with her Old Scratch-like investigation. I took the blame, as I always do.

"Uhhh, sorry about that Gruella…I opened a soda and it exploded (my daughter was shaking next to me, more because of her grandmother, but also because she sensed collateral damage standing so close to me…)."

"Well, that's really something (a dismissive haughty finality…I hate it when people speak like that…)! Did you ask the staff to help? Because if so, you will owe them money for their going beyond the call of duty (I'm happy to but do you know that they hate your guts and love my kids because we are human toward them?…)."

My kids didn't know whether to laugh or cry. She eventually had to lie down because this was so traumatic…you've never met such deranged narcissism and delusion. To her, it was as if someone died, she treated the soda tale that insanely emotionally. There wasn't a stain anywhere. It was simply a need of hers to be overly dramatic (hmmm, like mother like daughter) because there was a trapped audience and the world's a stage. You'll never meet any other human like her, I assure you.

My kids and I scampered over to the Jardin de Tivoli, leaving Gruella and Somers by themselves. On the way over and all during the vacation, I muttered a thousand times: *Va te fair foutre, putain d'espece d'encule!!* Not that Gruella would ever know what I was saying…she doesn't speak the language.

As Bogart said, "We'll always have Paris."

The Club Tennis Championship

My mind wasn't twisted, or even badly sprained for that matter…it was in shock trauma.

My heart? Well that was still alive, but barely. I wasn't that easily dissuaded by my unfolding personal disaster to simply waive the white flag, even to a Magical Narcissist celebutante. Marriage meant more to me than quick capitulation. I'd been in love in 1992 and assumed I'd always be…in spite of the ongoing felony murder, but my soul was in such rough shape I wasn't sure of my stamina.

Obviously I didn't bring up the Jewish heritage thing when we got back from Sun Valley. The less I said to Somers at this stage about anything outside the weather, the better.   Who knows, maybe we could survive.

I was devastated by the mothballing of the company. There went my $6 Million investment. There went my pride. There went my ego. There went ten years of hard work. And there went 25 employees and their families. There went everything frankly outside of my kids. I could resurrect it, but banking…argh. I just hate bankers, sorry.

The Adirondack house was now a $300K loss, not the manageable $150K that I alone needed to suffer by flying naked into the storm. Somers had impulsively allowed her worst instincts to get involved in something she never needed to get involved on, just another irrational emotional decision that you knew I'd pay for in the end.

I myself was in emotional meltdown, trying to find moments of clarity to determine what if any steps were available to me. In some weird way, I deluded myself into thinking that perhaps it wasn't so bad, because at least I no longer had to worry about all the employees. I could start over again, Somers and I could sell the house, pay off our debt, and we could rent again for a year or two while I recovered. My delusion came from thinking that Somers was in this at all with me…ha.

I knew I could run a company again, just this time without bankers. I wanted a real company with real people and real products. The kid wanted to stay in the picture!

Every August, Somers and I took the children to a private club in upstate New York for three weeks. Normally I would spend a solid week there and then bookend two long weekends. The Adirondack Club was even waspier than Stoney. The members can look a tad inbred after one too many generations of Anglicanism. You'd have to say that Somers and her three sisters were by far the most attractive women who visited, which genetic mixing can accomplish.

This was my favorite spot in the annual calendar of vacations. It was a comfort zone of outdoor goodness, with hiking, fishing, swimming, canoeing, golf, and tennis. Every night was blazer and tie at the main clubhouse. A couple of weeks there and you would be completely removed from reality. Which helps when reality is Manhattan. We loved it as a family. Somers insisted again on being the name member, even though I paid the dues and initiation fee…natch. That would end up being a brilliant signature move of hers, she's a total club kitten.

I was unsure if I should even go up that summer. I was gob-smacked business-wise and I needed to get back to work. I needed to find a company where I could make money again, for me, my family, and my partners. The problem was the world's economy had cratered. I could sit at a desk all I wanted, no one would be doing anything for a while, especially late August. So I went upstate. To be with my kids…and that wife of mine… She could re-energize me, no? She was about to pinch the oxygen hose to the terminally ill patient.

Every year I played in the men's tennis championships, which were considered to be the sine qua non of athletic events at the AC. Winning had become something of a mission for me, and the kids…they knew I had gotten some bum luck the prior few years. I thought that by playing in that year's tournament, at least I could take my mind off business if not possibly finally get that name on the board.

The previous year, Somers and I had watched the men's final from the club porch. Somers elected to stay for the entire match. It didn't strike me as strange that she wanted to watch it, because everyone knows everyone at the AC and its good form to stick around and cheer friends on. There were about sixty people watching that year. The same two guys had made the final for the last ten years, and neither was over 35 years yet.

I made it to the final in 2007, at nearly fifty years of age. There were about seventy-five people watching the match. I was pumped and playing well.

Somers came late to the match and left early, maybe she saw five games. That may not strike you as strange, but there isn't a match played in this tournament where the wives of the players don't stay and watch the entirety. Hell, most of the club stays and watches. My kids saw Somers leave during the second set and even they were confused why she would leave with Dad ahead. I noticed, but I was also focused on the game…oddly since I'd just lost $6 Million, so her leaving didn't trip me up too badly. If the match went three sets, maybe I would have been ground down by my opponent, who was fifteen years younger. Great guy by the way. It wasn't likely I'd be smelling the winner's podium again any day soon.

I won but the tournament had a hollow ring. My opponent and I hugged at the net…it had been a war, an honorable one. Somers had elected to take a Lake Road walk with another club member, a married man who had no interest in tennis. She was getting the best of me…laying me bare.

My kids were ecstatic and I was happy for them, but kids don't want to hear their Old Man brag forever about his accomplishments, they want to tell you about theirs!

I walked alone back to our cottage on the club's grounds, just off the second green. I opened the screen door and Somers was there stretching. She was dressed in her hiking outfit, red Patagonia shorts, Columbia hiking shoes, and gray long-sleeved shirt. Still hot as a society cougar can be. I was in my sweaty tennis whites, which isn't a great outfit to wear when you're about to enter into hand to hand combat. Beast hiker versus tennis preppy…I looked like such a pussy.

I held up the trophy so she could see, but she barely batted an eye, gave me the highway salute for no apparent reason, and just continued to stretch. May as well say something,

"Somers, how come you didn't watch the match today? The kids wanted you out there, and so did I. Why did you just flip me off?"

"Sebastian, there will be many more matches to watch. Tennis means nothing to me. Congratulations. You finally got what you wanted. I'm really happy for you. I have some things on my mind…it's got nothing to do with you (everything had everything to do with me by then…)."

Somers said this with the conviction of milquetoast. Burnt, stale, wet milquetoast with raccoon pee all over it.

"Thanks, I guess. If you're in a bad mood, we can skip it. I'm happy I won though. My name's gonna go on the board at least. Hey, there's something else I wanted to talk with you about. My company is really suffering. I need to mothball it for a while so we have got to cut back on family expenses. Everything is out of control. The clubs, the nanny, the parties, the annual funds. I guess saying this on a vacation is kind of ironic but it is what it is. Everything just needs to be more rational, okay? I don't have the ability to pay for it anymore. I'm sorry, I just don't. I need a few months to get my crap back together. This club is fine, because we don't come here often and the kids love it, so do you and I, but can we talk about everything else?"

"Sebastian, if we need money, I have money. But you have to pay that loan off first. That's your responsibility and I'm not helping you with it."

"Well, the loan isn't being paid 'off' any day soon. No one is going to buy my company when I'm icing it for a while…Why don't we just sell the house and start over…the kids won't care if we sell the house. It's more important to them that we stay together than anything. They could live in a tent for all they care. I figure I have $4-5 Million of excess equity by now. That would cover everything, leave us about $2miilion extra, and we could rent a great place for a year."

"We're not living in a tent Sebastian, for god's sake. Just get your act together. Money doesn't grow on trees! Go start for a hedge fund; those guys seem to make money. And it's my house, not yours. We'll sell it when and if I want to, and I don't want to, so drop it!"

I felt as if Rod Tidwell was in the room, shouting at me 'Show me the money!!!' I'd join her in some weird Gregorian chant exalting money. Somers would be a fantastic sports agent if she didn't prefer murdering husbands more. She wanted me back on the chain gang, not taking self-empowerment courses.

"Somers, I can't start a hedge fund. First off I have so much shite I still need to clean up in the old company; secondly I'm not much of a public stock guy."

"Well, if you don't start making money, then we are going to have serious problems, much more serious than what you have now. I know about your old company problems. Trust me (I did…)."

"I can make money Somers…I just need some time. And like what other serious problems?"

"I'm not going to say…but I will say this…I will not go down with you. I guarantee it (no shite…I got the sense you wouldn't go down after the eightieth call informing me about your affairs…). I worked too hard to get myself to where I am to be seen with someone who isn't what they claim to be. Mr. Big Shot Business-Man (what…?). And by the way, the house is mine; remember, you signed it over to me (yes, when you were having a psychotic meltdown in our front yard in front of the children and I didn't care anyway whose name it was in…did you?…)!"

Her words are weapons…believe me. Sharper than steel knives. The heartache and the pain were overwhelming. You can't easily remove her words once they're plunged and when she says something, she sticks to it, lunacy or not. A narcissist's worst trait.

"Is your goal to keep cutting me Somers? I'm bleeding, you've got me cut wide open, and you can't even see it. How about just doing something for us for once in your selfish life?"

"Spare me the drama you fucking fag!"

I hadn't been called a fag in a long time, certainly not by a female of the human species! Even gays didn't have the dramarama of this woman. I felt like I was talking to a first-grader. It was a YouTube moment.

Above all, love each other deeply, because love covers over a multitude of sins. Offer hospitality to one another without grumbling.
-- 1 Peter 4:8-9

I'm fairly sure of this…I never, ever said I was a 'big-shot businessman', far from it. If anyone ever asked me what I did, I'd always say my job was keeping my head above water, about as self-deprecating a guy you'll ever know. Somers was projecting again, something she wished I'd said. Her lack of empathy was a result of her grandiose self-absorption, her Special Narcissism, where she simply was and is better than you. Her vulgarity was simply a confirmation of the moral self-righteousness. My guess now is that she told her friends that I was a big-shot businessman.

I snapped.

"Somers, if we're talking about saying we're one thing, but when in fact we're something else, I heard another rumor, this time thankfully not about adultery… How come you never told me you're Jewish? I'm sure Locust Valley would love to know that."

The air hung still. She glowered at me. She knuckled up. I wanted to take the words back immediately. I needed a change of atmosphere quick.

The same flames that came when she tossed the plate of asparagus at my head were rising up inside her body, coming to her forehead. If Somers Gillette had a pistol on her that very second, there isn't one moment's doubt in the universe that she would have fired and never blinked. And she wouldn't miss either. And to be sure, she'd plug those extra few rounds into my skull, standing over me akimbo, laughing like a lunatic.

We were ten paces from each other in the large living room of the cottage, with twenty taxidermy animal heads hanging from the wall. They were all staring at our epic mental showdown, high noon again in the land of trust funds and country clubs. Somers sure could pick rental cottages by the way. The air was heavy with not just the craziness of asking about family secrets, but also the fact that taxidermy and I seemed to be on a one-way collision course. My head was on that wall next! The Princess of Darkness, the Lord of the Underworld, was coming at me. No wonder some animals eat their young.

Somers raised her fists as if she was going to come charging. She clenched them tightly. She thought long and hard for a minute, then…

She exhaled slowly, staring at me silently, like in the pool fifteen years before…that dreadful I'm taking a break in the battle quiet. And then, she just smiled, in an obviously phony, snarky way, loudly painting a mental image for me that I'd crossed the line of no return, that the seduction of me by a beautiful woman had worked it's magic and my soul now captured. I'd jumped the society shark and I wasn't coming back. Lower case voice,

"You know what Sebastian. No one knows what my Mom's background is. She's a mutt. And, you better never repeat what you just said to anyone, ever, or that will be the end of you. So far as the house, you may have paid for everything, but I have news for you…it's in my name. I get it no matter what. Get dressed for the cocktail party for profit. Thirty minutes. There will be about fifty people there tonight, so don't wear those fucking flip-flop Teva pieces of shit. Oh, and don't forget to pay your life insurance premium! Just kidding, sort of. Get a move on…"

That was weird. Somers didn't erupt like I thought she would, she was in total control. I thought she would go loco on me for asking about the Jewish thing, but instead, she had party plans. Another dreadful forced smile, shoulder surfing cocktail party with fifty of my nearest and dearest…ugh. Would she ever stop with the dog-park insanity? Guaranteed she doesn't make her next husband do this…

"You know what Somers, you don't know what you want and that scares the crap out of me. I'm not fearful of you because you're honest, I'm scared because you're flipping mental."

The rest of the vacation was awful, like avoiding a snake in a cage. I took a walk in the woods when we went to the cocktail party while Somers did her bad boundaries thing with the guests.

Here we were on Golden Pond practically, and there was no way she would ever be my Kate Hepburn…no way I'd ever hear, "Listen to me Mister. You're my knight in shining armor. Don't you forget it. You're going to get back on that horse, and I'm going to be right behind you, holding on tight, and away we're gonna go, go, go!" I think it was more likely that she'd spray rounds from her AR-15 at me as I kayaked the Lower Lake.

The end of summer shadows grew long. After breakfast Sunday, the five of us left for Locust Valley. Somers didn't say one word on the way down, but she pecked away on her Blackberry for the entire ride, huddled over in Blackberry Prayer.

The clock was ticking and a bomb was about to go off, stuffed up my sphincter as far as it could possibly go. I'd been a hero for all of three hours, winning the tennis championship for the kids. It was nearly time to tune my guitar to sad. Normally losers are the one who stand small. Good bye to all that…

A Week at The Links

I was withdrawing from my addiction to her, but like any withdrawal, the pain was intense. Sadly, the darkest hours of summer were upon us. So summer ended and school started, the private school Groundhog Day procession all over. My mental band was on strike.

On September 2, 2007, Somers surprised me (and ten couples from Locust Valley) with a birthday party at a nice-for-Long-Island Mexican restaurant, Besito. By the way, woe to the fool who throws Somers Gillette a surprise party…Somers had forever stated that if I ever threw her a surprise party, she'd kill me and she would (a woman in Locust Valley once put together a small surprise birthday lunch for Somers and Somers actually fainted…because of the surprise; when she got home that day, she cursed the woman out to me like you've never heard and that was the last we saw of her for two years). Surprises take control away, and Somers needs control. It's the Magical Narcissist in her.

The bill for my surprise birthday dinner was $10,892…Patron, Dom Perignon, etc… I guess we didn't have money problems. This was sheer audacity, an unsuspecting uppercut to my jaw.

We drove home silently. I was more than a little miffed that we'd spent that kind of money when she knew things were tight for us…or for me I guess. The tequila kicked in thankfully. We got in bed and pro-forma spooned. That led to an erection (mine, not hers, though few doubt she could do it), which led to the first marital sex we had in over a year. Whenever we had sex, I deceived myself into thinking we had made a turn for the better…Iblis was just teasing my brain nodes. It was a thin hope, but I could find footing on the smallest star.

After sex, Somers rolled toward me not away, something she had never done. She grabbed my hand and said,

"Remember Sweetie, it's not over til it's over. Things happen for a reason."

Whatever that meant… She fell asleep again like her usual light switch way…the sleep slut knew the E.L.E. was near. I was restless for hours, but I was worn out too. So tired I couldn't sleep.

I got out of bed at 5:30 AM the next day, potentially re-energized, got dressed, kissed a still-sleeping Somers on the forehead, and drove in to the city for work. That was our last kiss ever unless you want to include the times she told me to kiss her ass over the next few years. There was still a lot of pain inside, but I was determined to make it work. That wouldn't last long…or more precisely, it would last for just 3 more hours.

At 9:00 AM exactly, our thousand-dollar-an-hour Cravath lawyer, Jim Vander Hoorst, rang me at my Manhattan office. By that time, Somers and I had had sex all of nine hours ago. The markets were about to open…the futures were down as I remember. I took his call thinking he wanted to discuss the irrevocable life insurance trusts I had set up for Somers.

Unfortunately, he wanted to discuss something else. And he no longer represented us, he represented her. Last night had been her last dance, but the E.L.E. was not quite even this. Somers Gillette was now playing lawyer ball and Cravath had green-lit her fatwa….the suicide bombers were coming right behind.

Jim informed me that a Cravath process server in a Mets cap was standing outside my building with divorce papers (from my wife, not Cravath, though it felt one and the same…). If I didn't want to embarrass myself in front of colleagues he said, I should excuse myself, go outside, and accept service without a fuss. He said it would appear as if I was buying tickets to that night's game, Mets/ Cardinals. Rain was threatening, who would buy baseball tickets with that kind of forecast? Typical lawyer...What's up with Harvard grads anyway, does anyone there choose an honorable profession?

Either my toast to Somers was really god- awful, or that woman had it in for Labor Day. She just flat out pancaked the marriage. Smack.

And not that I am a stickler for the legal profession's code of ethics, but hadn't Jim and Cravath represented both wife and husband until that day? Was the firm allowed to choose sides like we were kids? Didn't they have to recuse themselves or had I been watching too much TV? And what did that word irrevocable mean anyway? Could I get my insurance back? Wouldn't she still be incentivized to kill me?

I walked out of the office building and greeted Mr. Met. He asked me my name.

"Are you Sebastian Graham?"

"Yes."

"Would you sign here please?"

He had a sealed package, the seal was in dark green. I could hear a violent thunderstorm in the distance. I could feel the earth being swallowed in the infinite abyss, the vials of sea, mankind, water, animal life, ships, crops, and land violently being torn apart. Sort of.

I signed, and then he said,

"Marriage sucks dude. Tried it twice, now I'm a process server. I could make more money at Home Depot than serving guys like you divorce papers, but Home Depot won't hire me because my ex-wife bankrupted me…Home Depot says I'm a credit risk and can't be trusted with cash registers! Cravath doesn't care about credit risk when all I have to do is deliver papers. And they have excellent medical plans…the best. Sorry to hand these to you. Women are real pains in the ass (you don't know the half of it mate…)."

He gave me two inches of white papers. All I could read, because the horror leapt out at me as if I was on the front page of the Journal, was….

Petitioner Gillette versus Defendant Graham

So, tell me again…why does it always rain on me? She had found her salvation…lawyers!   Avec l'horreur qui l'entourait, il a fallu qu'elle trouve une voie de sortie, un salut. L'avocat!

I'd loved Somers so deeply for so long and it was all going to waste…there's no worse feeling in the universe. The heart is such a debatably useless organ of emotion…I could really do better my next life without it!

I'd find out firsthand…how to live without a heart, that is. She'd tear it out later that morning, actually in just a few more minutes. I kept thinking, hadn't she just had sex with me nine hours before?! She'd have no guilt about that, I guess. Still, how weird… The sex was the last mental mind-fuck she'd toss my way, surely intended to destabilize the Defendant. Genius. She knew my ultimate weakness.   I applaud the depravity. I was certifiably insane, it worked.

I could hear a sad movie's end playing in the back of my head…Tears were streaming down my face and that woman didn't even have the physiological ability to cry…how's that for irony, or at least a horrible mismatch?   The process server stood there with me, hand on my shoulder,

"Hearts break every day Buddy. There's another woman somewhere out there for you…there always is."

I guess he was right. And then he disappeared into the Park Avenue human scrum.   He was an apparition. I wasn't sure I could handle it anymore, I was so tired of starting over again. Somers would be fine...me, a whole other story brother. I play golf…

The word divorce had never passed between our lips up until that moment…separation maybe, divorce never. So far as I knew, Somers and I were a couple determined to see things through to the end, no matter how brutal she could be or how many destructive shenanigans she would ever be up to. Nor did we ever see a marriage counselor or talk to a family friend before she filed…

I knew she was a lunatic about a lot, highly impetuous, not given to deep thought about anything except social climbing, but still…Wasn't this a tad abrupt? We'd had that sex that night… Who does that the night of the filing? Was that really her parting gift, so carefully thought through? Would this divorce hold up in court? We had three small children who needed us…

Somers wanted to blow the universe up in one explosion. Don't look in the mirror…just break the fucking glass and clean up the mess afterward. She knew the price of everything and the value of nothing.

There would be no way that she would sit down like a rational adult and debate the ripple effects this surely would have on the kids. Debating trivialities like collateral damage would be insignificant factor to her. If you know Somers, once she makes up her mind and announces it to others, there's not a thing in the world you can do to change it. She'd rather starve to death than admit a mistake. Somers and I were getting a divorce. I felt used. She'd leave with no love left to my name. I never thought it would end this way, no reasons offered, as if asking why was a threat to her.

Was I allowed back home that night…was it still my home? I'd slept there every night for ten years since we moved in and had practically built or conceived every nook and corner. It had everything that meant anything to me, my children, letters, pictures, videos. I had no emotional or mental equilibrium.

The kids talk to me about everything and they live in fear of Somers' volcanic temper. She could sell to them as long as she wanted, but nothing short of my death would convince them that their Dad wasn't there for them. She fully well understood that…. So death became an even better option, with a cash prize. The perfect sky of family was now ripped open and apart, compliments of Somers and her emotions.

As I was staring at the divorce filing, Somers called me on my cell phone, like she had a telescope trained from one of the skyscrapers watching down at me. I stared up at the buildings, looking for the scope and expecting the tracing arc of a bullet floating straight for my head. You never want to underestimate your enemy. General John Sedgwick's last words came when he remarked during a battle in the Civil War that , "They couldn't hit an elephant at this distance", and promptly was felled by a sniper's rifle. I had motivation to stay sharp.

"Sebastian (a very formal tone, like what I had heard fifteen years before on her home answering machine…). You need to spend the week in the city at The Links. I've told the kids that you are on a business trip, so just say that to them for now. Come meet me Friday at the house at 6 PM. The kids will be gone. We can speak then. I don't want you to call me before then. Thank you."

Click. The ultimate Hollywood hang-up, where you are expected to know what to do next, but I didn't. I could hear her reading off of a paper, and I also thought I heard another voice behind her.

*'…If I don't fall apart, will my memory stay clear, So you had to go, and I had to stay here, But the strangest thing to date, So far away, and yet you feel so close, '… **

I don't know if this is a common refrain from all divorced couples, but I hated the formality of our new relationship, as if you can just sweep the old relationship into the fire and pretend as if all of it never mattered. Someone you knew so well and loved, and you sense her only moves now were prepping for battle. The real Somers was about to surface.

I'd simply tried too hard, true love was her kryptonite. For every ounce I gave, she'd have to go backwards on the scale that much more, to permanently unglue us. Unfortunately, I'd given her my all, which meant…ugh.

The week ground by slowly. I called the kids every night, fibbing to them as asked that I was on a business trip. Somers had taken the liberty of booking me a room at The Links, even though that was my club and it was for men only. You can guess that Club employees had seen this picture a thousand times. When a member has marital troubles, they often go to one of the private clubs in Manhattan to sleep for a night or a month. I think this is what the clubs are really there for, divorces.

Friday came after what felt like a year, with me avoiding anyone I knew in the city for four days. I drove out to Locust Valley (it just so happened that that Monday I had driven in…meanwhile, my parking bill for four nights was $280…just another in the endless avoidable expenses I attributed to Somers).

I arrived at the house two hours later, sweating. Getting to Long Island on a Friday is crazy, as the drive should take about 25 minutes with no traffic. Everyone says the LA traffic is the worst, but I always figured that's because statisticians had just given up on Long Island. No traffic can be worse than our's.

The house looked the same, except it felt different, like the energy of the place had been sucked away. Somers hadn't done any major remodeling in those four days, but she had feng shue'd the place into a Hades-like felonious aura, Beelzebub's den. Only the children's presence would counter what she had wrought, but they weren't home.

I pulled into the front brick courtyard, parked, and got out, unsure on my feet, slightly nauseous, and supremely nervous. My dog came bounding out to greet me. I missed her. She licked my chin for a minute, until I sensed another, more ominous presence.

Somers was standing in the front doorway…like a cosmic raven's dark shadow. I wasn't hearing any music at all.

"I Want a Divorce"

"Come in Sebastian…First, I have something to say to you, so just listen to me, and then we can talk."

Here was practiced speech number 2, the initial anesthesia, the marksman's walking around the target to be sure of the best shot angle. I didn't sense I was still her arm candy, more her next taxidermy kill.

I guessed it wasn't the best time to bring up the fact that our picture memories were no longer scattered around the house…it appeared as if I'd been excised already. I also guessed I shouldn't bring up the fact that what I really needed now was the kids, not what she was about to unload.

Somers and I sat down in our living room, errr, her living room, the one with my paintings. The picture frames that used to have me in them were already missing…holy shite did she move fast! She was dressed in almost manly khaki pants, a plain white button down shirt, and chuck converse sneakers (like what young girls wear…). This must be the new look. She looked improbably younger, Dorian Graying backwards, while I'd metastized into a Quasimodo death spiral. And that was just my body, the damage to my soul was much worse.

She pulled out a two-page, typed fatwa, which she began to read with indecorous confidence. She should be a politician or sports agent, no doubt. Her lies flow like fine wine and if there's a hangover to pay, drugs compensate. This was Inflated, Special, Agentic, Selfish, Results Oriented Narcissism, with a marital contract as its bullseye.

"Sebastian. We need to talk (I got the sense immediately that only she would be talking…). I want to thank you for fifteen years of marriage, and for being a great father to our three children (this sounded more like a DMV employee telling me I failed a driver's test…). I want a divorce (if you've ever ordered a deli sandwich, the lack of your emotional content in ordering said sandwich would be the precise pitch of how she just said this…). The reasons for this are complex and will need months of deliberation, but I am resolute in my decision, so let's not debate the why and let's instead focus on how best to cocoon the children (here come the lies…). We will have time to settle our financial affairs and so that too is best left for a future date (though I suspect you want everything and then some…). I do not want you in my house. I do not want you to hang out at my house. We can split time with our children evenly, and we will always be together at major events for the children (when Somers tosses you overboard, there is no 'we' in the future…the spousal we is simply telling you that you just lost…). I need money (she didn't need a dime…). You should determine what amount you are best able to pay me every month, and you can send me a check for that amount (my choice…? doubtful…)…We will need to have lawyers determine the most appropriate alimony amount later on, so I am asking that you simply come up with a number that is workable for you in the meantime (here come the lawyers…). The house and all its contents are mine (uhhh, wait a sec, I bought everything…). If you want to have the children on the weekends, I will first need to see your new residence, and secondly will need to approve of it so the children can sleep there (I haven't exactly bought a second house yet, since this very second is the first we have ever discussed divorce…). I will end this letter by repeating what I started with. You are a fine father. No, you are the best father that I have ever known (this doesn't sound like it counts for much though does it…). I have told many people this in the last few days (who have you been discussing this with?…). Our children are fine individuals, and we both love them very much. Let's work together to make certain that they are OK (well, I will, but I get the sense you are about to go on a society bender, leaving the kids far behind…). Somers."

I didn't know if I could breathe. No break is clean I suppose. Still, the rehearsed legal speech was such a slap….I wanted to say to her man up, but I was the man, or you know, I hoped I was (depended on her mood swing du second). Maybe she needed the crutch of the rehearsed speech or else she'd break down crying...nahhh. Why do I constantly give her credit when she deserves none?

The words I want a divorce may not have the same ring of finality to a human as when a Somers Gillette utters them. When she says it, you're cooked. I didn't have the confidence in myself anymore to even think of challenging them. I guessed we wouldn't be seeing a marriage counselor or a church minister…ha. I was trying to count my few blessings while she spoke, because I was unsure of what to say.

Somers' steely grey eyes belied another, different, real deal she had in mind. With Somers, you always need to look behind the curtain, the divorce was only a loss-leader. What she really wanted was my blood, and perhaps a cash prize for the scalp. Little known to me, she'd already gone on her first officially sanctioned date that week…No more furtive hiding in the bushes, this bird was free.

She'd talked to other people? I hadn't said a word to anyone, I'd avoided everyone. I hadn't just lost this friend, but I was about to lose all my friends, she'd make damn sure of that. Who was other people? Somers was quickly becoming an even wilder version of indiscreet, a version even I'd never be willing to accept.

Somers was on a new tack of deception…I didn't know why, I didn't know how, and I didn't know what. My head was spinning again, the eddies and currents in full. I'd loved her so hard, but it had all gone to waste. So I had that going for me.

I was concerned about the kids. Again very unknown to me, Somers had already begun marketing to them, trying to convince them that dad wasn't as good a dad as they thought he was, in spite of her public protests that she said I was the best dad ever. There was no telling what lies she was telling whom. She knew the central truth about the kids and me: there was nothing I wouldn't do for them and the only thing I wanted out of life was: to be with them…For that reason alone, the work left to be done to destroy me would take on a whole new dimension. The kids were her hedge against the world knowing the real Somers. I mean look, the girl had already gone on her first date the week of the separation…

"I'm not trying to make your life harder. But you and I are done…there will be no turning around on that. It's a shame, because we have so much in common and I really like your sense of humor (it's gone Somers…). But there is too much mess and destruction here."

The kids were all I cared about. For Somers, the kids were accoutrements meant to buttress her public image. I could only think of the kids as my head flooded with anxiety and confusion; I couldn't even hear Somers speaking anymore. I'd heard enough.

I could see her lips move but I was sick from information and the heaviness of fifteen years ending like this… Just the wretched finality being lectured by her as if nothing had ever mattered. There was no way I would be able to control Somers once she was untethered, and there was no telling what damage she would inflict, on me and the kids. Was the material world so important like she was saying? Maybe it was and I'd underestimated what was necessary for my kids' happiness. Maybe I wasn't useful.

My entire universe was crumbling…I felt dizzy and confused. The stars were going from bright to turning blue. What I needed now more than anything was the kids and yet she had sent them somewhere for the night. I just kept thinking that the heartache and pain were mine alone, and there was no way I could lay that trip on my children. Her words came back into focus.

"Sebastian, this is Detective Arnold Rosario of the Nassau County Detective's bureau. He is not here for any other reason than I wanted to be sure you didn't hurt me. He's here simply to make sure you do not hit me (if I wanted to hit you Somers, I probably would have done it a long time ago. Couldn't you have just asked your dad to stop over, to keep our private matters from getting out into the community…I don't know this guy. Are you setting me up?…)."

A man in a suit that definitely could have been a detective's appeared from around the corner in the dining room. He flashed a badge at me, but I don't know what it said to be honest. It looked real enough. Somers chimed in, "Badges, we ain't got no badges! We don't need no badges! I don't have to show you no stinkin' badges!" At least that's what I thought I heard her say…it's what she would say if given a chance…

I also saw his holstered Glock. I was semi-conscious. Where's my shotgun by the way? Go ahead, make my day. I was losing it. She even brought a breakup buddy to her dramarama.

You have got to be kidding me…right? What in god's creation has ever given you the idea that I would think of hitting you? You're the mother to my children…not to mention the fact that you're a woman, or that I haven't hit even a man since 2nd Grade…Your stepfather or Vander Hoorst, OK, I could see hitting those guys; or actually, I can imagine them hitting a woman, but me? I wouldn't touch a fly! I'm the 'dog whisperer'. You're joking. That guy has a Glock in the house where my kids live! Are you fucking sane Somers? Or too sane and too devious?

Somers was setting me up right in front of my eyes. A man was standing in our dining room, and I had no idea if he was a detective or one of her lovers pretending to be a detective. All I knew was that I was super-pissed that some stranger was in my house with a loaded gun and she had just let this man hear everything. Completely private words between husband and wife, a Locust Valley husband and wife mind you where discretion is the better part of valor…Like I said, I'm embarrassed to talk with my banker, whereas Somers…ahhh, forget it. Let's just say she was getting in touch with her roots again, shedding generations of indiscretion by the second.

I'm tired of being what you want me to be. It probably was a good idea for Detective Whomever to be there.

I'd promised to stand by her always, and I had. She had had some rough shite of her own for the years we were married, and I was always by her side, always there….the hospital visits, family crises, etc… But those memories were now just a joke to her, discarded quickly and simply. We were at a crossroads, and the path she was choosing was my destruction, pure and simple. Everything to her was made to be broken. I was never coming back.

She'd asked me to fib that week to my kids, asking that I say to them I was away on a business trip , because we need to treat the kids gently, but obviously I hadn't been. Now she was mouthing something to the effect that she instead told the kids that daddy and mommy had an argument and that daddy was staying in the city that week… So while I lied to my kids about where I was, as she'd instructed me, Somers told the kids exactly where I was, in the city. So while I was trying to do the right thing and was asked to do the right thing, she'd simply set me up with my best friends bar none in the world…my children.

I can't tell you the number of times when she would do this to me over the proceeding two years. And I won't list them all…let's agree that she set me up with purposeful lies about once a week for two years, easy. I bought each time, like a trout hooked by the same fly over and over. Maybe I am still dumb.

The damage done was herculean.

My equilibrium wobbled. I had emotional vertigo. I couldn't make a sound. You think I was feeling all alone? Multiply that by infinity and you can get a small sense for how dark the hour was. Mental waves bashing against jetties and turning with ferocity against each other. The sea foam of mental nausea was at an all-time high. I couldn't distinguish fear from blame. She wanted to throw me away.

I'd lost $6 Million of my money and $5 Million of my partners, not for lack of trying but simply because we lost. I'd left a mess at the company level but I could deal with that. It might take a few years but I always recovered and I don't walk away from obligations. I don't walk away ever… How could I begin to repair all the damage in this emotional state? People were counting on me to deliver.

Up until that moment, I'd had a decent life. A psychotherapist would say I'd been a generally well-disposed human being….Everything non-disposed about me, I blame on the lack of marital sex, Somers' ass, and this Princess of the Quest Grigori, a woman who knew the difference between what was right and sinful… I'd be the man who'd have walked forever for his wife.

She was done and I was completely unaware of what she'd been up to behind my back.

Somers wanted me to deliver. Ed wanted me to deliver. The bank needed me to deliver. Company creditors needed me to deliver. My partners needed me to deliver. Everyone needed me for one thing: money.   And that was the only thing I had none of. Except for those life insurance policies…

She kept talking but I couldn't hear much. She never once asked me to say anything as she'd promised when I arrived. This was like a judge speaking to the defendant on sentencing day. She knew best and that was it. I wasn't asked for a defense.   And I didn't want the world to see me in this condition.

I'd become so tired.

I really didn't know what to say. I was speechless. The detective was staring at his feet, almost embarrassed that she'd done this…all he could see was a mortally wounded soul being berated by an evil slanderer, a man being pulverized into nothingness by a woman detached from humanity. Her flagitious narcissism had reached levels of comic totality and I was circling the drain.

"I will insist that you exercise discretion around the children with respect to any new girlfriends you want to bring around. It would be best if you could wait a few years before you see anyone, and perhaps even five years before you marry again. If you violate this, I will seek to keep the kids away from you. I intend to be loved again, but I won't bring that around my children like you."

I heard the words, but I didn't understand them. Why would I bring a girlfriend around…? I was still in love with her somewhat. I'd never considered seeing another woman. What was up was: Somers was doing her best ventriloquist projecting again, her Inflated Narcissism, where her views were contrary to reality. She was actually worried about herself and blaming me for her desires, entertaining others with fantasies of me. Jesus. I am so flipping stupid.

In less than two weeks from this speech, Somers would drunk-grind a stranger on the front porch of the clubhouse in the Adirondack's, have a serious boyfriend within a month, be engaged within a year, and sleep with no fewer than five men before snagging husband number two. 'Show discretion'…the third largest joke in her universal repertoire. Discretion…God if you only knew about Somers and her morals. Just ask me when you see me….This one probably hurts the most.

I was numb. I couldn't even feel my throat for words. Could I walk back to my room and get my stuff? Uhhh, actually….

Somers brought out from around a corner three suitcases stuffed with my clothes, like what you might see dropped at a Goodwill store. There were no pictures of the kids and me or anything of any real value like that. I wanted some pictures of the kids. And my paintings which I had so meticulously purchased and thought through, they hung on the walls like trophies for Somers, as if she'd bagged large cats on a safari. Those were my life, not her's. Looking at the art was like her sticking my nose in it all over again.

I finally scrounged up a word,

"Somers, can you get me the birthday cards and father day cards from the kids so I can take them now?"

"I burned them." Somers said this with the emotional content of a cold brick. She was really breaking crayons now.

For every year of my life, my children had either made me or given me cards for any and all important events and I kept them in the bottom drawer of a desk that Somers had given me when we got married. I treated the cards like gold bullion, and she knew it. She was hitting me hardest, there were no rules in her game anymore. Everything had been made to be broken...I could feel her rottenness in my bones.

"We are only going to communicate through lawyers anymore Sebastian. You have one option left, and you know what it is. I'm not offering you an apology and I don't want one. Do the right thing. Beat it. Walk out the door. Hit the road jack. Bye."

And that was it. My communication skills failed me dramatically, the same reason my college debate team was so happy to see me leave. I'd lost. I could feel myself going multi-ball.

Sometimes silence is all the communication you ever need to hear. My dreams were tossed away, they belonged to no one now, incinerated in the daze of a marital explosion. The door closed and

I was standing outside of my house with three bags, the house I'd built and lived in with my three children all my grownup life. Her smell was still on my clothes and her taste still in my mouth. I wasn't shaking, more decapitated. It was the moment when you realize that the enemy had been living with you all along…she was always among us. We had such different values and dreams.

Where do you go when you're that lonely? This was everything real in my life and now all I had to show for it were three suitcases of used underwear and shirts.

My dog Layla was inside the house staring at me from the living room window, oblivious to the shakedown that had just occurred. Even her tail-wagging couldn't bring me out of my funk. In fact, it only made it worse…Layla was my dog and I had to leave her behind as well?

And now my kids would stew on another night wondering if Dad had told them the truth, because she had asked me to lie to them to make them feel better…? I was sure that she had told them that she needed a detective to protect her from Dad…I could hear it already. If anyone needed protection, it was me, Somers was an unleashed monster, an assassin. I needed shelter in the worst way but I'd kept my mouth shut, and yet she was the one to sell the only version of the story. Jesus.

Would things ever get easier or brighter again? Should I go? What had she said? Could I ask for a redo? Nothing made sense, because there was no excuse given. She never said this is why we are divorcing. Just that we are divorcing.

I was devastated and crushed. I always thought it would be so hard to live without her. Alone as a human soul had ever been. I hadn't talked to my mother or brothers or friends in so long: I never bothered anyone when times were tough. I always assumed you dealt on your own. I never asked anything of anyone. But I would be the first to lend a hand when times were tough for anyone else. I desperately needed that hand now.

I had no destination. I was delirious. Rosebud?

Somers dealt with humans like they were perishable items on a supermarket stand. She had slowly sucked me in to a world controlled solely by her. Everything I had was dependant on her good graces (the irony in that…). The house wasn't mine, the clubs weren't mine, the friends weren't mine, the art wasn't mine, the dog wasn't mine, hell the air wasn't mine for all I knew. And yet I'd paid for everything. In fifteen years, Somers may have stroked one check, for the dachshund, and she could keep her…! I'd have nothing to show for the fifteen years because she'd gamed me, and I'd played along like a fool. My life was going down…I hadn't even gotten a blowjob in fifteen years, and that was a blasting reminder of how bad this really was!

I was no better than an overripe, flaccid banana…the leaves were brown even. I really was multi-balling.

A gentle mist was setting on my car. I would guess the nighttime temperature had dropped to an un-seasonable 55 degrees, cool for this time of year. I laboriously lifted the bags and put them in my trunk, and slowly drove away. Down our country lane, leaving behind the only house I had ever really known, my anchor in the storm of life. Leaving behind my kids, my dogs, my tool shed, my garden, my lacrosse goal, my landscaping, my clothes, my pictures, my basketball net, my pool, my roses, my vases, my outdoor furniture, my sound system, my rhodies, my ping-pong tables, my trophies, my video's, my Douglas firs, my paintings, my memories…my life.

It's just no good anymore, I'm only thinking of yesterdays. I couldn't go to the well again. I was spent, fully.

The side windows fogged up. I looked in the rear view mirror, looking for signs of life. It was dark already. I turned away. In my mind, I could see her face laughing, hers and the detective's. I was headed down the same sad road I always had known, but I'd actually built this one. The house lights were off. I didn't even know where I was. My mind was scrambled and confused.

I could hear the white pea gravel crunch beneath my tires, each tiny pebble individually crushed was a symphony of destruction in my ears, and my heart was being pulverized.

Board it up folks, I couldn't even trace my problems anymore, because the problems were me…I just felt dead. The world was no longer wide as I'd imagined it as a child. Somehow I'd lost and she'd won. Somers had just thrown the perfect game, no walks, no hits, no runs….no errors. I was out.

Sometime's good-bye's the only way…

*'…and I listen for voice inside my head, Nothing…I'll do this one myself,'… **

Marshmallow Clouds

I was suspended in space and time, tripping out on seeds of despair.
There were endless acres of marshmallow clouds and heavenly
voices in the distance, but I couldn't see shit. It was as if I was blind
to the action and yet the world seemed wonderful, peaceful, a
utopian dream of some kind of permanent settlement.

Bogart was right, I should have never switched from scotch to
martini's….

I'd come undone, fully… I'd fallen apart at the seams with my heart
lying in pieces on the floor. I was a fishing line spool that gets
tangled on a cast, and the likelihood of untangling it is less than
zero, so you simply cut bait. Who'd have known?

Someone appeared in my space, a woman without a face. I felt like
Capt. Jeffrey Spaulding, "One morning I shot an elephant in my

pajamas. How he got in my pajamas I don't know." This woman had a soothing mien,

"Mr. Graham. Good day. You've been out for a while. We're glad you're with us though. How are you feeling?"

She handed me a sealed envelope with the Roman number 5 on the face, "V". I tore open the seal and unleashed the letter. A thousand brown horses and riders came flying out, charging each other and everything, laughing, in some sort of young cub way, playfully. They were good guys, you could just sense. They were strong, chiseled and bearded. They must have been in that envelope for a long time.

I was trying to avoid them but they ran straight through, around, and behind me. The horses were thoroughbreds of the Roman Empire. I couldn't move from where I lay, it was if I was floating and yet incapable of movement, while these horsemen road through the air and turned when they wanted, as swiftly as if they were on solid ground.

One of the riders came up to me and halted, out of breath, but a face of happiness in a way I hadn't seen for a long time….I wondered if his wife was as wretched as mine. The woman without a face disappeared. The man looked to be a leader, he had an air of confidence but not an air of arrogance, my kind of guy.

"Mr. Graham (a knowing Mr. Graham way…), thanks for finally coming! We've been waiting for you for so long and the boys have built up a good deal of energy. I hope things weren't too rough for you. We heard some of it, and we know what she's still doing, but it's all good now."

"Uhhh, hi. How are you? Excuse me, but do we know each other? Because I feel a little lost to be honest, not exactly sure where I am. You guys seem like miniature toys, but yet you're real."

"You're here and so are we. That's all that matters mate (was this guy an Aussie…?). And yeah, we're real alright….we punch higher than our weight!"

"Uhhh, yeaahhh (perpelexed…). Ummm, ok, but how did you know my name?"

"Ha! You trained us…You know all of us. You know our mothers, our sisters, our brothers, our fathers. Because you asked us to be there for her! C'mon mate (imploring me to get with the program, but I had no clue what he was saying…)! I held your head when you died."

"Her? Somers? I died?"

"Awww, c'mon Seb. Not 'her'! Her! And you're alive now."

"Okay. Well, we have that settled. Not. Where the hell am I?"

"Not in 'hell' anymore! She's gone. You're here, with us. We were never going to let anything happen to you because the girl needs you. We need you. Nicolas and Joseph need you. We just have to get you back on your horse and we can go do our other work. Not much time. She's already at work again. You won't believe what she's doing as we speak! We have some scouts checking her out now."

"I'm assuming you're now talking about Somers…?"

"Yup. Man, you lasted a long time with that. How did you ever do it? What a witch! On my wife's worst day, she couldn't approximate 1/1000th what yours did to you with her weakest effort! She beat you every day, relentlessly, remorselessly, not an ounce of gratitude, pummeling you, pulverizing you, and you never said peep. For what it's worth, each additional day you took with her kept her from what she really wanted to be doing, so we all owe you a huge gratitude."

"So, what's she doing now?"

"Ahhhh, you probably don't want to know. But, I just got my first reports. This may be hard to hear, but for starters, she's called a few papers this morning. She called your mother and even yelled at her. She told the kids that you'd lied about spending the week at the Links. Telling anyone that you did this and that. She gave the wild green-light to her four horsemen, they're now spreading their pestilence. She's even got a date tonight, that didn't take long! Ahh she's vicious mate, but you don't need her anymore. Her damage will get worse, but you survived. You first need to get that. The apocalypse was yesterday, not in the future.

"You got to excuse me. No shit, I'm supposed to be at National in about an hour, my tee time is at 9 AM. It's gonna take me at least an hour to get there from LV. I am really confused."

"Seb, wake the hell up mate. No more golf. No more southsides. No more nassau's. You're done, at least for a few years. You think you just tee it up for 18 with that kind of violent disruption to your world. We held on because you held on. You were our beacon. That's it. You know how you were always saying how you couldn't believe how soft man had become, that all they did was bitch about this and that, that they gossiped instead of did, that the best sex they could ever have was if they could fuck themselves in a mirror (sorry for the word but you used to say it mate…)? You remember that? You really think it's changed since then to now? You call these modern men 'Facebook pussies', those Facebraggers, there were also agora phonies if you recall. And Angra Mainyu, Diavolus mate, she's been watching too. She hasn't been sitting on any sideline, I can assure you. She's got some Facebook pussies already lined up, and she's gonna Facebook-fuck you up."

"Look, I hear you. But how did you know I called them Facebook pussies? God, no real man should be on Facebook, don't you agree?"

"Agreed. Seb, you're not listening man. We've been in you, we are you. And we're all here. Ready. Now's the time. It's the end, but that's great, because now is the beginning. The Rapture is waiting. The Lamb needs you."

The soldier handed me a folder. It had no color, just like the continuum space I was floating in. I broke the seal and opened the envelope. Out spilled five letters I had written to myself and my family. The letters had water-seal marks which simply said, "Martyr". I couldn't actually read the writing on the letters, because the letters were floating on the paper as if they were plastic on a pool of water. Incongruously, the letters dissolved into sand as I held them, worthless testaments to my own false ego.

This soldier then said, "And there you are Seb. It's time. One more job. Congratulations."

"Hey what's your name?"

"It doesn't matter really Seb, you know me as an emotion. But if it helps you in any way, call me the Lion of Judah. How the hell did you hold on?! She was mine once as well...sad."

And then he vanished in a clouded dust-storm explosion, as did all the horsemen. It was quiet once more.

Love bears all things, believes all things, hopes all things, endures all things. Love never ends.
-- Corinthians 13:7-8

Perhaps the past fifteen years had been a dream, and maybe this was real. Maybe I had never met Somers Gillette and Gruella Kincaid. Psyched, not...ooops. Another man in white appeared, but this time he wasn't smiling and he had a face I dint love. It looked like he was the ticket taker at the Disney castle, but we weren't on any solid ground...

"Hello Mr. Graham. How are you?"

"Uhhh, I guess I'm fine. Where am I?"

"Mr. Graham, you're nowhere and you're everywhere. Do you want to talk about what happened?"

This was definitely going to be a long day. The irony of being married to a woman who has zero sex drive (for her husband anyway), but a phenomenally-gifted ass, is too great a burden for any heterosexual man to bear I gather.

"Jesus…I'm really sorry. I don't know, what happened? I really don't. My memory is a little hazy. Can you tell me what happened?"

"Sure. The music stopped and you tripped. We are going to get you back on your feet, no matter what."

"Does anyone know I'm here?"

"Yes, your wife knows. We reached her five hours ago. She's very concerned for you."

You know who you need when your life comes undone? Not your killer…or wife! Or both if they are the same!

"Yeah right (nervous laughter and sarcasm…this is all she'll ever need to bury me, mate…). I wanna be sedated. She's not really my wife anymore. Couldn't you have called anyone else, I mean anyone? I'd have taken my chances with Grinch, Scrooge, Freddy, Chucky, Jason, Kevorkian…anyone but her!"

"Mr. Graham. She's concerned (concerned about things you cannot begin to understand…). You and I need to discuss what happened. You need to let me know how you truly feel."

OK, so if I play along, I can get out of here…No problem. OK, is it any wonder I'm here? If I told you how I really feel, I won't be going anywhere for a long time. I'm trapped in the wrong time to the wrong woman; she never told me who she was. She has targeted me for the last ten years.

Whoever she is. Lucifer. Words were flowing out of his mouth and right through my empty mind…nothing was going to change what had happened. My world was changed forever.

"Mr. Graham…you don't seem like our normal type. And I'm not allowed to hold you if you refuse (thankfully…phew, because I blanking refuse!...). So, if you could, just give me your insurance identification and we will let you on your way."

"Uhhhh…small problem. My wallet was in my car last night, and my car is somewhere in Manhattan, and in my wallet is my new insurance ID card from United Health. I guess I could go get it if I could go retrieve my car…"

"You aren't allowed out of here unless you have the number. What's the insurance company?"

There was one person in the entire universe who had a second ID card and that would have been none other than Ms. Somers Gillette….natch fucking natch. Sorry for the curse word.

"United Health. My wife has my insurance card and ID. Can you call her and get it?"

"Mr. Graham, we already called her. She said 'you don't have insurance'…That you dreamt that up. You need to get the number on your own."

"Oh c'mon. Please. I swear to god we have insurance. I just got the new cards last week; we switched plans because my company was mothballed and we just got the new policy a few weeks ago. She's the only one who has a card besides me. She has it…I swear. United Health."

Even I thought I was sounding crazy. You sound crazy saying your wife is crazy. Circular logic is tragic for any defendant. I couldn't believe she said to them I dreamt up the insurance. She knew I had just spent the better part of the last two months dealing with those insurance companies, getting quotes, submitting the kids records, determining which company was best for our PCP's and all that junk. When we got the new cards, Somers was the one who was elated…it never even fazed me since I'd never gone to a doctor once in my life (which incidentally, she hated…she thought doctors were family members). I was livid bordering on psycho. Her plan was working to a tee, keeping me from my tee.

"Well, I guess we could try their main number and see if they have it, 'if they have it', but Saturdays are not great days to retrieve new account information from insurance companies. Do you think someone else could call your wife to ask her to reconsider telling us? I mean otherwise, you will have to stay for the weekend, and it's not so bad…after all, you were fairly miserable last night, and you seem better now."

"You must not be a mind reader, so trust me: I'm miserable now. Can I just call her?"

"She already said that you were not to call the house under any conditions (hmmm…I have children, is that even allowed?…)."

If this wasn't a catch-flipping-22, there's never been one.

"Look, I'm not staying here. You need to call my wife and demand the ID number. Jesus Christ. Somers is just being a pain in the ass. Let me call my lawyer."

"I'm telling you…we spoke with her earlier and I didn't get the sense that she wanted to help you in any way ('ya think?…). And no one here is allowed to call a lawyer. I'll try her again."

He walked out to the hall, where I could see him pick up a landline phone. He was staring back at me as he supposedly spoke to Somers. The way he looked at me reminded me of how a doctor looks in on a terminal patient while counseling in hushed tones the patient's family, preparing them for the worst.

There wasn't a doubt in my head that Somers was saying, OK, we've taught the fucker a lesson, here's the insurance number, let him go…Who would screw like this with the father to her kids? Uhhhh….Somers Gillette would! You just got a parting gift! Oh, livid had never seen such clarity…if I could only find her, elle a été condamnée à l'asile de fou.

He came back, looking like he had bad news and improbably even worse news. There was no smile or hopeful glint, just the executioner's blank stare.

"Look, Sebastian, she thinks you need to stay. She says she's scared (uhhh…buddy….Somers isn't scared of anything…don't give me that shite…she's always' award show'…), although we heard her laugh a few times. She won't give us the ID number no matter what. She did finally admit you have insurance, but she still refuses to give it to me, and I can't force her to hand it over. Sorry."

"You told her that I would have to stay for the weekend if she wouldn't give you the number? And she just admitted she lied to you initially, and she has it? But we have to defer to her?"

"Of course. I assumed that would make her give it to me."

"That's exactly what she wouldn't do! She's the Lord of the Underworld, the Angra Mainyu of Locust Valley! C'mon. Blasted…please get me out of this place. Look, I'm a rational guy. This isn't working for me. I'll get you the ID number Tuesday morning, I promise."

Marriage is a wonderful institution, but who wants to live in an institution (v. Groucho Marx).

"I'm very sorry Mr. Graham."

He walked out of my life as quickly as he walked in.

These would be long days, longer nights...all because a certain someone wouldn't give out over the phone a number on an ID card that the hospital needed. Never had to spend one night. I'd like to say one word here, but I think you'd think badly of me, so let me yell in my little box for a second… That @#$%!

I left immediately after getting the insurance ID information four days later, from United Health at 10:00 AM. I was back on solid ground, off that castle in the sky, but it was too late.

That Tuesday at 8:30 AM, strictly because of my ex-wife's refusal to give over an insurance identification number which would have allowed me to deal with many things, the company servers were disconnected (no one answered the phone when the tech company calling looking for an explanation of the late payment). With the servers shut down, my Blackberry and the company's mainframe servers were automatically and forever wiped of all historical information. Twenty-three years of business contacts, calendar items, data, and memo notes were permanently erased. You cannot imagine the problems that all this would cause. The only way back would be if I got a new job.

The kid wanted in the picture, but first I had to see my children.

Little did I know that Somers was setting off her bombs while I was away... My eschatology had begun, but I was trapped in a cage, just as she wanted.

Just One Lie Among Thousands

'...I got scratches all over my arms, One for each day since I fell apart,'... *

Things happened while I was away, away solely because a certain someone lied. Somers and Gruella would be the Mrs. Leary's cows of Locust Valley, tipping over my life, inflaming anyone and everyone about me but most poignantly, my kids…Despicable and reprehensible, and only a self-hater goes that low…More on self hating in the St. Dymphna's chapter…

I'm not certain how it's even possible, but they planted blind items about me in the New York Post that Monday morning as well as full page word for word rehash of her side in New York Social Diary. Since her broader family had been staple items in the gossip pages for so long and had become somewhat inured to the idea that it was actually okay to be in papers (unlike say most of the free world), the press thing never struck Somers as perhaps unseemly…it was what it was, standard business protocol for the high society narcissist. All press is good press. Disgusting. Because after the jump, it's you who has to pick up the pieces, not the narcissist.

Somers accidentally fat fingered me an email ('emaul' is more appropriate) intended for her lawyer, less than a week after the marshmallow clouds. This email was intended to go to several lawyers at her matrimonial lawyers' offices, one of whom had a first name that was similar to mine. This email was sent in response to an initial first cut at custody by her own lawyer, before we even legally separated (the standard 50/50 arrangement)! It's important also to note that this email was sent one year in advance of any legal trouble of mine business wise. Without further ado, allow me to simply put it out for the world to read,

"09-30-08

From: Somers Gillette

To: xxxx xxxxxxxx, xxx xxxxx, xxxxxxxxxx xxxxxxxxx, xxxx xxxxxxx

Re: 50/50 Custody

To All,

Fuck that! I will put him in jail before I agree to custody of 50/50! Fuck him!!"

That's verbatim. I guess you can make up your own mind as to whether Somers had it in mind that she would then proceed to make life miserable for me… The words in that email alone should serve as the beginning and ending arguments for her prosecution.

She ultimately called fifty-two people, planting blind items about me that were so illogical and misleading as to ultimately make lawyers of mine quit when I wouldn't sue her in return for libel. I don't sue.

Below is just one example of the outrageous conduct exhibited, and I could list hundreds of these, so hopefully this one anecdote puts her Dystopias in some perspective (the problem with recounting each incident is it begins to sound as if I'm putting on a defense, which I'm most certainly not…let this one snippet tell a story that can be retold hundreds more times with hundreds more incidents…). Somers would never come clean about this story to anyone, so allow me to help her now.

I made a real estate investment in 2003 in San Francisco, a relatively long time ago and well before any troubles. Those were better days obviously when I had money rolling in faster than even Somers could spend it. It wasn't a huge investment but I liked the probabilities and it had the salubrious double positive of being a recommendation of Ed Kincaid. Ed loves money as much as Somers, so partnering with Ed seemed like a decent way to ingratiate myself with him after many years of tension.

Anyway, unbeknownst to Somers, I placed the investment in her first name, but my last name ("Somers Graham")…an innocent error. Why I gave her the investment, I have no idea now. I guess I thought it was a decent gesture from husband to wife and I wanted to begin to build up assets in her name. That's what husbands do or so I thought. She certainly didn't need the money and at the time, neither did I. My company was doing fine. The reality is Somers couldn't give shite if I made her a billion dollars…she'd always want two.

Anyway, just prior to our separation, I told Somers that I'd made some investments for her and she took careful note…she notes everything when it comes to money. After the separation, one of her thug lawyers called the real estate company to ask about the real estate investment. No one ever called me to say they were doing this, and no one asked that I approve any independent communication between the real estate company and a third party. No, her lawyer simply called the company with the threat of a subpoena if they didn't cooperate!

I had never denied anything to Somers, no papers, records, communications, meetings….nothing. Of course, she'd burned my children's birthday cards to me and every other paper or file I ever kept at the house…all bank statements and brokerage account statements, all gone to the fireplace she loves. Yet, she and her lawyer determined on their own accord to go out and source assets that perhaps were not even theirs, and they would carpet bomb anyone in their way, especially me. Hers was a manic treasure quest.

The receptionist at the real estate company (please note this was the receptionist, not an MBA, JD, officer, or investor relations) could not locate my legal name or hers anywhere near any investment in her database, because I had her first name but my last name… So she politely informed Somers' lawyer that they were mistaken. The receptionist didn't ask any other company officer to handle the issue strictly because (in her words) Somers' lawyer badgered her on the phone to come up with the record immediately…or the receptionist herself would be considered an accomplice to a crime…!! Real words, real history, unreal… Who would ever hire a thug lawyer like that? Oh yeah, Somers Gillette would….

With the general agreement that no investment had ever been made (the real estate company didn't have my new cell phone number, and I couldn't even recall the real estate company's legal name…), Somers' lawyer and Somers made a second call to the real estate company to speak to the Managing Partner. He remembered me, he recalled that I'd intended to invest some money, but given that he and I hadn't spoken in over four years, he just couldn't recall much beyond that. That wasn't why Somers and her lawyer called him though….they weren't looking for a jackpot of assets, they were looking for a jackpot of slander.

The purpose of their second call was to ostensibly apologize for having wasted the time of the receptionist, but the broader purpose was: to cover their ass for having badgered the receptionist in the first place, and then to absolutely, unmitigatingly, and universally firebomb me like no tomorrow…You should read the affidavit from the company…it reads as if I personally underwrote Usamah bin Laden's entire life! I can't legally place the affidavit as an exhibit at the end, so just ask me when you see me and I'll fill you in on the details. I would say the net result of their second call was that the Managing Partner of the firm concluded that I was crazy. Which I am (I married Iblis…).

At this point, I'd ask the reader to kindly ask themselves how you might handle matters at this stage if you were Somers Gillette. Would you call me and ask if I could help you locate the investment that I told you I'd made? I mean, if you were so concerned about money, wouldn't you at least see if you could have all the facts before doing anything more or concluding that the investment was never made?

Of course, normal people would. But I know now that this wasn't even her real goal, and I realize that there's only one Somers Gillette, She in fact didn't even care about the investment in the first place…

For the next six months, while I worked outside the United States, oblivious to the ongoing carpet bombing, Somers and her lawyer informed everyone, and by that I mean everyone, that I was delusional and couldn't distinguish truth from fiction. I'd lied to

Somers, I never made an investment, I was not to be trusted, etc…Blah blah blah…

Trust me, that's exactly what went down….because six months after that first call to that receptionist, we saw an accidental filing in Nassau County matrimonial court where the real estate company's name had been curiously redacted. We innocently asked for the name of the company, and she and her lawyers refused to give it to us! I couldn't remember the name of the company, they knew they'd already spoken with the company, Ed was good friends with the Managing Partner of the company, so clearly they had the legal name and number. It confounded us. Why wouldn't they give us the name? Didn't they want the money I wanted to give them…?

I now had to spend another $5,000 filing motions simply to get the name of the company where I'd invested money many years before.

A normal human being, who's supposedly destitute, would simply have said, here you go, you try…But I was not married to a normal human being. The judge eventually ordered Somers to hand over the name of the real estate company. Again, I was wholly unaware of the bombs that had been thrown by Somers, so I'm thinking at the time that I'm helping her, if not a little confused as to why she wouldn't simply tell me the name of the company that I'd invested into...

I had the name of the company, so now I'm thinking aren't I the good guy, I'll call them, make sure all is in order, and then surprise Somers by letting her know that she's the recipient of an investment made on her behalf by me many years ago! Hell, I'd love that. She'll likely thank me and rethink this whole nonsense about divorce. Can you say, loudly in capital letters and, oh why not throw a fuck in there for good measure, FUCK NO?

I called the company. The receptionist, after a brief hello and with the extension of my name, literally fell to pieces over the phone. I felt as if I was on LSD, because I couldn't understand what was happening. Had we dated and I really screwed up in a prior life with this young girl? When she calmed down, she asked that I call back in an hour so she could be on the phone with their general counsel…she learned after one call from Somers that you best not allow the devil to feast on your weakness. That receptionist was smarter than me!

Anyway, when I called back, the general counsel let me know how berating Somers and her lawyer had been to the receptionist, how intimidating they'd been to this young girl, how they'd threatened her, and that even Ed had inserted himself into the affair. The three of them, Ed, Somers, and Somers' thug, had painted their van Gogh caricature of me for six months, not just to the real estate company, but to the world while I worked silently in Bermuda, completely unaware of what they were up to. They shamelessly lied and said I'd never made the investment that I said I made…and that indeed had been made…because,

It took no more than 22 seconds for the general counsel and me to locate the account name and the investment. Twenty-two seconds, about the same time it takes to read one paragraph in this novel. I stared at the watch. For 22 seconds, Somers and her legal quacks could have had the information they supposedly were after since day 1…had it been their goal. They could have saved me a mountain of headaches. In Somers' eyes though, her fantasies of me simply allowed her to do more damage, to be the queen narcissist of the day. She ran with this made-up story and spouted it to everyone, including my former partners, employees, creditors, investors, and the government…the main story line being that I couldn't be trusted, that I lied, and that I had absconded to Bermuda…! If it wasn't so flipping sad, it would be illegal.

I received a Fedex the next day from the company. Inside the package was a sealed envelope, with a distribution check made out to Somers. I opened the seal, and again I could hear a distant bass chord progression sound. Their check number was #144000, and the partnership agreement looked to me to be a heavenly sign, perhaps a way to regain my society fatwa imama's trust….Ahem…

If you can't understand the underlying story here, I haven't done a good job explaining. Somers needed fantasies to sell so she could wreck me, so she came up with a fantasy, kept me in the dark about what she was doing, and sold it to everyone while I wasn't looking… As they say, there are lies, damn lies, and statistics. The statistics are that Somers Gillette always had the investment and still has it to this day. If you are a woman and your husband made a very good investment on your behalf in your name from his checking account, I suppose it wouldn't be the worse bit of news to ever get…

Multiply the above anecdote by hundreds more, all of which were similarly proved false, and you get the idea of what Somers Gillette was really after…never money, but a soul. She couldn't allow custody going away from her and to the father. It was and is her worst fear…it's the narcissist's false moral outrage.

When it all came clear, a bit too late to minimize the damage by the way, I confronted her with the lie and here was her response in all its simplicity,

"Chalk it up to a misunderstanding Sebastian…"

No kidding, a verbatim response, as terse as it was final, the Hollywood hang-up special. A misunderstanding…? A misunderstanding is when you ask someone to come to dinner at 6, and they thought you said 7…simple, benign mistakes are misunderstandings. Misunderstandings are not universal libel gang rapes executed over multiple years when you know full well what the truth is and yet you persist. That isn't a misunderstanding…that's attempted murder.

"Marriage is give and take. You'd better give it to her or she'll take it anyway," Joey Adams.

Why did she have to make everything so complicated? What was I missing? Why was she doing this? How did it benefit Somers if I couldn't make money again? Why was she giving me the runaround on everything related to the kids? Hadn't we successfully handled all things for the kids together for fifteen years?

The libel flew without end for two years. She was like a nest of homosexualized, Africanized hornets dive-bombing my groin while being restrained on an operating table. Her only verbal testament to my character ever was to say he's a really good father, as if by saying that, somehow she was being objective about the rest of the bulldust.

'…Up here in my tree, Newspapers matter not to me, No more crowbars to my head, I'm trading stories with the leaves instead,'…*

The FBI was listening to every word and reading every column. And trust me, they don't care if you're a good dad. If they did, she'd be at Westchester Women's and I'd be the one driving the kids to school.

Post-Separation Grinding on the Adirondack Club Porch

My brother had arranged for Somers and me to speak that Friday at 6 PM. I was to call her at the house, the kids would be gone so we could speak freely. I was sure other, less family-centric friends of Somers' would also be in on the call. Somers had morphed into a latter-day Elliot Ness in Valentino.

I was still unaware of the gossip drops because my family wrongly concluded I was depressed enough without me reading the papers about me, so no one had prepped me about what Somers had done. I got on the phone as innocently as one can, albeit slightly ashamed. I only had the kids on my mind, she only had holy war.

Somers – "First of all, I'm glad you're okay (yeah right…). What the fuck were you thinking (not sure myself anymore…)? When I said I wanted a divorce, I only meant it as a warning (huh?…). I assumed you would have the balls to go back and earn a living (wasn't I earning a living for fourteen years?…). I was just testing you Sebastian. This is a huge mess! And I'm not fucking helping you (no, I know that, you are in fact hurting me…)!"

"Somers, if you were only 'testing' me, why wouldn't you say so? Who bluffs divorce? It's not poker. I was at the end of my rope and your shit caught up to me at the wrong time. You have got to be kidding me with the testing crap. I don't believe you. And why didn't you give them my insurance ID card number? What's wrong with you? I can't even remember the old you to this day; where is the old good you? You told them I was crazy! Who the hell are you anymore? Why didn't you just say you never met me?! That would have helped somewhat."

"The problem is you're still alive! Fuck you and your insurance. I'm getting my own now. You mean nothing to me!! You deserved it anyway (you try it sweetheart…). I'm not faking anymore. I can't be seen with you (no you can't, because you have a date this weekend...). I'll figure things out. I'm taking the kids to the Adirondacks for a few days. You can see them when we get back. Fuck off (such a pleasant woman…)!!!"

"Somers, I'd really like to see them now. I don't think they need another vacation for god's sake; why do you always have to spend so much money? And if you always had so much money, why didn't you ever pay for anything while we were married? I think what the kids need is to see me."

Her voice Upper Cased,

"I'M not in any mess; YOU are. FUCK you! We're going and that's that. If you don't like it, have your lawyer call my lawyers (she loves lawyers; the anti-me....)."

"Somers, I'm not having my lawyer call your lawyer. We are father and mother, not Sunni and Shiite. Give me a break."

You may have noticed that I had taken to saying her first name every time I spoke...you end up doing this when you sense the volcano rush of anger and emotion coming to the surface. It's a reflexive habit to try to tamper the blood flow. It doesn't work at all...It only makes her more mad. No one scratches Mephistopheles' tummy.

"You have no idea what's about to hit you. You will never have custody of my children so help me fucking god Sebastian! Fuck you! I am going to trash you to everyone! You're going to jail. Ahhhhhhhhh...."

Bat shit signal... Had I said anything about custody? By then, I wondered why I even made the call. After all these lies, I still got the strangest feeling she wasn't the worst. Having Gruella as your mother helps make anyone pale in comparison, the Pale Horseman rides...

"Somers, you're being slightly wacky right now. Calm down (never tell Somers to calm down...it's like telling a jihadist that Islam sucks...). I get it. I fucked up. How were you ever my one temptation? Do me a favor, outside the kids of course? Would you just give to any business colleague who calls the home my cell phone number, so I can deal with them directly? The company has too many loose ends, and I have to start dealing with it. I can do it, but I don't have anyone's contact data anymore. The servers wiped out my data. I can't even call anyone. So it's likely they will call the house. I need to speak with them so I can deal. Would you do me that one favor, because otherwise, it's not fair to them and it could really hurt me?"

And with that one sentence, my life would forever change to shite. Somers now knew the path to victory, I showed her the jackpot to my erasure. Her moral obligation to herself now was to screw me, and I lit the runway.

"Of course I will. Ha ha. You will never know what hits you. Fuck off and die. By the way, I already found a better man."

Click. Hollywood hang-up redux. What a pleasant human being. Nothing like a little hand when a brother is down. If the choice came down to the devil and Somers, I'd need extra time to deliberate. The irony was killing me... My head was on a silver platter somewhere and Somers Lecter was carrying it, 'I ate his liver with some fava beans and a nice Chianti'. And a new man had already taken my spot…bonus!

I wrongly assumed that Somers would have no interest in speaking to any former partners of mine or company creditors. It just never occurred to any of the lawyers to force her to redirect all business calls to me. I assumed she just would. I mean, who would take advantage of that? The only way for me to even reach any of my former partners was if they called the house and got my new cell number from Somers, and therefore it would be decent of her to simply tell the people to call me at the number I provided. Who would not do that? Who would have that kind of vicious heart? Hmmm, let me think…

I wanted to say hi to my kids. I wanted to smell their hair again, to let them know that Daddy was OK. A dose of seeing the kids might have given me the strength to go back and do battle business-wise and it also would have soothed them.   I'm a dad that has been in my kids' lives every day.

Somers had dramarama'd the event into a tale about her…Everything ultimately is about Somers. The phallic narcissist at work. Did Locust Valley even need to know about me? My family certainly wouldn't be saying anything. Would she talk? Does Rose Kennedy have a black dress?

I kept offering Somers lifelines that she didn't need. Somers had made a decision and that was fucking that. She had money to back her up and tie you in court for as long as she wanted. Fantasy revenge was definitely not beneath her, it was part of her.

Two weeks later, Somers took the kids to the Adirondack Club for their vacation. That would be three vacations in less than two months and supposedly we had money problems…knock me over with a feather. If we had money problems, then I wished I was having the same problems she seemed to be having. She even hosted a party for profit that weekend…Ugh… And yet, I was transferring her money each month.

What I got to learn later is that Somers hosted a large cocktail party for profit on the club veranda that Saturday night, with about twenty guests. She ended up sitting in some guy's lap for half the night and making out furiously, catching up for fifteen years of secret assignations…she was free now (technically not legally free, but who's splitting hairs…). This was two weeks after our separation.

The Bheliar was chewing up the earth with feverish abandon.

Supposedly Somers was distraught, because I heard that from about a hundred people I knew…Somers had put the word out to her gossip Horsemen that she was distraught over our breakup, so they regurgitated the story like good birds.

I just wanted to be with my children. I had no other desires. By the way, Somers' guy that night in the ADKS would not last long, but I gather he was useful for one month. And, most tellingly, he was first in the door. Kudos to number one.

She was always laughing at me…I was always her fool.

"Did She Just Say Physical Abandonment?"

Our first court appearance came two months later in Mineola. I expected the tag-hag mafia in their finest couture…I didn't even own a tie anymore.

I'd never stepped foot inside a courtroom. They really are imposing edifices that scare the crap out of people like me. This divorce was going to set records for speed because I wanted nothing to do with it and just wanted out… You heard about the new Barbie Doll? It comes with all of Ken's stuff. That was going to be us because I'd give her whatever she wanted.

I really hadn't been looking forward to seeing Somers or Gruella in a courtroom…this was a girl I'd been deeply in love with, not been arrested for assault and battery. I don't think she was on the same wavelength.

I was sure she was going to show in black dress, widow's veil, and a solemn string of matronly pearls, to make the courtroom empathize with her destitute plight. The whole event was just dreadful. I would have signed any piece of paper to get it over with…a murder confession even. I hate courtrooms and most lawyers. I'm really stranded in the wrong time.

Also, I needed time and space to get back on my feet professionally. I was a pretty weak competitor, that's for sure, and Somers Gillette loves weakness. I felt strung out.

Expensive divorce lawyers are the bottom of the moral barrel for the legal profession. They're exceedingly nasty, comically arrogant, often dumb, and super blunt: pure legal thugs, the pit bulls of the legal directory. Hers were no different, except they wore really expensive Chanel suits. Somers had two female lawyers who worked out of offices on 57th and Madison in Manhattan. Just like doctors who work on 72nd and Fifth, 57th and Madison doesn't come cheap…

I had a total schlep from Far Rockaway who worked in a second floor tenement house. My only advice to him was: get it over with quick, I don't care how much it costs. I needed my life back, my kids back, and I had to earn money for a lot of people. I was demanding freedom, but this society captor wouldn't let me go so easily.

I didn't know anything about how the courtroom scenario would play out. I half-expected that detective guy to show up and state that

I hit Somers like a punching bag…I had a feeling she would pay anyone to say anything about me at this stage…I just wish I knew how accurate that really was. I was clueless about what she was doing behind the scenes.

'…Every inch between us becomes light years now,'… *

Somers had been around this track before…she looked more comfortable here than anywhere I'd ever seen her. She was smiling, relaxed, a day at the beach, she showed up with umbrella's, coolers, and Frisbees.

She was big pimpin' in courtrooms, eventually bringing her whole family, a posse of 12th Man Cheering Section frenemies, society spin doctors, interior decorators that I'd paid millions to, and her Ashkenazi defense squad, as different from the white-shoe Cravath team I'd expected as could ever be (I gather she'd relegated Cravath to strictly trust work from here on out…this was war, and Cravath didn't do war…these two women, oh yeah, not only did they do war, they'd never lost…hot flashes when they smelled blood on the streets).

Somers finally rolled in the doorway of the cavernous courtroom with her two depressingly loathsome legal slugs, women who would never consider a child's best interests, not if their own lives depended on it. Somers, in her estimable way, had guided them into believing that I wanted to fight…not, so they showed up with claws extended, fangs bared, and saliva dripping from the corners of their mouths.

Somers also walked in with Gruella right by her side…they were dressed like you might see for the Wildlife Conservation Society Ball…happier than pigs in caca, a Mastema on tag-hag couture fire. I hadn't seen mother Drac in a while…"It's alive! It's alive!"…courts gave her menopausal ecstasy. A rat flees when sunlight streams through the glass, in here she was perched on a bale of hay lazily dreaming her days away, never more content.

Somers' 12th man cheering section was gratefully as confused as I was with respect to her choice of attack-dog counsel…her fans weren't exactly synagogue central casting (notwithstanding Gruella). It was the navy blazer Quest crowd sitting alongside Hempstead domestic violence victims. In spite of Somers' legal choice awkwardness, her friends still considered the event entertaining, just as Somers had promised. Party favors would be handed out upon the conclusion.

Somers was a traitor to marriage. Her narcissism had won out, her mother's King of Devil's mine had proven far deeper than my gold-panning of love. Somers' betrayal was Tarpeia, whose father was the keeper of the outer gates of the citadel of Rome. She betrayed the city of Rome by letting the Sabines enter the gates in exchange for "that which they wore on their left arms" (i.e: gold and silver). Even the Sabines disliked her for her traitorous ways, and they executed her for treason. Afterward, the rock from which condemned Roman criminals and traitors would be thrown to their deaths would forever be known as the Tarpeian Rock. We had Stoney Rock…

Somers was in her finest non-Somers outfit…black dress and pearls…natch. No veil, but that was probably because that was her ace up the sleeve. This was the time she throws it all out the window and reverts to form. Her dad's kindness was buried for the time being and Gruella's pestiferous platelets simply came to the surface and they swam in it. Somers showed the perfect amount of leg that day, enough to impress, but not enough for a judge to hold her in contempt. Which I desperately wished for him to do. No one wanted to see any leg from me I gathered.

My lawyer let word slip to her lawyers that perhaps it was best to leave family out of courtroom appearances, for the kids' sake, as this would only further harden resolve on any one person's side. My family heeded our direction of course, I wouldn't allow them to show. Somers' family never got that memo I guess…she wanted bitter feelings to harden, because she was up to even more shenanigans. Asking family to show for divorce is like asking someone to watch a vivisection…if you have the stomach, it can be fascinating and unforgettable. The cadaver isn't so keen on the event….

I was worn out already. We hadn't been there five minutes…she was just starting. I was never who she wanted me to be, and my overriding desire to protect my kids stood between her and a new life. Not to mention it threatened her reputation.

Somers hadn't paid her lawyers a Half Million Dollar retainer for only one day of pain (pain for me that is…). That retainer was intended to punish, inflict, and entertain over a long period of time, so nothing in this marital matter would proceed quickly as I'd hoped…and even though I agreed to everything, each time. It took her five minutes to trap me in 1992, but she wanted a lifetime to release me.

Oh, yeah, by the way, before we get too far…you heard that right: $500K for a divorce when we didn't argue about a.n.y.t.h.i.n.g.! I was honored in some small measure. Real destitute.

"Your Honor, Mr. Graham has left the family destitute. We respectfully ask that the court order Mr. Graham to pay Ms. Gillette $25,000 per month for living expenses."

This alimony thing would be the screwing I get for the screwing I got?

If a mathematician did a calculation of the amount of amorous relations I had over 15 years with my society Iblis, versus the dollar figure of the proposed alimony figure, I'd be somewhere south of the next lowest contestant…I'd be pitted against an 85-year old billionaire who croaked on his honeymoon!

The judge had already reviewed my bank statements (which just to get copies of, since Somers had burned the old statements at the house, I had to pay even more useless money), and he was fully aware that I was handing over 90% of my net income to her already…You can't squeeze blood from a rock. His response,

"I would suggest that Ms. Gillette get a job that pays her more than $200 per week. She is of able body and mind to do so, am I correct?"

"We believe that Mr. Graham is hiding assets overseas."

"Mr. Graham, are you hiding assets overseas?"

"Your Honor, no I'm not. I wish I was. What's actually happening here is, Ms. Gillette has become inverted, substituting fantasy for reality. She already threw out all my old records, making any problem worse. She caused all of my contacts and servers to be erased. She even threw out my letters from my children, all Father's day cards, all birthday cards from my kids, everything. She has an unusual way of getting what she wants I suppose. I'm giving her everything I have already as we have shown with the statements."

The judge smiled. He got her. Judges really don't believe anyone in court, especially people with highly paid legal thugs at their side.

In two years of court appearances, I never asked a friend to step inside the court with me for moral or any other kind of support. I gather Somers sort of fibbed her way into gaining even more undeserved sympathy by saying to everyone (when she wasn't sleeping around…) how intimidated she was with the process. Intimidated, Somers? She doesn't flinch from rattlesnakes.

But show up her paid fan section did…and she gave them parting gifts each time, natch. Somers was in total control of parents, friends, and eventually lovers. She wanted the judge to see that she had lifeline support beyond the two legal ogres sitting to her left, whereas I had one schleppy lawyer from the Rockaways. The matchup didn't look so strong to me.

Somers' childless assassin lawyers knew that Somers was conspiring against me behind the matrimonial courtroom….they assumed I knew about that already and therefore I hated her. I didn't know anything. I had no idea what she was doing, other than the adultery. I would have stood in the rain for her, even then, catching her if she fell. I'd taken her to so many hospital visits your head would spin. I couldn't erase memories just like that.

Her mongrel lawyers came back with even more delaying nonsense. They were sucking dollars from Somers' trusts as fast as they could…even Somers knew it, but she didn't care. She had plans for me that were much greater than a few hundred K on divorce lawyers. She was just getting amped up, and she needed time to manage a behind-the-scenes murder.

I wanted to get on with the business of being a dad and being back in business, so I could provide for my kids again and make some investors whole. Somers' divorce lawyers had a deliberate strategy for not getting to the finish line, until they gave Somers the time she needed to keep working her backdoor voodoo magic so others could plunge their daggers.

Every time I heard about the vacations, the legal bills, the new wardrobe, the new car, heard the kids tell me about the large hosted black-tie parties for profit at the house, I only had one thought: do we really have money troubles or is it only me that has money troubles?   Somers hosted thirty-eight parties in 2008…we counted. Somers spent four nights out of every seven away from the house…we counted. She spent money like a drunken Saudi prince, all the while claiming she was destitute…

And I sent her money every month like a chump. The lies she fed to the Locust Valley Horsemen was damaging, but the lie she fed to the courts was perjurous. And everyone else outside Locust Valley had begun to hear…

One my lawyers, Phil, said to me,

"First of all, where I'm from, if my wife did what she is doing to you, she wouldn't be fucking doing it…OK? You know what I mean Seb? She's fucking you like I've never seen a wife fuck a husband. You've got to stick up for yourself or those kids will be poisoned and you will pay for it professionally. Seb, she's fucking half of Locust Valley and spending your money on the condoms! I mean, get a fucking grip! She's gone and she's trying to wreck you…we have the proof. Want to read the emails? Wake the fuck up Buddy!"

"Look Phil, I get it man. The thing is, I feel like shite, I always wanted to provide for my wife. I feel sort of like I let her down."

"Get your fucking self-sorry ass off the deck Seb. You have to sue this bitch or she'll walk all over you. You want to see the emails she sent to her boyfriends the last ten years? You want to see how she lied to you about money issues? You want to see how great life is for her? She isn't destitute and yet you keep giving her money that you need. She doesn't need one fuckin shekel. She's fucking you, and I won't stand for it. Was she a great housekeeper Buddy? Because she's gonna 'keep the house', that you paid for and built."

Phil sounded like he wanted to whack Somers, and if you knew Phil's heritage, you could believe that.

"Phil, I don't sue people, it isn't me. Somers is going to eventually calm down. I'm still hung up on her, I guess"

"Seb, if you don't sue her now and she stops the bullshit, I walk. Her bitterness makes her happy; it sustains her, and those fucking lawyers of hers are goading her. I've never in thirty years of lawyering seen anything like this. They feed on others' misery. I can't allow you to lie down like a pussy and I won't be a party for profit to it. She doesn't respect that. You have to fight her. Sue her, or I walk. Your call."

Phil walked. I couldn't sue my own murderer, which ironically, Somers was fast becoming.

'...You can't be neutral on a moving train.'... *

Somers managed to wrangle the only socially acceptable job in Locust Valley for a society gal…she was now the assistant editor of the Locust Valley Gazette, which sounds impressive, as if she was actually working for a living…until you learned that her pay was $200/week. The paper is free if you want a copy. Somers trumpeted the news of her job as if she was the new head of the largest global multi-media corporation in the universe, and thank god she had a job because her family needs the money. The judge laughed.

And yet, in the courtroom, we heard the same refrain over and over and over: Mr. Graham has left the family destitute. The court had never seen a family spend so much money where there was such destitution. Somers lives in an alternative universe, complaining to people who earn no more than middle-income wages that she couldn't possibly live on the $12,500 per month that I handed over. One month I gave her $25,000. It still wasn't enough. I gave her 90% of my income; I signed over every asset I ever had; I voluntarily signed over the house and contents; and I bought my kids everything they needed for school and play. And yet, we were destitute. You've never seen a bigger farce. I don't know why the government didn't prosecute her.

She was all an act...the last thing Somers needed was money. She didn't want my money. What she wanted was my extinction...

She had been so erratic for so long, I didn't know who the hell I was anymore. How fucking bizarre can one woman be? She was bleeding me dry.

The destitution charade was an attempt to sell a version of me to others. I just didn't know it. Outside court, I never spoke to anyone about anything, so no one ever said anything back to me. I was working in Bermuda with a new cell phone and a new email. No one could reach me unless Somers handed over my contact data. I thought rectitude was the Protestant way. Meanwhile, she was selling her fantasies, and people were buying. She was The Slanderer, the Trickster, and The Accuser.

And yet, all of this was mere fodder to the ultimate marital insult, and I don't mean the murder. New York State is the last of the no/no-fault divorce states, so one of the two parties has to concoct a ruse to sell to the court for an expedited version of the event. Since Somers is good at ruses, she ran with it. One of Somers's legal trolls gurgled up this line,

"Your Honor, Mr. Graham has refused to have sex with my client, Ms. Gillette, for over a year, and because of this, we would ask that the court expedite the divorce proceeding so Ms. Gillette can establish normal relationships again shortly."

Hey-oahhhhh....! Could you repeat what you just said?! You're kidding, right?!?!!?

I almost choked. I stared at her legal swamp rat as if I was Charles Darwin in the Galapagos, fascinated by a new species that I'd come upon . A natural selection of inhumanity had emerged. Somers' cheering section was in the back of the courtroom, with their vuvuzela's momentarily quieted by the decorum of the court... Her lawyers were just the lowest of the low, the purest of lying callousness...you comb through lawyers and then down to divorce lawyers and then further down to whom Somers would hire, it simply goes no lower. Her lawyers had such a blasé indifference to telling lies, they too would need post-death autopsies for future scientists to study.

How do I breathe in this environment, how could I ever survive? Lawyers suck all the oxygen from a room.

I had three resoundingly horrific assessments, as I sat there transfixed by the new lawyer species...

- Excuse me, but I've been trying to have sex with The Plaintiff for fifteen years, every night without fail, and she stopped me at nearly every turn…'I need to be in Newport, the rooms are too close, I'm on my period, my Periods last a month now (capital P intended), I'm spending the night at my mom's, I'm too tired, I'm too hungry, American Idol is on, oh jesus Sebastian just stick it in'…I think the wrong person is being accused of physical abandonment your Honor. Like monumentally…Seriously, we're talking Biblical.
- The Plaintiff has been on a raging adulterous affair tour with no fewer than five men over the past fifteen years, and I've never said shite.
- Does anyone here care that the Plaintiff has never cracked her checkbook once in fifteen years, except for that rat dog she bought, and I spent every dime I ever made on this marriage, which is now being tarnished seconds by hours by these pestiferous clowns she calls lawyers?

You'd have to assume the judge thought so as well. As I came to learn later, he never believed a word of Somers and especially her lawyers. Still, the record shows for eternity that we divorced because I couldn't get wood for that piece of ass…as if. Is it any wonder I felt tired of her shite? Instead of getting married again, I'm gonna find a woman I don't like and just give her a house.

Bermuda Gales

It wasn't getting better…the Lion of Judah was wrong. She was trying to overwhelm me, not simply nick me. I was hearing it from all corners. It felt like she was in fifty states and fifty countries simultaneously. She'd Facebooked herself, spreading her tentacles to every corner of the globe. She would tell you about me if you were just a bum on the streets.

Somers spent more than $300,000 on two Manhattan pr flacks, the kind who trade society tidbits with gossip editors in exchange for favors down the road. In two years, here's what she spent on noncritical services: $2 million legal fees, $300k public relation, $200k catered parties for profit, $300k new wardrobe, $200k five country clubs, $100k travel, $398k interior decorating, and on and on…I wish I was that destitute! No wonder the judge laughed.

My professional reputation was trade-bait for her PR folks. I tried going silent, refusing to engage in conversations with anyone except my kids, but that only seemed to make matters worse. I never realized that society fills in the blanks when you won't. In Locust Valley, people need gossip like a sex addict needs pornography. You can't get enough until they commit you.

She had someone to blame, so she was on fire.

By the way, you'd think that our names only went in newspapers at birth and death…Episcopalians prefer that, especially country-club Wasps. Episcopalians don't do websites, reality TV, courtrooms, and papers. But the Episcopalian Church had a renegade in Somers Gillette.

Without my consulting business around to keep my bills paid, I never stood a chance. Somers pulled the dagger and plunged like a raving lunatic, over and over and over, feverishly spraying the walls with my blood and licking the drops in spasmodic ecstasy. She was painting the ceiling with my blood. I never felt the pain.

I took the first job I could get, consulting for two companies whose headquarters happened to be in Bermuda. I had to earn money. I still hadn't heard from anyone associated with the old company, which was strange. I could have sworn they would have called the house by then. I handed over to Somers my entire income. I barely had enough left to eat. But I thought it was the right thing to do, given the fact that she was so apparently destitute.

After being in Bermuda for two months (and flying home every weekend to be with the kids), I received my first call there from someone out of my previous life…our nanny of ten years, a woman from Peru called Betty. I was in my office on Front Street on a gorgeous Spring Day in the middle of the Atlantic Ocean, missing my kids terribly. Even Bermuda was depressing…the re-insurance world had cratered. Hearing Betty was like a shot of life…she had been in my world and the kids' for ten years. My own daughter preferred Betty to her mother by many factors, just like Lorna years before.

Betty had gotten my cell phone number from the boys, who weren't sure why she wanted it but gave it to her anyway. Somers kept a tight lid on house staff, jamming their cell phones around the property with radio frequency interrupters (not a cheap service, I assure you…you can add that to the non-essential fees services paid out). Somers wanted all calls to be made on the house landline phone, because she wanted to know who was with her. All house calls were tape recorded and Somers spent a fortune on an outside tech company to transcribe every call I ever made with the kids. Cha-ching.

Anyway, Betty called and asked me to hold what she was about to say in the strictest confidence. She was so nervous, she made me nervous. For Betty to even call me, something really dreadful had to have happened. This was that 3 AM call where you know something is wrong. Except this was 3 PM on a Wednesday. And when Betty gets nervous, her rough English gets even worse.

"Senor Graham. Hello. I miss you. How are you? I hope well. I am not so good at this. So excuse me. Your wife is acting crazy Senor. Graham. Mrs. Graham (Betty never knew that Somers kept her maiden name) tell me that no one is to get your cell number, like you asked me to do. She told me to no longer listen to you. She tell anyone who calls the house looking for you that you are criminal, and that they need to call a man that she is friends with (what?!...). I overhear his name. His name is Senor Thomas Spirella, and he will give them the name of someone at the FBI. I heard her one day. She saw me, and she asked to speak with me. She handed me the paper the next day, a confidential paper. She said I must sign. I don't sign, because I don't sign nothing in this country…you know. Anyway, I look up Mr. Spirella on my son's computer this weekend, and this guy is former federal prosecutor (great…). He definitely know Mr. Kincaid, because I see Mr. Kincaid, Mrs. Graham, and Mr. Spirella have lunch on the back porch. Mrs. Graham tell me that she is going to get you, that maybe my paper not so important because she can just sign my name anyway, and that I not to speak with you. Senor Graham, I think God works for all of us, and he ask me to call you. Mrs. Graham is trying to hurt you, and God wanted me to tell you. She says to me she is going to get you, and you will not know it before it does."

"Betty, thank you. I'm so sorry it has come to this, for all of us. Count me in as your friend. Yes, she's crazy, but it will all work out in the end. I won't tell her you called."

"Thank you Senor Graham. I need this job so much. If she fire me, maybe you can help. I love these children so much, and they so scared of her. I know they love you more than they love their own mother. And I don't know how to tell you this, because I not tell on no one…you know that. But Mrs. Graham had affair on you while you were married. I pray to God to forgive me for never telling you, but she told me Mr. Kincaid would deport me if I ever said anything to anyone. I know the man. You do too (double great…a rat and adulterer…)."

Well, maybe God was listening when I prayed at St. Bart's. No investor, but just desserts perhaps.

Betty then told me that Somers was sleeping around like crazy, and that she was telling the kids some awful lies about me, like a crazy woman…crazy as a fox. Betty told me she fished used condoms out of the master bathroom trashcan and she was concerned that my little daughter would eventually come across one and ask what it was. Betty said that Somers was out every night, drinking and carrying on. Betty was very religious and none of this made her very happy. You had to think that Somers had begun to question the need to have religious Betty so close to the scene of her nighttime crimes.

"Senor Graham…we have a Spanish saying in Peru, and it goes somewhat like this in English…'she was always looking out for herself'. I hope you realize your wife."

I recognized that name Spirella. I just couldn't place it. When I hung up with Betty, I did an Internet search of him and quickly I recalled why. He was an Astor lawyer involved in some large fraud case. But that wasn't the end of it. On his website, I saw that one of his clients was none other than Ed Kincaid's private holding company, which to the outside eye looked like an anonymous company, but to my eye simply said Ed Kincaid. Motherblaster.

"Senor Graham…one last thing. Ms. Graham is tracking where you are every minute. She has some device in her office that can pin down your location because of your cell phone. I know because she tell people at a party for profit one night at the house. That is wrong. She also tape records and listens to every phone call you have with the children. She is very bad, Ms. Graham. God will punish her one day."

What Betty told me about Somers' morals was nothing I didn't expect…the billion calls and emails already had confirmed that part. I was embarrassed for Somers mostly. But I didn't see the criminal thing at all. It was like it didn't compute. I was remembering the wife I took to the hospital for all of her cancer surgeries, practically carrying her to the car and driving her home each time, feeding her in bed when she was sick and defending her to nearly everyone (who talked about her behind her back in the game). Would she be so depraved as to toss our memories aside and lie about me in a criminal matter?

I didn't think I had done anything criminally wrong, then again I was well aware of the mess at the company level. I simply needed to talk with those guys and let them know what I was doing. I assumed they would call the house and get my phone and email information and I'd deal then. I didn't immediately go into lawyer overdrive with Betty's call. I thought mostly of what I would say to Somers when I saw her next. She was definitely trying to end me and yet I was handing her my income every week. Irony. Ain't love grand?

One month after Betty's call and still having yet to respond directly to Somers evil scheme, I received a second call in Bermuda, this time from an old friend from Kuwait, Talal. The former partners were finally starting to get through, so I thought. Talal had called the old Manhattan office number and it was obviously disconnected…he remembered that I lived in Locust Valley, so with the help of Google, he got my home number (you can't Google a Kuwaiti's home phone!). Somers wouldn't delist the house phone number even though hundreds of company creditors would call and speak with the kids. Somers wanted everyone's name, because she was organizing the offensive, while I underwrote her efforts...

Somers inexplicably gave Talal my number. In two years of post separation living, after hundreds of phone calls from old friends/enemies/creditors/partners asking her for my cell phone number, Talal was the only person she ever gave my number to even though we asked her to forward any calls to me so I could deal. She gave Talal the number because he agreed with her to work against me, and she was drunk one night. He insisted on speaking with me.

But he didn't get the number that easily…he had to pretend he was on her side. I guess that was the only way, faking the faker. She gave in. My guess is everyone else bought her story.

"Seb my friend. How is it going? What happened to you?"

When anyone would start a conversation like this, I assumed they knew my fragile state, so I immediately shriveled, hoping against hope they didn't really know about my emotions.

"Been better Talal to be honest with you. Living in Bermuda during the week, flying back to be with my kids every weekend. I'm really sorry about the company. I lost everything if that's any consolation. How's your wife, family?"

"Fine. Thank you for asking. I know how tough that must be for you, to be away from your kids. Seb, I need to tell you something very difficult. You have been a friend for over ten years, and although I'm not happy that we lost money instead of making a fortune, that's business and business is business. Friendships last forever and I love you like a brother. I called your house. Your wife, or ex-wife, answered the phone. I asked to speak with you, but she wasn't very interested in giving out your contact details. She said you had absconded the country (you have to be kidding me…?!...I come home every weekend to take my kids everywhere while she parties her lights out!...). Instead of giving me your number like I asked, she begged me to call an attorney she said was organizing people to arrest you. To be honest, she startled me and I'm not easily startled. She is after you my friend. She's a vicious, unforgiving, vengeful human being. We call her Iblis (I know the word…). Your children never came up, which I found odd, because I know you and I know how you love them. She wants to put a wall between you and them. I know. I come from a religion where we tolerate all of our family's mistakes, and I have seen trouble before with my own brother. But this is different. She's actively plotting against you. I actually played along with her, because I wanted to hear what she was up to. More for entertainment. But it was not so entertaining really. When she decided that I was on her side, I asked again for your cell phone number so I could yell at you. Ha! She said that she was not allowed to give the number out, but if I gave my word that I would testify against you, that she would give it to me. So, I did, and she did, and here I am on the phone, with you. For the record, I think she was drunk. And, you're my friend and she is the devil. I say this to you as my friend…I would never in a million years betray a friendship…I think you Americans are superb at handling that kind of evil, but I am simply warning you about your wife: she wants to destroy you, not a doubt in my head. You must protect yourself. Get a lawyer to shut her up before she does more damage. Or get someone worse than a lawyer. Friendships last forever, don't forget it."

I got off the phone with Talal…my ears singed. Here I was on Bermuda, so far away from my kids, giving my wife all of my hard-earned income every week, and she was conspiring to destroy me, for something she never had any involvement in. She never had any exposure to my old company and yet she was organizing anyone who had ever come across the company to team up against me?! Can you even consider the evil that it takes to do that, to the father of your three children?! Ahh, marriage. Seriously, passing kidney stones is more pleasant.

Somers was a silent assassin, doing her damage behind the scenes, using lawyers, thugs, and gossips to do her bidding. She shot me with a silencer because she didn't want to wake society…

I'd been in business for ten years, I'd met thousands of people, had hired and fired hundreds, had worked alongside hundreds of clients, and we'd transacted over a billion dollars of business. If you added it up, just assuming that ten percent of anyone you ever meet likely will not like you, then maybe 500 people would be willing to gang up on me, but only if there was a leader leading the effort. The leader had stuck her head out of the ground and she was an heiress with too much money and too much time, living in Locust Valley. Those are not good facts when you're on an island in the Atlantic.

I sat on the information for a month.

I didn't say a word to my lawyer, my brothers, my mother, or my friends. I was just embarrassed. For me, for her, trying to figure out if this was bulldust or if she actually had stooped that low…My kids' lives were in the balance. It certainly wasn't as if I never considered what she was doing…I was simply hoping that I could make a big comeback on the business scene and get back to the business of making money. And keep the kids safe. I could see things somewhat more clearly now: she was a fake plastic girl with a general lack of empathy for others. She was a Magical Narcissist.

And meanwhile, the party for profit raged in Locust Valley. Somers was now sleeping with partner #3. And all I ever wanted was to be with my kids…

Talal was the only friend who ever got my phone number from Somers in two years. Three hundred and forty two persons or companies called the Locust Valley house looking for me, asking for me. And only Talal from Kuwait got my number. Everyone was first sold a tragic version of me starting with the he told me he made an investment but didn't…and that story continued even after we confronted her…natch), a twenty minute assault by a supposedly destitute woman (spending $2 Million in one year on fees, clothes, and clubs), and then they were redirected to another man who methodically walked them through on how to conspire against me. And do you know that of those hundreds of people, how many eventually agreed to work against me, after all the marketing and lies and money…? Let's just say you don't need more than one hand.

Somers never wanted the father of her three to recover. She wanted him dead and buried. She knew I would stay by the kids' side if I had the choice, and the only way to prevent that was to bury me. Somers would kill herself to never stop. I needed two more Seals and a Revelation.

The Nanny Gets Fired, then Obliterated

The mayhem was building, and I was mentally stretched beyond my means. I didn't need her additional pain, so her answer was to provide even more. She had the world spitting at me by then. My heart was crippled.

Four weeks after Talal's call, I was in Locust Valley driving my children around to weekend events, while Somers partied it up in Manhattan. On Saturday at about 2 PM, I had to bring my sons back the house so they could get their lacrosse sticks for a game.

When we pulled into the driveway, I saw an empty 20 oz. Molson XX can lying near the garage and picked it up as if it was radioactive….I assumed it hadn't been drunk by my children. It's hard to explain why a small thing like an empty beer can trigger such deep emotion, but that beer can just seemed to represent Somers' willful disregard for the safety of the kids while she partied her guts out, and further while she and Ed conspired to destroy me. They were having a blast at my expense. It wasn't even a classic Molson! A Molson XX. You drink that to get drunk; that's what college kids drink.

While I waited by the car for my sons to get their sticks, Somers miraculously appeared inside the garage, looking like hell, like the wan vampire she had become. She saw me, frozen in her blue terry cloth bathrobe, at 2 PM. Clearly, she had gotten in kinda late the previous night. This was no longer the cheerful morning person I knew and loved. I held the beer can and said to her as she scurried around the garage…

"Somers, looks like your boyfriend left something last night."

Somers Gillette was high society's Messalina, the wife of Emperor Claudius, one of the wickedest women in the history of the Roman Empire, which was no small task. Messalina had numerous affairs. When Claudius left Rome for a visit to his troops in the fields, Messalina arranged to marry one of her lovers, Caius Silius, and install him on the throne instead of Caludius. Messalina was executed for her betrayals.

I'll grant you I could have just let it slide. But I just couldn't I help myself… I'd had it. I was fed up. And it felt so good saying something so wrong.

Somers being Somers wouldn't let me walk away so easily with a cheap shot…

"If you'd pay me more money, maybe I wouldn't fucking invite anyone over here."

"So, you're sleeping with men for money, is that it?"

Again, a little below the belt. I agree. Guilty. The explosion was imminent, the Upper Case Voice expected,

"FUCK YOU Sebastian! Just fuck you and your whole fucking family! I hope you fucking die! You're going to jail, trust me, I'll make sure of that! I'll do whatever the fuck I have to to make certain of that! We'll see who is good or not! Get off of my property before I call the POLICE!!"

Somers was a frequent flyer of 911, she called them more than she called directory assistance.

She'd have been an ideal patient inside Bellevue. The way she screamed, her constant obscenities, the way she waved her arms as if she was going to hit you…she was a caricature of whatever is opposite of normalcy. She is what they want at Bellevue. She was a narcissist's wet dream. The Director would be ecstatic to interview her.

And, for the record, this was only the eight hundredth time she said she was going to call the police, never for any reason of course…it's just another fallback line she loves. She fantasized that she owned the Old Brookville Police Department (the OB Police patrol Locust Valley), as her father was an honorary Commissioner (one of those only-in-Locust Valley unpaid roles, occupied solely by Stoney members). Somers understood the Commissioner role to mean that her father ran the police department … When someone cries wolf so often, you stop listening.

"Call them Somers. Before you do, would you have the kids come downstairs so we can leave and get the hell away from your moral desert? And by the way, I don't want to hear so much about used condoms floating around the house."

Now that statement I sincerely did regret, not because it hit Somers below the belt, but because I'd unwittingly revealed a source: Somers would take holy revenge on Betty. Only one person knew about the condoms and that was Betty. She was the only one who cleaned the house and emptied the garbage cans. I bummed out immediately.

Somers glowered. She was great at the glower. No words, just intensive menacing thoughts coursing through her demented head. She had a live mole in her house, and moles were not to be tolerated. I could see her head burbling with sheer hatred for many people, myself, Betty, others. The Agentic Narcissist.

The kids came down, Somers slammed the garage door as we were loading the lacrosse sticks, and once again, I had to explain to the kids that Mom was simply going through a phase…you know, that typical phase where she's actively plotting their Dad's arrest so she can have unencumbered custody to justify her life's wayward ways…Everyone goes through that, right?

Betty was fired that Monday when she came to work. Her bags were packed before she even got there, just like what had happened to me.

It wasn't Somers' right to go through Betty's stuff…Betty is a middle-aged woman who deserves some dignity. Somers handed Betty an indemnity statement to sign in exchange for money (likely my money again, since I was sending her money every month). Betty told her she would not sign anything, just like the last time when Somers had asked her to sign an agreement without anyone else looking at it. This was yet another example of Somers' feeling entitled and above it all. The Special Narcissist.

As Betty left in her small car, crying and confused, Somers was overhead by neighbors screaming the worst obscenities from the front porch, at our 55 year old Peruvian nanny of 11 years, the psycho society fatwa imama. God, I really wish Locust Valley knew the real Somers Gillette…it ain't the fake version they know. She's the master of artful deception…the real girl is about as opposite what they see as could ever be imagined. She slept with #4 that night.

Betty called me from a pay phone in Locust Valley, crying hysterically. I'd screwed up, but she was the one paying the price. When you mess up and it's only you paying the price, all well and good. But when you foul up and someone else pays the price, shame on you. Or me. I told her not to worry, it would be no problem, I'd help get her a new job. There is no greater nanny in the United States.

I felt really bad about what had happened to Betty. It was my entire fault. I let Somers get inside my head, and in a fit of stupidity, my aim hit the wrong person. Somers could care less about someone like Betty. Betty had worked for us for ten years, through some very difficult times, and she had never ever called in sick or was late. She was heroic in my book and the kids'. I'd give her the highest reference ever. To Somers, Betty was dispensable refuse, not even human.

There isn't anyone in the universe who knew more who the real Somers Gillette really was than Betty (and me). We had seen the warts and all side of Somers Gillette, and it's telling that we are the two who ended up on the outside. Unfortunately, both of us would remain silent, for different reasons.

So, if you ever have a doubt as to who the real Somers Gillette is, just remember: only two adults got to live with her every day, one for fifteen years (me) and one for ten (Betty). And neither of us lasted and both of us suffered Somers' attacks. You can call me the bitter ex of Locust Valley, but you can't call Betty anything…the woman is beyond reproach. Even friends of ours marveled at what a great nanny she was. Somers went after her like a sworn enemy and Betty never stood a chance. Somers waged a holy war on Betty that you cannot imagine.

Betty's headhunter called me a few days later. I gave Betty the great recommendation she deserved and needed. Within two days, Betty had gone on three interviews, all in Locust Valley, and had three conditional offers. Each prospective mother called me after their interview with Betty, and I said the same things to them…Betty is great; you can trust her with anything, etc…

They wanted to know why she had left or was terminated. I told them the unvarnished truth, excepting the mention of the condoms. I simply said that my ex-wife was a nutter, Betty felt closer to me, she called me with information about the kids because she knew I would be concerned, I accidentally repeated some of that to my wife, and my wife fired her, even after eleven loyal years of devoted service.

The next thing they all wanted to know was would it be possible for them to speak to my ex-wife. I couldn't exactly forbid them, that was their right, it's a free country still. Mom's want to talk with Mom's, which is odd, because Mom's I have news: Somers hates you, she hates all women just some more than others. I warned them that Somers would be unhinged about everything and she would likely make a mess of Betty even though Betty didn't deserve it. And sure enough that's exactly what happened.

Somers tore into Betty as if she was the devil incarnate (it takes one to know one…), when in fact she is the exact opposite. The ten years of service by Betty counted for less to Somers than the sweat off my ass. None of the three prospective hirers wanted to employ Betty after this, not necessarily because they didn't trust my assessment of what had happened, but mostly because Somers mentioned something about possibly suing Betty, and they may not want to put their kids in the way of the impending mess. Betty is a 55-year old Peruvian woman who served eight years in the US military as a cook, she attends church like a Pope, and she has never done anything bad at all in her entire life. She thought she had done the right thing. She was protecting the children. If she got sued, the courts would laugh the suit out. But that didn't mean Somers couldn't mess her up…Somers knew how.

Somers was out for blood from a woman who could not begin to defend herself. And Somers knew she could get away with it, because who would Betty complain to…?

I called Somers,

"Somers, do you think it's fair for you to be trying to deny Betty a new job? I mean, c'mon and give the poor woman a break. You're hassling a woman who needs the money. Fine if you don't want her to work for you… trust me, she doesn't want to work for you either. Is this what turns you on so much, hurting those less fortunate? No wonder everyone hates you so much."

The truth was people didn't hate Somers…they were intimidate by her. The last words stung,

"People don't hate me Sebastian…they respect me (that sounds so warm!…). Betty spoke to you about things that are private, to be kept between her and me (uhhh...she was protecting the kids, not telling me about your dating life…ooops, sorry, she did mention the condom thing, sorry…). That is a serious violation of our employment agreement with her. She is going to be lucky not to be deported (Betty had worked for the US Army for 8 years, which makes her more American than anything you've ever done Somers…). Ed is looking into it now with the State Department (this is how he spends his days?…). And you are FUCKED (as always…)!!"

Wait a minute, it was our agreement, as if we were still married? Presumably that meant I had liability here as well. Or liability when it suited Somers I guessed.

"Somers, the woman was concerned about the kids for god's sake, something you might consider every so often while you party like it's 1999. She's the only one between you and utter destruction. She worked for us for ten years without a hitch, never sick, never complained. Don't you think you could just say nothing at all about her, instead of something? She needs the job, she needs the money. And are you serious about Ed calling the State Department on a nanny? Doesn't he have anything better to do, like shoot your mother?"

Wayyyyyyy Upper Case,

"FUCK Betty Seb, and FUCK YOU! You can both rot in hell!! Ahhhh!!

Seriously, I knew more stabilized patients at Bellevue than this wife of mine. She was a complete lunatic, primal-yelling at the end of phone conversations. The Mara had come out of her cage.

Eventually I got a job for Betty, but far away from Locust Valley…

I also began to sense that things would not end well for me. These wayward jihadists of Manhattan society had too much pull and they knew how to wreck lives, but more importantly, they enjoyed wrecking lives. When I said I prefer doing things and not talking, they're the complete opposite…this was their life, their preferred way of dealing, the verbal destruction and gossiping and eschatology, they were gathering Gog and Magog from the four corners of the Earth, encamping themselves around their beloved city, so the Beast and the False Prophets could rule the world once again.

Maybe I should have married that Honda auto parts sales manager. I wonder where she was now. I bet her husband gets a blowjob.

The Decree of Dissolution

It had been a long while since I'd screwed things up this bad. Court dates always set new bars for me… When you can't recall much about today, it's even harder to remember the shite unloaded every day fifteen years prior. I needed peaceful days, not warfare.

Our final court appearance came in July of 2008. We were due that day to get the final judgment of divorce, otherwise known as the Decree of Dissolution, and we needed to be present to sign. She'd blast away without waiting for an answer, never a warning. She's my smokin' hot Harry Callahan in Manolo Blahnik's, a thigh strapped pistol for the perfect touch, a mouse tattoo on her inner thigh... I expected Somers Callahan to walk in to the courtroom with a .45 in her hands, point it at me, and say, "You've got ask yourself one question: 'Do I feel lucky?' Well, do ya, punk?"

Judgments of divorce are such anticlimactic events. Even Somers' family declined to attend this installment of Somers' entertainment review. No more live audiences and award show, and in fact on this day, she was all business, like we had asked her to be a year ago. Maybe she was simply sad that this installment of her life that she so loved, courtrooms and drama, was ending.

I wondered if Somers sensed that she could no longer beat up on me after that day. Naaah…she wasn't done just yet. The E.L.E. was still to come.

Somers walked into the room in your basic front button navy dress, looking sexy crypto-corporate with a strand of pearls (she never wore pearls before our courtroom appearances…). No .45 thank god. For some reason, I no longer fantasized about Somers naked…it probably had to do with the ruthless perpetual sodomizing of me. I only saw a con woman, an inveterate liar with no regulator on her depravity. She was a manipulator of human beings, covering up her heritage so she could live the life of Wasp Queen of Locust Valley and get custody.

What Gruella is to a rattlesnake, coiled and hiding in the tall grass snapping at unwary passers-by, Somers is to an anaconda…moving purposely, fully extended, unashamed of its outsized appetite for destruction, killing its victim with blunt force before devouring.

She'd never be an ex with benefits…

There was no way she was done with me because I was still free, I stood in the way of Somers' dreams and fantasies. I wondered who would take the place of me, staring at this pestiferous mess of an amoral Diablo. That guy would need cash, lawyers, how own kids, a house in Southampton, and a pitiful sex drive. When I saw Somers, the stars no longer shone, I saw nothing but blue. Time would relight that celestial sky, but for the time being, I was wayyyyyyyyyyy disillusioned…

One of her lawyers, the one with the lowest intelligence, stood up and asked the judge to revise a certain part of the custody agreement. The judge had never heard of such a last-minute request. The agreements had been signed months before, I'd offered and consented to everything, but now they wanted more, the proverbial blood from the rock, or as I liked to think of it, one last swift kick to my nuts.

"Your honor, Ms. Gillette believes that she needs to be granted sole custody at this stage, because it has come to our attention that Mr. Graham may be under a separate criminal investigation…"

I didn't even hear the rest. My ears were ringing red. Criminal?! Did she just say that in court, where records are made public and kept forever? The more I saw of Somers, the less I knew.

I said, as I often did in my relationship with this Shaitan, "Holy Christ."

There was no escape from this nightmare, this courtroom, like as a child when you wish to run through the field and escape. Somers was clamped onto my ankles with a ten-ton weight anvil, dragging me to the bottom of her dark sea. Seriously, my little private Armageddon was her dream fantasy. I was tuneless.

I had to keep repeating to myself to just don't look back…get on with it…don't let her drown you…

This was about as low as you could go…I felt like my kids' lives were at stake. There was no way I could allow this hebephrenic witch to manipulate my kids or my life anymore. She was organizing this so-called criminal case, completely unrelated to her original bulldust, and now she had placed it in the public record in an unrelated matter. It was more than a gratuitous slap. She had already done so many other things that I found distasteful, the condoms in the bathroom, the beer can in the driveway, the relentless adultery, the furious and unending flirtations, the money grab, stealing my art. I was at the end of the last strand of the past piece of fiber of my emotional rope.

She had crossed a serious line and yet it didn't matter to her. It only mattered to me and my kids.

I was so on the outside looking in on this divorce craziness, as if they were talking about someone else. I just wanted to get away from her. I figured that the divorce decree might cause her to stop with the criminal organizing thing…

I looked over at Somers…she didn't seen human anymore. She was rat-smug, cocooned by Harvard lawyers, spending two million on legal, PR, and investigative fees, just to ruin me. Destitution had never seemed so fun. I was a threat to her public image. She needed the kids by her side as an image shield for what she was really doing behind the scenes, that she was a good mother and all that, when in fact she was the worst in some ways. I knew the real Somers, and so did Betty, so she had to destroy us both to get away with it.

Once, many years before while holding my hand, she promised that she would stick around forever. She wasn't simply reneging on that promise…she was stomping all over it like rotten tomato's, peeing in the vat afterward for shits and giggles. Screw religion Seb. She had been living one big freakish lie.

I felt maligned, like a proctologist exam gone wildly bad. Of course her lawyer knew what she said in a court of law would be recorded forever in public transcripts. In fact anyone listening from the gallery that day, of which there were about ten other people for other cases, could have called the newspapers. There's no law so far as I know prohibiting the public from repeating to the press what they heard about my case. I had disappeared in her world, leaving nothing for me to reclaim.

Judge – "I want to see both counsels in my chambers immediately."

I was sure he was going to berate Somers' lawyer for unprofessional conduct. And he did…you could hear him through the closed doors yelling at this legally hapless dwarf….little good it did me though. He could yell at the lawyer all he wanted, it wouldn't change the direction my life was in, or the fact that the words had now been recorded. I'd never been a bitter guy, but two years of this constant scheming and fucking was draining even me.

I stared over at Somers, who jotted furiously on a yellow sheet of paper just like she had at the Cravath office. There she was, my formerly one and only temptation, still looking and smelling great, committing murder.

I was so pissed…something between us needed to live in order to keep the children safe, but she was burning that away as quickly as you can imagine… She was tearing apart my feelings one by one, no sign of guilt at all.

Howard Beale needed stage right, "I'm mad as hell and I'm not going to take it anymore."

She didn't want me to survive, whatever was going down. How could I ever tell the kids about her actions? That would only make me look like a weasel. I hate snitches, turncoats, betrayers, and fair-weather fans. I stay loyal to people once I swear loyalty, even to this witch, but mostly because we had children, though it never occurred to her that I was their dad.

When the judge returned to the courtroom with the two lawyers, he announced that he was striking from the court record what Fiona had bellowed, and that our previous agreement was to be signed, and we were to be granted a divorce. The custody would stay as written. He had one last announcement before we left.

"You two obviously have a tremendous amount of unresolved differences. But I want to offer you some guidance. Both of you seem like good parents. Try to keep things together for the sake of your kids. OK?"

He wasn't telling us to stay together, he wanted us simply to bury hatchets. For the first time in a year and a half of divorce court, I spoke up.

"Your honor, just so I am clear, am I allowed to come back in here when I am free to do so, to undo that custody agreement? Because for the record, this woman is unfit to have custody of a tadpole, let alone be a Custodial Parent."

Pins dropped. I could hear the other courtroom spectators shift in their seats…maybe they sensed fisticuffs. I couldn't believe I said anything. The judge was dumbfounded. He'd never heard me say a word in 18 months, except the occasional yes your honor, no your honor. Somers glowered. I stared back at her, impassively for once, our roles had reversed. Enough of the big lie, Somers. I got my words in the record though and the judge wouldn't strike it.

Somers' lawyer was rattling her small brain trying to find a legal precedent where she could have me tossed in jail for saying such a thing. She was rifling through an oversized Birkin bag, looking for legal books. The judge smiled…he knew the score.

"Mr. Graham, you're welcome back in this courtroom any time."

So bittersweet, a pyrrhic victory if ever there was one. No one was singing to me, but she was paying thousands to do the same to her. The judge rose to leave the courtroom for a bathroom break, or a few cocktails, even she could wear this man out. Doubtful he sees too many multi-million dollar society divorces where the woman exhibits narcissistic tendencies of no known computation.

I looked over at Somers,

"Bad taste in your mouth? Really, me? Cause you ought to look in the mirror one day, if it won't break first. I'd have given you my life! Instead, you keep screwing me over like you don't have any other purpose on earth. Do you ever recall that we have kids? Love is more than your disgraceful statist shithole of a diseased mind. If it's the last thing I ever do, I'll have custody of those kids…they need it. You're purposely ruining them to satisfy your own ego. I realize you enjoy lying to the world, but do you think you could at the very least ask your boyfriends to not spend the night at the house when the kids are there. I mean, come on…the kids aren't even teenagers yet. You're a disgrace to motherhood. Not immoral, just amoral. And can you cut the shite out and let me get back to making some money?"

Somers snatched her black raincoat, bared her frosty mien at me, and hustled out of the room in a Jamaican sprint, knocking over someone's papers on the way out, with her lawyer waddling behind her, everyone multitasking. The sunlight had hit the rat. I heard her say fuck you to the person with papers. Or maybe that was to me, actually.

I turned to my lawyer, John,

"Sorry John. They knew what they said earlier would go into the record, for others to read. But she's doing all the work to make a crime happen! How does that compute?! I can't take her shite anymore."

"Sebastian, I understand. But, you can't get down in the dirt with her either. She doesn't care how sloppy she gets; only you do. When you lie down with dogs, you get fleas. She'll pay a cleaning service to clean her off. You'll just scratch forever. Just remember that. Let it slide and drop her from your memory bank. You're going to need to."

Iceland, Milos, and A Bathroom Surprise

This was no ordinary world, the shoulder surfers of Locust Valley, and Somers Gillette was no ordinary girl. What I said in court in front of others simply demanded on overwhelming response on her part. She was coming back with Gehenna's Revenge, the Lake of Fire and Brimstone and Hell. The millennial war had begun.

Somers had been itching for my arrest. Who would ever believe that? The mother of my children, who didn't have to pay the

mortgage on her house but yet would tell anyone that she did. The
lies never seemed to stop.

Slowly but surely, I got my business life back together. It wasn't
easy, I was drained emotionally, but ultimately I found my groove
again. It isn't hard provided you're not an asshole. People will pay
you for being straight and working honestly. Of course, I had no
idea that Somers was denying my old friends and partner's access to
me when they called the house, selling them first about some tragic
version of me, and then redirecting them to her lawyer who was
conspiring with still others who really could make life tougher for
me. She would happily spend hours on the phone with anyone
regaling them with tales of my dastardly ways…

Talal had listened to Somers for over an hour when he called, and
she had never met the man…for all Somers knew, he could have
been a salesperson. It didn't stop her from blasting me to him
though…she had all the time in the world for her holy war.

If people couldn't reach me, I had no way to reach them. I had none
of my old contacts. They would call the house, Somers would do
her dance about what a horrible person I was and then give them
Spirella's number. What he did at that point is anyone's guess, but
its' fair to say that this all had a corrosive effect on my life. And it
could have been avoided. If someone felt they were owed money,
they just wanted the money…not my hide. Only one person wanted
my hide and there was only one way to get it…by denying others
access to me.

I was trying to make my way quietly, getting back on the bike,
sticking by the side of my kids. I was ignorant to it all. My phone
never rang. But people were thinking about me…

I had guaranteed way too much corporate debt personally from the company. Strangely, that was not a bummer for me. You sign up for this kind of beatdown when you launch your own company. But, when people can't reach you, you can only imagine their response when your wife freely laments an unexamined tale and then redirects them to criminal investigators.

My confidence began to emerge again with each successive new business meeting and each new business card contact entered into my new Blackberry. I swear losing my Blackberry was a hit to the gut that you just can't explain…Repairing that loss of information was what I needed. Pathetic but honest. These weren't old contacts but new ones. Still.

Once in a while, social friends would slip through her information dragnet and reach me. I began to hear about Somers' dating life. Not a week went by when one of my friends from Locust Valley wouldn't send me an email now saying you won't believe who she's sleeping with. I didn't really care if she was sleeping around, but it really bummed me out that she was so reckless in front of my kids. I had never thought she could be this way when I first met her at Hunter's.

I wanted to march back into that courtroom in Nassau County, and undo what was wrought, but the kids would be about 128 years old by the time I'd have the dosh to compete with her attack dog lawyers, so what good would it do me today while she did her damage. Somers knew all she had to was get the kids to the age of 18 without oversight by me. That has always been her goal. If she could last until then with them, in her head, she'd have won, just like her mother many years before.

Pride could tear us both apart if I allowed it.

My previous company problems were festering behind the scenes. What was once a small problem only got worse, a combination of my setting the table initially, losing my Blackberry contact database and data servers, and Somers' organizing everyone else with a complaint. Anyone. If you were an old girlfriend from high school and I hadn't bought you the proper corsage for the prom, you were fair game for her target universe. It's hard for me to overstate her aggressiveness to locate malcontents about Sebastian Graham. She had epically Bad Boundaries.

I was on others' minds, but the only way for them to reach me was Somers Gillette…again, the irony kills.

I've heard this now from a billion people, give or take, that whenever someone would call the house and ask specifically for me, Somers would launch into a veritable tirade about how Sebastian had left the kids penniless, that he was a crook, and that if it helped any, Somers just happened to have the phone number for a lawyer. If you had told me at the time of our separation that she was capable of that, I would have sworn she wasn't. I can't explain it. Only the later incidents confirmed that indeed she was capable of burning down the house in order to get what she thought was the prize, holding onto three kids until they reached 18 years of age, and breaking me so her other secret would never get out in Locust Valley.

Love is not self-seeking, nor easily angered.
It keeps no record of wrongdoing.
It does not delight in evil,
But rejoices in the truth.
-- 1 Corinthians 13:4-7

She schemed to cut my new life off at the knees. She knew that one of us chose the kids and one of us chose social prostration…any judge reviewing that would side with the parent who chose kids…so I had to be murdered. Trust me, that's exactly what she thought.

A small company out of Iceland had been referred to me for a possible acquisition. I didn't have the money to buy it, but I knew a way to recapitalize it. I could own a significant amount of the equity among other things. I began to laser in on this job as perhaps the surest way to repay others and also to have a meaningful salary.

Just to underscore how ridiculously naïve I still was about Somers, even though I was now circumspect about specifics on the job front with her, I stupidly let her know about the opportunity in Iceland. I assumed that she'd be happy that there was a light at the end of the tunnel….her locomotive was on the way!

Big flipping laugh. I had no idea that Somers didn't care about my money then…she only wanted me dead. And if I was getting close to redemption, she needed to expedite trouble.

"Somers, if you can just hold on until September, I am about to be named the CEO of a great apparel company, and although it's in Iceland, I am moving the management team to New York. This will really help with all the cash needs, as well as make the kids happy that I am back in New York full time."

"Whatever…"

Not exactly the confidence boost I was seeking…the conductor sped up.

I tried my best to ignore Somers' attitude, I burrowed in on the deal, spending all of my waking hours on it. I flew to Iceland several times, met the management team, and agreed with the current owners on the construct of a deal. I'd had a long two years but it seemed like maybe, just maybe, I could make it out of this whole affair with my integrity intact, and my head held high. The kids would be winners.

We arranged to hive off 25% of my equity to my former partners, giving them a preferred return on my own distributions until they were made whole. That wouldn't have been too hard to do in less than six months from the closing, as the revenues lines were set to double with one wholesale account I brought to the table. I had it all sussed out and everything would be good. This was all in contract language, vetted by some of the best lawyers (please go to the Epilogue to read the contract details).

Somers' reach didn't extend all the way to Iceland, not that it mattered… Somers Gillette was trying to derail this behind the scenes.

I should have taken out the British Airways Midtown Tunnel billboard to scream what I was doing…trying to make my former partners whole, instead I worked silently trying to get to the finish line.

I attended a dinner in Manhattan. The restaurant was Milos, a semi-famous Italian seafood restaurant on West 55th. I'd been invited by a friend who had allowed me to use an office of his for free while I pursued my Icelandic deal. The dinner was for his company and had nothing to do with Iceland. Other than being his friend, I didn't have any involvement in what the dinner was for.

I had to take a leak, and so I excused myself to the bathroom. While I was relieving myself, a man walked in the bathroom, and I recognized his face immediately…I had trouble remembering his name (will never change with the bad name memory trait…). He was one of the old outside partners from the old company.

"Hey Sebastian, how are you doing? I haven't seen you in a long time."

"Hey. How are you?"

This was Aaron Svednishman, a Swedish hedge fund manager whom I didn't know well, but he had been a participant in one of our deals.

"Well, no one has heard from you in two years, and we were just wondering what had happened to our investment."

He let the question hang, sort of like Somers does when she's about to castrate you. Of all the former partners, there were two I didn't care for and he was one (of all my former wives, there was only one I don't like…). There was something about him.

"Well, for starters, I don't have anyone's phone number, since the prior landlord took the servers and my blackberry got wiped, and your numbers are unlisted. You know where I lived, and even though I've asked my ex-wife to delist my number, it's still out there for the world to see. We all lost our investment Aaron. Me for $6 Million, and you for what, $250,000?"

"Didn't you think you had an obligation to keep me informed? By the way, I heard about what happened in Locust Valley (you mean my wife screwing me, and by that I don't mean conjugally…?)."

It sort of pissed me off the way the guy said this, as if it wasn't Somers' plan he was retelling…as if I had done something to Somers, he knew her marketing scheme, and once again, some a-hole had been exposed to my kids because of her.

"Aaron, your number is unlisted…hard to just dial you up. What happened in Locust Valley by the way?"

"We heard that you took your wife's money. Actually, that's what your wife told me (she talked to you too? Doesn't she have better things to do, like be a mother?…). She doesn't have very many good things to say about you Seb."

Really? Cause I could have sworn she ended up with a $6 Million house and no debt, all my assets, she just spent $2Mil on fees last year, etc etc etc…should I go one?…And I'm so glad my wife had decided to befriend my business associates, which was ironic, because when I had wanted her to play the corporate wife when I was just starting out, she acted like I wanted her to store nuclear fuel in her closet. But now she wants to help…? I asked her to forward all calls to me.

"Look Aaron, I'm not going to talk about my wife; I never have. She's nuts, and if you care to believe her, that's your right. I know you spoke with the attorney for the company, what do you want?"

"I just want to know what happened to my money."

"Aaron, I'm actually glad to see you, because I need everyone's contact details. I'm also happy to meet with you anytime to discuss the old company, but tonight isn't the time. I happen to be a guest of someone, and I'm headed back upstairs. If you want to call me, here's my phone number. I'd like to get together shortly, at your convenience. Tomorrow even if it works."

I handed him my number. Freely, happily. I knew Aaron knew two other former partners, and I figured he would give me their email addresses. I even sent him an email that night asking for their contact data. It's good to get problems behind you. He never replied to the request.

The next day Aaron called me. He wasn't alone.

'Lucy' Pulls the Ball Yet Again

Aaron and I agreed to meet at Tom's Restaurant on the Upper West Side in three weeks' time. This place is otherwise known as the exterior shot of a diner for the Seinfeld show. It was a fairly nondescript place, but it was near his office. I asked him about the other partners' contact data, but all he said was he would let them know we had been in touch… The thing was, I was really happy to run into the guy, because I really wanted to begin the process of getting the past behind me.

I continued to get my own deal done and recapitalized. The fees and income and equity were going to get me out of my old mess, and I would be back…The kid stays in the picture.

It had taken me six months but I had everything arranged for the Icelandic deal. I was over the moon looking forward to running this company for any number of reasons, but the biggest by far was I'd be with my kids full-time again. Ski apparel was in an industry that I loved and knew. I could double the sales volume with one call. We'd be eating North Face's lunch within two years and my kids would be so pumped to see Dad back in the hunt. I would have no partners and no investors. It was perfect…I didn't quite like Bjork, but some localized Icelandic rock wasn't the worst.

In hindsight, everything was too perfect.

Anything too perfect in my life has always come crashing down eventually. Mostly because of my ex-wife. Life is the zero-sum game, as ever. In spite of her perfidy, I keep getting back up off the mat. You'd think that after 45 years of that kind of self-flagellating confidence beatdown that I'd be working for a big chain somewhere, abandoning the entrepreneurial spirit along the way. But my goddamn heritage keeps raising the ugly head of eternal optimism…And hers the opposite.

Aaron and I had tea and coffee. He seemed nervous and had a set list of questions about a business deal from three years ago. He pressed me for details, I answered honestly, and then he left.

The Alphabet Boys came swarming in and arrested me…I gather the government hadn't cut back on expenses, like I had. I was ham-sandwiched.

By then in my life, I figured I had coughed up approximately $20 Million in taxes to the government, and my first thought was, this is what I get for that… Not a wholesome and timely thought, but nothing good was in my head then…I was numb. This was Somers' E.L.E, her extinction level event. I was running to kick a ball, she yanked it away, as I flew into the air prepared to fall on my back, she whipped an AR-15 automatic from inside her Versace and sprayed me …

Are you Sebastian Graham of Locust Valley?

Well, technically no, I don't live in Locust Valley anymore because my wife took my house…but yes, I'm Seb, what's happening? Wait a sec, I'm not Seb, I'm Terry Malloy, "You don't understand, I coulda had class. I coulda been a contender. I could've been somebody, instead of a bum, which is what I am."

And on and on…The kid wasn't staying in the picture. Lucy had pulled the ball again and Charlie Brown would take the blame.

I'm cutting through this whole mess because, well, that's for another book another time. Hey, it's a novel, but still, I owe it to the government to not discuss my case or my thoughts on it.

Somers had the DA pumped with her right and with her left she was strangling me. It's hard to overestimate the sheer craziness of this coming from a place like Locust Valley. Not much ugliness ever happened out there. It's easy to bear Hester Prynne's scar in a small town where nothing goes unnoticed.

Somers now had a new set of lies and a new story to sell to her friends: she would say she had nothing to do with anything, when in fact it was always her. She couldn't allow a man who was getting custody (if given the chance) from being that father…The courts would have taken the kids away from her, and she'd be exposed. Ironies. Blasted.

People knew full well what had happened in Locust Valley, they were armed to the teeth with her stories. It wasn't hard to figure out how. Her saga ended up being more prurient to them and could help build a case, but these people thought on substance 'she was full of shite'. They knew she actually made out like a bandit. I could have told anyone that.

And these people knew she was trumpeting to anyone who would listen (including the kids) that she was destitute, even though I had given her all my money and 'she was in great shape'. People also had a copy of the letter I had signed at the Cravath offices a year and a half prior. They wanted to know why I had signed it, and I answered plainly…because I thought we were married forever and I think I would have agreed to say I could run the 100 meter dash in five seconds if asked. They understood and were fascinated by the lawyer's dereliction of code of professional conduct.

People told me I was married to a raving lunatic. But they were also very unfamiliar with how to navigate marital shoals, as if the subject made them queasy. They asked that we stick to the business subject. Still, I couldn't help but wonder how low I could slide…Crazy thoughts can rule your mind when you are arrested and don't think they didn't capture my fantasies some that day.

I wasn't hiding anything. No one bothered to tell anyone that I was the largest loser when the company went out of business. You could have just called. People were told that I wouldn't speak…when in fact what had happened was no one was given my new phone number…natch. Guess who fed them that lie.

Here's a generic conversation with some people…it happened many times over…

"Mr. Graham…May we call you Sebastian?"

"Seb's fine…don't worry."

"Your wife sabotaged you Buddy. I mean Seb."

"I'm beginning to get that…"

"Sherlock Holmes called it a Masterpiece of Villainy."

"Boys, she's smarter than Sherlock. And if you couldn't tell, she's cray-cray, crazier than crazy."

"You're going to pay for her anger. She drew a masterpiece, with you as her bulls-eye. When she first spoke, we thought she was a lunatic. But she had done her homework with very expensive lawyers showing the way. She had you dead to rights, because she sold everyone else so damn well. We've never seen a woman do this and we've been around a while. In some ways, we're really sorry. In other ways, excuse the cold line, you're cooked. She bought you, and then she sold you. It was heartless like we've never seen."

People thought I was leading the life of Reilly. Someone had really misled them. Wonder who?

Your chances of escaping prosecution (even on charges not related to the original offense) stand at less than 3%....meaning, 97% of the time, you lose. But you say, well if you did nothing wrong, then you have nothing to worry about...you don't know the half of it... I'd like to speak more about this, but I won't. If you know those numbers going in...

I needed to face the music, the consequences of a horrible business.

I didn't even ask for a lawyer. Don't have anything to hide, never did, never will. I'm not necessarily a fan of the US Justice Department, but I'm no enemy either. I'd never met anyone from there prior to this mess. Somers...well, let me save that information for the next installment. I kept repeating to them that they sure did waste a lot of money when they could have just called me...I guess Somers failed to tell people I had a cell phone...

I'd never had one Internet picture or story about me except for that goddamn New York Times wedding blurb (which I objected to in the first place, but someone else desperately wanted to have...and natch, she of course demanded that it include a line that I had been married once before...). Still, none of that would matter, because I had one old company problem I couldn't escape from without my Iceland deal closing, and that looked unlikely now. The original problem didn't seem large to me, but it became large with Somers fanning the flames, and a small issue can bring a large man down.

When my court appointed lawyer met me for the first time, she told me to shut the hell up.

"What did you tell them?"

"Whatever they wanted to know. I don't have anything to hide….I'm quite happy to talk about my old company…I lost the most money…I wouldn't mind slitting my throat…you know, the normal stuff."

The quickest way to lose your lawyer's trust is to tell them that you've just spent six hours willingly talking to FBI agents in a government office. I thought I had been helping the Government. She shot me a look that confirmed my worst instincts…I am stupid beyond repair. Honest, but perhaps torpidly stupid.

You're probably thinking my life had gone from hell to worse, but the truth was things were not getting any worse than they'd been. Worse was a year ago when I was at my absolute rock bottom emotionally.

Did this have to happen? Absolutely not. Somers could have prevented everything, with one call. I knew I would have to deal with the business mess at some stage. I wanted to, but no server and Blackberry, and Somers' meddling, was a horrible prescription to try to overcome that. I'd been hoping to get the Icelandic deal under my belt so I could start over again and clean up the small mess that I'd left behind, but that would now have to wait obviously. I thought quiet rectitude was the right way. My silence was Shaitan's fuel.

The larger threat to me was Somers showing up in a courtroom, either as a target or as a witness. I was still shielding her, and people laughed. Someone had the following exchange with me, me going first,

"You mean she would be called up to the stand, or they would prosecute her? Which one? What has she done? I'm just a little confused."

"Mr. Graham, we never tell a defendant how they proceed, they just do. They'd prefer to minimize the costs of this affair, and they think there is an offer on the table for you. But, it's your choice at the end of the day. What happens to Somers is an unknown. If you feel that bringing your wife into the proceedings is a good thing, then by all means they are prepared to go forward."

"I want to be clear about something. So if I agree to a plea, then there is nothing, and I mean nothing, that she can do to influence the proceedings, and they will agree to not prosecute her for anything? Is that a correct reading?"

"That is correct but why in the hell are you concerned about her…she screwed you!"

"Alright, then let's end this bulldust. I don't have a ton of life left. She's the last person I should be protecting, but I don't think the kids would want to see both parents going through this ordeal…One's too much, two would be life-altering. Let's get a deal done…but remember, I don't want to ever hear her name around this plea."

"You won't. She doesn't want to harm you anymore…she told people she was done (you know, she tells everyone that, but then she keeps cutting me anyway…)."

By the way, if Somers was arrested for anything (witchcraft perhaps), she would never be so dumb as to talk to the government without a lawyer. She'd be turned on. She'd likely call Gruella before she'd call a lawyer, because those witches stick together man. I'd bet dollars to a doughnut Gruella would find a way to spring her from prison, a daring nighttime raid, flying off on their brooms.

Where would my friend be when I needed her the most? The thought haunted me.

For the arrest day, I was mostly concerned about my kids. I needed to protect them from the Locust Valley gossip mill. Somers wanted to feed them to it. She had her own mole obviously, because she had already told the kids everything that morning, before I was arrested. She had also called the papers and gossip websites. Her Four Horsemen were on the clock again, spreading the news. Her mother was dropping leaflets all over Fairfield, Nassau, and Westchester Counties (okay, perhaps not that extensive, but you get the picture).

A smashing victory was in her sights. She had effectively blocked me out of custody, which had always ever been her real concern. Why she wanted custody was not the innocent reason you might think though…

The Stealth Victim and Her Impact Statement

I don't cry about yesterdays anymore. Just looking forward to tomorrow.

The kids had been at the Adirondack Club the day of my arrest, so I couldn't reach them easily. And Somers knew it. She wasn't exactly with the kids…she was hosting parties for profit and had social engagements to attend… Just as she wanted.

On September 8, I was supposed to be signing the executed contacts with the Icelandic company….22 calendar days from arrest day.

My society jihadist called me the day after the arrest, she couldn't help herself. She shouldn't have called because she had no right to speak with me, but she'd forgotten to be real anymore. She didn't know at that time that I knew about the extent of her involvement. She had crossed over to the other side so long ago, she couldn't even consider how low she had gotten. Her voice was one of glee and mirth, wrapped in a plastic plate of too clever by half…an Antichrist's full stomach rumble.

Initially, she faked the omigod I can't believe what's happened to you how are you are you okay I was so worried when I heard demeanor over the phone. Insert a valley girl patois and that is how I heard it…the least real, most phony, most staged concern from one human to another in the history of mankind.

I had a photograph of her from when she was 30 cupped into my hands while we spoke. I'd been married to a thief of souls. I could hear her voice but I didn't recognize the human behind it. The photo was of someone else, as stunning as she could be. The voice was real though, the owner of the most dystoptic, Leviathanic, most Fallen Angel in the history of the world. She had left her own habitation, to become a Judas within a family surrounded by love.

Obviously, I knew by then that she had participated all along. My lawyers had spoken with people behind closed doors. They said they had never come across a crazier more vindictive wife, who wanted her husband dead but simultaneously said was the world's best dad. Which was I? There was no option but to go after me when she led others down her mine-laden path.

You might think I was armed for bear when she called. The reality was that when we spoke, I didn't have the energy anymore to blast her. I was focused on my children and how to make things right for them, someday. I just wanted to be straight.

"Somers, no need for your phony bullshit. I don't know if you can tape record this call or not from up there, but I know what you did and how you organized it. Why wouldn't you let people have my phone number when they called the house? They didn't want to screw me, only you did. They just wanted to get things right and it would have been too easy to do so. All I know is that some day, and it may not be today, my kids are going to know what you did. And when they know, they're going to abandon you if I give them the green light. You know me, that's not who I am, it's who you are, but it's not me. I have more compassion in my fingernail than you do in your entire soul. So, just don't bullshit me anymore, and I'll keep things straight with the kids. I don't know yet what I will do later. Count on that. I once said that only the worst thing can make a guy like me snap…well, you may have found the mechanism. Your narcissism had no equal. This is a saga for the Ages, a biblical fuck."

"Don't threaten me Sebastian. I will do more than what's been done!!"

She's not an easy mark, is she? Even the arrest wouldn't end my nightmare. She was baiting me with everything she had, and it was fortunate we were three hundred miles and a Thomas Edison line away from each other.

"Somers, I'm not threatening you. I'll never threaten you. I hope you had the time of your life. I'll just deal on my end without saying a word. I'm just wondering though, what did you just mean by saying you will do more than what's been done? What more can be done by you at this point? And do you think that someday you could give me "Witness" back, since the artist signed it to me (Witness is a piece of art that a friend of mine made for me, which means a lot to me, not as much as the kids' letters, but a second place; it's unseemly that she continues to hang it in the house if you knew the backstory…)? Forget that…I don't even care. You know what I care about?! My kids. You're spitting on my children, and you won't even admit it."

"Fuck you and fuck Ashley (Ashley is my artist friend…)! Be tougher in your next life you faggot!!"

Somers is high society's Anne Bonny, a notorious female pirate who ended up being Captain Jack Rackham's lover, Calico Jack, the dashing pirate of the high seas. When Calico Jack and Anne Bonny were captured, Anne "pled her belly", meaning she lied about being pregnant in order to save her life. Calico Jack asked for a final meeting with Anne, who by then had turned on him for losing the battle of the ship. She scornfully said to him, "If you'd fought like a man, you needn't hang like a dog". Somers Gillette had channeled Anne Bonny's spirit for the millennial age.

"You know what Somers, time might change things, but I won't change my contempt for your craziness…never has any human ever been so reckless about another human, all to cover up your adultery and the fact that no court would ever give you custody if they really knew the full set of facts, and not your mythology. I don't quite know how to say I feel…What I want to say seems so insufficient, so not enough. You never had an honest word with me in fifteen years."

I agreed to a plea, like anyone of sound mind. I'm not even going to address my feelings or my thoughts on the legal issues or why I agreed to the plea. Somers hovering around the table had a tremendous weight on my decision…I didn't want her bulldust entered into the court record, because then I'd have to spend time defending myself over even more inanities, not to mention my kids would then be exposed to a complete breakdown of the world. You don't want to sit in front of twelve jurors blaming your ex-wife for anything, burned toast or worse…

One assessment of the plea I'm allowed to write is this: what you think is obvious, may not be so, and if you think you know the full story, you don't know a hundredth of it. I have tremendously conflicted feelings but for many reasons I can't really write them for now. My friends know who I am…generous, caring, compassionate, and thoughtful. I'll let those words stand as my defense.

Tomorrow's another day…

Somers' actions ultimately reminded me of the adage that a lioness never goes after the strong, they only attack the weak.

Long story short, my lawyers and I geared up for sentencing day with tremendous weariness but also cautious optimism. I mean, I hadn't impeded anything, I had voluntarily accepted blame. I just wanted to get it all behind me so I could work again and be with my kids…two noble pursuits.

Still, bottom line, bad things happen to good people.

Somers made my visits with the kids as hellish as could be. She was reaching new highs, or lows depending on your perspective. Clinically speaking, she had become certifiably unhinged. Please read Exhibit #1 at the end.

I am the only one who knew her as well as I did, therefore I needed to be terminated. She couldn't allow the one man who wanted to be the responsible party for profit for her children to walk free, because he would have been given custody. That was her Hobson's choice: terminate me or lose the kids.

My lawyers and I finally got to see the Victim Impact statements. We sat at my lawyers' conference room while we each had copies set in front of us. These are written statements by victims that detail what the aggrieved feels about the defendant. Out of thousands of business and personal relationships I had had over ten years of being in business and 46 years of just being alive, the court received no more than a handful of Statements. Mostly they were dry and factual recitations of the charges, not even of the groups, and they seemed like they were written perhaps by lawyers. I couldn't argue frankly. It is what it was.

"Wait a minute, wait a minute, you ain't heard nothin' yet!!", v. Jakie Rabinowitz.

Maybe not so dry and factual... There was one victim impact statement that came in late and you could say it caught our eyes....it would have caught Al Jolson's eyes. You could say it made our eyes pop out of their sockets. This victim impact statement was from none other than Somers C. Gillette, faux social arbiter of Locust Valley. A non-victim who had no basis in this courtroom or my trial. She was never part of the securities fraud. She was simply the mother of my three children, bent on destroying their relationship with their father.

I almost couldn't read the statement in full, it was so hellish. It was written by a woman who had become unhinged from reality, someone whose ethos had metastasized into a lustful macabre devolution. Her statements were so erroneous, so baseless, and so vitriolic...it was hard to know where to even begin. This wasn't even a fatwa, more a general call to my public stoning.

The essential construct of the statement was that I was the worst father in the universe of man…You know, sometimes in life we aren't sure where we are or even where we're going, and I've felt both ways from time to time. The one thing I can state with more than just a little emphasis is that I'm the best father I'll ever know…there's nothing I wouldn't do for my children, and I've done it… And anyone who has ever met me knows the same.

The only way to undo that accomplishment would be to paint the complete opposite picture. Even though she had trumpeted to all wide and far before this day that I was the best father in the world…now I was not. What was up was down, and what she loved she hated. I wonder now if she hates those large parties for profit…

When we finished reading it, my lawyers were agape. No one spoke for ten minutes….everyone was too embarrassed, too stunned, or too confused to say a word. We simply stared at each other and at the paper.

I can't get it all out now, what was in my head then. It was a raging shitstorm, with me desperately trying to understand if she had just abandoned any hope of being a fit custodial parent. All I could say was what naturally came to me in times of crisis or ecstasy,

"Holy Christ."

All of us were speechless. I had a vision of Somers as a mad, evil scientist doing her devil work behind a curtain. A vicious Oz. This latest science project of hers, a complete atomic bomb of character assassination, was almost too horrific to be true. She had way outdone herself, and that is saying something.

Randi (lawyer) finally spoke up and went first.

"Well, if Somers wanted you put away, this should do the trick. But, is it fair of me to ask you Seb, does she really want to lose her kids' love later on? I mean, there isn't a kid in the world that wouldn't turn their back on a Mom for having done this. She didn't need to write this…she's not a victim in this courtroom, or any courtroom. And no one asked her to. This is simply spite, malice, anger, horror, revenge, destruction, pure evil. I don't think she's of sound mind, if you don't mind my saying."

"Randi, what do I do? Did the judge read this? I mean, it's so inaccurate, okay forget the issue of her doing it, but it's so inaccurate, can I at least correct the statements to him? Can she be tried for perjury? This is blasphemy. There isn't anything she's written in here that isn't documentably, categorically false. I own the mortgage, not Somers. I gave her the investments and she continues to lie about that. I mean come on. This is nuts. Who will ever stop her lies? Seriously, she should be arrested. You can't lie in a VI statement, can you? Isn't there some method for rebutting? It's as if she wanted to throw everything on the wall, and hope for one small drop to stick."

I was about to blow a gasket.

"The judge would have already read this. The fact is, anyone can send a VI statement in. Anyone. Even old girlfriends. And it doesn't have to be truthful necessarily. It speaks to your decency that only a handful did. You were in business for over ten years. Most guys in business for ten years, they go down, about five hundred statements get sent in saying this guy is a con. You only had a few individual statements sent. But this one is going to stick out in the judge's eyes. No doubt. There isn't time to undo her statement. It would take a month at least, and they aren't going to delay sentencing now. The fact is your kids will abandon her when they hear she did this…I'm not sure you should say anything to them though, not yet anyway, because they may ironically need her while we deal with you (that didn't sound so promising…)."

Fiona – "Let's think this over for the night. Do not send your wife, err ex-wife, an email (too late…just emailed her telling her I couldn't believe it…she had outdone even herself, possibly her Mom…again, everyone seemed to be enthusiastic outdoing each other on their way to the Fire Lake…). We'll need to address it though. It's really damaging. We had everything organized perfectly for you Seb. I'm really sorry; I don't know why she would do this (I do…she's evil in a way that you can never imagine…). Justice would never ask her to send it in. I'm thinking that one tack might be we could say to the judge that this is merely the ranting of a deranged ex-wife (I know that part…will anyone else? I think her father knows she's nuts, and her family, but she lies to everyone…). That might fly. It doesn't mean he'll forget it though. She's really after you; I've never seen anything like it. We've known you for a while; you're a good guy. I think you married a lunatic ('ya think?…)."

Randi and Fiona had been with me now for a year, and they understood who Somers was and what she was about. They had even spoken to someone who had good inside information on her. They knew she was a maniac but would the judge know that. I would find out in two days. Time is never time enough.

When we arrived in court for sentencing day, we all expected Somers to show and make a dramarama scene in black dress, teased hair, push-up bra, leg-reveal, veil, and pearls. Why she didn't show is anyone's guess, but I think even she knew she'd done enough damage. Barely anyone was in the large cavernous room at 500 Pearl. The US Attorney was there, as was the arresting FBI agent. Pleasant guys. We shook hands and waited for the judge to appear.

He did, we rose, we sat, and he spoke. Forty one months. I'm not allowed to write what he said, how the decision was rendered, or whether Somers' statement impacted him or not.

And that was that. This chapter ended. All I could think was: I chose my kids, she chose death, and she won….for now.

Somers called me three hours later while I was walking the city streets alone. She was ecstatic to the point of being daffy,

"I told you I would nail you! Fuck you! You'll never have those kids now!"

"Somers, I thought it wasn't possible for you to sink any lower, but I guess you found a way…Victim? Let' me get this right…I give you 90% of my net income, you have a house with no debt, you have all the contents, you took my life's treasures and threw them away, you have my investments…Oh yeah, that's right, I have nothing. And that's the way I want it...which you never understood, I never wanted a thing and wanted you to have it always. And, you slept around on me with no fewer than five men…and now, you seem like you're beginning to do things in front of the kids that's almost incomprehensible. And yet, and yet, you're a "victim"? Can you even for a second imagine what the kids will do to you once they are old enough to understand that Mommy submitted a letter to the court asking that the judge punish their daddy, even though this case has absolutely one hundred and ten percent NOTHING to do with you? You were willing to take that gamble? Because if so, you will lose, there is not a doubt in my mind, and anyone else's. You are pure evil, and if cancer doesn't strike you down first, I'm sure the bitterness will. No heart outlasts those kinds of vicious ways. Way to stick together as a family, so loyal, sort of like what our kids rely on us as adults to do. My Judas in Lilly Pullitzer."

Triple Upper Case voice,

"Sebastian, fuck off and die! ROT IN HELL! Loyalty extends only as far as my options, and my options here were clear…to fuck you first and remove you from the kids. You're not getting custody, I didn't give birth to three kids to see their father walk away with them!!! I'd kill you before that happened! Eat shit and die in prison, and I'll keep you in there longer than you can ever imagine…Trust me, I'm already working on it!! FUCK YOU!"

Prolonged Silence… me considering an adequate response, Somers praying I hadn't tape recorded her words…So morally righteous, never stopping her unleashed disgust to tell me what I'd done wrong…because that wasn't the point anyway.

"Somers, freedom means nothing left to lose. I think I qualify, don't you? Ahhh, forget it…No use arguing with someone so utterly self-absorbed. Everything will be just fine with me and the kids, eventually. Not for you. Your blazing sun of parties for profit, men, and revenge will set for you sooner than you ever want…Trust me."

"How dare you! I'll get you Sebastian…this sandbox was never for morons!!"

Click. That is an exact transcription. It is my one and only tape recording. Loyalty extends only as far as my options…how will I ever forget that gem! It needs to go on her epitaph. She had sunk to a level not known in human history. Who knew, besides Satan himself?

Dymphna's Corner

I made a special trip back one night to that corner where Somers and I first kissed so many years ago, to 78th and 2nd... It was the same, but so different too. I wanted to see the beginning again. It was almost surreal to stand there, knowing this is where the snake bit the victim. I was dizzy looking up at the stars, and heard a voice,

"Seb, over here."

Behind me on 2nd Avenue was a 2nd Floor walk-in tarot card reader. A woman in a blue burqa was calling my name from the window. I was right below her window. The sign on the door said "$10 Tarot. Your Future." The voice was hypnotic.

I walked over to the door and looked up, she still completely unknown to me.

"Hi. How are things? Hey, did you just say my name? Do I know you?"

"You definitely know me. I've been waiting for you for a long time. Honestly, I wasn't sure they had given me the right man. But you're here. And guess what, you're coming up, you don't even have a choice."

"The last woman I blindly took direction from ended up screwing me pretty bad. Why would I trust a tarot card reader any more than that? And it happened right here by the way."

"Yes, I'm well aware of what happened. I was here. And I don't read tarots…I'm a fortune teller of another nature. "

She removed her hijab, and I saw her face for the first time. If I wasn't so logical, I'd say that an angel had just descended from heaven. Her face was that of a real angel, a soft unblemished skin whose very touch could heal a thousand lepers. Her hair was a beautiful golden blond of such warmth that armies could be hypnotized by it. Her eyes were of a blue that you simply could not describe, they had a hue of no known description, a blue of such purity and grace that they could solve epic conflicts and global discord. Her face, interestingly, looked almost identical to a singer called Jewel.

"Sebastian, it's time."

I was powerless to not do what she said, my legs started moving without my asking them to. I entered the door and walked up into her second floor space. The floor gave way and I was standing in air, there was nothing below me, above me, behind me, or in front. It wasn't light and it wasn't dark, it was simply nothing, and my soul was suspended as if I were next on the firing line. Now this is what it really felt like I thought. Yet, I wasn't ready to leave, not anymore. Jewel had disappeared but music filled the room, a colliding symphony of the best songs of my life (see Dymphna's Playlist at the end of the book).

"Hey, where did you go? Hey, Jewel? Hey, you told me to come up, I did. What the f-"

"Don't curse! That was always a problem for you Seb."

She reappeared right in front of me and we were now seated on floating throw pillows. They were massive Egyptian cotton balls of pure comfort. And I hadn't moved, so how did I sit like that? The space continuum had now become dark, with the exception of a lone candle on a non-floor underneath us, lighting our faces. Her skin was beyond just perfect…it was milk and honey.

This she-angel had a summer dress on and she clearly was no Muslim. She had a figure that could not be easily drawn…it simply was it, artists would quake trying to match her lines If you recall what I felt about Somers all those years ago, multiply that by a billion and that is what this Jewel was. Her breasts were fountains of life, civilizations of babies would be taken care of. Her shoulder, arm, and body skin was simply life. She had a voice that was mellifluous in country twang, alluring and assuring. It was without equal on this planet. It was the purest woman's voice you would ever hear. It was at once sexy as it was innocent as it was real as it was knowing. Her eyes were honest.

"Okay. Hey, this is tripping me out. What's going on? I had only come to see the corner where my ex-wife and I first kissed. That didn't work out great, but this…man, I don't know what's happening."

"Seb, it's time you understand many things, especially the higher law of love. Let's start with my name. My name is not Jewel, however if that is what you prefer to call me, feel free. My real name is Dymphna, I'm an Irish Saint. We made love with each other before my death a thousand years ago, under the stars on St. Stephen's Green in Dublin, Ireland. And for the record, you weren't a great lover even then (why does this hurt so much?...my epitaph is going to read 'Here Lies NOT Casanova'…)! Somers was right! Then again, obviously I wasn't that memorable to you either…Everyone thought I died a virgin, which is why they wanted me so badly. Men, geez…can't live with them, can't shoot 'em! Second, I have to explain Somers to you. Third, I want to explain why you and who you are. And finally, I have to tell you about the Seventh Seal."

"Uhh, okay. Sounds heavy for a felon. But, that's okay. Hey, do you need anything?"

"Seb, this is no time for pleasantries, and I take care of myself thank you very much. Will you ever change?!"

"Okay, okay, sorry. What's your last name?"

"Don't have one."

"Alrighty then. ET?"

"Enough wasted time. Let's get down to it. Let's begin with your wife, Somers Gillette. Do you remember Rev. Warren's admonition about John 14:2-3. Did you ever figure that out…Don't bother. Let me deal. Somers is not as evil as you think, she's more mental patient than evil. There's more to her than meets the eye. You will be the only soul ever to consider her as badly as you do, and you have that right and then some. But, she won't do what she did to you to anyone else. I promise. Her days of extreme pestilence are ended. She was the Lion of Judah's former wife a few thousand years ago…she is the Lioness, the best protector of cubs, or Lambs even. Not a great wife, perhaps a tad too much perma-PMS as you like to call it, but a great mother. She had to reflect the mirror back at you, for every ounce you gave, she needed to take that back and then some. Consider it a compliment that she went to such extreme depravity to hose you!"

"Great. Lucky me."

"Somers is not the self-hating Jew her mother is. Somers is actually worse…she's a husband-hating Jew…now that's the toughest woman in the universe!"

"Would have been nice to know that a few years ago…"

"I'm just kidding. Somers is reclaimable, and we intend to reclaim her, but she'll fight it. She answers to no one it appears. You used to know this in a previous life but I don't have enough time to explain past lives. Here's the story….Give me Ten Jews, I can build a city. Give me One Hundred, I'll build a civilization. That's not the case for any other religion, Seb, is it? Have you ever wondered why they call them the Chosen People? Because they were "chosen"…By God. And he wanted them to have the Promised Land. So many other cultures have despised the Jews' accomplishments, the Buddhists, Brahmins, Islam, Hindu, Pagans, Satanism, and yes, Christians."

"The world against Judaism?"

"More or less. Mr. Darwin was studying the wrong species Seb…he should have been studying the Jewish people specifically, to understand why they have excelled so much greater than other cultures. Look what natural selection has wrought, an imbalance of talent in the arts, business, and sciences, against the greatest odds. You yourself are so focused on your own shortcomings of sex and nurturing from Somers, you never considered that she's simply a product of generations of survival. That's what they have done…survived. And per person, they're the wealthiest religious group of all and there's no close second…and I'm not referring to what you think I am. I'm talking family. They have the world beaten in spades. They have family. Look at your's. Divorce, wreckage, drugs, suicide, drinking, gambling, cursing….and that's just Episcopalians! Don't get me started on the Pagans. You think Jews are the whiney, moaning Miracle Mile crowd that you sniff at sometimes…that's not Judaism Seb, you're smarter than that. Among other things, I'm also here to snap you out of a thousand year old intellectual slumber. You used to rule people, and you will again someday."

She continued,

"There's one person, however, that we are all careful of, and that's the self-hater, the Slanderer, the Accuser, the Hitler in many of us.

The self-hater wants to wreck humanity because she hates humanity. Satan has grabbed hold of the Slanderers and he won't let go. Why is a self-hating Jew or a self-hating anyone so dangerous?! Because they're so gifted in so many other ways and their motivation is unmatched unfortunately. They're smart, they're motivated, they're talented, and how's this for irony….they have more love than any of us. But they hate that love of theirs, it's a scab they can't pick enough. They want to bury that love. For as you yourself went out on the line of marriage for Somers, she had to reverse it that much more in order to ruin you…she hated what you gave her. It was a given that she would do what she did to you, because you gave that much to her. Do you understand? It's not to excuse them but to understand them. I realize this is difficult to see but you will. And ultimately you will forgive her, because you're a forgiver, you don't have it in your heart to hate, even your own murderer, but you will."

"If I forgive her, that will only piss her off more."

"Exactly…Chalk it up to a "misunderstanding"! Just kidding! That's what Gruella is though, a self hater…and as Somers said to you once, 'it ain't over 'til it's over'. So who knows. I wouldn't hold my breath on Gruella, but stranger things have happened. So just be yourself when this all over, quiet, pleasant, helpful, kind. You always had the most remarkable capacity to forgive, you could take pain like no other warrior in the Kingdom. That's why you were chosen. We underestimated your heart. You will continue to be generous, empathetic, and full of grace. That's who you were, and that's who you shall be. Your children will have the man they always wanted, the man they need. If Somers doesn't change, she'll lose them, she's already losing them and it frightens her so. She has so much to atone for, but we see in her heart that she has lost the fight to continue the assault. We're not so certain that Satan could have ever succeeded with her…I think even he found her obstreperous! You're in a whole new category if Satan can't beat you and Somers Gillete just might be that black swan. We're not certain we want her on our side or his…She's a strange one. But she'll never realize she has the Lamb in her until it's likely too late."

"Yeah, you could say that again."

"The Devil is an angel, a Fallen Angel. God would like for that Angel to come back into the fold, but first there will be a battle. This battle will involve Satan who's been stewing in his pit for almost 1,000 years now. You put him there, but let's not get all crazy now so don't ask me about that one. He's about to come out and he'll surround the 'beloved city, and the heavens will rain fire. Someone will need to put him and The False Prophet back into Gehenna. It's you again."

"Wait a second…You never told me 'why me?'…So, why me?"

"I already told you…See above! We don't have time to go over it again, and so if I can be so bold, and I'm not supposed to use such words, because you're not a Facebook pussy! We need men not stalkers, strength not manicures, cowboys not hats. Avoir des coquilles. You've never complained ever, you've never gossiped, you're stoic but in the right way. And almost as importantly, you have the key to the seventh seal."

"You keep saying that, but I don't get it. What's this seventh seal you keep referring to?"

"The Seventh Seal can only be opened by the Lamb of God. Unfortunately, you aren't exactly the Lamb of God! I mean the blowjobs, the premarital sex, sheesh…it was enough to kill me watching that nonsense the last thirty years! Men! It's all you think about. I'm a big believer in condoms, ahem."

"Are you really a Saint, Dymphna? Saints can't discuss this stuff, Jewel maybe, but you?"

"Oh please Seb, get a life. There are a lot of Saints and don't think they don't enjoy sex like you do. Babies aren't conceived immaculately, as you learned, ahem. Mary wasn't a virgin and Mary Magdalene isn't a whore. We're all somewhere in the middle, mostly anyway. I should have taught you better in Sunday School."

"Whoah there Jewel, I mean Dymphna. None of my Sunday School teachers looked like you!"

"Whoah there back to you Sebastian Graham! That was me…I can be whoever I want to be, and you should be looking at my character and not my boobs. I knew if I looked like Jewel you'd pay more attention. I never realized that back in 1972."

"My bad. Okay, so what about the Seventh Seal?"

"Do you remember signing a document in 1998 in Irkutsk Russia, and placing it in safekeeping with a lawyer in London? You know what was in there?"

"How do you know all my secrets?! I feel like you've been spying on me… Even Cravath couldn't get that out of me, and those guys are like God…"

"God would never go to Harvard Law!"

"Okay, yeah, I agree. And I also know what's in that document. So what…it's a numbered bank statement. So?"

"It's not just that. It's why you will live, and it's why she's living among us, she's breathing, growing. The Only Daughter of God."

"You mean the Only Son of God?"

"No... I said what I meant. The Only Daughter."

Jewel evaporated, into a fine mist in the darkness, a sprite pixie of magic dust. A wind blew out the candle and I felt as if I were free floating into space. Shooting stars and holographic Milky Way's spun around me at warp speed. I definitely wasn't at 78th and 2nd anymore. I was on the best LSD trip man had ever taken, except I had never taken a drug. The odd thing was, events in my past, my long agoooo past, started to flow into my head, as if I was being transfused with intellect and my brain had an endless receptacle to it.

I still didn't understand what Jewel had said to me, or whatever her name was, Dymphna. And then bam, I was there, standing under the pedestrian sign again at 78th and 2nd at 10 PM. Taxis whizzed by and young couples were arm in arm, dogs were being walked. Physically dazed but no longer dizzy in the head, I was clear headed, if I could be so bold, like I hadn't in a very long time.

What was that all about?!

I walked away, alone in the night air, back toward 3rd and 79th to catch the Subway at 77th. I was humming that song, I and Love and You, and I walked by what used to be Hunter's. It's a new restaurant now and there was a new crowd, neck buttons securely fastened again (the more things change, the more they stay the same...). I could hear a Foreigner tune wedgie inside, the DJ had tuned up "Waiting for a Girl Like You". The kids were living it up, like in 1992, and they all knew the words. I was jealous about the atmosphere but horrified about the song…still more horrified that they knew the words.

A bum was sitting cross-legged on the street outside, almost in yoga style. He had a long beard and baggy clothes. I stooped down to give him a dollar…figured he needed it more than me, even if I was the one headed to the bing.

He looked up at me, and he had bluest eyes I'd ever seen, they startled me. I remembered this guy…I had seen him seventeen years before, at the same place, but he hadn't aged, and his face still had the same grace and dignity that I recalled. He spoke before I could give him the dollar,

"So, do you get it yet Sebastian? Is it all clear? Are you with us?"

By now, I simply had to expect this kind of thing. I answered,

"If you're with Jewel, I mean, Dymphna, then I'm with you. You have to pardon my not being as eloquent last time we met. I know you. I'm seeing strange things in my head. I think I may have always been with you. I fought for you, I died for you."

"Yes you're goddamn right you did (and then he laughed so hard I thought he'd have a heart attack…he had a sense of humor obviously…). But please remember: only The Lamb can open the seal. Don't forget."

"Who is the Lamb?"

"Oh, that's never been too hard to figure out. And I think you'd get it shortly now that the cobwebs are clearing out of your brain. So let me speed things up. The Fallen Angel had three children. The Book of Revelation 13:17-18. 'Do you know the number of a man', Sebastian?"

"666."

"That's correct. And who is the anti-Devil, who is the opposite of Angra Mainyu, the Antichrist, Kolski, Leviathan, Mephistopheles, Iblis? How can one invert that kind of evil? How can one turn such awesome pestilence on it head? If I say I love something but yet I hate it, is my world upside down? "

"Yes."

"So turn the Beast upside down and tell me your new number! We inverted the Beast, we inverted her with the Lamb. Even gave her an extra 9 to be sure! AOL Keyword: "Nine"!"

Thunder cracked and Manhattan shook.

"999?"

"Add the keyword."

"9999"

"You're not as dumb as you look! The lamb, 9.9.99, premillenial, it had to be the year before the millennium, I'd run out of time. Do you see? The inversion of 666, the Lamb is now among you."

"Holy Christ…"

I was no longer Icarus mindlessly flying into the sun but rather a starburst of knowledge returning to earth.

"You've always known her. I'm an equal opportunity resurrection man. It's a new age…got to give the women a shot at immortality, don't cha think? (Another hearty laugh…) Good luck Sebastian, sorry about your lot in life, but for what's worth: I've only identified with dysfunctional people. I've also left Joseph of Arimathea and Nicodemus to aid you in protecting her. I think you know who they are too, don't you (he winked…)? And by the way, enough with the Jesus complex musicians! And always kill 'em with kindness, they hate that the worst! Au-revoir!! See you in a thousand years! "

The bum vanished in a shower of light, a street lamp exploded. My eyes blinked. I knew exactly who the Lamb was. And I finally knew why it was me chosen for the pain.

And suffering I received! And Somers, Ed, and Gruella got what they wanted: me in the bing. If you don't think that was their overriding goal, you don't know them, so count your blessings you don't know them. They killed the Icelandic deal because I needed it so badly. Whatever I needed, they took. The champagne must have tasted sweet, this was the time of their lives. Don't sell these three hellish fiends short. This will be a never ending quest of theirs for three full years, to ruin me more.

What they don't realize is I'll have little to lose when I get freedom again. But, I will have something to gain, the love of three of the most precious human beings ever in the world…

The End

I heard a new sound, a country roots tune which was so bare, so clean, so stripped as to almost be non-professional. Lyrics that came straight from the heart, college day loves and energy and communal trust. A piano's lead, a defiant spirit, temporarily forlorn but hopeful, a southern twang and rusted, but that was the beauty of it. A sporadic percussion beat, and what sounded like a background cello. Three words. That was all. I and love and you. Just remembering what makes it all worthwhile, no matter the gutter we end up in sometimes. Just keep your eyes looking up at stars always. And let the audience sing along. No large society cocktail party for profit with this playlist. The smalltown boy had a new sound, and yet, the song remains the same...it's always about love and leaving.

There's not a doubt in my head that I am the least capable locked up man in the universe...meaning, I love my kids to no end. The bigger picture was the heaviest rains had passed a year before. Judges got to decide the result at the end...and Somers wanted that. She would have shot me if it hadn't worked out for her. You don't believe me? There were no handshakes afterward.

The emotional beatdowns from Somers continued, if not even more persistently. She would slam doors in front of the kids, she cursed at all of us, she tossed gifts onto sidewalks like trash, she carelessly brought boyfriends into the house and into the bedroom in front of the kids. She was socially reckless, if you consider bringing male companions to sleep at the house within seconds after our separation an act of recklessness, which I did since I was the kids' dad and would never consider doing the same (you know, the warning she threw at me in front of the detective when we separated...but which was all about her...ahhh, it was always about herself, I just never knew...).

Somers would send emails about an hour before a child's pickup, telling me I could no longer get the kids unless I paid her more money, money I didn't have and money which meant nothing to her. She just wanted to pick at any scab she could, which wasn't too hard with me by then. I ignored it all, not even responding to her emails and simply showing up to get the kids. They wanted to be with me, and I them, and Somers wasn't around anyway.

She didn't exactly love this part of her life though. She hadn't quite snagged the next husband and she needed a new husband to begin the steady beatdowns that made life worth living. Once she got her new man, she would mercifully leave us alone. I foresee great trouble with the ex-wife of husband number 2. Just wait until Somers insists that her kids wear certain clothes or act certain ways. Somers likely has it all figured out already.

Somehow, she managed to insert Gruella back into the kids' lives, which grated on me like nothing else frankly. If the kids knew how involved Gruella and Ed were in this mess, they would disown them too. I hope they eventually do. Those two are lousy human beings, unfit to be around goldfish let alone children. Maybe too harsh on Ed, since he has suffered being in Gruella's lair for too long. But Gruella definitely needs to be locked up in an asylum.

For Somers, it's always been about her and no one else. It will always be about her, just as in Gruella's world it has always been about Gruella. Gruella couldn't get in the Social Register so she made life hell for those who could.

One interesting exchange happened in front of the kids recently. In Somers' never ending quest to prove her bon fides as the ideal Jekyll and Hyde 50/50 split personality wonder, she offered to give me money one day when one of my tires went flat (while returning the kids from a weekend). But as you must know her, her kindness has invisible strings…so I declined,

"I'd rather starve than take a cent from you Somers…no thanks. You have zero compassion, this is all a fake as well."

She couldn't let that lie, so she went in for a counterattack, unleashing a volley of punches that were impressive even for her.

"Does it look like a give a flying fuck (D.i.l.l.i.g.a.f.{f.})?!!! You better be careful around me Sebastian, because I will see to it, and

Ed too, that you suffer even greater than what you think you're up against today! Trust me! I will fuck you up even worse than this! I will, I swear, and I'll have no shame about it. Dreamers aren't meant to last long, dickface…Want to hear something funny?! I own you, now and forever! Fuck you and your dreams, Dreamer Douchebag! What do you think of that?!!!"

She literally was throwing air punches as she said this, like a possessed Kolski. She stared at me waiting for my rejoinder. She'd served up the juiciest meatball ever…and the thing is, she was on another of her hallucinogenic benders and the fact is I am a dreamer.

"Frankly my dear, I don't give a damn, dot com!!" Clark Gable never had it better than that! She wheeled away, diminished because her boundaries hadn't been respected. She was the one good thing in my life before my kids, but that girl's gone away for good.

'…He floated back down because he wanted to share, The keys to the locks on the chains he saw everywhere, But first he was stripped and then he was stabbed, By faceless men, but fuckers…he still stands, And he still gives his love he just gives it away'…. *

I have a ski apparel company to run when I get out and I think we will be something remarkable. No partners, no debt, and no investors…I learned where I'm weak and I won't make the same mistakes again. We'll have dozens if not hundreds of employees within five years of restarting. I know because my wholesale buyers have all stood behind me, even now, and they want me back in the ring.

I'm so looking forward to battling Somers again…not. I'm praying she finds another soul to project her angst and bitterness onto, perhaps her new husband's ex-wife will be that person. Somers still wants me dead, not alive and making money. She has three kids whom she sees as pure chattel, not little humans to adore. The evil scientist is hard at work and she doesn't have an off-switch.

I always thought Somers would be the type of assassin to stand over her target's dead body and plug a few extra rounds into the target's eyes, just because... Then, quite effortlessly and after the carnage, she'd go to a society cocktail party for profit in high-fashion bore, with not a trace of trauma. A sociopathic, murderous, cannibalistic, high-society, ravishing thug: that's Somers.

How did it come to this? I'm still astounded.

Oddly, I still half-love her, even after the marital bloodshed and her feverish adultery. In the end, I guess I prefer the murderer/cocktail-party variety wife. She just shouldn't have custody. She wants people to think she's the everything woman, when she's anything but. And so a poisonous kiss started all this, this new millennial Rapture, Armageddon, and Final Judgement?

Her ass is still perfect…the nonparallel Modigliani sculpture whose heritage could never have been pure wasp. No wasp was ever that fine, but no wasp was ever this evil. I try but I just can't forget the curves of her body…I also can't forget the rottenness of her soul. She's back in her ring, throwing air punches at imaginary enemies and the narcissism is cuter than ever.

The name "narcissism" by the way is derived from Greek mythology. Narcissus was a handsome Greek youth who'd never seen his reflection. As Narcissus was walking along a path one afternoon, he got thirsty and stopped to take a drink from a pool of water. He saw his reflection for the first time and not knowing any better, started talking to it. Echo, who had been following him, started repeating the last thing Narcissus said back. Not knowing about reflections, Narcissus thought his reflection was speaking to him. Unable to consummate his love, Narcissus pined away at the pool and changed into the flower that bears his name, the <u>narcissus</u>. I'm going to send Somers a bouquet of narcissus for Christmas this year. Narcissus had the ultimate Bad Boundaries.

"You're not really in love with someone unless you've thought of killing them." I thought Somers Gillette was only kidding. She never wanted to die by my side…from the beginning, she was always killing me. When the sun set for me, the sun rose for her…so when I lost, she won. It was the ultimate 'Holy Christ' revelation. Mon dieu, I refuse to have her hold my balls anymore.

Here's the end, where we begin again.

\

Epilogue

Lord Byron said that all tragedies are finished by death and all comedies by marriage. I almost batted two for two, but the hitting instructor didn't quite finish me off. At St. Thomas' Church, I wanted Beethoven's Ode to Joy…she wanted Love Stinks (just one more ear worm from the 70's…).

You're probably wondering why I ever loved Somers so much. I've asked myself the same question, how could I have been attracted to someone so utterly profane, so wildly vulgar, so thoroughly immoral, so completely devoid of human compassion.   And what I'll say is this…when Somers was able to channel her father's good grace, and it wasn't often, what you got was a woman of such incredible fun and humor, that it was impossible to resist her. At the same time, you could never reconcile that side of her with the epic destructive side of her mother's that ultimately ran me over. The girl has the best father of any human being in the universe, an American man who deserves his own Washington Monument, so people can understand what being a great person is all about. And that's that.

I got her adultery thing, heck I should have expected it. If her own mother couldn't resist her own wandering instincts, and she was married to a billionaire, then you can only imagine how easy it was for Somers to run from me!

You should know what I was contractually guaranteed on September 8th 2009, Twenty-Two calendar days from the arrest day. Twenty-two…I could count the hours it was that close. Guaranteed personal fees and points, and we were pre-funded… Here they are:

- $4 Million closing fee;
- $1 Million guaranteed salary per year for five years;
- 10% Commission, $4.675 Million First Year Alone
- 5% Net Income (who knows)
- 40% of a company conservatively valued at $80 Million.

All guaranteed. All pre-funded. You say you have doubts? Well, there's a tiny law firm based in Manhattan with over 1,000 partners that still has the paperwork…so go ask them. I'd have repaid the only part of the old company I considered a total fuckup on my part (for which I am now paying the penalty), making others whole and happy, and I'd have had significant assets and income to cover anything else for my kids forever. And maybe Somers would have been satisfied…nah.

If you think Somers cared about the money, you'd be wrong… Does it really look like she gives a flying frig (the clean dilligaff enunciation)? Go ask the Nanny. Somers had parties to plan and dates to go on and my having custody of the kids interfered with the master plan.   Once Somers set out to destroy me, there'd have been no turning back. Everything for Somers is impulsive and yesterday and face-saving is the only priority. She had a holy war of revenge to execute. I just needed 22 more days…my rectitude was a tragic error, I should have been marketing. No one but Talal got my new cell phone.

The kid would have been in the picture.

What's become of Somers? Well, firstly, I don't think she even thought that all this would work out for her as well as it did. She kept feeding and everyone kept eating.   Somers went yard on emotions and actions because they suited her needs and fantasies, the atheism could never just be agnosticism, the large parties could never just be three couples, the adultery could never just be one guy because five gave her an addiction-out, and the obliteration of me allowed her to escape seemingly as an innocent, when only Betty and I knew what she was really all about.

On the dating front, she immediately went Facebook yard: Facebook flirting, Facebook crushes, Facebook foreplay, Facebook ehaircutting, Buddy pouncing, Facebragging… Facebook is dreadful.

She still ego searches the Internet, checking to see what media outlet has talked her up this week. She gives herself email promotions whenever she wants.

She has what we call technolust, which accounts for the new guy, a total disconnection from humanity and reality. I'm not sure if she's Facebook official with him yet, 'in a relationship', but even that won't stop her from entertaining better offers…it never stopped her mom. Her guy is a bluetool technosexual, natch.

If I do the half my age plus seven for my next serious girlfriend, her husband and my date will have at least two decades difference between them. They'll probably marry each other after Somers hits the eject button…

Just as someone can have an emotional breakdown, where the loss is pure and complete, Somers had an anger breakdown, where she pitched so high that there was no emotion left afterward. She's weirdly neutered now, outwardly sweet to the rest of humanity for the time being, and inwardly dead of feeling. She got an enragement ring from husband the new guy.

She's still at the business of selling mirages…she doesn't even allow the gardener to cut the grass every week because she figures she still needs to convince people that she's hamstrung financially, when that's the furthest problem she's got. God…If you only knew how many parties she hosts…It's amazing, this need to feed the world a lie.

My being away gives her the necessary time to hook the new guy, who would always need to bring his own kids to the table (a hedge against the possibility of her own children fleeing her when they learn the truth). As importantly it gives her time to sell a version of false history to the kids, and to try and Rip van Winkle me. She'll stay at it until she's won because it's her only goal now, outside the large parties for profit.

So far as the Jewish heritage, I'm not sure that's huge anymore in Somers' head…she's more jihadist terrorist than Ashkenazi anyway. She seems to have accepted the fact that a percentage of the LV community now knows and doesn't care. The recession scared people's prejudices out of their system and made for new bedfellows. And the funny thing is, she doesn't look Jewish…mazel tov.

Somers' hatred for humanity was deeper than the earth's core. It was as if all of her collective misery simply rose up in a funnel cloud of destruction and consumed her, but feasted on me…it needed my soul to sustain her. All narcissists need a bogey man and selling a myth never seemed so easy.

Her makeup, once so soft and muted, has gone neo-gothic, a pathological celebration of plaintive youthful re-identity, eyeliner heavy like coal, rouge splotchy as a clown, lipstick thick as blood, nails sharper than knives. Her outfits have trended age-inappropriately higher and tighter, no longer causing young men to wonder with awe…I knew she'd go down that road. Her hair no longer carries its natural tint of golden blonde nor is it effortlessly windswept…it's caked in cement salon care, stiff as cardboard, yellow as mustard. In form and presentation, she has become one and the same as Gruella. From behind, you wouldn't know who was who except for the ass.

Somers ultimately slept/tried out five new suitors post marriage adultery, the first starting the week of our separation. She sank her fangs into and got a huge enragement ring from pro-forma husband number two/suitor number five, the bluetool hedge fund operations executive, an in-line skating, boarding school, 70's light rock loving, mini-dachshund, Mini-Cooper divorced yuppie ('I give bonuses to my people'…natch). Aaaah, he's a nice leprechaun, I know, just busting his chops.

He'll be a much better son-in-law to Gruella, because he saw what happened to me and he certainly doesn't want the same. Gruella is ready for another half-her-age Oedipal flirtation, and Somers' new husband will play that game...Gruella likes compliance in a man, and he's willing to cave before the battle even begins. He'll love that mongrel dog of hers. And she will be smugly content again.

Anyone have a silver cross I can borrow? I'll be happy to wipe it off afterward.

If you really want to know why Somers wanted me dead, besides the many things I've laid out, just read Exhibit #1 behind the Epilogue. She knew we were going forward with a custody battle if I was free to do so and she knew she would have lost...her actions demanded it. Angry ex-wives have gone to jail for 1/100th less, let alone lose custody of their children. There's no sense filing it for the time being.

Somers Gillette never needed my money...rather, she needed me to be unable to make money. No one ever understood that. My silence was my worst mistake and her best gambit. Somers never had a vested interest in my success...she had a vested interest in my failure. And everyone went along because they were scared of her.

She needed the kids wholly and entirely dependent on her. Two million in legal fees didn't buy Somers a divorce, it bought her a murder, mine. The master always teaches the apprentice but one better. Somers knew she wasn't a fit mother, just like her mom. She also knew that Betty was the only one who knew the whole story besides me and she was showing up in court to testify against Somers, so Somers had to deny her a new job as well. Insane that anyone else who knows those facts could trust Somers for half a second, because Betty gave her life to my kids, and Somers' reward to her was a total character assassination... Unreal.

There was only one way for Somers to stay on top when the clock ended, by pushing her husband and the father of her kids to the bottom. Chesterton said that marriage is an adventure, like going to war. That's my ex's primary concept of marriage, to kill, cripple, or emasculate her husband.

Read the Exhibit…it explains why she went all in. For me, these are simply times to learn to love again. See you soon I hope.

SG

Letter For Somers

"Only you have ever understood me ... and you got it wrong." Hegel

Somers,

*Once I thought I saw you in a crowded hazy bar, dancing on the light from star to star. Far across the moonbeam, I know that's who you are. (*Neil Young)*

You were right: dreamers never stand a chance.

I found someone I was willing to risk it all on, the one thing that meant more to me than anything, someone I'd have gone to the end of the world for no questions asked. It's not always about doing the right thing and all that bullshit, because I've done that my whole life and still do....if you need, I give, to anyone and I treat every human the same, regardless of their background. You know what though, that stuff is all fine, but ultimately life comes down to and is all about love, not just doing the right thing. I fought for you, I put you in front of anything else in my life, I gave it all and then some, and I remained faithful... And even after all the bullshite you threw my way, the setup, the betrayals, the holy war, it's still worth it to me, because although I can't love you like I always did, I've got those three great kids from it.

Your illusions became real, the perception became reality. I was so weak you could have knocked me over with a feather duster, instead you brought out ICBM's. To think you were my only temptation ever, and your secrets that I held and still hold...what a shame. Every day was one more missed kick, one more pulled ball by your Lucy to my Charlie.

You and I know that this has been the biggest tragedy (travesty) in the history of mankind, or at least Locust Valley, and only you and I get to look in the mirror and know that it was you who orchestrated nearly every step. You were never the contradiction like I thought - guilt and honesty, sin and holiness, sex and chastity – you were always just you, and I'll let people figure out what I mean by that on their own.

You did do three things I still can't quite believe (I can believe the adultery because that's what your mom did; and for the Victim Statement...you had become unhuman by that point)...actually, no one can believe the below three now that they know the full story,

- When someone asked you for a health insurance number which you alone had, and you had it, you wouldn't tell them; because of that, I lost everyone's contacts, all agreements, all records, everything.
- You never told me about any calls to the house…not once, making a problem an eschatology, because you knew I would have met any problem head-on, because that's who I am.
- You burned my children's birthday and Father's Day cards that they painstakingly made for me every year…15 years of life's treasures, things I would have buried with me… for this act alone, aaah, forget it… It should be self-evident to anyone who wants to understand you and wants to trust you.

When I first saw you in that doorway in Millbrook, when I saw the backlight of your figure, all I could say was Holy Christ. All I can say now is…Holy Christ.

You're a one woman wrecking crew of souls…a storm of insults that started the day we married (and hasn't ended yet!). There has to be a terminal date on your craziness…right? Even the kids asked you to stop going out at night, and yet you told them they didn't know what they were saying! They're kids…they can't lie about things they see!

You never told anyone about Iceland…you only sped up to deny me the opportunity to get back on my feet. You, Betty, and I knew that there was no way you would have ended up with custody, not after what you did during and after the separation. It must have made you mental that I never said anything negative about you to the kids…not once and never will.

You were so flagrant with respect to sleeping around with so many men right in front of the children's eyes, during the separation and after the divorce. I'm hoping you still hate sex but with my luck, you actually enjoy it now. Gawd.

Your only miscalculation at all so far as I can tell was believing that the rats you did business with wouldn't come to me once you discarded them. Rats have no loyalty…they came as quickly as they could. That's how the information came to me…

I never appreciated the society thing…your manic going out every night swamped me, I never had a second to react. And as you know, I'll never be on Facebook…real men don't do Facebook. What real man goes on Facebook? That should be illegal. I'll never hustle an image, real men should figure out who's who based on experience.

Life is a series of events and we have to be amused by most of it. The only thing I don't find amusing is the kids…that's where you and I part ways. For you, it's always been about you…for me it's always been about the kids. And of course you understood that.

Did you really get away with it? Don't be so sure. It will keep being about you and you alone, likely forever, making the mother-daughter axis complete, a ring of hellish fire, the Furies circling.

*'…I know someday you'll have a beautiful life, I know you'll be a star in somebody else's sky, But why can't it be mine?'**

That's how I felt about you since the day we met because I didn't know how to control my heart. I just wanted to die by your side. If it's any consolation, I still think you're hot as hell…if there was ever a double entendre, that's it!

And don't worry: if you're wondering by the end of The Dream, I won't show up at your 50th. Because I do give a flying fuck.

Zut alors,

S

PS…fifteen years and you never asked if I played guitar…

PSS….Oh yeah…one other thing.

Remember when Jim Vander Hoorst poked and prodded about how I made my early money and when you couldn't figure it out, you simply put the lie out there that I had stolen it?…Here's your answer.

February 1999…

I arrive in Irkutsk Russia in Siberia. It's cold, a cold like I've never felt. 20 Degrees below Zero. My nostrils are in pain from the frigid air. I don't have the right clothes so I sprint to a waiting ZIL-41041 on the tarmac.

I'm driven to a gated dacha on the evergreen-forested shores of Lake Baikal. The dacha is a Georgian-brick colonial, not a common sight in Russia. There's a large, gently-sloping lawn leading to the Lake. On the ground are ten inches of pure white snow. On the vast expanse of snowy lawn stand four Sikorsky S-76 helicopters in red and white trim; mechanics and pilots are milling about, dressed in military parka's…they look like technicians on Mir. There appear to be about fifty dark-suited military sharpshooters walking around the property.

To the northern side of the dacha is an attached glass structure, an octagonal room approximately 100 feet in diameter and thirty feet high; it's large, looking almost like a funky greenhouse. The huge glass panes are covered in thick steam and condensation. Inside the room is a large Hydropool hot tub, large enough for twenty people. The water is heated to a comfortable 102 Degrees.

I'm shown to a changing room where a bathing suit is hanging waiting for me. I put it on and then go to the room where the hot tub lies.

Inside the tub are four men and eight women. I get in. I'm the only person who has any clothing on, in my case blue-checked shorts. There's a Saudi royal, an important and known executive from a large private equity firm in Washington DC, a budding metals oligarch who will eventually own global sports franchises and mega-yachts, a senior Russian Politburo member we'll call 'Boris', and six Russian women who could be supermodels, except I think the Russian Federation pays them more than they could earn in the west. They're the most stunning visual human specimens I've ever seen, and they're bone naked.

The ladies are seated at the side of each man except me, and they're giggling at anything and everything. I don't think they speak English.

'Boris' orders some vodka shots for the men and proceeds to launch into a toast given in Russian. A man in a suit is translating 'Boris'' words from the side. The ten of us are holding chilled shot glasses. 'Boris' is saying something about platinum, palladium, nickel, patriarchal societies, future riches, and Mother Russia. This is a real toast for real men…I don't think any of these guys will end up on Facebook. With the word Nostrovia, the vodka pours into our throats. The liquor is so strong it takes your breath away.

The man in the suit walks behind me and asks me to step out of the tub. He leads me to an antique wooden credenza to the side of the room where four manila folders are sitting face-up…I can see my name Graham written on one in Cyrillic and English. I towel off. The man opens my folder and lays out six items. On the credenza now lie i) a one-page agreement, ii) a Russian Central bank check made out to a Bermuda company I now control in the amount of $7.5 Million, iii) a white sheet of paper with drawings of Seven Angels, Seven Trumpets, a written number, and Cypriot Bank name, and iv) three envelopes.

I sign the i) agreement and take the ii) check , paper, and envelopes.

Written on the iii) one-page letter is a sixteen-digit bank account number and a bank's name. The account, though numbered, it's an irrevocable trust funded and established for my children. Somers' name is purposely nowhere near the trust. By design, the assets transfer once a year for 20 years. I know where the trust will end up in 2017 and I know what it will be worth. There are also two lawyers in London who know, in fact one will safe-keep the envelope in his office for the next twenty years…I'm going to deliver it to him in about twelve hours. I've always trusted Englishmen.

I exhale deeply. I'm not entirely sure one of the sharpshooters won't take me out when I walk away from this place, but that's the risk I assumed when I signed up for this particular job. I think it's worked out for everyone…It was never about the risk, it was always about my children.

I look back to 'Boris', who has two girls in his lap. He's happy, but he also looks like a heart attack waiting to happen. He smiles. In clipped, Russian-accented English, he says to me,

"Graham, sposeba, my friend. You, you earned dese. Don't let ever no woman take dis from you or your sons (my daughter is growing as he speaks...). You have a reason to live, even when you can't find one friend. Dos vadanya"

"Don't worry about that, Boris. See 'ya."

I walk away from the party, oblivious to the hot tub fun, thinking only of my children back in the States. I remember the plate of asparagus and how unhinged Somers became like a wild animal, no justifiable provocation, and then leaving for the night unexplained. I get dressed in the anteroom alone. A long way from country boy to this. The sealed envelope is safely in my pocket now and an asset is forever protected for my kids. One of the helicopters has started its engines and the blades are turning over.

I don't think I was of sound mind when I married. But my head was on straight in Russia, always. It had to be. You see, with me, it was never about the party for profit...my kids would always win with this dad.

For where your treasure is, there your heart will be also.-- Matthew 6:21

Dumbed down and numbed by time and age.
You're dreams that catch the world the cage.
The highway sets the travelers stage.
All exits look the same.

Three words that became hard to say.
I and Love and You.

(v. The Avett Brothers, North Carolina/Brooklyn)

Exhibit

May XX, 2009

Nassau County Matrimonial Court
1200 Old Country Road
Mineola, NY 11590

Attention: The Hon. xxxxx xxxxxxxxx
Ph: (516) xxx-xxxx
Fax: (516) xxx--xxxx

RE: Graham v Gillette, Civ. xxxxxxx (2007)

Dear Judge xxxxxxxxx,

Please accept this letter as an addendum to the motion being filed today, to award sole custody of the three children in the above referenced case (Civ. xxxxxxx...2007), to the undersigned (the "Petitioner"), effective immediately.

Your last words to my ex-wife and me in court were as such: "Please keep yourselves together for the sake of your children". You meant obviously our mental wherewithal and ability to function to preserve the children's peace of mind. One of us has heeded your advice, whereas one of us has done nothing but thumb her nose in the direction of it. As Mark Twain famously said, 'there are lies, damn lies, and then there are statistics'. I am submitting to the court taped phone record conversations, documented emails to and from Ms. Gillette, documented text messages to and from Ms. Gillette, and affidavits from independent parties supporting the 17 charges found below.

We ask for an immediate court-supervised transfer of full custodial rights to the Petitioner, away from Ms. Gillette, as the Court can expect an unrestrained, vituperative, and ultimately injurious (to the children), emotional reaction by Ms. Gillette (the "Ms. Gillette") to this filing. Upon the many occasions of Ms. Gillette's extraordinarily dangerous outbursts and extreme displays of physical and verbal anger, we would expect this filing to cause no less to and around the children; the children will be at extreme risk of further emotional damage. I am a Pro Se litigant; counsel representing Ms. Gillette has been served as evidenced by the Certificate of Service attached.

We have patiently waited for one year to make this filing, and in that time we have noted every action and every instance of parental disenfranchisement. We had been highly reluctant to sign the previous custody agreement, however we felt that it was in the best interests of the children to do so given Mr. Graham's other predicament, which ironically Ms. Gillete had no uncertain hand in. We had been hoping that Ms. Gillette could behave like a rational party for profit and help assist in the continuance of co-parenting rights.

All of our best wishes have proven unfounded. Ms. Gillette is a disturbed litigant evidencing the most contemptible behavior around the children.

Given a choice, without emotional pressures being exerted by Ms. Gillette, the three children would elect to be in the care of Petitioner. I have been unable to express my urgent and deepest objections to Ms. Gillette's actions since we were last in your courtroom, but I am now free to do so. On the kids' behalf, we have absolutely no alternative than to pursue judicial intervention.

As but one example of Ms. Gillette's skewed priorities, but a very telling example, Ms. Gillette asked the children to sleep elsewhere (away from the domestic residence) the night before Mother's Day, so the children could not wake up in their house with their Mother on Mother's Day (give her their presents, make her breakfast, etc…). Rather, Ms. Gillette hosted a party for profit that night at the residence, and a male romantic partner spent the night with her in her bedroom, while the children were forced to sleep elsewhere, away from their bedrooms, though they did not wish to.

Please note that Petitioner has pleaded with Ms. Gillette via email many times to alter or modify her vengeful dereliction of the custody agreement and parental rights, to no avail. Indeed, Ms. Gillette's responses generally fall in the category of extreme and unpleasant vituperations and vulgarity, with almost zero direct response to the real issues that Petitioner has raised with respect to the children, their contact details, their health, their education, and their welfare.

In the January 2010 Custody Agreement of this matrimonial action, at the time, Petitioner agreed to award voluntarily custody over the children's mother for the sole and express purpose of expediting and facilitating ease of paperwork for the children when and if necessary; he thought that (ease of paperwork) might be useful for all, given the other issues he was facing. He did not anticipate that Ms. Gillette would become vengeful, would deny Petitioner with even the most basic information of education, health, contact data, and welfare, even when such lack of information placed the children in harm's way, and this has caused significant irreparable emotional damage to the children. He did not cede, nor asked, ever, to be removed from any affairs of the children, and yet this is precisely what Ms. Gillette has sought to do, with astonishing levels of denial, vulgarity, parental absenteeism, and extreme moral depravity.

In the face of this storm, Petitioner has continued to stay as involved as he can with the kids, being with them every weekend, taking them to games, buying them clothes, shoes, and items related to their various activities, and taking them on vacations.

So that the Children are no longer exposed to the vituperative, volcanic, unstable character of Ms. Gillette, and because of her demonstrated actions which are willfully ignorant of their impact on the children, it is in the Court and County's interests that these children are removed from Ms. Gillette without any delay. I and others are convinced without a shadow of doubt that this would be in the children's best interests.

Ms. Gillette has summarily:

-cut off all communication regarding any data concerning the children to the Petitioner, such as contacts, health, and educational welfare
-denied Petitioner previously agreed access to his children
-set up erratic communication roadblocks to previously agreed weekends and vacations
-deliberately set out to deny Petitioner any and all access to the children's -educational records and meetings, by calling and communicating with current and future school administrators and demanding that they not involve the father in any further meetings (this after the Petitioner never once failed to show for any of his children's teacher meetings in 15 years)

-harassed the children about all access to Petitioner and any conversations that they may have had with him, by badgering the young children for information

-secretly and illegally tape recorded all calls by Petitioner with the children on the home phone line, again causing the children to devise their own ways to avoid Ms. Gillette's eavesdropping

-Maintained several adulterous affairs during the marriage and forced the children to sleep under the same roof as one male partner on at least one vacation and at the domestic residence.

-Currently Ms. Gillette is in a fifth documented active romance, with multiple sleepovers both at the residence and away with the newest partner, in front of the children and with the full knowledge of the children, leaving children no fewer than three nights out of every week.

-Stayed away from the household for four to five nights per week prior to this calendar year, in the company of male relations, leaving the children in the care of illegal immigrants or at the homes of neighbors, where basic activities like homework were neglected

-Repeatedly lied to the children on so many occasions that it would not be in the court's interest for them to be listed individually, but just several would be: "Dad and I will sit together for all school events", "the bank is foreclosing on the house", etc…; these statements, made directly to the children, are outright fabrications, leaving the children confused as to what the truth is

-Repeatedly lied to the children about the welfare of the Petitioner

-Committed xxxxxxxxx xxxxxxxxxxxxxxxx, with no input from Petitioner

-Arranged summer camps for the children, with no input nor warning to Petitioner

-Deliberately and falsely stated to xxxxxxxxxxxxxx was applying to a new school xxxxxxxxxxxxxx, when in fact Ms. Gillette had applied in his name xxxxxxxxxxxxxx.…this was done with no warning nor input to Petitioner

-Took xxxxxxxxxxxxxxxxxxxxxxxxxxxxxxxxxxx without informing Petitioner beforehand

-Asked all schools to "only deal with Ms. Gillette" on all matters; school administrators would be happy to provide corroborative statements. Threatened schools with penalties if they did not comply!

-Badgers Petitioner continuously in front of the children, alternately changing agreements on weekends with the children.

We respectfully submit that if any one of the above seventeen actions constitutes a dangerous dereliction of the custody agreement, that Ms. Gillette would be forced to renounce her rights as custodian, and all rights should be shifted over to the Petitioner, who would never engage in such callous and wanton disenfranchisement of the Ms. Gillette should Petitioner have custody.

As it is, all seventeen actions have occurred, repeatedly, and Ms. Gillette has shown no sign of remorse, nor change; indeed, if anything, this situation has been aggravated even more with each passing day. Ms. Gillette recently began having unilateral discussions with the middle child on boarding schools, again in the face of and in violation of a custody requirement to first discuss these educational issues with Petitioner, prior to any unilateral discussions with the children.

The children are legitimately frightened of Ms. Gillette, and this will not end unless the court intervenes immediately.

It is of no pleasure to ask the court to step in; this is a last effort situation, and one that Petitioner has pleaded with Ms. Gillette to avoid. Ms. Gillette's actions indicate a summary dismissal of any objections and therefore Petitioner has exhausted his available recourse actions.

This is as dire a situation as can be envisioned; Ms. Gillette seems bent on making the disenfranchisement of Petitioner even more acute (if that can even be envisioned) unless enjoined from doing so. The court will likely be shocked by the dangerous actions of Ms. Gillette. Petitioner will if necessary file several hundred emails and texts to support his claims, and if necessary, ask the Court to appoint a psychologist to stabilize Ms. Gillette.

After repeated requests by petitioner to reconsider her actions, Ms. Gillette has ignored all requests and seems only more determined to do further damage. We ask for immediate relief and possible contempt of Ms. Gillette if she elects to ignore the court's direction.

We will end by repeating something that Ms. Gillette repeated in court several times, in front of you and recorded by the court stenographer, "Mr. Graham is an excellent father and positive force for the children, and I want him to remain in the children's lives."

While Ms. Gillette was saying this, she was simultaneously orchestrating an effort by others to criminally prosecute Mr. Graham. When her own attempts to include her supposed defrauding failed to make any impact with law enforcement, Ms. Gillette astonishingly and voluntarily submitted a Victim Impact Statement to the Southern District of New York, for a securities case wholly unrelated to her own perceived problems. The purpose of her statement was crystal clear to anyone who read it: she had no basis to submit a statement in a securities trial wholly unrelated to her, and therefore she wanted the Petitioner to suffer and spend as much time away from his children as possible.

So what is it with Ms. Gillette: was she then lying to this court when she unequivocally stated to your Honor that she wished for Petitioner to remain the positive force that she claimed he was (and that your Honor, I am more than, as my own children would willingly attest), or is she so morally corrupt as to lie to this court and thereby constitute a complete and utter dereliction of custodial rights?

We plead with the court for immediate intervention.

Respectfully,

Sebastian Graham
(xxx) xxx-xxxx

A Country Club Dream

It's the Year 2014, early October. I've waited my whole life for this one night; so has she…

The men's' grill room at The Stoney Rock Club in Locust Valley New York, the Gold Coast of Long Island. It's October and inside is the ultimate Quest crowd, men in navy blazers and Hermes (natch…) ties, and women in DVF cocktail dress. No beards, tattoos, Kiki de Montparnesse, Brazilian waxes, or hair gel. Ironically, someone has a gun. The room is filled with ten white linen tables of twelve…the wait-staff is black tie (too many staff as always). The table queen, my ex, has carefully though through who sits where. It's a Saturday night, dark outside, cool but not cold…tree leaves have begun their inexorable fall. The grill room is festive, adorned like only real money can, with cutesy silver-picture frames of a younger woman and carefree times. I recognize the face in the frames because I slept next to it for fifteen years. God I hate large parties for profit like this.

Stoney is the premier club on Long Island and my ex is now on the board (she desperately wanted to be on that board and she always knew how to get there). The evening is an uber-narcissistic celebration of her 50th birthday, something she's been planning for fifty years…no shite! This girl doesn't do parties light…she goes yard. The night is beyond important to her, so of course there are no children present (she's starting to behave like her mother who hates children…reminds her of lost innocence).   Her Surprise 50th is a surprise to no one there since she organized it, just like she organized her surprise 30th birthday at the Puck twenty years before.

I see a number of faces I know (mostly Stoney members I used to play golf with…their handicaps are pretty impressive, mine now sucks though I think I could take most of them with a day of practice). None of the mouthpieces she used to trash me with are there…their shelf lives ended years ago so they're useless to her anymore. Somers' new husband is seated to her right…he's a successful short guy (thank god!). If she had married a successful tall guy, that would have really pissed me off. He dances really well from what I hear, which doesn't surprise me…there's a direct causal relationship between male height and dance floor skill (short, Fred Astaire; tall, mosh pit). In a similar vein, the shorter the man, the more intense the Facebook activity…I can't dance for shite and I'm not on Facebook. She wanted the anti-me, and it looks like she got it. This Bluetool even drives a Mini-Cooper!

Bob Hardwick is leading his eight piece band. He played at our wedding twenty years ago (good irony there…only two people know about Bob's two-fer tonight).

Toasts begin praising my ex (but not me of course…). They culminate with the penultimate one given by the new Willie Wonka Oompah-Loompah husband, drolling on about how lucky he was to have found such an eligible woman in Locust Valley (she wasn't so much eligible as hungry…I need to have a word with him on that one day). He's eloquent of course, and I have to give him semi-credit for that. That man's put her first, but so did I…the thing is, he's much smoother in front of 120. Still, fuck him, that should be me up there! I wanted to toast her, but I'd rather roast her like no one's business. Oddly she'd find it hilarious, as would everyone else. Her sense of humor is still sharp. I always loved it and she loved mine.   Anyway, that husband is so much shorter than me, did I mention that yet? Looks like a munchkin, an oompa-loompa…I'm ecstatic for small favors…They say that when a man steals your wife, the best revenge is to let him keep her, so have at it Tiny Tim. Bet he has a huge ego wall at the office with all his academic and business plaques.

I see my ex. God she's hot, an ageless beauty queen even after 50 years of unrestrained lunacy and incurable bitterness. I have mixed feelings about her hotness, like my mother-in-law driving over a cliff in my new Ferrari…The ex is in a stunning off-the-shoulder, floor length, silky red gown that teasingly drips off of her ridiculously perfect shoulders; it must be worth north of $10k, to be worn only once tonight…She's a cool narcissist, that's for sure.

She's absorbing everything like a phantasma sponge, pretending not to calculate everyone's words, but she sees and hears it all…the night is designed to inflate her self-love. She's secretly tape recording everyone's toasts. She'll play the tape a thousand times after the evening, allocating to each toast-giver fantasy evil-league points for levels of their prostrate obsequiousness to her. She enjoys her time in the spotlight, she used to rule Manhattan back in the day, an important person in an important city, but she's too preoccupied tonight remembering the toasts and adding the points up like a Shenzhen accountant. She craves the game. She never really became someone else like I thought…this is who she always was, a schizophrenic split personality narcissistic wonder, a lover of large society parties for profit. Life's not complicated when you stay the same, even when you're posing. A poser is a poser after all.

She rises from her seat to give the reciprocal toast, remembering to mention every person there. That's a real talent with 120 people to recall. You couldn't envision a more exquisite woman at 50…she's defied gravity's odds, which I can believe. I knew she'd hold up well. That chick has been having sex for the past three years while I haven't had anything…that's perhaps the biggest crime in the world. It would really throw me if I heard she likes giving head now…don't even start me on that.

In heels, she stands six feet tall; every man there wants be with her. Her speech is written out on twenty sheets of paper, typed and spell-checked, making it as spontaneous as pre-meditated murder. She'll fake the evening, about how tonight was such a surprise and how affected she is by everyone's love, because after all, she certainly had to go through so much to get here, but satisfied things worked out in the end (that's a subtle knock on me, her ex… still trashing me because she loves that more than anything; it's anger as pleasure all over again). She gives a wink and nod to the new and shorter husband (I pray he has a small penis…my luck he's in the Guinness Book of World Records going the other way). That technosexual is wearing a Rolex…argh, so typical. I bet he says my people.

I'm standing on the practice green looking through the large glass window, chuckling mostly, with a Scotty Cameron putter in one hand and a Budweiser in the other, looking for all the world like a drunken golfing fugitive...which I guess I am. I'm wearing prison issue blues. I'm quasi-incoherent, channeling my inner-Carl

Spackler, "Cinderella story. Outta nowhere. A former groundskeeper, now, about to become the Masters Champion…"

I can't contain myself, she's really starting to get under my skin. Her narcissism has gone on too long, and my time on the outside is fast drawing to a close. I can hear distant helicopters and muffled sirens; the bloodhounds and their handlers are already coming up the 1st and 18th fairways. I could reach them with a three-iron by now.

This is a woman no one really knows, they don't begin to understand, and they're definitely afraid of. She's smoking, but perhaps too hot to touch in other ways. Only the nanny and I ever really knew her, and she showed us both out the door. Her guests are aware of what she did to me, but not the nanny, and they don't want the same done to them, so they'll show up and air-kiss. No one wants to be pulverized into sand.

She finally finishes her demented oratorical fantasia with my reputation slightly worse for the wear, which is remarkable given there wasn't much left anyway. Before Bob strikes up the band for a song by fucking Journey (argh…), I quickly enter stage left, much uninvited and exquisitely inebriated, holding my Scotty Cameron (that sucker is going into my grave with me…). I haven't been to the club in three years (pre-occupied…). I spent over $500,000 there during my supposedly sane years…I feel the Board owes me one last panache…I paid the woman's initiation fee for god's sake, not that she'd ever admit that to anyone. Hell, I paid all the club dues, come to think of it. I see Pedro, one of the bartenders and an old friend, and ask him for a fresh Bud. He says hi and tosses one to me. I pop the top and take a long gulp. We're about to rock…

My presence in the room stops a Mack truck; jaws drop, trays tip, glasses crash, hearts defibrillate, men pee, women orgasm, musicians laugh, someone calls security. I'll need to hustle. I grab the microphone from Bob, who isn't quite sure what's going on, but like most musicians, he senses delicious pandemonium in the air and does his part. He stops the band. I sneak a glance at my ex…she isn't so much pissed as about to go nuclear-native on me.

Here we go (alternative conversation in parentheses…). Deep breath, tap the mic, cough, quickly review my redneck teleprompter (scribbled notes on my hand…),

"First off, how ya doin'? You guys had the loyalty of hyenas in heat during mating season: (extended pronunciation coming, nervous giggle)… Jesus (now exhale….). OK? Why did you ever allow that witch to over-control you like that?! Don't you get her? That's all I really have to say (actually I have a lot more, but the Old Brookville Police and US Marshal's are on the way…). No offense intended to anyone specific of course. Mostly you're not bad, but I've waited a few years to get that off my chest, not to any one person in particular, just a general happy 'toss off' for allowing her to over-control things. Actually the three phonies I really wanted to really say toss off to aren't even here…damn! I feel so much better though…Sorry. Thanks. Go back to your meal (keep getting fat…). I really miss the golf and pong. No texting security or the police (they're almost at the door…). Oh yeah, wait…"

My ex and short husband blue-techno are staring at me agape…she's reaching in her purse for her handgun, it's pre-loaded just like security instructed her. He's flummoxed beyond words, looking shorter every second. How does she sleep with that guy, he's a tenth her height-appropriate level…he looks like a kewpie doll. Go Shorty, it's your birthday, drink Bacardi…whatever Fitty…

"To the birthday girl: what can I say that hasn't already been said? (a bullet whizzes by my head, but she can't figure out the automatic trigger to shoot again…not yet anyway) Nice shot, Sweetie! You're supposed to warn someone first before firing at them! Ha! Good analogy there, huh?! Oh yeah…actually I have a ton to say!"

She's really fidgeting with her gun now, her guitar face is all distorted, the night is NOT going as planned…

"No words are sufficient to describe what you accomplished…You're the tops! Everyone's capable of wickedness, self-importance, and lots of it, but none more so than you; so hat's off…You bested your own Mom for god's sakes, and she wrote the friggin Book on Narcissism (that's an understatement!….)! You lied to me from the start, not a minute went by when you didn't concoct some fantasy and sell it. You lied to all of them…The nanny knew it and I knew it. But no one out here ever did. They can't begin to understand what you did then or know you even now, but I do… (knowing smile from me to her; btw, why in the world did I ever call you Sweetie…? You're the "anti-Sweetie"…)."

I hear the chamber click…she's taking aim.

"I'm the only one who feels the way I do about you, because I trusted you completely and look how you treated that…I guess we hate those who love us the most? But, you didn't kill me so I can at least still speak (if you don't get that gun firing again first…btw, I can't believe New York State gave you a 'license to carry'!!!…you should be locked up in an asylum, not carrying a gun…). So allow me this ….Johnny, I hardly knew ye."

Only my ex would understand where I'd be headed with that subtle entendre; the bullets would start flying, the dance floor clears, Quest would have their November cover story, a Murder in Locust Valley. I'd have to run.

<u>Dymphna's Playlist</u>

I Wanna Be Sedated…The Ramones
Heartbreak Beat…Psychedelic Furs
Heroes…David Bowie
Hey Man Nice Shot…Filter
Pennyroyal Tea…Nirvana
High and Dry…Radiohead
The Shadow of the Day…Linkin Park

Both Sides Now....Joni Mitchell
Starlight....Muse
Standing on the Corner....The Script
I and Love and You...The Avett Brothers
And the Many Poems of Pearl Jam

Better take care,
Laughing at danger,
Virtue a stranger,
Better beware!

Life's a bitter foe!
With fate it's no use competing,
Youth is so terribly fleeting,
By dancing much faster,
You're chancing disaster,
Time alone will show.

v. Noel Coward (1925)